C000228931

Deemed 'the father of the scie[...] **Austin Freeman** had a long and [...] a writer of detective fiction. He v[...] tailor who went on to train as a pharmacist. After graduating as a surgeon at the Middlesex Hospital Medical College, Freeman taught for a while and joined the colonial service, offering his skills as an assistant surgeon along the Gold Coast of Africa. He became embroiled in a diplomatic mission when a British expeditionary party was sent to investigate the activities of the French. Through his tact and formidable intelligence, a massacre was narrowly avoided. His future was assured in the colonial service. However, after becoming ill with blackwater fever, Freeman was sent back to England to recover and, finding his finances precarious, embarked on a career as acting physician in Holloway Prison. In desperation, he turned to writing and went on to dominate the world of British detective fiction, taking pride in testing different criminal techniques. So keen were his powers as a writer that part of one of his best novels was written in a bomb shelter.

A CERTAIN DR THORNDYKE

THE D'ARBLAY MYSTERY

DR THORNDYKE INTERVENES

DR THORNDYKE'S CASEBOOK

THE EYE OF OSIRIS

FELO DE SE

FLIGHTY PHYLLIS

THE GOLDEN POOL: A STORY OF A FORGOTTEN MINE

THE GREAT PORTRAIT MYSTERY

HELEN VARDON'S CONFESSION

JOHN THORNDYKE'S CASES

MR POLTON EXPLAINS

MR POTTERMACK'S OVERSIGHT

THE MYSTERY OF 31 NEW INN

THE MYSTERY OF ANGELINA FROOD

THE PENROSE MYSTERY

THE PUZZLE LOCK

THE RED THUMB MARK

THE SHADOW OF THE WOLF

A SILENT WITNESS

THE SINGING BONE

The Cat's Eye

R Austin Freeman

HOUSE OF
STRATUS

This edition published in 2001 by House of Stratus, an imprint of
House of Stratus Ltd, Thirsk Industrial Park, York Road, Thirsk,
North Yorkshire, YO7 3BX, UK.

www.houseofstratus.com

Typeset, printed and bound by House of Stratus.

A catalogue record for this book is available from the British Library
and the Library of Congress.

ISBN 0-7551-0348-3

PREFACE

By one of those coincidences which are quite inadmissible in fiction, but of frequent occurrence in real life, an incident in the story of *The Cat's Eye* has found an almost exact duplicate in an actual case which has been reported in the Press.

The real case was concerned with a most alarming misadventure which befell a distinguished police official of high rank. The fictitious incident occurs in Chapter ten of this book; and the reading of that chapter will inevitably convey the impression that I have appropriated the real case and incorporated it in my story; a proceeding that the reader might properly consider to be in questionable taste.

It seems, therefore, desirable to explain that Chapter ten was written some months before the real tragedy occurred. Indeed, by that time, the book was so nearly completed that it was impracticable to eliminate the incident, which was an integral part of the plot.

The coincidence is to be regretted; but worse things might easily have happened. But for the circumstance that I had to lay this book aside to complete some other work, *The Cat's Eye* would have been in print when the crime was committed; and it might then have been difficult for any one – even for the author – to believe that the fictitious crime had not furnished the suggestion for the real one.

RAF
Gravesend, *19th June 1923.*

CONTENTS

1	In the Midst of Life –	1
2	Sir Lawrence declares a Vendetta	14
3	Thorndyke takes up the Inquiry	23
4	The Lady of Shalott	39
5	Mr Halliburton's Mascot	50
6	Introduces an Ant-eater and a Detective	62
7	The Vanished Heirloom	76
8	A Jacobite Romance	92
9	Exit Moakey	104
10	A Timely Warning	115
11	The Blue Hair	129
12	From the Jaws of Death	145
13	Thorndyke states his Position	163
14	Beauchamp Blake	170
15	The Squire and the Sleuth-hound	183
16	Mr Brodribb's Embassy	192
17	The Secret Chamber	202
18	The Cat's Eye	218
19	A Relic of the '45	234
20	QED	247

CHAPTER ONE

In the Midst of Life –

I am not a superstitious man. Indeed superstition, which is inseparably
bound up with ignorance or disregard of evidence, would ill accord
with the silken gown of a King's Counsel. And still less am I tainted
with that particular form of superstition in which the fetishism of
barbarous and primitive man is incongruously revived in a population
of, at least nominally, educated persons, by the use of charms, amulets,
mascots and the like.

Had it been otherwise; had I been the subject of this curious
atavistic tendency, I should surely have been led to believe that from
the simple gem whose name I have used to give a title to this
chronicle, some subtle influence exhaled whereby the whole course
of my life was directed into new channels. But I do not believe
anything of the kind; and therefore, though it did actually happen that
the appearance of the Cat's Eye was coincident with a radical change
in the course and manner of my life, and even, as it seemed, with my
very personality; and though with the Cat's Eye the unfolding of the
new life seemed constantly associated; still I would have it understood
that I use the name merely as a label to docket together a succession
of events that form a consistent and natural group.

The particular train of events with which this history deals began
on a certain evening near the end of the long vacation. It was a cloudy
evening, I remember, and very dark, for it was past eight o'clock and
the days were drawing in rapidly. I was returning across Hampstead

Heath towards my lodgings in the village, and was crossing the broken, gorse-covered and wooded hollow to the west of the Spaniards Road, when I heard the footsteps of some one running, and running swiftly, as I could judge by the rapid rhythm of the footfalls and the sound of scattering gravel. I halted to listen, noting that the rhythm of the footsteps was slightly irregular, like the ticking of an ill-adjusted clock; and even as I halted, I saw the runner. But only for a moment, and then but dimly. The vague shape of a man came out of the gloom, passed swiftly across my field of vision, and was gone. I could not see what he was like. The dim shape appeared and vanished into the darkness, leaving me standing motionless, listening with vague suspicion to the now faint footfalls and wondering what I ought to do.

Suddenly the silence was rent by a piercing cry, the cry of a woman calling for help. And, strangely enough, it came from the opposite direction to that towards which the fugitive was running. In an instant I turned and raced across the rugged hollow towards the spot from whence the sound seemed to come, and as I scrambled up a gravelly hillock I saw, faintly silhouetted on the murky skyline of some rising ground ahead, the figures of a man and a woman struggling together; and I had just noted that the man seemed to be trying to escape when I saw him deal the woman a blow, on which she uttered a shriek and fell, while the man, having wrenched himself free, darted down the farther slope and vanished into the encompassing darkness.

When I reached the woman she was sitting up with her right hand pressed to her side, and as I approached she called out sharply:

'Follow him! Follow that man! Never mind me!'

I stood for a moment irresolute, for on the hand that was pressed to her side I had noticed a smear of blood. But as I hesitated, she repeated: 'Follow him! Don't let him escape! He has just committed a dreadful murder!'

On this I ran down the slope in the direction that the man had taken and stumbled on over the rugged, gravelly hillocks and hollows, among the furze bushes and the birches and other small trees. But it was a hopeless pursuit. The man had vanished utterly, and from the

2

dark health not a sound came to give a hint as to the direction in which he had gone. There was no definite path, nor was it likely that he would have followed one; and as I ran forward, tripping over roots and sandy hummocks, the futility of the pursuit became every moment more obvious, while I felt a growing uneasiness as to the condition of the woman I had left sitting on the ground and apparently bleeding from a wound. At length I gave up the chase and began to retrace my steps, now full of anxiety lest I should be unable to find the spot where I had left her, and speculating on the possibility that the victim of the murder of which she had spoken might yet be alive and in urgent need of help.

I returned as quickly as I could, watching the direction anxiously and trying vainly to pick up landmarks. But the uneven, gorse-covered ground was a mere formless expanse intersected in all directions by indistinct tracks, confused by the numbers of birch-trees and stunted oaks, and shut in on all sides by a wall of darkness. Presently I halted with a despairing conviction that I had lost my way hopelessly, and at that moment I discerned dimly through the gloom the shape of a piece of rising ground lying away to the right. Instantly I hurried towards it, and as I climbed the slope, I thought I recognised it as the place from which I had started. A moment later, the identity of the place was confirmed beyond all doubt, for I perceived lying on the ground a shawl or scarf which I now remembered to have seen lying near the woman as she sat with her hand pressed to her side, urging me to follow her assailant.

But the woman herself had disappeared. I picked up the shawl, and throwing it over my arm, stood for a few moments, peering about me and listening intently. Not a sound could I distinguish, however, nor could I perceive any trace of the vanished woman. Then I noticed, a few yards away, a defined path leading towards a patch of deeper darkness that looked like a copse or plantation, and following this, I presently came upon her, standing by a fence and clinging to it for support.

'The man has got away,' said I. 'There is no sign of him. But what about you? Are you hurt much?'

3

'I don't think so,' she answered faintly. 'The wretch tried to stab me, but I don't think – ' Here her voice faded away, as she fell forward against the fence and seemed about to collapse. I caught her, and lifting her bodily, carried her along the path, which appeared to lead to a house. Presently I came to an open gate, and entering the enclosed grounds, saw before me an old-fashioned house, the door of which stood ajar, showing a faint light from within. As I approached the door, a telephone bell rang and a woman's voice, harsh and terrified, smote my ear:

'Are you there? This is Rowan Lodge. Send to the police immediately! Mr Drayton has been robbed and murdered! Yes, Mr Drayton. He is lying dead in his room. I am his housekeeper. Send the police and a doctor!'

At this moment I pushed open the door and entered; and at my appearance, with the insensible woman in my arms, the housekeeper shrieked aloud, and dropping the receiver, started back with a gesture of wild terror.

'My God!' she exclaimed, 'What is this? Not another!'

'I hope not,' I replied, not, however, without misgivings. 'This lady tried to hold the man as he was escaping and the villain stabbed her. Where can I lay her down?'

The whimpering housekeeper flung open a door, and snatching a match-box from the hall table, struck a match and preceded me into a room where, by the light of the match that flickered in her shaking hand, I made out a sofa and laid my burden on it, rolling up the shawl and placing it under her head. Then the housekeeper lit the gas and came and stood by the sofa, wringing her hands and gazing down with horrified pity at the corpse-like figure.

'Poor dear!' she sobbed. 'Such a pretty creature, too, and quite a lady! God help us! What can we do for her? She may be bleeding to death!'

The same thought was in my mind, and the same question, but as I answered that we could do nothing until the doctor arrived, the woman – or rather girl, for she was not more than twenty-six – opened her eyes and asked in a faint voice: 'Is Mr Drayton dead?'

The housekeeper sobbed an indistinct affirmative and then added: 'But try not to think about it, my dear. Just keep yourself quite quiet until the doctor comes.'

'Are you sure he is dead?' I asked in a low voice.

'I wish I were not,' she sobbed. Then, with an earnest look at the young lady – who seemed now to be reviving somewhat – she added: 'Come with me and see; and do you lie quite still until I come back, my dear.'

With this she led me out of the room, and turning from the hall into a short corridor, passed quickly along it and stopped at a door. 'He is in there,' she said in a shaky voice that was half a sob. She opened the door softly, peered in, and then, with a shuddering cry, turned and ran back to the room that we had just left.

When she had gone I entered the room half-reluctantly, for the atmosphere of tragedy and horror was affecting me most profoundly. It was a smallish room, almost unfurnished save for a range of cabinets such as insect collectors use; and opposite one of these a man lay motionless on the floor, looking, with his set, marble-white face and fixed, staring eyes, like some horrible waxwork figure. I stooped over him to see if there were any sign of life. But even to a layman's eye the fixity, the utter immobility was unmistakable. The man was dead beyond all doubt. I listened with my ear at his mouth and laid my finger on the chilly wrist. But the first glance had told me all. The man was dead.

As I stood up, still with my eyes riveted on the face, set in that ghastly stare, I became conscious of a certain dim sense of recognition. It was a strong, resolute face, and even in death, the fixed expression spoke rather of anger than of fear. Where had I seen that face? And then in a flash I recalled the name that the housekeeper had called through the telephone – Mr Drayton. Of course. This was the brother of my neighbour in the Temple, Sir Lawrence Drayton, the famous Chancery lawyer. He had spoken to me of a brother who lived at Hampstead, and there could be no doubt that this was he. The likeness was unmistakable.

But, as I realised this, I realised also the certainty that this crime would become my professional concern. Sir Lawrence would undoubtedly put the case in the hands of my friend John Thorndyke – the highest medico-legal authority and the greatest criminal lawyer of our time – and my association with Thorndyke would make me a party to the investigation. And that being so, it behoved me to gather what data I could before the police arrived and took possession.

The mechanism of the crime was obvious enough, though there were one or two mysterious features. Of the cabinet opposite which the body lay, one drawer was pulled out, and its loose glass cover had been removed and lay shattered on the floor beside the corpse. The contents of this drawer explained the motive of the crime, for they consisted of specimens of jewellery, all more or less antique, and many of them quite simple and rustic in character, but still jewels. A number had evidently been taken, to judge by the empty trays, but the greater part of the contents of the drawer remained intact.

The rifled drawer was the second from the top. Having turned up the gas and lit a second burner, I drew out the top drawer. The contents of this were untouched, though the drawer appeared to have been opened, for the cover-glass was marked by a number of rather conspicuous fingerprints. Of course these were not necessarily the prints of the robber's fingers, but they probably were, for their extreme distinctness suggested a dirty and sweaty hand such as would naturally appertain to a professional thief in a state of some bodily fear. Moreover the reason why this drawer should have been passed over was quite obvious. Its contents were of no intrinsic value, consisting chiefly of Buckinghamshire lace bobbins with carved inscriptions and similar simple objects.

I next drew out the third drawer, which I found quite untouched, and the absence of any fingerprints on the cover-glass confirmed the probable identity of those on the glass of the top drawer. By way of further settling this question, I picked up the fragments of the broken glass and looked them over carefully; and when I found several of them marked with similar distinct fingerprints, the probability that they were those of the murderer became so great as nearly to amount to certainty.

I did not suppose that these fingerprints would be of much interest to Thorndyke. They were rather the concern of the police and the Habitual Criminals Registry. But still I knew that if he had been in my place he would have secured specimens, on the chance of their being of use hereafter, and I could do no less than take the opportunity that offered. Looking over the broken fragments again, I selected two pieces, each about four inches square, both of which bore several fingerprints. I placed them carefully face to face in a large envelope from my pocket, having first wrapped their corners in paper to prevent the surfaces from touching.

I had just bestowed the envelope in my letter-case and slipped the latter into my pocket when I heard a man's voice in the hall. I opened the door, and walking along the corridor, found a police inspector and a sergeant in earnest conversation with the housekeeper, while an elderly man, whom I judged to be the doctor, stood behind, listening attentively.

'Well,' said the inspector, 'we'd better see to the lady. Will you have a look at her, doctor, and when you've attended to her, perhaps you will let us know whether she is in a fit state to answer questions. But you might just take a look at the body first.' Here he observed me and inquired: 'Let me see, who is this gentleman?'

I explained briefly my connection with the case as we walked down the corridor, and the inspector made no comment at the moment. We all entered the room, and the doctor stooped over the body and made a rapid inspection.

'Yes,' he said, rising and shaking his head, 'there's no doubt that he is dead, poor fellow. A shocking affair. But I had better go and see to this poor lady before I make any detailed examination.'

With this he bustled away, and the inspector and the sergeant knelt down beside the corpse but refrained from touching it.

'Knife wound, apparently,' said the inspector, nodding gloomily at a small pool of blood that appeared between the outstretched right arm and the side. 'Seems to have been a left-handed man, too, unless he struck from behind, which he pretty evidently did not.' He stood up, and once more looking at me, somewhat inquisitively, said: 'I had better have your name and address, sir.'

'My name is Anstey – Robert Anstey, KC, and my address is 8A King's Bench Walk, Inner Temple.'

'Oh, I know you, sir,' said the inspector with a sudden change of manner. 'You are Dr Thorndyke's leading counsel. Well, well. What an odd thing that you should happen to come upon this affair by mere chance. It's quite in your own line.'

'I don't know about that,' said I. 'It looks to me rather more in yours. If they have got these fingerprints in the files at Scotland Yard you won't have much trouble in finding your man or getting a conviction.'

As I spoke, I drew his attention to the fingerprints on the broken glass, saying nothing, however, about those on the upper drawer.

The two officers examined the incriminating marks with deep interest, and the inspector proceeded carefully and skilfully to pack several of the fragments for subsequent examination, remarking, as he laid them tenderly on the top of a cabinet: 'This looks like a regular windfall, but it's almost too good to be true. The professional crook, nowadays, knows too much to go dabbing his trade-marks about in this fashion. These prints and the knife rather suggest a casual or amateur of some kind. The fellow not only didn't wear gloves, he didn't even trouble to wipe his hands. And they wanted wiping pretty badly. Are all these cabinets full of jewellery?'

'I really don't know what they contain, but they are pretty insecure if their contents are valuable.'

'Yes,' he agreed. 'A single locked batten to each cabinet. One wrench of a jemmy and the whole cabinet is open. Well, we'd better have a few words with the housekeeper before we go over the room in detail. And she won't want to talk to us in here.'

With this he led the way back to the hall, and I could not but admire the diplomatic way in which he managed to get me away from the scene of his intended investigation.

As we entered the hall, we met the doctor, who was repacking his emergency bag at the door of the room.

'I think,' said he, 'my patient is well enough to give you a few necessary particulars. But don't tire her with needless questions.'

'She is not seriously hurt, then?' said I, with considerable relief.

'No. But she has had a mighty narrow escape. The brute must have aimed badly, for he struck viciously enough, but the point of the knife glanced off a rib and came out farther back, just transfixing a fold of skin and muscle. It is a nasty wound, but quite superficial and not at all dangerous.'

'Well, I'm glad it's no worse than that,' said the inspector, and with this he pushed open the door of the room and we all entered, though I noticed that the sergeant regarded me with a somewhat dubious eye. And now, for the first time, I observed the injured lady with some attention, which I was able to do at my leisure while the examination was proceeding. And a very remarkable-looking girl she was. Whether she would have been considered beautiful by the majority of persons I cannot say; she certainly appeared so to me. But I have always felt a great admiration of the pictures of Burne-Jones and of the peculiar type of womanhood that he loved to paint; and this girl, with her soft aureole of reddish-gold hair, her earnest grey eyes, her clear, blonde skin – now pale as marble – the characteristic mouth and cast of features, might have been the model whose presentment gave those pictures, to me, their peculiar charm. She seemed not of the common, everyday world, but like some visitor from the regions of legend and romance. And the distinction of her appearance was supported by her speech – by a singularly sweet voice, an accent of notable refinement, and a manner at once gentle, grave, and dignified.

'Do you feel able to tell us what you know of this terrible affair, Madam?' the inspector asked.

'Oh yes,' she replied. 'I am quite recovered now.'

'Was Mr Drayton a friend of yours?'

'No. I never met him until this evening. But perhaps I had better tell you how I came to be here and exactly what happened.'

'Yes,' the inspector agreed, 'that will be the shortest way.'

'Mr Drayton,' she began, 'was, as you probably know, the owner of a collection of what he called "inscribed objects" – jewels, ornaments, and small personal effects bearing inscriptions connecting them with some person or event or period. I saw a description of the collection in the *Connoisseur* a short time ago, and as I am greatly interested in inscribed jewels, I wrote to Mr Drayton asking if I could be allowed to see the collection; and I asked, since I am occupied all day, if he could make it convenient to show me the collection one evening. I also asked him some questions about the specimens of jewellery. In reply he wrote me a most kind letter – I have it in my pocket if you would like to see it – answering my questions and not only inviting me most cordially to come and look at his treasures, but offering to meet me at the station and show me the way to the house. Of course I accepted his very kind offer and gave him a few particulars of my appearance so that he should be able to identify me, and this evening he met me at the station and we walked up here together. There was no one in the house when we arrived – at least he thought there was not, for he mentioned to me that his housekeeper had gone out for an hour or so. He let himself in with a key and showed me into this room. Then he went away, leaving the door ajar. I heard him walk down the corridor and I heard a door open. Almost at the same moment, he called out loudly and angrily. Then I heard the report of a pistol, followed immediately by a heavy fall.'

'A pistol!' exclaimed the inspector. 'I thought it was a knife wound. But I mustn't interrupt you.'

'When I heard the report I ran out into the hall and down the corridor. As I went, I heard a sound as of a scuffle, and when I reached the door of the museum, which was wide open, I saw Mr Drayton lying on the floor, quite still, and a man climbing out of the window. I ran to the window to try to stop him, but before I could get there he was gone. I waited an instant to look at Mr Drayton, and noticed that he seemed to be already dead and that the room was full of the reek from the pistol; then I ran back to the hall and out through the garden and along the fence to where I supposed the window to be. But for a few moments I could not see any one. Then, suddenly, a man sprang over the fence and dropped quite near me, and before he could recover his balance, I had run to him and seized him by both wrists. He struggled violently, though he did not seem very strong, but he dragged me quite a long way before he got free.'

'Did he say anything to you?' the inspector asked.

'Yes. He used most horrible language, and more than once he said: "Let go, you fool. The man who did it has got away." '

'That might possibly be true,' I interposed, 'for, just before I heard this lady call for help, a man passed me at a little distance, running so hard that I was half inclined to follow him.'

'Did you see what he was like?' the inspector demanded eagerly.

'No. I hardly saw him at all. He passed me at a distance of about thirty yards and was gone in an instant. Then I heard this lady call out and, of course, ran towards her.'

'Yes,' said the inspector, 'naturally. But it's a pity you didn't see what the man was like.' Then, once more addressing the lady, he asked:

'Did this man stab you without warning, Miss – '

'Blake is my name,' she replied. 'No. He threatened several times to "knife" me if I didn't let go. At last he managed to get his left hand free. I think he was holding something in it, but he must have dropped it, whatever it was, for the next moment I saw him draw a knife from under his coat. Then I got hold of his arm again, and that is probably the reason that he wounded me so slightly. But when he stabbed me I suddenly went quite faint and fell down, and then he escaped.'

'He held the knife in his left hand, then?' the inspector asked. 'You are sure of that?'

'Quite sure. Of course it happened to be the free hand, but – '

'But if he had been a right-handed man he would probably have got his right hand free. Did you see which side he carried his knife?'

'Yes. He drew it from under his coat on the left side.'

'Can you give us any description of the man?'

'I am afraid I can't. I am sure I should recognise him if I were to see him again, but I can't describe him. It was all very confused, and, of course, it was very dark. I should say that he was a smallish man, rather slightly built. He wore a cloth cap and his hair seemed rather short but bushy. He had a thin face, with a very peculiar expression – but, of course, he was extremely excited and furious – and large, staring eyes, and a rather pronounced, curved nose.'

'Oh, come,' said the inspector approvingly, 'that isn't such a bad description. Can you say whether he was dark or fair, clean shaved or bearded?'

'He was clean shaved, and I should say decidedly dark.'

'And how was he dressed?'

'He wore a cloth cap, and, I think, a tweed suit. Oh, and he wore gloves – thin, smooth gloves – very thin kid, I should say – '

'Gloves!' exclaimed the inspector. 'Then the fingerprints must be the other man's. Are you sure he had gloves on both hands?'

'Yes, perfectly sure. I saw them and felt them.'

'Well,' said the inspector, 'this is a facer. It looks as if the other man had really done the job while this fellow kept watch outside. It's a mysterious affair altogether. There's the extraordinary time they chose to break into the house. Eight o'clock in the evening. It would almost seem as if they had known about Mr Drayton's movements.'

'They must have done,' said the housekeeper. 'Mr Drayton went out regularly every evening a little after seven. He went down to the village to play chess at the club, and he usually came back between half-past nine and ten. And I generally sat and worked in the kitchen on the other side of the house from the museum.'

'And did he take no sort of precautions against robbery?'

'He used to lock the museum when he went out. That was all. He was not at all a nervous man, and he used to say that there was no danger of robbery because the things in the museum were not the kind of things that burglars go for. They wouldn't be of any value to melt or sell.'

'We must just look over the museum presently and see what the collection consists of,' said the inspector. 'And we must see how they got in and what they have taken. I suppose there is a catalogue?'

'No, there isn't,' replied the housekeeper. 'I did suggest to Mr Drayton that he ought to draw up a list of the things, but he said it was not a public collection, and as he knew all the specimens himself, there was no need to number them or keep a catalogue.'

'That is unfortunate,' said the inspector. 'We shan't be able to find out what is missing or circulate any descriptions unless you can remember what was in the cabinets. By the way, did Mr Drayton ever show his collection to visitors other than his personal friends?'

'Occasionally. After the *Connoisseur* article that Miss Blake was speaking of, two or three strangers wrote to Mr Drayton asking to be allowed to see the jewellery, and he invited them to come and showed them everything.'

'Did Mr Drayton keep a visitors' book, or record of any kind?'

'No. I don't remember any of the visitors, excepting a Mr Halliburton, who wrote from the Baltic Hotel in the Marylebone Road. I remember him because Mr Drayton was so annoyed about him. He put himself to great inconvenience to meet Mr Halliburton and show him the jewellery that he had asked to see, and then, he told me, when he came, it was quite obvious that he didn't know anything at all about jewellery, either ancient or modern. He must have come just from idle curiosity.'

'I'm not so sure of that,' said the inspector. 'Looks a bit suspicious. We shall have to make some inquiries at the Baltic. And now we had better go and have a look at the museum, and perhaps, doctor, you would like to make a preliminary examination of the body before it is moved.'

On this we all rose, and the inspector was just moving towards the hall when there came a sharp sound of knocking at the outer door, followed by a loud peal of the bell.

CHAPTER TWO

Sir Lawrence declares a Vendetta

At the first stroke of the knocker we all stood stock still, and so remained until the harsh jangling of the bell gradually died away. There was nothing abnormal in either sound, but I suppose we were all somewhat overstrung, for there seemed in the clamorous summons, which shattered the silence so abruptly, something ominous and threatening. Especially did this appear in the case of the housekeeper, who threw up her hands and whimpered audibly.

'Dear Lord!' she ejaculated. 'It is Sir Lawrence – his brother! I know his knock. Who is to tell him?'

As no one answered, she crept reluctantly across the room, murmuring and shaking her head, and went out into the hall. I heard the door open and caught the sound of voices, though not very distinctly. Then the housekeeper re-entered the room quickly, and a man who was following her said in a brisk, somewhat bantering tone: 'You are very mysterious, Mrs Benham.' The next moment the speaker came into view; and instantly he stopped dead and stood staring into the room with a frown of stern surprise.

'What the devil is this?' he demanded, glaring first at the two officers and then at me. 'What is going on, Anstey?'

For a few moments I was tongue-tied. But an appealing glance from the housekeeper seemed to put the duty on me.

'A dreadful thing has happened, Drayton,' I replied. 'The house has been broken into and your brother has been killed.'

Sir Lawrence turned deathly pale and his face set hard and rigid, until it seemed the very counterpart of that white, set face that I had looked on but a few minutes age. For a while he stared at me frowningly, neither moving nor uttering a word. Then he asked gruffly: 'Where is he?'

'He is lying where he fell, in the museum,' I replied.

On this he turned abruptly and walked out of the room. I heard him pass quickly down the corridor, and then I heard the museum door shut. We all looked at one another uncomfortably, but no one spoke. The housekeeper sobbed almost inaudibly and now and again uttered a low moan. Miss Blake wept silently, and the two officers and the doctor stood looking gloomily at the floor.

Presently Sir Lawrence came back. He was still very pale. But though his eyes were red, and indeed were still humid, there was no softness of grief in his face. With its clenched jaw and frowning brows, it was grim and stern and inexorable as Fate.

'Tell me,' he said, in a quiet voice, looking from me to the inspector, 'exactly how this happened.'

'I don't think any one knows yet,' I replied. 'This lady, Miss Blake, is the only person who saw the murderer. She tried to detain him and held on to him until he stabbed her.'

'Stabbed her!' he exclaimed, casting a glance of intense apprehension at the recumbent figure on the sofa and stepping softly across the room.

'I am not really hurt,' Miss Blake hastened to assure him. 'It is only quite a trifling wound.'

He bent over her with a strange softening of the grim face, touching her hand with his and tenderly adjusting the rug that the housekeeper had spread over her.

'I pray to God that it is as you say,' he replied. Then, turning to me, he asked: 'Has this brave young lady been properly attended to?'

'Yes,' I answered. 'The doctor here – Dr – '

'Nichols,' said the medicus. 'I have examined the wound thoroughly and dressed it, and I think I can assure you that no danger is to be apprehended from it. But, having regard to the shock she has sustained, I think she ought to be got home as soon as possible.'

'Yes,' Sir Lawrence agreed, 'and if she is fit to be moved, I will convey her to her home. My car is waiting in the road. And I will ask you, Anstey, to come with me, if you can.'

Of course I assented, and he continued, addressing the inspector: 'When I have taken this lady home I shall go straight to Dr Thorndyke and ask him to assist the police in investigating this crime. Probably he will return here with me at once, and I will ask you to see that nothing – not even the body – is disturbed until he has made his inspection.'

At this the officer looked a little dubious, but he answered courteously enough: 'So far as I am concerned, Sir Lawrence, your wishes shall certainly be attended to. But I notified Scotland Yard before I came on here, and this case will probably be dealt with by the Criminal Investigation Department, and, of course, I can enter into no undertakings on their behalf.'

'No,' Sir Lawrence rejoined, 'of course you can't. I will deal with the Scotland Yard people myself. And now we had better start. Is Miss Blake able to walk to the car, Doctor? It is only a few yards to the road.'

'I am quite able to walk,' said Miss Blake; and as Dr Nichols assented, we assisted her to rise, and Sir Lawrence carefully wrapped her in the rug that Mrs Benham had thrown over her. Then I picked up the shawl, and tucking it under my arm, followed her as she walked slowly out supported by Sir Lawrence.

At the garden gate we turned to the left, and passing along the path, came very shortly to a road on which two cars were standing, a large closed car, which I recognised as Sir Lawrence's, and a smaller one, presumably Dr Nichols'. Into the former Miss Blake was assisted, and when the carriage rug had been wrapped around her, I entered and took the opposite seat.

'What address shall I tell the driver, Miss Blake?' Sir Lawrence asked.

'Sixty-three Jacob Street, Hampstead Road,' she replied; and then, as neither the driver nor either of us could locate the street, she added: 'It is two or three turnings past Mornington Crescent on the same side of the road.'

Having given this direction to the driver, Sir Lawrence entered and took the vacant seat and the car moved off smoothly, silently, and with unperceived swiftness.

During the journey hardly a word was spoken. The darkness of the heath gave place to the passing lights of the streets, the rural quiet to the clamour of traffic. In a few minutes, as it seemed, we were at the wide crossing by the Mother Red-Cap, and in a few more were turning into a narrow, dingy, and rather sordid by-street. Up this the car travelled slowly as the driver threw the light of a powerful lamp on the shabby doors, and at length drew up opposite a wide, wooden gate on which the number sixty-three was exhibited in large brass figures. I got out of the car and approached the gate in no little surprise, for its appearance and the paved truckway that led through it suggested the entrance to a factory or builder's yard. However, there was no doubt that it was the right house, for the evidence of the number was confirmed by a small brass plate at the side, legibly inscribed 'Miss Blake' and surmounted by a bell-pull. At the latter I gave a vigorous tug and was immediately aware of the far-away jangling of a large bell, which sounded as if it were ringing in an open yard.

In a few moments I detected quick footsteps which seemed to be approaching along a paved passage; then a wicket in the gate opened and a boy of about twelve looked out.

'Whom did you want, please?' he asked in a pleasant, refined voice and with a courteous, self-possessed manner which 'placed' him instantly in a social sense. Before I had time to reply, he had looked past me and observed Miss Blake, who, having been helped out of the car, was now approaching the gate; on which he sprang through the wicket and ran to meet her.

'You needn't be alarmed, Percy,' she said in a cheerful voice. 'I have had a little accident and these gentlemen have very kindly brought me home. But it is nothing to worry about.'

'You look awfully white and tired, Winnie,' he replied; and then, addressing me, he asked: 'Is my sister hurt much, sir?'

'No,' I answered. 'The doctor who attended to her thought that she would soon be quite well again, and I hope she will. Is there anything that we can do for you, Miss Blake?'

'Thank you, no,' she replied. 'My brother and a friend will look after me now, but I can't thank you enough for all your kindness.'

'It is I,' said Sir Lawrence, 'who am in your debt – deeply in your debt. And I do pray that you may suffer no ill consequences from your heroism. But we mustn't keep you standing here. Goodbye, dear Miss Blake, and God bless you.'

He shook her hand warmly and her brother's with old-fashioned courtesy. I handed the boy the folded shawl, and having shaken hands with both, followed my friend to the car.

'Do you think Thorndyke will be at home?' he asked as the car turned round and returned to the Hampstead Road.

'I expect so,' I replied. 'But I don't suppose there will be very much for him to do. There were plenty of fingerprints in evidence. I should think the police will be able to trace the man without difficulty.'

'Police be damned!' he retorted gruffly. 'I want Thorndyke. And as to fingerprints, weren't you the leading counsel in that Hornby case?'

'Yes, but that was exceptional. You can't assume – '

'That case,' he interrupted, 'knocked the bottom out of fingerprint evidence. And these fingerprints may not be on the files at the registry, and if they are not, the police have no clue to this man's identity, and are not likely to get any.'

It seemed to me that he was hardly doing the police justice, but there was no use in discussing the matter, as we were, in fact, going to put the case in Thorndyke's hands. I accordingly gave a colourless assent, and for the rest of the short journey we sat in silence, each busy with his own reflections.

At length the car drew up at the Inner Temple gate. Drayton sprang out, and signing to the driver to wait, passed through the wicket and strode swiftly down the narrow lane. As we came out at the end of Crown Office Row, he looked eagerly across at King's Bench Walk.

'There's a light in Thorndyke's chambers,' he said, and quickening his pace almost to a run, he crossed the wide space, and plunging into the entry of number 5A, ascended the stairs two at a time. I followed, not without effort, and as I reached the landing the door opened in response to his peremptory knock and Thorndyke appeared in the opening.

'My dear Drayton!' he exclaimed, 'you really ought not, at your age –' he stopped short, and looking anxiously at our friend, asked: 'Is anything amiss?'

'Yes,' Drayton replied quietly, though breathlessly. 'My brother Andrew – you remember him, I expect – has been murdered by some accursed housebreaker. He is lying on the floor of his room now. I told them to leave him there until you had seen him. Can you come?'

'I will come with you immediately,' was the reply; and as with grave face and quick but unhurried movements, he made the necessary preparations, I noticed that – characteristically – he asked no questions, but concentrated his attention on providing for all contingencies. He had laid a small, green, canvas-covered case upon the table, and opening it, was making a rapid inspection of the apparatus that it contained, when suddenly I bethought me of the pieces of glass in my pocket.

'Before we start,' said I, 'I had better give you these. The fingerprints on them are almost certainly those of the murderer.' As I spoke, I carefully unwrapped the two pieces of glass and handed them to Thorndyke, who took them from me, holding them daintily by their edges, and scrutinising them closely.

'I am glad you brought these, Anstey,' he said. 'They make us to some extent independent of the police. Do they know you have them?'

'No,' I replied. 'I took possession of them before the police arrived.'

'Then, in that case,' said he 'it will be as well to say nothing about them.' He held the pieces of glass up against the light, examining them closely and comparing them, first with the naked eye and then with the aid of a lens. Finally he lifted the microscope from its shelf, and placing it on the table, laid one of the pieces of glass on the stage and examined it through the instrument. His inspection occupied only a few seconds, then he rose, and turning to Drayton, who had been watching him eagerly, said: 'It may be highly important for us to have these fingerprints with us. But we can't produce the originals before the police, and besides, they are too valuable to carry about at the risk of spoiling them. But I could make rough, temporary photographs of them in five minutes if you will consent to the delay.'

'I am in your hands, Thorndyke,' replied Drayton. 'Do whatever you think is necessary.'

'Then let us go to the laboratory at once,' said Thorndyke; and taking the two pieces of glass, he led the way across the landing and up the stairs to the upper floor on which the laboratory and workshop were situated. And as we went, I could not but appreciate Thorndyke's tact and sympathy in taking Drayton up with him, so that the tedium of delay might be relieved by the sense of purposeful action.

The laboratory and its methods were characteristic of Thorndyke. Everything was ready and all procedure was prearranged. As we entered, the assistant, Polton, put down the work on which he was engaged, and at a word, took up the present task without either hesitation or hurry. While Thorndyke fixed the pieces of glass in the copying frame of the great standing camera, Polton arranged the light and the condensers and produced a dark-slide loaded with bromide paper. In less than a minute the exposure was made; in another three minutes the print had been developed, roughly fixed, rinsed, squeegeed, soaked in spirit, cut in two, and trimmed with scissors, and the damp but rapidly drying halves attached with drawing pins to a small hinged board specially designed for carrying wet prints in the pocket.

'Now,' said Thorndyke, slipping the folded board into his pocket and taking from a shelf a powerful electric inspection lamp, 'I think we are ready to start. These few minutes have not been wasted.'

We returned to the lower room, where Thorndyke, having bestowed the lamp in the canvas-covered 'research-case,' put on his hat and overcoat and took up the case, and we all set forth, walking quickly and in silence up Inner Temple Lane to the gate, and taking our seats in the waiting car when Drayton had given a few laconic instructions to the driver.

Up to this point Thorndyke had asked not a single question about the crime. Now, as the car started, he said to Drayton: 'We had better be ready to begin the investigation as soon as we arrive. Could you give me a short account of what has happened?'

'Anstey knows more about it than I do,' was the reply. 'He was there within a few minutes of the murder.'

The question being thus referred to me, I gave an account of all that I had seen and heard, to which Thorndyke listened with deep attention, interrupting me only once or twice to elucidate some point that was not quite clear.

'I understand,' said he when I had finished, 'that there is no catalogue or record of the collection and no written description of the specimens?'

'No,' replied Drayton. 'But I have looked over the cabinets a good many times, and taken the pieces out to examine them, so I think I shall be able to tell roughly what is missing, and give a working description of the pieces. And I could certainly identify most of them if they should be produced.'

'They are not very likely to be traced,' said Thorndyke. 'It is highly improbable that the murderer will attempt to dispose of things stolen in such circumstances. Still, the possibility of identifying them may be of the greatest importance, for the folly of criminals is often beyond belief.'

As he finished speaking the car slowed down in the hollow, sandy road that skirted the grounds of 'The Rowans' and presently drew up opposite the gate, when we all alighted and made our way through the garden to the door of the house.

CHAPTER THREE

Thorndyke takes up the Inquiry

The outer door of the house was shut, although the lower rooms were all lighted up, but at the first sound of the bell it was opened by a uniformed constable who regarded us stolidly and inquired as to our business. Before there was time to answer, however, a man whom I at once recognised as Inspector Badger of the Criminal Investigation Department came out into the hall and asked sharply: 'Who is that, Martin?'

'It is Sir Lawrence Drayton, Dr Thorndyke, and Mr Anstey,' I replied; and as the constable backed out of the way we all entered.

'This is a terrible catastrophe, Sir Lawrence,' said Badger. 'Dreadful, dreadful. If sincere sympathy would be any consolation – '

'It wouldn't,' interrupted Drayton, 'though I thank you all the same. The only thing that would console me – and that little enough – would be the sight of the ruffian who did it dangling at the end of a rope. The local officer told you, I suppose, that I was asking Dr Thorndyke to lend his valuable aid in investigating the crime?'

'Yes, Sir Lawrence,' replied Badger, 'but I don't know that I am in a position to authorise any unofficial – '

'Tut, tut, man!' Drayton broke in impatiently, 'I am not asking you to authorise anything. I am the murdered man's sole executor and his only brother. In the one capacity his entire estate is vested in me until it has been disposed of in accordance with the will; in the other capacity, the duty devolves on me of seeing that his murderer is brought to account. I give you every liberty and facility to examine these premises, but I am not going to surrender possession of them. Has any discovery been made?'

'No, sir,' Badger replied a little sulkily. 'We have only been here a few minutes. I was taking some particulars from the housekeeper.'

'Possibly I can give you some information while Dr Thorndyke is making his inspection of my poor brother's body,' said Drayton. 'When he has finished and the body has been laid decently in his bedroom, I will come with you to the museum and we will see if anything is missing.'

Badger assented, with evident unwillingness, to this arrangement. He and Drayton entered the drawing-room, from which the inspector had just come, while I conducted Thorndyke to the museum.

The room was just as I had seen it last, excepting that the open drawer had been closed. The stark, rigid figure still lay on the floor, the set, white face still stared with stern fixity at the ceiling. As I looked, the events of the interval faded from my mind and all the horror of the sudden tragedy came back.

Just inside the door Thorndyke halted and slowly ran his eye round the room, taking in its arrangement, and no doubt fixing it in his memory. Presently he stepped over to where the body lay, and stood a while looking down on the dead man. Then he stopped and closely examined a spot on the right breast.

'Isn't there more bleeding than is usual in the case of a bullet-wound?' I asked.

'Yes,' he replied, 'but that blood hasn't come from the wound in front. There must be another at the back, possibly a wound of exit.' As he spoke, he stood up and again looked searchingly round the room, more especially at the side in which the door opened. Suddenly his glance became fixed and he strode quickly across to a cabinet that stood beside the door; and as I followed him, I perceived a ragged hole in the front of one of the drawers.

'Do you mean, Thorndyke,' I exclaimed, 'that the bullet passed right through him?'

'That is what it looks like,' he replied. 'But we shall be able to judge better when we get the drawer open – which we can't do until Badger comes. But there is one thing that we had better do at once.' Stepping over to the table on which he had placed the research-case, he opened the latter, and taking from it a stick of blackboard chalk, went back to the body. 'We must assume,' said he, 'that he fell where he was standing when he was struck, and if that is so he would have been standing here.' He marked on the carpet two rough outlines to indicate the position of the feet when the murdered man fell, and having put the chalk back in the case, continued: 'The next thing is to verify the existence of the wound at the back. Will you help me to turn him over?'

We turned the body gently on to its right side, and immediately there came into view a large, blood-stained patch under the left shoulder, and at the centre of it a ragged burst in the fabric of the coat.

'That will do,' said Thorndyke. 'It is an unmistakable exit wound. The bullet probably missed the ribs both in entering and emerging, and passed through the heart or the great vessels. The appearances suggest almost instantaneous death. The face is set, the eyes wide open, and both the hands tightly clenched in a cadaveric spasm. And the right hand seems to be grasping something, but we had better leave that until Badger has seen it.'

At this moment footsteps became audible coming along the corridor, and Badger entered the room accompanied by the local inspector. The two officers looked inquiringly at Thorndyke, who proceeded at once to give them a brief statement of the facts that he had observed.

'There can't be much doubt,' said Badger when he had examined the hole in the drawer front, 'that this was made by a spent bullet. But we may as well settle the question now. We shall want the keys in any case.'

He passed his hand over the dead man's clothes, and having located the pocket which contained the keys, drew out a good-sized bunch, with which he went over to the cabinet. A few trials with likely-looking keys resulted in the discovery of the right one, and when this had been turned and the hinged batten swung back, all the drawers of the cabinet were released. The inspector pulled out the one with the damaged front and looked in inquisitively. Its contents consisted principally of latten and pewter spoons, now evidently disarranged and mingled with a litter of splinters of wood; and in the bowl of a spoon near the back of the drawer lay a distorted bullet, which Badger picked up and examined critically.

'Browning automatic, I should say,' was his comment, 'and if so we ought to find the cartridge case somewhere on the floor. We must look for it presently, but we'd better get the body moved first, if you have finished your inspection, Doctor.'

'There is something grasped in the right hand,' said Thorndyke. 'It looks like a wisp of hair. Perhaps we had better look at that before the body is moved, in case it should fall out.'

We returned to the body, and the two officers stooped and watched eagerly as Thorndyke, with some difficulty, opened the rigid hand sufficiently to draw from it a small tuft of hair.

'The spasm is very marked,' he observed as he scrutinised the hair and felt in his pocket for a lens; and when, with the aid of the latter, he had made a further examination, he continued: 'The state of the root-bulbs shows that the hair was actually plucked out – which, of course, is what we should expect.'

'Can you form any opinion as to what sort of man he was?' Badger asked.

'No,' replied Thorndyke, 'excepting that he was not a recently released convict. But the appearance of the hair agrees with Miss Blake's description of the man who stabbed her. I understand that she described him as a having rather short but bushy hair. This hair is rather short, though we can't say whether it was bushy or not. Perhaps more complete examination of it may tell us something further.'

'Possibly,' Badger agreed. 'I will have it thoroughly examined, and get a report on it. Shall I take charge of it?' he added, holding out his hand.

'Yes, you had better,' replied Thorndyke, 'but I will take a small sample for further examination, if you don't mind.'

'There is no need for that,' protested Badger. 'You can always have access to what we've got if you want to refer to it.'

'I know,' said Thorndyke, 'and it is very good of you to offer. Still this will save time and trouble.' And without more ado he separated a third of the tuft and handed the remainder to the inspector, who wrapped it in a sheet of note-paper that he had taken from his pocket and sourly watched Thorndyke bestow his portion in a seed-envelope from his pocket-book, and after writing on it a brief description, return it to the latter receptacle.

'You were saying,' said Badger, 'that this hair agrees with Miss Blake's description. But it was suggested that it was the other man who really committed the murder. Isn't that rather a contradiction?'

'I don't think so,' replied Thorndyke. 'The probabilities seem to me to point to the other man as the murderer.'

'But how can that be?' objected Badger. 'You say that this hair agrees with Miss Blake's description of the man. But this hair is obviously the hair of the murderer. And that man was left-handed and the wound is on the right breast, suggesting that the murderer held his pistol in his left hand.'

'Not at all,' said Thorndyke. 'I submit that this hair is obviously not the hair of the murderer. Look at those chalk marks that I have made on the floor. They mark the spot on which the deceased was standing when the bullet struck him. Now go back to the cabinet and look at the chalk marks and see what is in a direct line with them.'

The inspector did so. 'I see,' said he. 'You mean the window.'

'Yes, it was open, since the robber evidently came in by it, and the sill is barely five feet from the ground. I suggest – but merely as a probability, since the bullet may have been deflected – that the other man was keeping guard outside, and that when he heard a noise from this room he looked in through the window and saw his confederate on the point of being captured by the deceased, that he then fired, and when he saw deceased fall, he made his escape. That would account for the man who was seen by Miss Blake making appearance after the other man had gone. He may have had to extricate himself from the dead man's grasp, and then he had to climb out of the window. But the position of the empty cartridge-case – if we find it – will settle the question. If the pistol was fired into the room through the window, the cartridge-case will be on the ground outside.'

He opened his research-case, and taking from it the electric lamp, walked slowly to the window, throwing the bright light on the floor as he went. The two officers followed, and all scrutinised the floor closely, but in vain. Then Thorndyke leaned out of the window and threw the light of his lamp on the ground outside, moving the bright beam slowly to and fro while the inspector craned forward eagerly. Suddenly Badger uttered an exclamation.

'There it is, Doctor! Don't move the light. Keep it there while I go out and pick the case up.'

'One moment, Badger,' said Thorndyke. 'We mustn't be impetuous. There are some other things out there more important than the cartridge-case. I can see two distinct sets of footprints, and it is above all things necessary that they should not be confused by being trodden into. Let us get the body moved first. Then we can take some mats out and examine the footprints systematically and recover the cartridge-case at the same time. If we are careful we can leave the ground in such a condition that it will be possible to go over it again by daylight.'

The wisdom of this suggestion was obvious, and the inspector proceeded at once to act on it. The sergeant and the constable were sent for, and by them the body of the murdered man was carried, under the inspector's supervision, to the bedroom above. Then a couple of large mats were procured from Mrs Benham and we all issued from the front door into the garden. Here, however, a halt was called, and at Thorndyke's suggestion, the party was separated into two, he and Badger to explore the grounds inside the fence, while the local inspector and the others endeavoured to follow the tracks outside.

I did not join either party, nor did Sir Lawrence. We both realised the futility of any attempt to trace the fugitives, and recognised that the suggestion was made by Thorndyke merely to get rid of the unwanted supernumeraries. Accordingly we took up a position outside the fence, which we could just look over, and watched the proceedings of Thorndyke and Inspector Badger, as they passed slowly along the side of the house, each with the light of his lantern thrown full on the ground.

They had gone but a few paces when they picked up on the soft, loamy path the fairly clear impressions of two pairs of feet going towards the back of the house. Both the investigators paused and stooped to examine them, and Badger remarked: 'So they came in at the front gate – naturally, as it was the easiest way. But they must have been pretty sure that there was no one in the house to see them. And that suggests that they knew the ways of the household and that they had lurked about to watch Mr Drayton and Mrs Benham off the premises.'

'Is it possible to distinguish one man from the other?' Drayton asked.

'Yes, quite easily,' Badger replied. 'One of them is a biggish man – close on six feet, I should say – while the other is quite a small man. That will be the one that Miss Blake saw.'

They followed the tracks to the back of the house, and as we followed on our side of the fence Thorndyke called out: 'Be careful, Anstey, not to tread in the tracks where they came over the fence. We ought to get specially clear prints of their feet where they jumped down. Could you get a light?'

'I'll go and get one of the acetylene lamps from the car,' said Drayton. 'You stay where you are until I come back.'

He was but a short time absent, and when he returned he was provided with a powerful lamp and a couple of small mats. 'I have brought these,' he explained, 'to lay on any particularly clear footprints to protect them from chance injury. We mustn't lose the faintest shadow of a clue.'

With the aid of the brilliant light Drayton and I explored the ground at the foot of the fence. Suddenly Sir Lawrence exclaimed: 'Why, these look like a woman's footprints!' and he pointed to a set of rather indistinct impressions running parallel to the fence.

'They will be Miss Blake's,' said I. 'She ran round this way. Yes, here is the place where the man came over. What extraordinarily clear impressions this ground takes. It shows the very brads in the heels.'

'Yes,' he agreed; 'this is the Hampstead sand, you know; one of the finest foundry-sands in the country.'

He laid one of the mats carefully on the pair of footprints, and we continued our explorations towards the back of the house. Here we saw Thorndyke and the inspector, each kneeling on a mat, examining a confused mass of footprints on the ground between the museum window and the fence.

'Have you found the cartridge-case?' I asked.

'Yes,' replied Thorndyke. 'Badger has it. It is a "Baby Browning." And I think we have seen all there is to see here by this light. Can you see where the big man came down from the fence? He went over where I am throwing the light.'

We approached the spot cautiously, and at the place indicated perceived the very clear and deep impression of a large right foot with a much less distinct print of a left foot, both having the heels towards the fence; and a short distance in front of them the soft, loamy earth bore a clear impression of a left hand with the fingers spread out, and a fainter print of a right hand.

I reported these facts to Thorndyke, who at once decided to come over and examine the prints. Handing his lamp over a few paces farther along the fence, he climbed up and dropped lightly by my side, followed almost immediately by Inspector Badger.

'This,' said the inspector, gazing down at the foot and hand-prints, 'bears out what we saw from the inside. He wasn't any too active, this chappie. Probably fat – a big, heavy, awkward man. Had to pull the garden seat up to the fence to enable him to get over, though it was an easy fence to climb with those big cross-rails; and here, you see, he comes down all of a heap on his hands and knees. However, that doesn't help us a great deal. He isn't the only fat man in the world. We had better go indoors now and have a look at the room and see if we can find out what has been taken.'

We turned to retrace our steps towards the gate, pausing on our way to lift the mats and inspect the footprints of the smaller man; and as we went Drayton asked if anything of interest had been discovered.

'No,' replied Badger. 'They got in without any difficulty by forcing back the catch of the window – unless the window was open already. It isn't quite clear whether they both got in. The big man walked part of the way round the house and along the fence in both directions, and he pulled a garden seat up to the fence to help himself up. The small man came out of the window last, if they were both inside, and I expect it was he who dropped this – must have had it in his hand when he climbed out' – and here the inspector produced from his pocket a ring, set with a single round stone, which he handed to Sir Lawrence.

'Ah,' said the latter, 'a posy-ring, one of the cat's eye series. There were several of these and a set of moonstone rings in the same drawer.'

'You know the collection pretty well, then, Sir Lawrence?'

'Fairly well. I often used to look over the things with my poor brother. But, of course, I can't remember all the specimens, though I think I can show you the drawer that this came from.'

By this time we had entered the house and were making our way to the museum. On entering the room, Drayton walked straight to the cabinet which I remembered to have seen open, and pulled out the second drawer from the top.

'This is the one,' said he. 'They have taken out the glass top – I suppose those are the pieces of it on the floor.'

'Yes,' said Badger. 'We found it open, and it seems to be the only drawer that has been tampered with.'

Drayton pulled out the top drawer, and having looked closely at the glass cover, remarked: 'They have had this one open, too. There are distinct fingerprints on the glass; and they have had the cover off for there are finger-marks on the inside of the glass. I wonder why they did that.'

'I can't imagine,' said Badger. 'They don't seem to have taken anything – there wasn't anything worth taking, for that matter. But they could see that without lifting off the glass. However, it is all for the best. We'll hand this glass cover to the Fingerprint Department and hope they will be able to spot the man that the fingers belong to.'

As he spoke, he made as if he would lift off the cover, but he was anticipated by Thorndyke, who carefully raised the glass by its leather tab, and taking it up by the edges, held it against the light and examined the fingerprints minutely both on the upper and under surfaces.

'The thumbs are on the upper surface,' he remarked, 'and the fingers underneath; so the glass was lifted right out and held with both hands.'

He handed the glass to the inspector, who had been watching him uneasily, and now took the cover from him with evident relief; and as Badger proceeded to deposit it in a safe place, he pushed in the top drawer and returned to the consideration of the second.

'There are evidently several pieces missing from this drawer,' said he, 'and it may be important to know what they are, though it is rather unlikely that the thieves will try to dispose of them. Can you tell us what they are, Drayton?'

'I can tell you roughly,' was the reply. 'This drawer contained the collection of posy-rings, and most of them are there still, as you can see. The front row were rings set with moonstone and cat's eye, and most of those are gone. Then there was a group of moonstone and cat's eye ornaments, mostly brooches and earrings, and one pendant. Those have all disappeared. And there is another thing that was in this drawer that has apparently been taken; a locket. It was shaped like a book and had a Greek inscription on the front.'

'So far as you can see, Sir Lawrence,' said Badger, 'has anything of value been taken – of real value, I mean?'

'Of negotiable value, you mean,' Drayton corrected. 'No. Most of the things were of gold, though not all, but the stones were probably worth no more than a few shillings each. The value was principally in the associations and individual character of the pieces. All of them had inscriptions, and several of them had recorded histories. But that would be of no use to a thief.'

'Exactly,' said Badger. 'That was what was in my mind. There is something rather amateurish about this robbery. It isn't quite like the work of a regular hand. The time was foolish, and then all this shooting and stabbing is more like the work of some stray foreign crooks than of a regular tradesman; and as you say, the stuff wasn't worth the risk – unless there's something else of more value. Perhaps we had better go through the other cabinets.'

He produced the bunch of keys from his pocket and had just inserted one into the lock of the next cabinet when Drayton interposed.

'There is no need for that, Inspector. If the cabinets are locked and have not been broken open, their contents are intact; and I can tell you that those contents are of no considerable intrinsic value.' With this he drew the key from the lock and dropped the bunch in his pocket, a proceeding whereat the inspector smiled sourly and remarked: 'Then in that case, I think I have finished for the present. I'll just pack up this glass cover and see if those others were able to follow the tracks of either of these men. And I'll wish you gentleman "goodnight." '

Sir Lawrence accompanied him to the drawing-room, and as I learned later, provided the official party with refreshment, and when we were alone I turned to Thorndyke.

'I suppose we have finished, too?'

'Not quite,' he replied. 'There are one or two little matters to be attended to, but we will wait until the police are clear of the premises. They will keep their own counsel and I propose to keep mine, unless I can give them a straight lead.' He opened his research-case and was thoughtfully looking over its contents when Drayton returned and announced that the police had departed.

'Is there anything more that you want to do, Thorndyke?' he asked.

'Yes,' was the reply. 'For one thing, I should like to see if there are any more fingerprints.' As he spoke, he pulled out the drawers of the cabinet one after the other, and examined the glass covers. But apparently they had not been touched. At any rate, there were no marks on any of the glasses.

33

'They must have been disturbed soon after they got to work,' said Drayton, 'as they opened only two drawers.'

'Probably,' Thorndyke agreed, taking from his case a little glass jar filled with a yellowish powder and fitted with two glass tubes and a rubber bulb. With this apparatus he blew a cloud of the fine powder over the woodwork of the rifled cabinet, and when a thin coating had settled on the polished surface, he tapped the wood gently with the handle of his pocket-knife. At each tap a portion of the coating of powder was jarred off the surface, and then there appeared several oval spots to which it still adhered. Then he gently blew away the rest of the powder, when the oval spots were revealed as fingerprints, standing out white and distinct against the dark wood. Thorndyke now produced from his pocket the hinged board, and opening it, compared the photographs with these new fingerprints, while Drayton and I looked over his shoulder.

'They are undoubtedly the same,' said I, a little surprised at the ease with which I identified these curious markings. 'Absolutely the same – which is rather odd, seeing that there are the marks of only two digits of the left hand and four of the right. It almost looks as if those particular fingers had got soiled with some greasy material and that the other fingers were clean and had left no mark.'

'An admirable suggestion, Anstey,' said Thorndyke. 'The same idea had occurred to me, for the prints of these particular fingers are certainly abnormally distinct. Let us see if we can get any confirmation.' He blew upon each of the fingerprints in turn until most of the powder was dislodged and the markings had become almost invisible. Then, taking his handkerchief, which was of soft silk, and rolling it into a ball, he began to wipe the woodwork with a circular motion, at first very lightly but gradually increasing the pressure until he was rubbing quite vigorously. The result seemed to justify my suggestion, for as the rubbing proceeded, I could see, by the light of Drayton's lamp, thrown on at various angles, that the fingerprints seemed to have spread out into oval, glistening patches, having a lustre somewhat different from that of the polished wood.

Sir Lawrence looked on with keen interest, and as Thorndyke paused to examine the woodwork, he asked: 'What is the exact purpose of this experiment?'

'The point is,' replied Thorndyke, 'that whereas the fingerprint of the mathematical theorists is a mere abstraction of form devoid of any other properties, the actual or real fingerprint is a material thing which has physical and chemical properties, and these properties may have considerable evidential significance. These fingerprints, for instance, contain some substance other than the natural secretions of the skin. The questions then arise, What is that substance? How came it here? And is it usually associated with any particular kind of person or activity? The specimens that Anstey so judiciously captured may help us to answer the first question, and our native wits may enable us to answer the others. So we have some data for consideration. And that reminds me that there are some other data that we must secure.'

'What are they?' Drayton asked eagerly.

'There are those impressions in the sand outside the fence. I must have permanent records of them. Shall we go and do them now? I shall want a jug of water and a light.'

While Drayton went to fetch the water Thorndyke and I took our way out through the garden to the outside of the fence, he carrying his research-case, and I bearing Drayton's lamp. At the spot where we had laid down the mat we halted, and Thorndyke, having set down his case, once more lifted the mat.

'They are small feet,' he remarked, glancing at the footprints before stooping to open the case. 'A striking contrast to the other man's.'

He took from his case a tin of plaster of Paris, and dipping up a small quantity in a spoon, proceeded very carefully to dust the footprints with the fine, white powder until they were covered with a thin, even coating. Then he produced a bottle of water fitted with a rubber ball-spray diffuser, and with this blew a copious spray of water over the footprints. As a result, the white powder gradually shrank until the footprints looked as if they had received a thin coat of whitewash.

'Why not fill the footprints up with liquid plaster?' asked Drayton, who came up at this moment carrying a large jug.

'It would probably disturb the sand,' was the reply, 'and moreover, the water would soak in at once and leave the plaster a crumbling mass. But when this thin layer has set it will be possible to fill up and get a solid cast.'

He repeated the application of the spray once or twice, and then we went on to the place where the other man had come over. Here the same process was carried out, not only with the footprints but also with those of the hands. Then we went back to the first place, and when Thorndyke had gently touched the edge of the footprints and ascertained that the thin coating of plaster had set into a solid shell, he produced a small rubber basin, and having half filled it with water, added a quantity of plaster and stirred it until it assumed the consistency of cream; when he carefully poured it into the white-coated footprints until they were full and slightly overflowing.

'You see the advantage of this?' said Thorndyke as he cleaned out the basin and started to walk slowly back to the site of the second set of prints.

'I do, indeed,' replied Drayton, 'and I am astonished that Badger did not take a permanent record. These casts will enable you to put the actual feet of the accused in evidence if need be.'

'Precisely; besides giving us the opportunity to study them at our leisure, and refer to them if any fresh evidence should become available.'

The second set of footprints and the impressions of the hands received similar treatment, and when they had been filled, Thorndyke proceeded to pack up his appliances.

'We ought to give the casts a good twenty minutes to set hard,' he said, 'though it is the best plaster and quite fresh and has a little powdered alum mixed with it to accelerate setting and make the cast harder. But we mustn't be impatient.'

'I am in no hurry,' said Drayton. 'I shall stay here tonight – one couldn't leave Mrs Benham in the house all alone. The car can take you back to your chambers and drop Anstey at his lodgings.

Tomorrow we must make some arrangements of a more permanent kind. But the great thing is to get on the track of these two villains. Nothing else seems to matter. There is my poor brother's corpse, crying aloud to Heaven for justice, and I shall never rest until his murderers have paid their debt.'

'I sympathise with you most cordially, Drayton,' said Thorndyke, 'and it is no mere verbal sympathy. I promise you that every resource at my disposal shall be called in to aid, that no stone shall be left unturned. It is not only the office of friendship; it is a public duty to ensure that an inexcusable crime of this kind shall be visited with the most complete retribution.'

'Thank you, Thorndyke,' Sir Lawrence said with gruff earnestness. And then after a short pause, he continued: 'I suppose it is premature to ask you, but do you see any glimmer of hope? Is there anything to lay hold of? I can see for myself that it is a very difficult and obscure case.'

'It is,' Thorndyke agreed. 'Of course the fingerprints may dispose of the whole difficulty, if they happen to be on the files at the Habitual Criminals Registry. Otherwise there is very little evidence. Still, there is some, and we may build up more by inference. I have seen more unpromising cases come to a successful issue.'

By this time the stipulated twenty minutes had expired, and we proceeded to the first set of footprints. The plaster, on being tested, was found to be quite firm and hard, and Thorndyke was able, with great care, to lift the two chalky-looking plates from their bed in the ground. And even in the rather unfavourable light of the lamp their appearance was somewhat startling, for, as Thorndyke turned them over, each cast presented the semblance of a white foot, surprisingly complete in detail so far as the sole was concerned.

But if the appearance of these casts was striking, much more so was that of the second set; for the latter included casts of the handprints, the aspect of which was positively uncanny, especially in the case of the deeper impression, the effect of which was that of a snowy hand with outspread, crooked, clutching fingers. And here again the fine loam had yielded an unexpected amount of detail. The creases and markings of the palm were all perfectly clear and distinct, and I even thought that I could perceive a trace of the ridges of the fingertips.

Before leaving the spot we carefully removed all traces of plaster, for it was certain that the footprints would be examined by daylight, and Thorndyke considered it better that the existence of these casts should be known only to ourselves. The footprints were left practically intact, and it was open to the police to make casts if they saw fit.

'I think,' said Thorndyke when we had re-entered the house and were inspecting the casts afresh as they lay on the table, 'it would be a wise precaution to attach our signatures to each of them, in case it should be necessary at any time to put them in evidence. Their genuineness would then be attested beyond any possibility of dispute.'

To this Drayton and I agreed most emphatically, and accordingly each of us wrote his name, with the date, on the smooth back of each cast. Then the 'records' were carefully packed and bestowed in the research-case, and Thorndyke and I shook our host's hand and went forth to the car.

CHAPTER FOUR

The Lady of Shalott

The modern London suburb seems to have an inherent incapacity for attaining a decent old age. City streets and those of country towns contrive to gather from the passing years some quality of mellowness that does but add to their charm. But with suburbs it is otherwise. Whatever charm they have appertains to their garish youth and shares its ephemeral character. Cities and towns grow venerable with age, the suburb merely grows shabby.

The above profound reflections were occasioned by my approach to the vicinity of Jacob Street, Hampstead Road, and by a growing sense of the drab – not to say sordid atmosphere that enveloped it, and its incongruity with the appearance and manner of the lady whose residence I was approaching. However, I consoled myself with the consideration that if 'Honesty lives in a poor house, like your fair pearl in your foul oyster,' perhaps Beauty might make shift with no better lodging; and these cogitations having brought me to the factory-like gateway, I gave a brisk tug at the bell above the brass plate.

After a short interval the wicket was opened by my young acquaintance of the previous night, who greeted me with a sedate smile of recognition.

'Good afternoon,' I said, holding out my hand. 'I have just called to learn how your sister is. I hope she is not much the worse for her rather terrifying experiences last night.'

39

'Thank you,' he replied with quaint politeness, 'she seems to be all right today. But the doctor won't let her do any work. He's fixed her arm in a sling. But won't you come in and see her, sir?'

I hesitated, dubious as to whether she would care to receive a stranger of her own class in these rather mean surroundings, but when he added: 'She would like to see you, I am sure, sir,' my scruples gave way to my very definite inclination and I stepped through the wicket.

My young friend – who wore a blue linen smock – conducted me down a paved passage, the walls of which bore each a long shelf on which was a row of plaster busts and statuettes, into an open yard in which a small, elderly man was working with chisel and mallet on a somewhat ornate marble tombstone, amidst a sort of miniature Avebury of blocks and slabs of stone and marble. Across the yard rose a great barn-like building with one enormous window high up the wall, a great double door, and a small side door. Into the latter my conductor entered and held it open for me, and as I passed in, I found myself in total darkness. Only for a moment, however, for my young host, having shut the door, drew aside a heavy curtain and gave me a view of huge, bare hall with lofty, whitewashed walls, an open timber roof, and a plank floor relieved from absolute nakedness by one or two rugs. A couple of studio easels stood opposite the window, and in a corner I observed a spectral lay-figure shrouded in what looked like a sheet. At the farther end, by a large, open fireplace, Miss Blake sat in an easy-chair with a book in her hand. She looked up as I entered, and then rose and advanced to meet me, holding out her left hand.

'How kind of you, Mr Anstey, to come and see me!' she exclaimed. 'And how good it was of you to take such care of me last night!'

'Not at all,' I replied. 'But I hope you are not very much the worse for your adventures. Are you suffering much pain?'

'I have no pain at all,' she replied with a smile, 'and I don't believe this sling is in the least necessary. But one must obey the doctor's orders.'

'Yes,' interposed her brother, 'and that is what the sling is for. To prevent your from getting into mischief, Winnie.'

'It prevents me from doing any work, if that is what you mean, Percy,' said she, 'and I suppose the doctor is right in that.'

'I am sure he is,' said I. 'Rest is most essential to enable the wound to heal quickly. What sort of night did you have?'

'I didn't sleep much,' she replied. 'It kept coming back to me, you know – that awful moment when I went into the museum and saw that poor man lying on the floor. It was a dreadful experience. So horribly sudden, too. One moment I saw him go away, full of life and energy, and the next I was looking on his corpse. Do you think those wretches will really escape?'

'It is difficult to say. The police have the fingerprints of one of them, and if that person is a regular criminal, they will be able to identify him.'

'Will they really?' she exclaimed. 'It sounds very wonderful. How are they able to do it?'

'It is really quite simple. When a man is convicted of a crime, a complete set of his fingerprints is taken at the prison by pressing his fingers on an inked slab and putting them down on a sheet of paper – there is a special form for the purpose with a space for each finger. This form is deposited, with photographs of the prisoner, in one of the files of the Habitual Criminals Registry at Scotland Yard. Then, when a strange fingerprint turns up, it is compared with those in the files, and if one is found that is an exact facsimile, the name attached to it is the name of the man who is wanted.'

'But how are they ever able to find the facsimile in such a huge collection, for the numbers in the files must be enormous?'

'That also is more simple than it looks. The lines on fingertips form very definite patterns – spirals, or whorls, closed loops like the end grain of wood, open curves, or arches, and so on. Now each fingerprint is filed under its particular heading – whorl, loop, arch, etc. – and also in accordance with the particular finger that bears the pattern, so the inquiry is narrowed down to a comparatively small number from the start. Let us take an instance. Suppose we have found some fingerprints of which the left little finger has a spiral pattern and the ring finger adjoining has a closed loop. Then we look in the file which contains the spiral left little fingers and in the file of looped left ring fingers and we glance through the lists of names. There will be certain names that will appear in both lists, and one of those will be the name of the man that we want. All that remains is to compare our prints with each of them in turn until we come to the one that is an exact facsimile. The name attached to that one is the name of our man. Of course, in practice, the process is more elaborate, but that is the principle.'

'It is wonderfully ingenious,' said Miss Blake, 'and really simple, as you say, and it sounds as if it were perfectly infallible.'

'That is the claim that the police make. But, as you see, the utility of the system for the detection of crime is limited to the cases of those criminals whose fingerprints have been registered. That is what our chance depends on now. The man who murdered Mr Drayton left prints of his fingers on the glass of the cabinet, and the police have taken the glass away to examine. If they find facsimiles of those fingerprints in the register, then they will know who murdered Mr Drayton. But if those fingerprints are not in the register, they won't help us at all. And as far as I know, there is no other clue to the identity of the murderer.'

Miss Blake appeared to reflect earnestly on what I had said, and in the ensuing silence I continued my somewhat furtive observation of the great studio and its occupants. Particularly did I notice a number of paintings, apparently executed in tempera on huge sheets of brown paper, pinned on the walls somewhat above the level of the eye; figure subjects of an allegorical character, strongly recalling the manner of Burne-Jones, and painted with something considerably beyond ordinary competence. And from the paintings my eye strayed to the painter – as I assumed and hoped her to be – and a very striking and picturesque figure she appeared, with her waxen complexion, delicately tinged with pink, her earnest grey eyes, a short, slightly retroussé nose, the soft mass of red-gold hair and the lissom form, actually full and plump though with the deceptive appearance of slimness that one notes in the figures of the artist whose style she followed. I noted with pleasure – not wholly aesthetic, I suspect – the graceful pose into which she seemed naturally to fall, and when my roving eye took in a 'planchette' hanging on the wall and a crystal ball reposing on a black velvet cushion on a little altar-like table in a corner, I forbore to scoff inwardly as I should have done in other circumstances, for somehow the hint of occultism, even of superstition, seemed not out of character. She reminded me of the Lady of Shalott, and the whispered suggestion of Merlinesque magic gave a note of harmony that sounded pleasantly.

While we had been talking, her brother had been pursuing his own affairs with silent concentration, though I had noticed that he had paused to listen to my exposition on the subject of fingerprints. In the middle of the studio floor was a massive stone slab – a relic of some former sculptor tenant – and on this the boy was erecting, very methodically, a model of some sort of building with toy bricks of a kind that I had not seen before. I was watching him and noting the marked difference between him and his sister – for he was a somewhat dark lad with a strong, aquiline face – when Miss Blake spoke again.

'Did you find out what had been stolen?'

'Yes,' I answered, 'approximately. There was nothing missing of any considerable value. Only a few pieces had been taken, and those were mostly simple jewels set with moonstones or cat's eyes.'

'Cat's eyes!' she exclaimed.

'Yes, a few posy-rings, some earrings, and, I think, one pendant.'

'Was the pendant stolen?'

'Yes, apparently. Sir Lawrence mentioned a cat's-eye pendant as one of the things that he missed from the drawer. Does the pendant interest you specially?'

'Yes,' she answered thoughtfully, 'it was this pendant that I went there to see. It was illustrated in the *Connoisseur* article, and I wrote to poor Mr Drayton because I wanted to examine it. And so,' she added in a lower tone and with an expression of deep sadness, 'the pendant became, through me, the cause of his death. But for it and me, he would not have gone to the house at that time.'

'It is impossible to say whether he would or not,' said I, and then, to change the subject, as this seemed to distress her, I continued: 'there was another thing missing that was figured in the *Connoisseur* — a locket — '

'Of course!' she exclaimed. 'How silly of me to forget it.' She rose hastily, and stepping over to an old walnut bureau that stood under the window, pulled out one of the little drawers and picked some small object out of it.

'There,' she said, holding out her hand, in which lay a small gold locket, 'this is the one. I recognised it instantly. And now see if you can guess how it came into my possession.'

I was completely mystified, and said so, though I hazarded a guess that it had in some way caught in her clothing.

'Yes,' said she, 'it was in my shawl. You remember I said that the man whom I was trying to hold had something in his hand and that he must have dropped it when he drew his knife. Now it happened that my shawl had just then slipped off in the struggle and that he was standing on it. The locket must have dropped on the shawl, and this little brass hook, which some one has fastened to the ring of the locket, must have hooked itself into the meshes of the shawl — which is of crocheted silk, you will remember. Then you picked the shawl up and rolled it into a bundle, and it was never unrolled until this morning. When I shook it out to hang it up, the locket fell out, and most unfortunately, as it fell it opened and the glass inside got broken. I am most vexed about it, for it is such an extremely charming little thing. Don't you think so?'

I took the little bauble in my hand, and, to speak the literal truth, was not deeply smitten with its appearance. But policy, and the desire to make myself agreeable, bade me dissemble. 'It is a quaint and curious little object,' I admitted.

'It is a perfectly fascinating little thing,' she exclaimed enthusiastically. 'And so secret and mysterious, too. I am sure there is some hidden meaning in those references inside, and then there is something delightfully cabalistic and magical about that weird-looking inscription on the front.'

'Yes,' I agreed, 'Greek capitals make picturesque inscriptions, especially this uncial form of lettering, but there is nothing very recondite in the matter; in fact it is rather hackneyed. "Life is short but Art is long." '

'So that is what it means. Percy couldn't quite make it out, and I don't know any Greek at all. But it is a beautiful motto, though I am not sure that I don't prefer the more usual form, "Art is long but Life is short." '

'That is the Latin version, "Ars longa, Vita brevis." Yes, I think I agree with you. The Latin form is rather more epigrammatic. But what other inscription were you referring to?'

'There are some references to passages of Scripture inside. I have looked them out, all but one. Shall I get my notes and let you see what the references are?' She looked at me so expectantly and with such charming animation that I assented eagerly. Not that I cared particularly what the references were, but the occupation of looking them out promised to put us on a delightfully companionable footing. And if I was not profoundly interested in the locket, I found myself very deeply interested in the Lady of Shalott.

While she was searching for her notes, I examined the little bauble more closely. It was a simple trinket, well made and neatly finished. The workmanship was plain, though very solid, and I judged it to be of some considerable age, though not what one would call antique. It was fashioned in the form of a tiny book with a hinge at the back and a strong loop of gold on each half, the two loops forming a double suspension ring. To one of the loops a small brass hook had been attached, probably to hang it in a show-case. On the front was engraved in bold Greek uncials 'Ο ΒΙΟC ΒΡΑΧΥΟ Η ΔΕ ΤΕΧΝΗ ΜΑΚΡΗ' without any other ornament, and on turning the locket over I found the back – or under-side as a bookbinder would say – quite plain save for the hallmark near the top. Then I opened the little volume. In the back half was a circular cell, framed with a border of small pearls and containing a tiny plait of black hair coiled into a close spiral. It had been enclosed by a glass cover, but this was broken and only a few fragments remained. The interior of the front half was covered with extremely minute engraved lettering which, on close inspection, appeared to be references to certain passages of Holy Scripture, the titles of the books being given in Latin.

I had just concluded these observations when Miss Blake returned with a manuscript book, a Bible, and a small reading-glass.

'This,' she said, handing me the latter, 'will help you to make out the tiny lettering. If you will read out the references one at a time, I will read out the passages that they refer to. And if any of them suggest to you any meaning beyond what is apparent, do, please, tell me, for I can make nothing of them.'

I promised to do so, and focusing the glass on the microscopic writing, read out the first reference: 'Leviticus 25.41.'

'That verse,' she said, 'reads: "And then shall he depart from thee, both he and his children with him, and shall return unto his own family, and unto the possession of his fathers shall he return." '

'The next reference,' said I, 'is "Psalms 121.1." '

'The reading is: "I will lift up mine eyes unto the hills, from whence cometh my help." What do you make of that?'

'Nothing,' I replied, 'unless one can regard it as a pious exhortation, and it is extraordinarily indefinite at that.'

'Yes, it does seem vague, but I feel convinced that it means more than it seems to, if we could only fathom its significance.'

'It might easily do that,' said I, and as I spoke I caught the eye of her brother, who had paused in his work and was watching us with an indulgent smile, and I wondered egotistically if he was writing me down a consummate ass.

'The next,' said I, 'is Acts 10.5.'

'The reading is: "And now send men to Joppa, and call for one Simon, whose surname is Peter." '

'I begin to think you must be right,' said I, 'for that passage is sheer nonsense unless it covers something in the nature of a code. Taken by itself, it has not the faintest bearing on either doctrine or morals. Let us try the next one, Nehemiah 8.4.'

'That one is just as cryptic as the others,' said she. 'It reads: "And Ezra the scribe stood upon a pulpit of wood, which they had made for the purpose; and beside him stood Mattithiah, and Shema, and

Anaiah, and Urijah, and Hilkiah, and Maaseiah, on his right hand; and on his left hand, Pedaiah, and Mishael, and Malchiah, and Hashum, and Hashbadana, Zechariah, and Meshullam." '

At this point an audible snigger proceeding from the direction of the builder revived my misgivings. There is something slightly alarming about a schoolboy with an acute perception of the ridiculous.

'What is the joke, Percy?' his sister asked.

'Those fellows' names, Winnie. Do you suppose there really was a chap called Hashed Banana?'

'Hashbadana, Percy,' she corrected.

'Very well. Hashed Badada then. But that only makes it worse. Sounds as if you'd got a cold.'

'What an absurd boy you are, Percy,' exclaimed Miss Blake, regarding her brother with a fond smile. Then, reverting to her notes, she said: 'The next reference appears to be a mistake, at least I don't understand it. It says "3 Kings 7.41." Isn't that so?'

'Yes. "3 Lib. Regum 7.41." But what is wrong with it?'

'Why, there are only two Books of Kings.'

'Oh, I see. But it isn't a mistake. In the Authorised Version the two books of Samuel have the alternative title of the First and Second Books of Kings, and the First Book of Kings has the subtitle "Commonly called the Third Book of the Kings." But at the present day the books are invariably referred to as the First and Second Books of Samuel and the First and Second Books of Kings. Shall we look it up?'

She opened the Bible and turned over the leaves to the First Book of Kings.

'Yes,' she said, 'it is as you say. How odd that I should never have noticed it, or at any rate, not have remembered it. Then this reference is really 1 Kings 7.41. And yet it can't be. What sense can you possibly make of this: "The two pillars, and the two bowls of the chapiters that were on the top of the two pillars; and the two networks, to cover the two bowls of the chapiters which were upon the top of the pillars." It seems quite meaningless, separated from its context.'

47

'It certainly is rather enigmatical,' I agreed. 'This is an excerpt from what was virtually an inventory of Solomon's Temple. If the purpose of this collection of Scripture texts was to inculcate some religious or moral truths, I don't see the bearing of this quotation at all. But we may take it that these passages had some meaning to the original owner of the locket.'

'They must have had,' she replied earnestly. 'Perhaps we may be able to find the key to the riddle if we consider the whole series together.'

'Possibly,' I agreed, not very enthusiastically. 'The next reference is Psalms 31.7.'

'The verse is: "I will be glad and rejoice in thy mercy: for thou hast considered my trouble; thou hast known my soul in adversities." '

'That doesn't throw much light on the subject,' said I. 'The last reference is 2 Timothy 4.13.'

'It reads: "The cloak that I left at Troas with Carpus, when thou comest, bring with thee, and the books, but especially the parchments." ' She laid down her notes, and looking at me with the most intense gravity, exclaimed: 'Isn't that extraordinary? It is the most astonishing of them all. You see, it is perfectly trivial, just a message from St Paul to Timothy on a purely personal matter of no importance to anybody but himself. But the whole collection of texts is very odd. They seem utterly unconnected with one another, and, as you say, without any significance in respect of either faith or morals. What is your opinion of them?'

'I don't know what to think,' I replied. 'They may have had some significance to the original owner of the locket only, something personal and reminiscent. Or they may have been addressed to some other person in terms previously agreed on. That is to say, they may have formed something in the nature of a code.'

'Exactly,' she agreed eagerly. 'That is what I think. And I am just devoured by curiosity as to what the message was that they were meant to convey. I shan't rest until I have solved the mystery.'

I smiled, and again my glance wandered to the planchette on the wall and the crystal ball on the table. Evidently my new and charming friend was an inveterate mystic, an enthusiastic explorer of the dubious regions of the occult and the supernormal. And though my own matter-of-fact temperament engendered little sympathy with such matters, I found in this very mysticism an additional charm. It seemed entirely congruous with her eminently picturesque personality.

But at this moment I became suddenly aware that I had made a most outrageously long visit and rose with profuse apologies for my disregard of time.

'There is no need to apologise,' she assured me cordially. 'It is most kind of you to have given so much time to a mere counterfeit invalid. But won't you stay and have tea with us? Can't you really? Well, I hope you will come and see us again when you can spare an hour. Oh, and hadn't I better give you this locket to hand to Sir Lawrence Drayton?'

'Certainly not,' I replied. 'You had better keep it until you see him, and perhaps in the interval you may be able to extract its secret. But I will tell him that it is in safe hands.' I shook her hand warmly, and when I had made a brief inspection of Master Percy's building, that promising architect piloted me across the yard and finally launched me, with a hearty farewell and a cordial invitation to 'come again soon,' into the desert expanse of Jacob Street.

CHAPTER FIVE

Mr Halliburton's Mascot

Emerging into the grey and cheerless street I sauntered towards the Hampstead Road, and having reached that thoroughfare, halted at the corner and looked at my watch. It was barely four o'clock, and as I had arranged to meet Thorndyke at the Euston Road corner at half-past four, I had half an hour in which to cover something less than half a mile. I began to be regretful that I had refused the proffered tea, and when my leisurely progress brought me to the door of an establishment in which that beverage was dispensed, I entered and called for refreshment.

And as I sat by the shabby little marble-topped table, my thoughts strayed back to the great bare studio in Jacob Street and the strange, enigmatical but decidedly alluring personality of its tenant. To say that I had been favourably impressed by her would be to understate the case. I found myself considering her with a degree of interest and admiration that no other woman had ever aroused in me. She was – or, at least, she appeared to me – a strikingly beautiful girl, but that was not the whole, or even the main, attraction. Her courage and strength of character, as shown in the tragic circumstances of the previous night; her refinement of manner and easy, well-bred courtesy, her intelligence and evident amiability, and her frank friendliness, without any sacrifice of dignity, had all combined to make her personality gracious and pleasant. Then there were the paintings. If they were her work, she was an artist of some talent. I had meant cautiously to inquire into that, but the investigation of the locket had excluded everything else. And the thought of the locket and the almost childish eagerness that she had shown to extract its (assumed) secret, led naturally to the planchette and the crystal globe. In general I was disposed to scoff at such things, but on her the mysticism and occultism – I would not call it superstition – seemed to settle naturally and to add a certain piquancy to her mediaeval grace. And so reflecting, I suddenly bethought me of the cat's eye pendant. What was the nature of her interest in that? At first I had assumed that she was a connoisseur in jewels, and possibly I was right. But her curious interest in the locket suggested other possibilities, and into these I determined to inquire on my next visit – for I had already decided that the friendly invitations should not find me unresponsive. In short, the Lady of Shalott had awakened in me a very lively curiosity.

My speculations and reflections very effectively filled out the spare half-hour and brought me on the stroke of half-past four to the corner of the Euston Road; and I had barely arrived when I perceived the tall, upright figure of my colleague swinging easily up Tottenham Court Road. In a few moments he joined me, and we both turned our faces westward.

'We needn't hurry,' said he. 'I said I would be there at five.'

'I don't quite understand what you are going for,' said I. 'This man, Halliburton, seems to have been no more than a chance stranger. What do you expect to get out of him?'

'I have nothing definite in my mind,' he replied. 'The whole case is in the air at present. The position is this: a murder has been committed and the murderers have got away almost without leaving a trace. If the fingerprint people cannot identify the one man, we may say that we have no clue to the identity of either. But that murder had certain antecedents. Halliburton's visit was one of them, though there was probably no causal relation.'

'You don't suspect Halliburton?'

'My dear fellow, I suspect nobody. We haven't got as far as that. But we have to investigate every thing, person, or circumstance that makes the smallest contact with the crime. But here is our destination, and I need not remark, Anstey, that our purpose is to acquire information, not to give it.'

The 'Baltic' Hotel was a large private house not far from the Great Central Station, distinguished from other private houses only by an open street door and by the name inconspicuously inscribed on the fanlight. As we ascended the steps and entered the hall, a short, pleasant-faced man emerged from an office and looked inquiringly from one of us to the other. 'Dr Thorndyke?' he asked.

'Yes,' replied my colleague, 'and I assume that you are the manager, Mr Simpson. I must thank you for making the appointment and hope I am not inconveniencing you.'

'Not at all,' rejoined the other. 'I know your name very well, sir, and shall be delighted to give you any assistance that I can. I understand that you want Mr Halliburton's address.'

'If you have no objection, I should like to have it. I want to write to him.'

'I can give it to you off-hand,' said the manager. 'It is "Oscar Halliburton, Esquire, Wimbledon." '

'That doesn't seem a very sufficient address,' remarked Thorndyke.

'It is not,' said the manager. 'I had occasion to write to him myself and my letter was returned, marked "insufficiently addressed." '

'Then, in effect, you have not got his address?'

'That is what it amounts to. Would you like to see the visitors' book? If you will step into my private office I will bring it to you.'

He showed us into his office, and in a few moments entered with the book, which he laid on the table and opened at the page on which the signature appeared.

'This does not appear to have been written with the hotel pen,' Thorndyke remarked when he had glanced at the adjoining signatures.

'No,' the manager agreed. 'Apparently he used his own fountain pen.'

'I see that this entry is dated the 13th of September. How long did he stay?'

'He left on the 16th of September – five days ago.'

'And he received at least one letter while he was here?'

'Yes, one only, I believe. It came on the morning of the 16th, I remember, and he left in the evening.'

'Do you know if he went out much while he was here?'

'No, he stayed indoors nearly all day, and he spent most of his time in the billiard-room practising fancy strokes.'

'What sort of man was he – in appearance, for instance?'

'Well,' said Simpson rather hesitatingly, 'I didn't see much of him, and I see a good many people. I should say he was a biggish man, medium colour and rather sunburnt.'

'Any beard or moustache?'

'No, clean shaved and a good deal of hair – rather long, wanted a crop.'

'Any distinctive accent or peculiarity of voice?'

'I didn't have much talk with him – nor did anybody else, I think. He was a gruffish, taciturn man. Nothing peculiar about his voice, and as to his accent, well, it was just ordinary, very ordinary, with perhaps jut a trace of the cockney, but only a trace. It wasn't exactly the accent of an English gentleman.'

'And that is all that you remember about him?'

'That is all.'

'Would you have any objection to my taking a photograph of this signature?'

The manager looked rather dubious. 'It would hardly do for it to be known – ' he began, when Thorndyke interrupted:

'I suggest, Mr Simpson, that whatever passes between us shall be regarded as strictly confidential on both sides. The least said, the soonest mended, you know.'

'There's a good deal of truth in that,' said the manager with a smile, 'especially in the hotel business. Well, if that is understood, I don't know that I have any objection to your taking a photograph. But how are you going to manage it?'

'I have a camera,' replied Thorndyke, 'and I see that your table lamp is a sixty Watt. It won't take an unreasonably long exposure.'

He propped the book up in a suitable position, and having arranged the lamp so as to illuminate the page obliquely, produced from his pocket a small folding camera and a leather case of dark slides, at which Mr Simpson gazed in astonishment. 'You'll never get a useful photograph with a toy like that,' said he.

'Not such a toy as you think,' replied Thorndyke as he opened the little instrument. 'This lens is specially constructed for close range work, and will give me the signature the full size of the original.' He laid a measuring tape on the table, and having adjusted the camera by its engraved scale, inserted the dark slide, looked at his watch, and opened the shutter.

'You were saying just now, Mr Simpson,' he resumed as we sat round the table watching the camera, 'that you had occasion to write to Mr Halliburton. Should I be indiscreet if I were to ask what the occasion was?'

'Not at all,' replied the manager. 'It was a ridiculous affair. It seems that Mr Halliburton had a sort of charm or mascot which he wore suspended by a gold ring from a cord under his waistcoat; a silly little bone thing, of no value whatever, though he appears to have set great store by it. Well, after he had left the hotel he missed it. The ring had broken and the thing had dropped off the cord – presumably, he supposed, when he was undressing. So a couple of days later – on the eighteenth – back he came in a rare twitter to know if it had been picked up. I asked the chambermaids if any of them had found the mascot in his room or elsewhere, but none of them had. Then he was frightfully upset and begged me to ask them again and to say that he would give ten pounds to any one who should have found it and would hand it to him. Ten pounds!' Mr Simpson repeated with contemptuous emphasis. 'Just think of it! The price of a gold watch for a thing that looked like a common rabbit bone! Why, a man like that oughtn't to be at large.'

I could see that my colleague was deeply interested, though his impassive face suggested nothing but close attention. He put away his watch, closed the lens-shutter and the dark slide, and finally bestowed the little apparatus in his pocket. Then he asked the manager: 'Can you give us anything like a detailed description of this mascot?'

'I can show you the thing itself,' replied Simpson. 'That is the irony of the affair. Mr Halliburton hadn't been out of the house half and hour when the boy who looks after the billiard-room came bursting into my office in the devil's own excitement. He had heard of the ten pounds reward and had proceeded at once to take up all the rugs and mats in the billiard-room, and there, under the edge of a strip of cocoa-nut matting, he had found the precious thing. No doubt the ring had broken when Halliburton was leaning over the table to make a long shot. So I took it from the boy and put it in the safe, and I wrote forthwith to the address given in the book to say that the mascot had come to light, but, as I told you just now, the letter was returned marked "insufficiently addressed." So there it is, and unless he calls again, or writes, he won't get his mascot, and the boy won't get his ten pounds. Would you like to see the treasure?'

'I should, very much,' replied Thorndyke; whereupon the manager stepped over to a safe in the corner of the room, and having unlocked it, came back to the table holding a small object in the palm of his hand.

'There it is,' said he, dropping it on the table before Thorndyke, 'and I think you will agree with me that it is a mighty dear ten pounds' worth.'

I looked curiously at the little object as my colleague turned it about in his hand. It was evidently a bone of some kind, roughly triangular in shape and perforated by three holes, one large and two smaller. In addition to these, a fourth hole had been drilled through near the apex to take a gold suspension ring, and this was still in position, though it was broken, having chafed quite thin with wear in one part and apparently given way under some sudden strain. The surface of the bone was covered with minute incised carving of a simple and rather barbaric type, and the whole bone had been stained a deep, yellowish brown, which had worn lighter in the parts most exposed to friction; and the entire surface had that unmistakable polish and patina that comes with years of handling and wear.

'What do you make of it, sir?' asked Mr Simpson.

'It is the neck bone of some small animal,' Thorndyke replied. 'But not a rabbit. And, of course, the markings on it give it an individual character.'

'Would you give ten pounds for it?' the manager asked with a grin.

'I am not sure that I wouldn't,' Thorndyke replied, 'though not for its intrinsic value. But yours is not a "firm offer." You are not a vendor. But I should like very much to borrow it for a few hours.'

'I don't quite see how I could agree to that,' said Simpson. 'You see, the thing isn't mine. I'm just a trustee. And Mr Halliburton might call and ask for it at any moment.'

'I would give you a receipt for it and undertake to let you have it back by ten o'clock tomorrow morning,' said Thorndyke.

'M'yes,' said Simpson reflectively and with evident signs of weakening. 'Of course, I could say I had deposited it at my bank. But is it of any importance? Would you mind telling me why you want to borrow the thing?'

'I want to compare it carefully with some similar objects, the existence of which is known to me. I could do that tonight, and, if necessary, send the specimen back forthwith. As to the importance of the comparison, who can say? If Halliburton should turn up and give a practicable address there would be nothing in it. But if he should never reappear and it should become necessary to trace him, the information gathered from an exhaustive examination of this object might be of great value.'

'I see,' said Simpson. 'In a sense it is a matter of public policy. Of course that puts a different complexion on the affair. And having regard to your position and character, I don't see why I shouldn't agree to your having a short loan of the thing. But I should like to have it back by nine o'clock tomorrow morning, if you could manage it.'

'I promise you that it shall be delivered into your hand by a responsible person not later than nine o'clock,' said Thorndyke. 'I will now give you a receipt, which I will ask you to hand to my messenger in exchange for your property; and again, Mr Simpson, I would suggest that we make no confidences to anyone concerning this transaction.'

To this the manager assented with decided emphasis, and our business being now concluded, we thanked Mr Simpson warmly for his courtesy and his very helpful attitude and took our departure.

'You seem extraordinarily keen about that precious bone, Thorndyke,' I remarked as we walked back along the Marylebone Road, 'but I'm hanged if I see why. It won't tell you much about Halliburton. And if it would, I don't quite see what you want to know. He is obviously a fool. You don't need much investigation to ascertain that, and like most fools, he seems easily parted from his money. What more do you want to know?'

'My learned friend,' replied Thorndyke, 'is not profiting sufficiently by his legal experience. One of the most vital principles that years of practice have impressed on me is that in the early stages of an inquiry, no fact, relevant or irrelevant, that is in any way connected with the subject of the inquiry should be neglected or ignored. Indeed, no such fact can be regarded as irrelevant, since, until all the data are assembled and collated, it is impossible to judge the bearing or value of any one of them.

'Take the present case. Who is Mr Halliburton? We don't know. Why did he want to examine Mr Drayton's collection? We don't know. What passed between him and Mr Drayton when he made his visit? Again we don't know. Perhaps there is nothing of any significance to know. The probability is that Halliburton has no connection with this case at all. But there is no denying that he is in the picture.'

'Yes, as a background figure. His name has been mentioned as one of the visitors who had come to see the collection. There were other visitors, you remember.'

'Yes, and if we knew who they were we should want to know something about them, too. But Halliburton is the only one known to us. And your presentation of his position in relation to what has happened does not state the case fairly at all. The position is really this:

Halliburton – a complete stranger to Drayton – took considerable trouble to obtain an opportunity to examine the collection. Why did he do this? You have quoted Mrs Benham as saying that he apparently knew nothing about jewellery, either ancient or modern. He was not a connoisseur. Then, why did he want to see the collection? Again, he wrote for the appointment, not from his own residence but from an hotel; and when we come to that hotel we find that he has left no verifiable address, and the vague locality that he gave may quite possibly be a false address. And further, that this apparent concealment of his place of abode coincides with a very excellent reason for giving a correct address, the fact that he has lost – and lost in the hotel, as he believes – certain property on which he sets a high value. And if you add to this the facts that within four days of his visit to Drayton the collection was robbed; that the robbers clearly knew exactly where it was kept and had some knowledge of the inmates of the house and their habits, you must admit that Halliburton is something more than a background figure in the picture.'

I was secretly impressed by the way in which Thorndyke had 'placed' Mr Halliburton in respect of the inquiry, but, of course, it wouldn't do to say so. It was necessary to assert my position.

'That,' I replied, 'is the case for the prosecution, and very persuasively stated. On the other hand it might be said for the defence: "Here is a gentleman who lives in the country and who comes up to spend a few days in town – " '

'For the apparent purpose,' Thorndyke interrupted, 'of practising the art of billiards, a sport peculiar to London.'

'Exactly. And while he is in London he takes the opportunity of inspecting a collection which has been described in the Press. A few days after his visit the collection is robbed by some persons who have probably also seen the published description. There is no positive fact of any kind that connects him with those persons, and I assert that the assumption that any such connection exists is entirely gratuitous.'

Thorndyke smiled indulgently. 'It seems a pity,' he remarked, 'that my learned friend should waste the sweetness of his jury flourishes on the desert air of Marylebone Road. But we needn't fash ourselves, as

I believe they say in the North. There was a lady named Mrs Glasse whose advice to cooks seems to be applicable to the present case. We had better catch our hare before we proceed to jug him – the word "jug" being used without any malicious intent to perpetrate a pun.'

'And do I understand that the capture is to be accomplished by the agency of the rabbit-bone that my learned senior carries in his reverend pocket?'

'If you do,' replied Thorndyke, 'your understanding is a good deal in advance of mine. I am taking this little object to examine merely on the remote chance that it may yield some information as to this man's antecedents, habits, and perhaps even his identity. The chance is not so remote as it looks. There are very few things which have been habitually carried on a man's person which will not tell you something about the person who has carried them. And this object, as you probably noticed, is in many respects highly characteristic.'

'I can't say that I found the thing itself particularly characteristic. The fact that the man should have carried it and have set such a ridiculous value on it is illuminating. That writes him down a superstitious ass. But superstitious asses form a fairly large class. In what respects do you find this thing so highly characteristic, and what kind of information do you expect to extract from it?'

'As to the latter question,' he replied, 'an investigator doesn't form expectations in advance; and as to the former, you will have an opportunity of examining the object for yourself and of forming your own conclusions.'

I determined to make a minute and exhaustive inspection of our treasure trove as soon as we arrived home. For obviously I had missed something. It was clear to me that Thorndyke attached more importance to this object than would have been warranted by anything that I had observed. There was some point that I had overlooked and I meant to find out what it was.

But the opportunity did not offer immediately, for, on our arrival at his chambers, Thorndyke proceeded straight up to the laboratory, where we found his assistant, Polton, seated at a jeweller's bench, making some structural alterations in a somewhat elaborate form of pedometer.

'I've got a job for you, Polton,' said Thorndyke, laying the mascot on the bench. 'Quite a nice, delicate little job, after your own heart. I want a replica of this thing – as perfect as you can make it. And I have to return the original before nine o'clock tomorrow morning. And,' he added, taking the camera and dark slides from his pocket, 'there is a photograph to be developed, but there is no particular hurry for that.'

Polton picked the mascot up daintily, and laying it in the palm of his hand, stuck a watchmaker's glass in his eye and inspected it minutely.

'It's a queer little thing, sir,' he remarked. 'Seems to have been made out of a small cervical vertebra. I suppose you want the copy of the same colour as this and as hard as possible?'

'I want as faithful a copy as you can make, similar in all respects, excepting that the reproduction can scarcely be as hard as the original. Will there be time to make a gelatine mould?'

'There'll have to be, sir. It couldn't be done any other way, with these undercuttings. But I shan't lose any time on that. If I have to match the colour I shall have to make some experiments, and I can do those while the gelatine is setting.'

'Very well, Polton,' said Thorndyke. 'Then I'll leave the thing in your hands and consider it as good as done. Of course the original must not be damaged in any way.'

'Oh, certainly not, sir'; and forthwith the little man, having carefully deposited the mascot in a small, glass-topped box on the bench, fell to work on his preparations beaming with happiness. I have never seen a man who enjoyed his work so thoroughly as Polton did.

'I am going round to the College of Surgeons now,' said Thorndyke. 'No callers are expected, I think, but if any one should come and want to see me, I shall be back in about an hour. Are you coming with me, Anstey?'

'Why not? I've nothing to do, and if I keep an eye on you I may pick up a crumb or two of information.' Here I caught Polton's eye, and a queer, crinkly smile overspread that artificer's countenance. 'A good many people try to do that, sir,' he remarked. 'I hope you will have better luck than most of them have.'

'It occurs to me,' Thorndyke observed as we descended the stairs, 'that if the scribe who wrote the Book of Genesis had happened to look in on Polton he would have come to the conclusion that he had grossly overestimated the curse of labour.'

'He was not much different from most other scribes,' said I. 'A bookish man – like myself, for instance – constantly fails to appreciate the joy of manual work. I find Polton an invaluable object lesson.'

'So do I,' said Thorndyke. 'He is a shining example of the social virtues – industry, loyalty, integrity, and contentment – and as an artificer he is a positive genius.' With this warm appreciation of his faithful follower he swung round into Fleet Street and crossed towards the Law Courts.

CHAPTER SIX

Introduces an Ant-eater and
a Detective

As we entered the hall of the College of Surgeons Thorndyke glanced at the board on which the names of the staff were painted and gave a little grunt of satisfaction.

'I see,' he said, addressing the porter, 'that Mr Saltwood hasn't gone yet.'

'No, sir,' was the reply. 'He is working up at the top tonight. Shall I take you up to him?'

'If you please,' answered Thorndyke, and the porter accordingly took us in charge and led the way to the lift. From the latter we emerged into a region tenanted by great earthenware pans and jars and pervaded by a curious aroma, half spirituous, half cadaveric, on which I commented unfavourably.

'Yes,' said Thorndyke, sniffing appreciatively, 'the good old museum bouquet. You smell it in all curators' rooms, and though, I suppose, it is not physically agreeable, I find it by no means unpleasant. The effects of odours are largely a matter of association.'

'The present odour,' said I, 'seems to suggest the association of a very overripe Duke of Clarence and a butt of shockingly bad malmsey.'

Thorndyke smiled tolerantly as we ascended a flight of stairs that led to a yet higher storey, and abandoned the discussion. At the top, we passed through several long galleries, past ranges of tables piled up

62

with incredible numbers of bones, apparently awaiting disposal, until we were finally led by our conductor to a room in which two men were working at a long bench, on which were several partially articulated skeletons of animals. They both looked up as we entered, and one of them, a keen-faced, middle-aged man, exclaimed: 'Well, this is an unexpected pleasure. I haven't seen you for donkey's years, Thorndyke. Thought you had deserted the old shop. And I wonder what brings you here now.'

'The usual thing, Saltwood. Self-interest. I have come to negotiate a loan. Have you got any loose bones of the Echidna?'

Saltwood stroked his chin and turned interrogatively to his assistant. 'Do you know if there are any, Robson?' he asked.

'There is a set waiting to be articulated, sir. Shall I fetch them?'

'If you would, please, Robson,' replied Saltwood. Then turning to my colleague, he asked: 'What bones do you want, Thorndyke?'

'The middle cervical vertebrae – about the third or fourth,' was the reply, at which I pricked up my ears.

In a few minutes Robson returned carrying a cardboard box on which was a label inscribed 'Echidna hystrix.'

Saltwood lifted the lid, disclosing a collection of small bones, including a queer little elongated skull.

'Here you are,' said he, picking out a sort of necklace formed of the joints of the backbone; 'here is the whole vertebral column, minus the tail, strung together. Will you take it as it is?'

'No,' replied Thorndyke, 'I will just take the three vertebrae that I want – the third, fourth, and fifth cervical, and if I let you have them back in the course of the week, will that do?'

'Perfectly. I wouldn't bother you to return them at all if it were not for spoiling the set.' He separated the three little bones from the string, and having wrapped them in tissue paper and handed them to Thorndyke, asked; 'How is Jervis? I haven't seem him very lately, either.'

'Jervis,' replied Thorndyke, 'is at present enjoying a sort of professional holiday in New York. He is retained, in an advisory capacity, in the Rosenbaum case, of which you may have read in the papers. My friend Anstey here is very kindly filling his place during his absence.'

'I'm glad to hear that I'm filling it,' said I, as Saltwood bowed and shook hands. 'I was afraid I was only half filling it, being but a mere lawyer destitute of medical knowledge.'

'Well,' said Saltwood, 'medical knowledge is important, of course, but you've always got Thorndyke to help you out. Oh – and that reminds me, Thorndyke, that I've got some new preparations that I should like you to see, a series of tumours from wild animals. Will you come and have a look at them? They are in the next room.'

Thorndyke assented with enthusiasm, and the two men went out of the room, leaving me to the society of Robson and the box of bones. Into the latter I peered curiously, again noting the odd shape of the skull; then I proceeded to improve the occasion by a discreet question or two.

'What sort of beast in an Echidna?' I asked.

'Echidna hystrix,' replied Robson in a somewhat pompously didactic tone, 'is the zoological name of the porcupine ant-eater.'

'Indeed,' said I, and then tempted by his owlish solemnity to ask foolish questions, I inquired: 'Does that mean that he is an eater of porcupine ants?'

'No, sir,' he replied gravely (he was evidently a little slow in the uptake). 'It is not the ants which are porcupines. It is the ant-eater.'

'But,' I objected, 'how can an ant-eater be a porcupine? It is a contradiction in terms.'

This seemed to floor him for a moment, but he pulled himself together and explained: 'The name signifies a porcupine which resembles an ant-eater, or perhaps one should say, an ant-eater, which resembles a porcupine. It is a very peculiar animal.'

'It must be,' I agreed. 'And what is there peculiar about its cervical vertebrae?'

He pondered profoundly, and I judged that he did not know but was not going to give himself away, a suspicion that his rather ambiguous explanation tended to confirm.

'The cervical vertebrae,' he expounded, 'are very much alike in most animals. There are exceptions, of course, as in the case of the porpoise, which has no neck, and the giraffe, which has a good deal of neck. But in general, cervical vertebrae seem to be turned out pretty much to one pattern, whereas the tail vertebrae present great differences. Now, if you look at this animal's tail −' here he fished a second necklace out of the box and proceeded to expound the peculiarities of its constituent bones, to which exposition I am afraid I turned an inattentive ear. The Echidna's tail had no bearing on the identity of Mr Halliburton.

The rather windy discourse had just come to an end when my two friends reappeared and Saltwood conducted us down to the hall. As we stepped out of the lift he shook our hands heartily, and with a cheery adieu, pressed the button and soared aloft like a stage fairy.

From the great portico of the College we turned eastward and walked homewards across Lincoln's Inn, each of us wrapped in his own reflections. Presently I asked:

'Supposing this mascot of Halliburton's to be the neck bone of an Echidna, what is the significance of the fact?'

'Ah!' he replied. 'There you have me, Anstey. At present I am concerning myself only with the fact, hoping that its significance may appear later. To us it may have no significance at all. Of course there is some reason why this particular bone should have been used rather than some other kind of bone, but that set of circumstances may have − probably has − no connection with our inquiry. It is quite probable that Halliburton himself has no such connection. On the other hand, the circumstances which determined the use of an Echidna's vertebra as a mascot may have an important bearing on the case. So we can only secure the fact and wait for time and further knowledge to show whether it is or is not a relevant fact.'

'And do you mean to say that you are taking all this trouble on the mere chance that this apparently trivial and meaningless circumstance may possibly have some bearing?'

'That is so. But your question, Anstey, exhibits the difference between the legal and the scientific outlook. The lawyer's investigations tend to proceed along the line of information wanted: the scientist's tend to proceed along the line of information available. The business of the man of science is impartially to acquire all the knowledge that is obtainable; the lawyer tends to concern himself only with that which is material to the issue.'

'Then the scientist must accumulate a vast number of irrelevant facts.'

'Every fact,' replied Thorndyke, 'is relevant to something, and if you accumulate a great mass of facts, inspection of the mass shows that the facts can be sorted out into related groups from which certain general truths can be inferred. The difference between the lawyer and the scientist is that one is seeking to establish some particular truth while the other seeks to establish any truth that emerges from the available facts.'

'But,' I objected, 'surely even a scientist must select his facts to some extent. Every science has its own province. The chemist, for instance, is not concerned with the metamorphoses of insects.'

'That is true,' he admitted. 'But then, are we not keeping within our own province? We are not collecting facts indiscriminately, but are selecting those facts which make some sort of contact with the circumstances of this crime and which may therefore conceivably be relevant to our inquiry. But methinks I perceive another collector. Isn't that our friend Superintendent Miller crossing to King's Bench Walk and apparently bearing down on our chambers?'

I looked at the tall figure, indistinctly seen by the light of a lamp, and even as I looked, it ascended the steps and vanished into our entry; and when, a couple of minutes later, we arrived on our landing, we found Polton in the act of admitting the Superintendent.

'Well, gentlemen,' the officer said genially, as he subsided into an armchair and selected a cigar from the box which Thorndyke handed to him, 'I've just dropped in to give you the news – about this Drayton case, you know. I thought you'd be interested to hear what our people are doing. Well, I don't think you need trouble yourselves about it any more. We've got one of the men, at any rate.'

'In custody?' asked Thorndyke.

'No, we haven't actually made the arrest, but there will be no difficulty about that. We know who he is. I just passed those fingerprints in to Mr Singleton and he gave me the name straight away. And who do you think it is? It is our old friend, Moakey – Joe Hedges, you know.'

'Is it really!' said Thorndyke.

'Yes, Moakey it is. You're surprised. So was I. I really did think he had learned a little sense at last, especially as he seemed to be taking some reasonable precautions last time. But he always was a fool. Do you remember the asinine thing that he did on that last job?'

'No,' replied Thorndyke, 'I don't remember that case.'

'It was a small country house job, and Moakey did it all on his own. And it did look as if he had learned his lesson, for he undoubtedly wore gloves. We found them in his bag and there was not a trace at the house. But would you believe it, when he'd finished up, all neat and ship-shape, he must stop somewhere in the grounds to repack the swag – after he had taken his gloves off. Just then the alarm was raised and a dog let loose, and away went Moakey, like a hare, for the place in the fence where he had hidden his bicycle. He nipped over the fence, mounted his bike, and got clear away, and all trace of him seemed to be lost. But in the morning, when the local police came to search the grounds, they found a silver tray that Moakey had evidently had to drop when he heard the dog, with a most beautiful set of fingerprints on it. The police got a pair of photographs at once – there happened to be a dark room and a set of apparatus in the house – and sent a special messenger with them to Scotland Yard. And then the murder was out. They were Moakey's prints, and Moakey was arrested the same day with all the stuff in his possession. He hadn't had time to go to a fence with it. So the fingerprints didn't have to be put in evidence.'

'Did Moakey ever hear about the fingerprints?' Thorndyke asked.

'Yes. Some fool of a warder told him. And that's what makes this case so odd; to think that after coming a cropper twice he should have gone dabbing his trademarks over the furniture as he has, is perfectly incredible. And that isn't the only queer feature in the case. There's the stuff. I got Sir Lawrence to show it to me this morning, and I assure you that when I saw what it was, you could have knocked me down with a feather. To say nothing of the crockery and wineglasses and rubbish of that sort and the pewter spoons and brass spoons and bone bobbins, the jewellery was a fair knockout. There was only one cabinet of it, and you'll hardly believe me, Doctor, when I tell you that the greater part of it was silver, and even pinchbeck and brass – or latten, as Sir Lawrence calls it – set with the sort of stones that you can buy in Poland Street for ten bob a dozen. You never saw such trash!'

'Oh come, Miller,' Thorndyke protested, 'don't call it trash. It is one of the most interesting and reasonable collections that I have ever seen.'

'So it may be,' said the Superintendent, 'but I am looking at it from the trade point of view. Why, there isn't a fence outside Bedlam who'd give a fiver for the whole boiling. It's perfectly astonishing to me that an experienced tradesman like Moakey should have wasted his time on it. He might just as well have cracked an ironmonger's.'

'I expect,' said I, 'he embarked on the job under a mistake. Probably he saw, or heard of, that article in the *Connoisseur* and thought that this was a great collection of jewels.'

'That seems likely,' Miller agreed. 'And that may account for his having worked with a chum this time instead of doing the job single-handed as he usually does. But it doesn't account for his having used a pistol. That wasn't his way at all. There has never been a charge of violence against him before. I always took him for the good old-fashioned, sporting crook who played the game with us and expected us to play the game with him.'

'Is it clear that it was Moakey who fired the shot?' asked Thorndyke.

'Well, no, I don't know that it is. But he'll have to stand the racket unless he can prove that somebody else did it. And that won't be so very easy, for even if he gives us the name of the other man – the small man – and Miss Blake can identify him, still it will be difficult for Moakey to prove that the other man fired the shot, and the other chap isn't likely to be boastful about it.'

'No,' said Thorndyke, 'he will pretty certainly put it on to Moakey. But between the two we may get at the truth as to what happened.'

'We will hope so,' said Miller, rising and picking up his hat. 'At any rate, that is how the matter stands. I understand that Sir Lawrence wants you to keep an eye on the case, but there's really no need. It isn't in your line at all. We shall arrest Moakey and he will be committed for trial. If he likes to make a statement we may get the other man, but in any case there is nothing for you to do.'

For some minutes after the Superintendent's departure, Thorndyke sat looking into the fire with an air of deep reflection. Presently he looked up as if he had disposed of some question that he had been propounding to himself and remarked: 'It's a curious affair, isn't it?'

'Very,' I agreed. 'It seems as if this man, Moakey, had thrown all precaution to the winds. By the way, do you suppose those fingerprint people ever make mistakes? They seem pretty cocksure.'

'They would be more than human if they never made a mistake,' Thorndyke replied. 'But, on the other hand, the identification of a whole set of fingerprints doesn't leave much room for error. You might get two prints that were similar enough to admit of a mistake, but you would hardly get two sets that could be mistaken for one another.'

'No, I suppose not. So the mystery remains unexplained.'

'It remains unexplained in any case,' said Thorndyke.

'How do you mean?' I asked. 'If they had made a mistake and these were really the fingerprints of some unknown person, that person might be a novice and there would be no mystery about his having taken no precautions.'

'Yes, but that is not the mystery. The real mystery is the presence of a third man who has left no other traces.'

'A third man!' I exclaimed. 'What evidence is there of the presence of a third man?'

'It is very obvious,' replied Thorndyke. 'These fingerprints are not those of the small man, because he wore gloves. And they are not the fingerprints of the tall man.'

'How do you know that?' I asked.

Thorndyke rose, and opening a cabinet, took out the plaster cast of the tall man's left hand, which he had made on the previous night, and the pair of photographs.

'Now,' said he, 'look at the print of the left forefinger in the photograph. You see that the pattern is quite clear and unbroken. Now look at the cast of the forefinger. Do you see what I mean?'

'You mean that pit or dent in the bulb of the finger. But isn't that due to an irregularity of the ground on which the finger was pressed?'

'No, it is the puckered scar of an old whitlow or deep wound of some kind. It is quite characteristic. And the print of this finger would show a blank white space in the middle of the pattern. So it is certain that those fingerprints did not belong to either of these two men.'

'Then, really,' said I, 'the fact that these are Moakey's fingerprints serves to explain this other mystery.'

'To some extent. But you see, Anstey, that it introduces a further mystery. If there were three men in that room, or on the premises, how comes it that there were only two sets of footprints?'

'Yes, that is rather extraordinary. Can you suggest any explanation?'

'The only explanation that occurs to me is that one of these men may have let Moakey into the house by the front door, that he may have been in the room when Miss Blake entered – he might, for instance, have been behind the door – and have slipped out when she ran to the window. He could then have to run into the drawing-room and waited until she rushed out of the house, when it would be easy for him to slip out at the front door and escape.'

'Yes,' I said dubiously, 'I suppose that is possible, but it doesn't sound very probable.'

'It doesn't,' he agreed. 'But it is the only solution that I can think of at the moment. Of course there must be some explanation, for there are the facts. Inside the house are traces of three men. Outside are traces of only two. Have you any suggestion to offer?'

I shook my head. 'It is beyond me, Thorndyke. Why didn't you ask Miller?'

'Because I am not proposing to take the police into my confidence until I have evidence that they are prepared to do the same by me.

They will probably assume that the tall man was Moakey – he is about the same height. The information that we obtain from the cast of that man's hand is not, you must remember, in their possession.'

'No, I had forgotten that. And now I begin to appreciate my learned senior's foresight in taking a permanent record of that handprint.'

'Yes,' said Thorndyke. 'A permanent record is invaluable. It allows of reference at one's leisure and in connection with fresh evidence, as in the present case. And, moreover, it allows of study under the most favourable conditions. That scar on the finger was not noticeable in the impression in the sand, especially by the imperfect light of the lamp. But on the cast, which we can examine at our ease, by daylight if necessary, it is plainly visible. And we have it here to compare with the finger, if ever that finger should be forthcoming. I now make a rule of securing a plaster cast of any object that I cannot retain in my possession.'

Here, as if in illustration of this last statement, Polton entered the room bearing a small tray lined with blotting paper, on which lay three objects – a diminutive glass negative and two mascots. He laid the tray on the table and invited us to inspect his works, tendering a watchmaker's eyeglass to assist the inspection.

Thorndyke picked up the two mascots and examined them separately through the glass, then with a faint smile, but without remark, he passed the tray to me. I stuck the glass in my eye and scrutinised first one and then the other of the mascots, and finally looked up at Polton, who was watching me with a smile that covered his face with wrinkles of satisfaction.

'I suppose, Polton,' I said, 'You have some means of telling which is which, but I'm hanged if I can see a particle of difference.'

'I can tell 'em by the feel, sir,' he replied, 'but I took the precaution to weigh the original in the chemical balance before I made the copy. I think the colour matches pretty well.'

'It is a perfect reproduction, Polton,' said Thorndyke. 'If we were to show it to Superintendent Miller he would want to take your fingerprints right away. He would say that you were not a safe person to be at large.'

At this commendation Polton's countenance crinkled until he looked like a species of human walnut, and when the photograph of the signature had been examined and pronounced fit for the making of an enlargement, he departed, chuckling audibly.

When he had gone, I picked up one of the mascots and again examined it closely while Thorndyke made a similar inspection of its twin.

'Had you any definite purpose in your mind,' I asked 'when you instructed Polton to make this indistinguishable copy?'

'No,' he replied. 'I thought it wise to preserve a record of the thing, but, for my own information, a plain plaster cast would have answered quite well. Still, as it would not take much more trouble to imitate the colour and texture, I decided that there might be some advantage in having a perfect replica. There are certain imaginable circumstances in which it might be useful. I shall get Polton to make a cast of the Echidna's vertebra, so that we may have the means of demonstrating the nature of the object to others, if necessary; and by the way, we may as well make the comparison now and confirm my opinion that the animal really was an Echidna.'

He produced the little packet that Saltwood had given him, and laying the little bones on the table, compared them carefully with the mascot.

'Yes,' he said at length, 'I was right. Mr Halliburton's treasure is the third cervical vertebra of a young but full-grown Echidna.'

'How did you recognise this as an Echidna's vertebra?' I asked, recalling Mr Robson's rather obscure exposition on the subject. 'Aren't neck vertebrae a good deal alike in most animals?'

'In animals of the same class they are usually very much alike. But the Echidna is a transitional form. Although it is a mammal, it has many well-marked reptilian characters. This vertebra shows one of them. If you look at those corner-pieces – the transverse processes – you will see that they are separate from the rest of the bone, that they are joined to it by a seam or suture. But in all other mammals, with a single exception, the transverse processes are fused with the rest of the bone. There is no separating line. That suture was the distinguishing feature which attracted my attention.'

'And does the fact of its being an Echidna's bone suggest any particular significance to your mind?'

'Well,' he replied, 'the Echidna is far from a common animal. And this particular bone seems to have been worked on by some barbarian artist, which suggests that it may have been originally a barbaric ornament or charm or fetish, which again suggests personal connections and a traceable history. You will notice that the two letters seem to have been impressed on the ornament and have no connection with it, which suggests that the bone was already covered with these decorations when it came into the late owner's possession.'

I took up the glass and once more examined the mascot. The whole surface of the little bone, on both sides, was covered with an intricate mass of ornament consisting principally of scrolls or spirals, crude and barbaric in design but very minutely and delicately executed. In the centre of the solid part of the bone an extremely small o had been indented on one side and on the same spot on the reverse side an equally minute h. And through the glass I could see that the letters cut into the pattern, whereas the hole for the suspension ring was part of the original work and was incorporated into the design.

'I wonder why he used small letters for his initials instead of capitals,' said I.

'For the reason, I imagine, that they were small letters. He wanted them merely for identification, and no doubt wished them to be as inconspicuous as possible. Any letters are a disfigurement when they are not part of the design, and capitals would have been much worse than small letters.'

'These seem to have been punched, on with printer's types,' I remarked.

'They have been punched, not cut, but not, I should say, with printer's types. Type metal – even the hard variety which would be used for casting these little "Pearl" or "Diamond" types – is comparatively soft and the harder varieties are brittle. It would scarcely be strong enough to bear hammering into bone. I should say these letters were indented with steel punches.'

'Well,' I said, 'we have got a vast amount of entertainment out of Mr Halliburton and his mascot. But it looks rather as if that were going to be the end of it, for if Moakey is one of the robbers, we may take it that the others are just professional crooks. And thereupon Mr Halliburton recedes once more into the background. Isn't that the position?'

'Apparently it is,' replied Thorndyke. 'But we shall see what happens at the inquest. Possibly some further evidence may be forthcoming when the witnesses give their accounts in detail. And possibly Moakey himself may be able to throw some further light on the matter. They will probably have him in custody within a day or two.'

'By the way,' I said, 'have you examined the hair that poor Drayton had grasped in his hand?'

'Yes. There is nothing very characteristic about it. It is dark in colour and the hairs are rather small in diameter. But there was one slightly odd circumstance. Among the tuft of dark hairs there was one light one – not white – a blonde hair. It had no root and no tip. It was just a broken fragment. What do you make of that?'

'I don't know that I make anything of it. I understand that a man may sometimes find a woman's hair sticking to his coat in the neighbourhood of the shoulder or chest, though I have no personal experience of such things. But if on the coat, why not on the head. My learned senior's powerful constructive imagination might conceive circumstances in which such a transfer of hair might occur. Or has he some more recondite explanation?'

'There are other possible explanations,' Thorndyke replied. 'And as the hour seems to preclude a return to Hampstead tonight, and seems to suggest a temporary tenancy of Jervis's bedroom, I would recommend the problem for my learned friend's consideration while awaiting the approach of Morpheus or Hypnos, whichever deity he elects to patronise.'

This gentle hint, enforced by a glance at my watch, brought our discussion to an end, and very shortly afterwards we betook ourselves to our respective sleeping apartments.

CHAPTER SEVEN

The Vanished Heirloom

The tragic events at 'The Rowans' had excited a considerable amount of public interest, and naturally that interest was manifested in a specially intense form by the residents in the locality. I realised this when, in obedience to the summons which had been left at my lodgings, I made my way to the premises adjoining the High Street in which the inquest was to be held. As I approached the building I observed that quite a considerable crowd had gathered round the doors awaiting their opening, and noticed with some surprise the proportion of well-dressed women composing it.

Observing that the crowd contained no one whom I knew, I began to suspect that there was some other entrance reserved for authorised visitors, and was just looking round in search of it when the doors were opened and the crowd began to surge in; and at that moment I saw Miss Blake approaching. I waited for her to arrive, and when we had exchanged greetings I proceeded to pilot her through the crowd, which passed in with increasing slowness, suggesting that the accommodation was already being somewhat taxed.

I was not the only person who observed the symptoms of a 'full house.' A woman whom I had already noticed making her way through the throng with more skill and energy than politeness, came abreast of me just as I had struggled to the door and made a determined effort to squeeze past. Perhaps if she had been a different type of woman I might have accepted the customary masculine defeat, but her bad manners, combined with her unprepossessing appearance, banished any scruples of chivalry. She was a kind of woman that I dislike most cordially; loudly dressed, flashy, scented like a civet cat; with glaring golden hair – manifestly peroxided, as was evident by her dark eyebrows – pencilled eyelids, and a coat of powder that stared even through her spotted veil. My gorge rose at her, and as she stuck her elbow in my ribs and made a final burst to get in before me, I maintained a stolid resistance.

'You must excuse me,' I said, 'but I am a witness, and so is this lady.'

She cast a quick glance at me, and from me to Miss Blake; then – with a bad enough grace and without replying – she withdrew to let us pass, and ostentatiously turned her back on us.

The room was already crowded, but that was no concern of ours. We were present, and when our names should be called, the coroner's officer would do all that was necessary.

'I suppose,' said Miss Blake, 'we ought to have come in by another door. I see Sir Lawrence and Mrs Benham are sitting by the table; and isn't that Dr Thorndyke next to Sir Lawrence?'

'Yes,' I replied. 'I don't think he has been summoned, but, of course, he would be here to watch the case. I see Inspector Badger, too. I wonder if he is going to give evidence. Ah! You were right. There is another door. Here come the coroner and the jury. They will probably call you first as you are the principal witness, unless they begin with the medical evidence or Sir Lawrence. I see Dr Nichols has just come in.'

As the coroner and the jury took their seats at the table, the loud hum of conversation died away and an air of silent expectancy settled on the closely-packed audience. The coroner looked over a sheaf of type-written papers, and then opened the proceedings with a short address to the jury in which he recited the general facts of the case.

'And now, gentlemen,' he said in conclusion, 'we will proceed to take the evidence, and we had better begin with that of the medical witness.'

Hereupon Dr Nichols was called, and having been sworn, described the circumstances under which he was summoned to 'The

Rowans' on the night of the 20th of September, and the result of his subsequent examination of the body of the deceased. 'The cause of death,' he stated, 'was a bullet-wound of the chest. The bullet entered on the right side between the third and fourth ribs, and passed completely through the chest, emerging on the left side of the back between the fourth and fifth ribs. In its passage it perforated the aorta – the greater central artery – and this injury might have produced almost instantaneous death.'

'Could the wound have been self-inflicted?' the coroner asked.

'Under the circumstances, it could not, for although death was practically instantaneous, no weapon was discovered. If the injury had been self-inflicted, the weapon would have been found either grasped in the hand or lying by the body.'

'Was the weapon fired at close quarters?'

'Apparently not. At any rate there was no singeing of the clothes or any other sign indicating a very close range.'

That was the sum of Dr Nichols' evidence, and on its conclusion the local inspector was called. His evidence, however, was of merely formal character, setting forth the time at which he received the alarm call from Mrs Benham and the conditions existing when he arrived. When it was finished there was a short pause. Then the next witness was called. This was Sir Lawrence Drayton, who, after giving evidence as to the identity of the deceased, answered a few questions respecting the collection and his brother's manner of life, and the articles which had been stolen.

'The report, then,' said the coroner, 'that this was a collection of valuable jewellery was erroneous?'

'Quite erroneous. Deceased never desired, nor could he afford, to accumulate things of great intrinsic value.'

'Do you know if many strangers came to see the collection?'

'Very few. In fact I never heard of any excepting those who came after an article on the collection had appeared in the *Connoisseur.*'

'Do you know how may came then?'

'There was a small party of Americans who came by appointment and were introduced by one of the staff of the South Kensington

Museum. And there was a Mr Halliburton who wrote from some hotel for an appointment. All I know about him is that he was apparently not specially interested in anything in the collection excepting the pieces that were illustrated in the magazine. I believe he wanted to buy one of those, but I don't remember which it was.'

That was the substance of Drayton's evidence, and when he had returned to his seat, the next witness was called.

'Winifred Blake.'

Miss Blake rose, and having made her way to the table, took the oath and proceeded to give her evidence. After one or two preliminary questions, the coroner allowed her to make her statement without interruption, while the jury and the audience listened with absorbed interest to her clear and vivid account of the events connected with the crime. When she had finished her narration – which was substantially the same as that which I had heard from her on the night of the tragedy – the coroner thanked her for the very lucid manner in which she had given her evidence and then proceeded to enlarge upon one or two points relating to the possible antecedents of the tragedy.

'You have mentioned, Miss Blake, that you were led to communicate with deceased by a certain article which appeared in the *Connoisseur*. Did that article give you the impression that the collection described was an important collection of valuable jewellery?'

'No. The article explicitly stated that the chief value of the pieces was in their history and associations'

'Are you an expert or connoisseur in jewellery?'

'No. As an artist I am, of course, interested in goldsmith's and jeweller's work, but I have no special knowledge of it. My interest in this collection was purely personal. I wished to examine one of the pieces that was illustrated.'

'Would you tell us exactly what you mean by a personal interest?'

'The *Connoisseur* article was illustrated with two photographs, one of a locket and the other of a pendant. The pendant appeared to me to resemble one which was an heirloom in my own family and which disappeared about a hundred and fifty years ago and has never been seen since. I wanted to examine that pendant and see if it really was the missing jewel.'

'Was the missing pendant of any considerable value?'

'No. It was a small, plain gold pendant set with a single cat's eye, and the pendant shown in the photograph appeared to answer the description exactly so far as I could judge. Its actual value would be quite small.'

'You say that the actual, or intrinsic, value of this jewel would be trifling. Had it, so far as you know, any special value?'

'Yes. It appears to have been greatly prized in the family, and I believe a good many efforts have been made to trace it. There was a tradition, or superstition, connected with it which gave it its value to members of the family.'

'Can you tell us what was the nature of that tradition?'

'It connected the possession of the jewel with the succession to the estates. The custom had been for the head of the family to wear the jewel, usually under the clothing, and the belief was that so long as he wore the jewel, or at any rate had it in his possession, the estates would remain in the possession of the branch of the family to which he belonged; but if the jewel passed into the possession of a member of some other branch of the family, then the estates would also pass into the possession of that branch.'

The coroner smiled. 'Your ancestors,' he remarked, 'appear to have taken small account of property law. But you say that efforts have been made to trace this jewel and that a good deal of value was set on it. Now, do you suppose that this tradition was taken at all seriously by any of the members of your family?'

'I cannot say very positively, but I should suppose that any one who might have a claim in the event of the failure of the existing line, would be glad to have the jewel in his possession.'

'Is there, so far as you know, any probability of a change in the succession to this property?'

'I believe that the present tenant is unmarried and that if he should die there would be several claimants from other branches of the family.'

'And then,' said the coroner with a smile, 'the one who possessed the cat's eye pendant would be the successful claimant. Is that the position?'

'It is possible that some of them entertain that belief.'

'Have you any expectations yourself?'

'Personally I have not. But my brother Percival is, properly speaking, the direct heir to this estate.'

'Then why is he not in possession? And what do you mean exactly by the "direct heir"?'

'I mean that he is the direct descendant of the head of the senior branch of the family. Our ancestor disappeared at the same time as the jewel – he took it with him, in fact. The reason that my brother is not in possession is that we cannot prove the legality of our ancestor's marriage. But it is always possible that the documents may be discovered – they are known to exist; and then, if a change in the succession should occur, my brother's claim would certainly take precedence of the others.'

'This is very interesting,' said the coroner, 'and not without importance to this inquiry. Now tell us, Miss Blake, would you yourself attach any significance to the possession of this jewel?'

Miss Blake coloured slightly as she replied: 'I don't suppose it would affect the succession to the property, but I should like to know that the jewel was in my brother's possession.'

'In case there might be some truth in the belief, h'm? Well, it's not unnatural. And now, to return for a moment to the man whom you tried so pluckily to detain. You have given us a very clear description of him. Do you think you would be able to recognise him?'

'I feel no doubt that I could. As an artist with some experience as a portrait painter I have been accustomed to study faces closely and quickly and to remember them. I can form quite a clear mental picture of this man's face.'

'Do you think you could make a drawing of it from memory?'

'I don't think my drawing would be reliable for identification. It is principally the man's expression that I remember so clearly. I might be wrong as to the details of the features, but if I were to see the man again I am sure I should know him.'

'I hope you will have an opportunity,' said the coroner. Then, turning to the jury, he asked: 'Do you wish to ask this witness any questions, gentlemen?' and on receiving a negative reply, he thanked Miss Blake and dismissed her with a bow.

My own evidence was taken next, but I need not repeat it since it was concerned only with those experiences which I have already related in detail. I was followed by Mrs Benham, who, like the preceding witnesses, was allowed to begin with a statement describing her experiences.

'How did it happen,' the coroner asked when she had finished her statement, 'that there was no one in the house when the thieves broke in?'

'I had to take a message for Mr Drayton to a gentleman who lives at North End. It is quite a short distance, but I was detained there more than a quarter of an hour.'

'Was the house often left?'

'No, very seldom. During the day I had a maid to help me. She went home at six, and after that I hardly ever went out.'

'Were you alone in the house in the evenings when Mr Drayton was at the club?'

'Yes. From about seven to between half-past nine and ten. Mr Drayton used to lock the museum and take the key with him.'

'Did many persons know that deceased was away from the house every evening?'

'A good many must have known, as he was a regular chess-player. And anybody who cared to know could have seen him go out and come back.'

'On the night of the murder did he go out at his usual time?'

'Yes, a little after seven. But, unfortunately, he came back nearly two hours earlier than usual. That was the cause of the disaster.'

'Exactly. And now, Mrs Benham, I want you to tell us all you know about the visitors who came to see the collection after the article had appeared in the *Connoisseur*. There were some Americans, I believe?'

'Yes. A small party – four or five – who came together in a large car. They sent a letter of introduction, and I think Mr Drayton knew pretty well who they were. Then about a week later Mr Halliburton wrote from the Baltic Hotel to ask if he might look over the collection, and naming a particular day – the sixteenth of this month – and Mr Drayton made the appointment, although it was very inconvenient.'

'Was Mr Halliburton known to deceased?'

'No, he was a complete stranger.'

'And did he come and inspect the collection?'

'Yes; he came, and Mr Drayton spent a long time with him showing him all the things and telling him all about them. I remember it very well because Mr Drayton was so very vexed that he should have put himself to so much inconvenience for nothing.'

'Why "for nothing"?' asked the coroner.

'He said that Mr Halliburton didn't seem to know anything about jewellery nor to care about any of the things but the two that had been shown in the photographs. He seemed to have come from mere idle curiosity. And then he rather offended Mr Drayton by offering to buy one of the pieces. He said that he wanted to give it for a wedding present.'

'Do you know which piece it was that he wanted to buy?'

'The pendant. The other piece – the locket – didn't seem to interest him at all.'

'Did you see Mr Halliburton?'

'I only saw his back as he went out. Mr Drayton let him in and took him to the museum. I could see that he was rather a big man, but I couldn't see what he was like.'

'And are these the only strangers that have been to the house lately?'

'Yes; the only ones for quite a long time.'

The coroner reflected for a few moments, then, as the jury had no questions to ask, he thanked the witness and dismissed her.

The next witness was Inspector Badger, and a very cautious witness he was, and like his namesake, very unwilling to be drawn. To me, who knew pretty well what information he held, his evasive manoeuvres and his portentous secrecy were decidedly amusing, and the foxy glances that he occasionally cast in Thorndyke's direction made me suspect that he was unaware of Superintendent Miller's visit to our chambers. He began by setting forth that, in consequence of a telephone message from the local police, he proceeded on the evening of the twentieth instant to 'The Rowans' to examine the premises and obtain particulars of the crime. He had obtained a rough list of the stolen property from Sir Lawrence Drayton. It included the pendant and the locket which had been illustrated in the article referred to.

'Should you say there was any evidence of selection as to the articles stolen?' the coroner asked.

'No. Only two drawers had been opened, and they were the two upper ones. The top drawer contained nothing of any value, and I infer that the thieves had only just got the second drawer open when they were disturbed.'

'Did you ascertain how many men were on the premises?'

'There were two men. We found their footprints in the grounds, and moreover, both of them were seen. And certain other traces were found.'

'Dr Nichols has mentioned that some hair was found grasped in the hand of deceased. Has that been examined?'

'I believe it has, but hair isn't much use until you have got the man to compare it with.'

'I suppose not. And with regard to the other traces. What were they?'

The inspector pursed up his lips and assumed a portentous expression.

'I hope, sir,' said he, 'that you will not press that question. It is not desirable in the interests of justice that the information that is in our possession should become public property.'

'I quite agree with you,' said the coroner. 'But may we take it that you have some clue to the identity of these two men?'

'We have several very promising clues,' the inspector replied with some disregard, I suspected, for the exact wording of the oath that he had just taken.

'Well,' said the coroner, 'that is all that really concerns us'; and I could not but reflect that it was all that really concerned Mr Joseph Hedges, *alias* Moakey, and that the inspector's secrecy was somewhat pointless when the cat had been let out of the bag to this extent. 'I suppose,' he continued, 'it would be indiscreet to ask if any information is available about the Mr Halliburton whose name has been mentioned.'

'I should rather not make any detailed statement on the subject,' replied Badger, 'but I may say that our information is of a very definite kind and points very clearly in a particular direction.'

'That is very satisfactory,' said the coroner. 'This is a peculiarly atrocious crime, and I am sure that all law-abiding persons will be glad to hear that there is a good prospect of the wrongdoers being brought to justice. And I think if you have nothing more to tell us, Inspector, that we need not trouble you any further.' He paused, and as Badger resumed his seat, he took a final glance over his notes; then, turning to the jury, he said: 'You have now, gentlemen, heard all the evidence, excepting those details which the police have very properly reserved and which really do not concern us. For I may remind you that this is not a criminal court. It is not our object to fix the guilt on any particular persons but to ascertain how this poor gentlemen met with his most deplorable death; and I am sure that the evidence which you have heard will be sufficient to enable you, without difficulty, to arrive at a verdict.'

On the conclusion of the coroner's address, the jury rapidly conferred for a few moments; then the foreman rose and announced that they had agreed unanimously on a verdict of wilful murder committed by some person or persons unknown, and they desired to express their deep sympathy with the brother of the deceased, Sir

Lawrence Drayton; and when the latter had briefly thanked the jury, through the coroner, the proceedings terminated and the court rose.

As the audience were slowly filing out, Sir Lawrence approached Miss Blake, and having shaken hands cordially and inquired as to her convalescence, said: 'That was a very remarkable story that you told in your evidence; I mean the simultaneous disappearance of your ancestor and this curious heirloom. As a Chancery barrister, unusual circumstances affecting the devolution of landed property naturally interest me. In the court in which I practise one sees, from time to time, some very odd turns of the wheel of Fortune. May I ask if any claim has ever been advanced by your branch of the family?'

'Yes. My father began some proceedings soon after my brother was born, but his counsel advised him not to go on with the case. He considered that without documentary evidence of my ancestor's marriage, it was useless to take the case into court.'

'Probably he was right,' said Drayton. 'Still, as a matter of professional interest – to say nothing of the interest that one naturally feels in the welfare of one's friends – I should like to know more about this quaint piece of family history. What do you think, Anstey?'

'I think it would be interesting to know just at what point the evidence of the relationship breaks off, and how large the gap is.'

'Precisely,' said Drayton. 'And one would like to know how the other parties are placed. What, for instance, would be the position if the present tenant were to die without issue, who are the heirs, and so on.'

'If it would interest you,' said Miss Blake, 'I could give you fairly full particulars of all that is known. My grandfather, who was a lawyer, wrote out an abstract for the guidance of his descendants; quite a full and very clear narrative. I could let you have that or a copy of it, if I didn't feel ashamed to take up your time with it.'

'Let me have the copy,' said Drayton. 'I don't suppose anything will come of it from your point of view, but it strikes me as an interesting case which is at least worth elucidating. Do you know Dr Thorndyke?'

'We know one another by repute,' said Thorndyke. 'Miss Blake used to board with Polton's sister. You were speaking of the curious circumstances that Miss Blake mentioned in reference to the cat's eye pendant.'

'Yes,' said Drayton. 'I was saying that it would be worth while to get the facts of the case sorted out.'

'I quite agree with you,' said Thorndyke. 'The same idea had occurred to me when Miss Blake was giving her evidence. Do I understand that there are documents available?'

'I have a full *résumé* of the facts relating to the change in the succession,' said Miss Blake, 'and a copy which I am going to hand to Sir Lawrence.'

'Then,' said Thorndyke, 'I shall crave your kind permission to look through that copy. I am not much of an authority on property law, but –'

'*Nihil quod tetigit non ornavit,*' I murmured, quoting Johnson's famous epitaph on the versatile 'Goldie.'

'Quite right, Anstey,' Drayton agreed warmly. 'All knowledge is Thorndyke's province. Then you will let me have that copy at your convenience, Miss Blake?'

'Thank you, yes, Sir Lawrence,' she replied. 'You shall have it by tomorrow. Oh, and there is something else that I have to give you, and I may as well give it to you now. Did Mr Anstey tell you that I had found the missing locket? I have brought it tied round my neck for safety. Has any one got a knife?' As she spoke she unfastened the top button of her dress and drew out the little gold volume which was attached to a silken cord.

'Don't cut the cord,' said Drayton. 'I want you to keep the locket as a souvenir of my poor brother. Now don't raise objections. Anstey has told me that the little bauble has found favour in your eyes, and I very much wish you to have it. It was a great favourite of my brother's. He used to call it "the little Sphinx" because it always seemed to be propounding a riddle; and it will be a great satisfaction to me to feel that it has passed into friendly and sympathetic hands instead of going to a museum with the other things.'

'It is exceedingly kind of you, Sir Lawrence,' she began, but he interrupted: 'It is nothing of the kind. I am doing myself a kindness in finding a good home for poor Andrew's little favourite. Are you going by train or tram?'

'I shall wait for the tram,' she replied.

'Then we part here. Dr Thorndyke and I are taking the train to Broad Street. Goodbye! Don't forget to send me that copy of the documents.'

The two men swung off down the road to the station, and as a tram appeared in the offing, a resolution which had been forming in my mind took definite shape.

'I don't see,' said I, 'why I should be left out in the cold in regard to this family romance of yours. Why shouldn't I come and collect the copy to deliver to Sir Lawrence and have a surreptitious read at it myself?'

'It would be very nice of you if you could spare the time,' she replied. 'I will even offer special inducements. I will give you some tea, which you must be wanting by this time, I should think, and I will show you not only the copy but the original documents. One of them is quite curious.'

'That settles it then,' said I. 'Tea and documents, combined with your society and that of your ingenious brother, form what the theatrical people would call a galaxy of attractions. Here is our tram. Do we go inside or outside?'

'Oh, outside, please. There is quite a crowd waiting.'

I was relieved at this decision, for I was hankering for a smoke; and as soon as we had taken our places in a front seat on the roof, I began secretly to feel in the pocket where the friendly pipe reposed and to debate within myself whether I might crave permission to bring it forth. At length the tobacco-hunger conquered my scruples and I ventured to make the request.'

'Oh, of course,' she replied. 'Do smoke. I love the smell of tobacco, especially from a pipe.'

Thus encouraged, I joyfully produced the calumet and felt in my pocket for my pouch. And then came a dreadful disappointment. The pouch was there, sure enough, but its lean sides announced the hideous fact that it was empty. There were not even a few grains wherewith to stave off imminent starvation.

'How provoking!' my companion exclaimed tragically. 'I *am* sorry. But you shan't be deprived for long. You must get down at a tobacconist's and restock your pouch, and then after tea you shall smoke your pipe while I show you the documents, as you call them.'

'Then I am comforted,' said I. 'The galaxy of attractions has received a further addition.' Resignedly I put away the pipe and pouch, and reverting to a question that had occurred to me while she was giving her evidence, I said: 'There was one statement of yours that I did not quite follow. It was with regard to the man whom you were trying to hold. You said that you were quite confident that you would recognise him and that you could call up quite a clear and vivid mental picture of his face, but yet you thought that, if you were to draw a memory portrait of him, that portrait might be misleading. How could that be? You would know whether your portrait was like your recollection of the man, and if it was, surely it would be like the man himself.'

'I suppose it would,' she replied thoughtfully. 'But there might be some false details which wouldn't matter to me but which might mislead others who might take those details for the essential characters.'

'But if the details were wrong, wouldn't that destroy the likeness?'

'Not necessarily, I think. Of course, a likeness is ultimately dependent on the features, particularly on their proportion and the spaces between them. But you must have noticed that when children and beginners draw portraits, although they produce the most frightful caricatures – all wrong and all out of drawing – yet those portraits are often unmistakable likenesses.'

'Yes, I have noticed that. But don't you think the likeness is probably due to the caricature? To the exaggeration of some one or two characteristic peculiarities?'

'Very likely. But that rather bears out what I said. For those caricatures, though easily recognisable, are mostly false; and if one of them got into the hands of a stranger who had never seen the subject of the portrait, for purposes of identification, he would as probably as not look for some one having those characteristics which had been quite falsely represented.'

'Yes; and then he would be looking for the wrong kind of person altogether.'

'Exactly. And then my drawing would probably be far from a correct representation of my recollection of the face. It isn't as if one could take a photograph of a mental image. So I am afraid that the idea of a memory drawing for the purpose of identification must be abandoned. Besides, it would be of no use unless we could get hold of the man.'

'No. But that is not impossible. The police have apparently identified one of the men and expect to have him in custody at any moment. He may give information as to the other, but even if he does not, the police may be able to find out who his associates were, and in that case a memory drawing which was far from accurate might help them to pick out the particular man.'

'That is possible,' she agreed. 'But then if the police could get hold of this man's associates and let me see them, I could pick out the particular man with certainty and without any drawing at all. Isn't that a tobacconist's shop that we are approaching?'

'It is. I think I will get off and make my purchase and then come along to the studio.'

'Do,' she said, 'and I will run on ahead and see that the preparations for tea are started.'

I ran down the steps and dropped off the tram without stopping it, but by this time we had passed the shop by some little distance and I had to walk back. I secured the new supply, and having stuffed it into my pouch, came out of the shop just in time to see the tram stop nearly a quarter of a mile ahead and Miss Blake get off, followed by a couple of other passengers, and walk quickly into Jacob Street. I strode forward at a brisk pace in the same direction, but when I reached the corner of the street she had already disappeared. I was just about to cross to the side on which the studio was situated when my attention was attracted by a woman who was walking slowly up the street on my side. At the first glance I was struck by something familiar in her appearance and a second glance confirmed the impression. She was smartly — and something more than smartly — dressed, and in particular I noted a rather large, elaborate, and gaudy hat. In short, she was very singularly like the woman who had jostled me in the doorway of the hall in which the inquest was held.

I slowed down to avoid overtaking her, and as I did so she crossed the road and walked straight up to the gate of the studio. For an instant I thought she was going to ring the bell, for after a glance at the number on the gate she turned to the side and read the little nameplate, leaning forward and putting her face close to it as if she were near-sighted. At that moment the wicket opened and Master Percy stepped out on to the threshold; whereupon the woman, after one swift, intense glance at the boy, turned away and walked quickly up the street. I was half disposed to follow her and confirm my suspicion as to her identity; but Master Percy had already observed me, and it seemed, perhaps, more expedient to get out of sight myself than to reveal my presence in attempting to verify a suspicion of which I had practically no doubt, and which, even if confirmed, had no obvious significance. Accordingly I crossed the road, and having greeted my host, was by him conducted down the passage to the studio.

CHAPTER EIGHT
A Jacobite Romance

In the minds of many of us, including myself, there appears to be a natural association between the ideas of tea and tobacco. Whether it is that both substances are exotic products, adopted from alien races, or that each is connected with a confirmed and accepted drug habit, I am not quite clear. But there seems to be no doubt that the association exists and that the realisation of the one idea begets an imperative impulse to realise the other. In conformity with which natural law, when the tea-things had been, by the joint efforts of Miss Blake and her brother, removed to the curtained repository – where also dwelt a gas ring and a kettle – I proceeded complacently to bring forth my pipe and the bulging tobacco-pouch and to transfer some of the contents of the latter to the former.

'I am glad to see you smoking,' said Miss Blake as the first cloud of incense ascended. 'It gives me the feeling that you are provided with an antidote to the documents. I shall have less compunction about the reading.'

'You think that the "tuneless pipe" is similar to the tuneful one in its effects on the "savage breast." But I don't want any antidote. I am all agog to hear your romance of a cat's eye, that is, if you are going to read out the documents.'

'I thought I would read the copy aloud and get you to check it by the originals. Then you can assure Sir Lawrence that it is a true copy.'

'Yes. I think that is quite a good plan. It is always well to have a copy checked and certified correct.'

'Then I will get the books and we will begin at once. Do you want to hear the reading, Percy, or are you going on with your building?'

'I should like to come and listen, if you don't mind, Winnie,' he replied; and as his sister unlocked the cabinet under the window, he seated himself on a chair by the now vacant table. Miss Blake took from the cabinet three books, one of which — an ordinary school exercise-book — she placed on the table by her chair.

'That,' she said, 'is the copy of both originals. This' — handing to me a little leather-covered book, the pages of which were filled with small, clearly-written, though faded, handwriting — 'is the abstract of which I spoke. This other little book is the fragmentary original which is referred to in the abstract. If you are ready I will begin. We will take the abstract first.'

I provided myself with a pencil with which to mark any errors, and having opened the little book announced that I was ready.

'The abstract,' said she, 'was written in 1821, and reads as follows:

' "A SHORT HISTORY OF THE BLAKES OF
BEAUCHAMP BLAKE NEAR WENDOVER IN THE
COUNTY OF BUCKINGHAMSHIRE, FROM THE
YEAR OF OUR LORD 1708.

' "This history has been written by me for the purpose of preserving a record of certain events for the information of my descendants, to whom a knowledge of those events may prove of great importance; and its writing has become necessary by the circumstance that, whereas the only existing written record has been reduced by Time and Ill-usage to a collection of disconnected fragments, the traditions passed on orally from generation to generation become year by year more indistinct and unreliable.

' "I shall begin with the year 1708, at which time the estate of Beauchamp Blake was held by Harold Blake. In this year was born Percival Blake, the only son of Harold aforesaid. Seven years later occurred a rising in favour of the Royal House of the Stuarts, in which act of rebellion the said Harold Blake was suspected (but never accused) of having taken part. In the year

1743, Harold Blake died and his only son, Percival, succeeded to the property.

' "In or about the year 1742, Percival Blake married a lady named Judith Weston (or Western). For some unknown reason this marriage took place secretly, and was, for a time at least, kept secret. Possibly the marriage would not have been acceptable to Percival's father, or the lady may have been a Papist. This latter seems the more probable, inasmuch as the marriage was solemnised, not at the church of St Margaret at Beauchamp Blake, but at a little church in London near to Aldgate, called St Peter by the Shambles, the rector of which, the Reverend Stephen Rumbold, an intimate friend of Percival's, became subsequently not only a Papist but a Jesuit. In the next year, 1743, a son was born and was christened James. No entry of this birth appears in the registers of St Margaret's, so it is probable that it was registered at the London church. Unfortunately, this register is incomplete. Several pages have been torn out, and as these missing pages belong to the years 1742 and 1743, it is to be presumed that they contained the records of the marriage and the birth.

' "About the year 1725 Percival came to London to study medicine; and about 1729 or 1730 he completed his studies and took his degree at Cambridge, of which University he was already a Bachelor of Arts. From this time onwards he appears to have practised in London as a physician, and it was probably at this period that he made the acquaintance of Judith Western and Stephen Rumbold. Even after the death of his father and his own succession to the property, he continued to practise his profession, making only occasional visits to his estate in Buckinghamshire.

' "Like his father, Percival Blake was an ardent supporter of the Stuarts, and it is believed that he took an active part in the various Jacobite plots that were heard of about this time; and when, in 1745, the great rising took place, Percival was one of those who hastened to join the forces of the young Pretender; a disastrous act, to which all the subsequent misfortunes of the family are due.

' "On the collapse of the Jacobite cause, Percival took immediate measures to avert the consequences of his ill-judged action from his own family; and in these he displayed a degree of foresight that might well have been exhibited earlier. From Scotland he made his way to Beauchamp Blake and there, in one of the numerous hiding-places of the old mansion, concealed certain important documents connected with the property. It is not quite clear what these documents were. Among them appear to have been some of the title-deeds, and there is no doubt that they included documents proving the validity of his marriage with Judith and the legitimacy of his son James. Meanwhile, he had sent his wife and child, with a servant named Jenifer Gray, to Hamburg, where they were to wait until he joined them. He himself made his way to a port on the East Coast, believed to have been King's Lynn, where he embarked, under a false name, on a small vessel bound for Hamburg; but while he was waiting for the vessel to sail, he circulated a very circumstantial account of his own death by drowning while attempting to escape in an open boat.

' "This was at once a fortunate and unfortunate act; fortunate inasmuch as it completely achieved his purpose of preventing the confiscation of the property; unfortunate inasmuch as it effectually shut out his own descendants from the succession. On the report of his death (unmarried, as was believed, and so without issue) a distant cousin, of unquestionable loyalty to the reigning house, took possession of the estate without opposition and without any suggestion of confiscation.

' "One thing only, appertaining to the inheritance, Percival took with him. Among the family heirlooms was a jewel consisting of a small pendant set with a single cymophane (vulgarly known as a cat's eye) and bearing an inscription, of which the actual words are unknown, but of which the purport was that whosoever should possess the jewel should also possess the Blake estate; a foolish statement that seems to have been generally believed in the family and to which Percival evidently attached incredible weight. For not only did he take the jewel with him, but, as will presently appear, he made careful provision for its disposal.

'"From this time onward the history becomes more and more vague. It seems that Percival joined his wife and child at Hamburg, and thereafter travelled about Germany, plying his profession as a physician. But soon he was overtaken by a terrible misfortune. It appears that a robbery had been committed by a woman who was said to be a foreigner, and suspicion fell upon Judith. She was arrested, and on false evidence, convicted and sent, as a punishment, to labour in the mines somewhere in the Harz Mountains. Percival made unceasing efforts to obtain her release, but it was three years before his efforts were crowned with success. But then, alas, it was too late. The poor lady came back to him aged by privation and broken by long-standing sickness, only to linger on a few months and then to die in his arms. On her release he carried her away to France, and there, at Paris, about the year 1751, she passed away and is believed to have been buried in the cemetery of Père Lachaise.

'"The death of his wife, to whom he seems to have been devotedly attached, left Percival a broken man; and about eighteen months later, he himself died, and is believed to have been buried beside Judith. But in these sad months he occupied himself in making provision for the recovery of the family inheritance by his posterity when circumstances should have become more favourable. To this end he wrote a summary of the events connected with and following the Jacobite rising and had it sewn into a little illustrated Book of Hours, which, together with the cymophane jewel, he gave into the keeping of Jenifer Gray, to be by her given to the child James when he should be old enough to be trusted with them. The exact contents of the little book we can only surmise from the fragments that remain, but they seem to have been a short account of his own actions and vicissitudes, and no doubt gave at least a clue to the place in which the documents were hidden. Nor can we tell what the exact form of the jewel was or the nature of the inscription, for Percival's references to the latter as 'a guide' to his descendants are not clearly understandable. At any rate, the jewel has disappeared and the written record is reduced to a few fragments. Jenifer Gray (who seems to have been an illiterate and foolish woman) apparently gave the little book to the child to play with, for the few leaves that remain are covered with childish scrawls; and she may have sold the jewel to buy the necessaries of life, for she and the boy were evidently but poorly provided for.

' "On reaching the age of fourteen, James was apprenticed to a cabinetmaker in Paris and apparently became very skilful workman. When he was out of his time (Jenifer Gray having died in the meantime) he came to England and settled in London, where, in time, he established an excellent business.

' "Into this his son William (my father), was taken, first as an apprentice, then as partner and finally as principal. By my father the prosperity of the house was so well maintained that he was able to article me to an attorney, to whom I am chief clerk at this time of writing.

' "This record, together with what remains of Percival Blake's manuscript, will, I trust, be preserved by my descendants in the hope that it may be the instrument by which Providence may hereafter reinstate them in the inheritance of their forefathers.

' "JOHN BLAKE.

' "16 SYMOND'S INN, LONDON,
' "20th *June* 1821." '

As she finished reading, Miss Blake let the book fall into her lap and looked at me as if inviting criticism. I closed the little original, and laying it on the table, remarked: 'A very singular and romantic history, and a very valuable record. The detailed narrative presents a much more convincing case than one would have expected from the bare statement that you gave in your evidence. Your great-grandfather was a wise man to commit the facts to writing while the memory of the events was comparatively recent. How much is there left of Percival's manuscript?'

'Very little, I am sorry to say,' she replied, picking up the remaining volume and handing it to me; 'but I have made a copy of these fragments, too. It follows the copy of John Blake's abstract, and I will read it out to you if you will check it by the original.'

I turned the little book over in my hand and examined it curiously. It was a tiny volume, bound in gold-tooled calf, now rusty and worn and badly broken at the joints. The title-page showed it to be a Book of Hours – *Horae Beatae Mariae Virginis* – printed at Antwerp by Balthasar Moretus and dated 1634, and on turning over the leaves I perceived that it was illustrated with a number of quaint but decorative woodcuts. The inside of the cover seemed to have been used as a sort of unofficial birth register. At the top, in very faded writing, was inscribed 'Judith Weston,' and underneath a succession of names beginning with 'James, son of Percival and Judith Blake, born 3rd April 1743,' and ending with Winifred and Percival, the daughter and son of Peter and Agnes Blake. Between the cover and the title-page a number of fly-leaves of very thin paper had been stitched in, and those that remained were covered with minute writing of a pale, ghostly brown, largely defaced by spots, smears, scribblings and childish drawings. But most of them had disappeared, and the few that were left hung insecurely to the loosened stitches.

When I had completed my inspection, I opened the book at the first fly-leaf, and adjusting the reading-glass which Miss Blake had placed on the table, announced that I was ready; whereupon she resumed her reading.

'The first page reads: "…to my cousin Leonard, who, as the heir-at-law, would, I knew, be watching the course of events. Indeed, I doubt not that if he had known of my marriage, he would have used his influence at the Court to oust me. But the news of my death I felt sure would bring him forward at once, and his loyalty to the German King would make him secure to the succession. So he and his brood should keep the nest warm until the clouds had passed and the present troubles should be forgotten. Only to my own posterity, the true heirs, must be provided a key wherewith to re-enter on their inheritance, and to this end I searched the muniment chest and took therefrom all the – " '

This was the end of the page, and as she broke off, Miss Blake looked up.

'Isn't it exasperating?' said she. 'There seems to be only one page missing in this place, but it is the one that contains the vital information.'

'It is not very difficult to guess what he took,' said I. 'Evidently he abstracted the title-deeds. But the question is, what did he do with them?'

'Yes,' said Miss Blake, 'that is the important question, and unfortunately we cannot answer it. That he hid them in a secure hiding-place is evident from the next two pages. The first reads: "Will Bateman, the plumber, made me a tall leaden jar like a black-jack to hold the documents, with a close-fitting lid, which we luted on with wax when we had put the documents into it. And this jar I set in the hiding-place, and on top of it the great two-handled posset-pot that old Martin, the potter, made for my mother when I was born; which I prize dearly and would not have it fall into the hands of strangers. When all was ready, we sent for the carpenter, who is a safe man and loyal to the Prince, and bade him close the chamber, which he did so that no eye could detect the opening. So the writings shall be safe until such time – "

'The next page reads: "…and the other documents which I obtained from Mr Halford, the attorney. I had feared that their absence might be a bar to the succession, but he assured me it was not so, but only that it would hinder the sale of the property. So I am satisfied; and I am confident that Leonard will never guess the hiding-place in which they are bestowed, nor will he ever dream what that hiding-place conceals.

' "When I had done this I began forthwith to spread the report of my death among strangers, both in the coffee-houses and at the inn whereat I lodged while I was waiting for the ship to sail from – " There the page ends, and there seems to be quite a lot missing, for the next one speaks of the disaster as having already occurred.

' "Nor, indeed, would they listen to her protestations (spoken, as they were, in a strange tongue), and still less to my entreaties. And so she was borne away from my sight, brave, cheerful, and dignified to the last, as befitted an English gentlewoman, though it seemed then as

if we should never look on one another again. So I left with the child
and Jenifer and must needs continue to live at Eisenach (that I might
be near my darling, though I could never see her) and must minister
for my daily bread to the wretches who people that accursed land – "

'There seems to be only one or two pages missing here, for the
next page runs: "…this joyful day (as I had hoped it would be) and
set forth from Eisenach with the child and Jenifer to meet my poor
darling on the road. A few miles out we saw the cart approaching,
filled with the prisoners released from the mines. I looked among
them, but at first saw her not. Then a haggard old woman held out her
arms to me and I looked again. The old woman was Judith, my wife!
But, O God, what a wreck! She was wasted to a very skeleton, her skin
was like old parchment, her hair, that had been like spun gold, was
turned to a strange black and her whole aspect – "' Miss Blake paused
and said in a low voice: 'It is a dreadful picture. Poor Judith! And poor
Percival! And the rest of the story is just as sad. The next page takes up
the thread just after Judith's death.

' "And when it was over and I saw them shovel in the earth, I felt
moved to beg them not to fill the grave but to leave room for me. I
went away through the snow with Jenifer and the boy. But I was
alone. Judith had been all to me, and my heart was under the new-
turned sods. Yet I bethought me, if it should please God to take me, I
must not go without leaving some chart to guide my son back to our
home, should such return be possible in his lifetime, or to guide his
children or his children's children. Therefore, that same sad day I began
to write this history on the fly-leaves that my dear wife had had sewn
into her little book of – "

'There seems to be only one page missing before the next, but it
was an important one, so far as we can judge. Indeed, it almost appears
as if all the most significant pages were lost. The next page reads:
"…gave me a string from his bass viol, which he says will be the best
of all. So that matter is as secure as care and judgement can make it.
This book and the precious bauble I purpose to hold until I feel the
hand of death upon me, and then I shall give both into the keeping
of Jenifer, bidding her guard them jealously as treasures beyond price,
until my son attains the age of fourteen. Then she shall give them
to him, adjuring him to preserve the book in a safe place and never to

lend or show it to any person whatsoever, and to wear the trinket hung around his neck under his clothing so that none shall know – "

'That is the last complete page. There remains a half-page, which seems to have been the concluding one. It reads: "…and that is all that I can do, since one cannot look into the future. When the time is ripe, my son, or his descendants, can go forward with open eyes. This history and the trinket shall guide them. Wherefore I pray that both may be treasured by them to whom I thus pass on the inheritance." '

As Miss Blake finished her reading she closed the book and sat looking thoughtfully at her brother, who had listened with rapt attention to the pathetic story. Half-reluctantly I shut the little Book of Hours and laid it on the table.

'It is a tragic little history,' I said, 'and these soiled and tattered leaves and the faded writing and the old-fashioned phraseology make it somehow very real and vivid. I wonder what became of the cat's eye pendant. Is nothing at all known of the way in which it was lost?'

'Nothing,' she replied. 'The boy James was only seven years old when his father died, so he would hardly have remembered, even if he knew of the existence of the jewel. It may have been lost or stolen, or, more probably, Jenifer sold it to buy the necessaries of life. She must have been pretty hard pressed at times.'

'She must have been a duffer,' said Percy, 'if she sold it after what she had been told. Couldn't she have popped it and kept up the interest?'

'You seem to know a good deal about these matters, Percy,' his sister remarked with a smile.

'Well,' said he, 'I should think everybody knows how to raise the wind if they are hard up. There's no need to sell things when you've got an uncle.'

'We don't know that she did sell it,' said Miss Blake. 'She may even have "popped" it, to use your elegant expression. All that we know is that it disappeared. And now it has disappeared again, if this pendant that was stolen was really the Blake pendant.'

'Is there any reason to suppose that it was?' I asked.

'Only that it agreed with what little we know of the missing jewel, and cat's eye pendants must be very rare. Unfortunately, the *Connoisseur* article doesn't help us much. It gives a photograph, from which we could identify the pendant if we knew exactly what it was like, but the description fails just at the vital point. It doesn't say anything about the inscription on the back. It was in order to find out what that inscription was that I asked poor Mr Drayton to let me see the jewel. Would you like to see the photograph?'

'I should, very much, if you have a copy.'

She fetched from the cabinet a copy of the *Connoisseur*, and having found the article, handed the open magazine to me. There were two photographs on the page, one of the little book-locket and the other of a simple, lozenge-shaped pendant of somewhat plain design, set with a single, rather large stone, smooth-cut and nearly circular. The letterpress gave no particulars and did not even mention the inscription.

'I suppose,' said I, 'there is no doubt that this pendant did bear an inscription of some kind. There is no reference to it here.'

'No particular reference, unfortunately. But this was a collection of inscribed objects. Every specimen bore an inscription if it was only a name and a date. The article, you will see, says so, and Mr Drayton told me so himself.'

'You didn't ask him what was written on this pendant?'

'No; I didn't want to tell him about our family tradition unless I found that it really was the Blake pendant. Perhaps I might not have told him even then, for the inscription might have told us all we wanted to know; though I must confess to a certain superstitious hankering to possess the jewel, or, at least, to see it in Percy's possession.'

'You were telling Sir Lawrence that proceedings to establish a claim were actually begun by your father.'

'Yes, but our solicitor was not at all hopeful, and the counsel whom he retained very strongly advised my father not to go on. He thought that, with the apparently well-founded belief in Percival's death and the absence of any real evidence of his marriage and survival, we had no case. So the action was settled out of court and the tenant at the time agreed to pay most of the costs.'

'Do you remember who was the solicitor for the tenant?'

'Yes. His name was Brodribb, and my father thought he treated us very fairly.'

'He probably did. I know Mr Brodribb very well, and I have the highest opinion of him as a lawyer and as a man. I have often been retained by him, and I have usually been very well satisfied to be associated with him. Do you know what the position was when your father began his action? I mean as to the possible heirs. Was the present tenant then in possession?'

'No; he was a Mr Arnold Blake, a widower with no surviving children. But he knew the present tenant, Arthur Blake, although they were not very near relatives, and was prepared to contest the claim on his behalf. Arthur Blake was then, I think, in Australia.'

'And I gather that you don't know much about him?'

'No, excepting that I understand that he is unmarried, which is all that really matters to us.'

'And did Brodribb know about this little book and John Blake's abstract?'

'I think my father must have told him that we had some authentic details of the family history, but I don't know whether he actually showed him the originals.'

'And with regard to the pedigree since Percival. Have the marriages and births all been proved?'

'Yes. My father had them investigated, and obtained certificates of all of them, and I have those certificates, though I am afraid they are never likely to be called for.'

'Well,' I said, 'as a lawyer, I shouldn't like to hold out any hopes even if the death of the present tenant without issue should seem to create a favourable situation. But, of course, if it should ever become possible to prove the marriage of Percival and Judith and the birth of James, that would alter the position very materially. And now I must tear myself away. I have been most keenly interested in hearing your romance, and I have no doubt that Sir Lawrence will be equally so. If you will give me the copy, I will leave it at his chambers tonight or tomorrow morning.'

She gave me the manuscript book, which I slipped into my pocket, and then she and Percy escorted me across the yard and let me out at the wicket.

CHAPTER NINE

Exit Moakey

From Jacob Street I made my way to the Temple with the intention of letting Thorndyke look through Miss Blake's manuscript – since he had expressed a wish to see it – before delivering it to Drayton. And as I sat on the omnibus roof I reflected on the events of the afternoon. In spite of my legal training and experience the romance of the lost inheritance had taken a strong hold on me. The two narratives, and especially the older one, diffused an atmosphere of reality that was very convincing. It was practically certain that the two manuscripts were genuine, and if they were, there could be no doubt that my young friend Percy was the direct descendant of the Jacobite fugitive, Percival Blake. Nor could there be much reasonable doubt that the descent was legitimate. Percival plainly referred to Judith as his wife and there seemed to be no reason for supposing that the marriage had not taken place at the time stated in John Blake's abstract. In short, I found myself wondering whether Mr Peter Blake's counsel had not been a little over-cautious, or whether he might not have been influenced by a possible financial straitness on the part of the said Peter unfavourable to a warmly-contested action at law.

If he had been over-cautious, it was unfortunate, for he had missed an opportunity. The death of Arnold Blake without a direct successor would have made things comparatively easy for a new claimant with a good case, whereas now, with Arthur Blake in possession, the difficulties would be much greater. It is one thing to maintain a claim against other claimants, but quite another to oust a tenant who has established a title by actual possession. And, to judge by their surroundings and mode of life, my friends were but poorly equipped for any action at all.

From the manuscripts and their story my thoughts strayed to the woman whom I had seen examining Miss Blake's nameplate. I did not like that incident at all. It might mean nothing. The woman might happen to live in the neighbourhood and have made her inspection from mere idle curiosity. But that was not what the appearances suggested. The woman had been at the inquest, and from Hampstead she must have travelled in the same tramcar that had conveyed Miss Blake and me. Then she had seemed to have followed Miss Blake, at some distance, on the opposite side of the road. There was a suggestion of purpose in the whole proceeding that I found disquieting and rather sinister, and it was not made less so by the very unprepossessing appearance of the woman herself.

When I let myself into our chambers with my key – or rather Jervis' – I found the sitting-room vacant; but as an inspection of the hat-rack in the lobby suggested that Thorndyke was somewhere on the premises, I went up to the laboratory, and there I found him in company with Polton and an uncanny-looking apparatus consisting of a microscope with an attachment of miniature hot-water pipes.

'This is a new form of magic,' said I, 'at least it is new to me. What is going on?'

'This is just a microscope with a warm stage,' Thorndyke explained. 'We are making it a hot stage for the purposes of the present experiment.'

'And what is the experiment?' I asked with sudden curiosity, for I had just observed that the object on the microscope stage was an irregular-shaped piece of glass on which I could distinguish a very clear fingerprint.

'The experiment is connected with the fingerprints on the piece of glass that you so very fortunately secured at "The Rowans." This is a portion of it which I have cut off with a glazier's diamond and which bears a duplicate print. You remember my pointing out to you that a real fingerprint – as distinguished from a statistical or mathematical fingerprint – has chemical and physical properties. Well, we are endeavouring to determine the chemical nature of the substance of which this fingerprint is composed by inference from its physical properties. We are now ascertaining its melting-point; in fact I may say that we have ascertained it. It is fifty-three degrees centigrade. And this fact, in conjunction with its other observed physical properties, tells us that it is Japanese wax.'

'Indeed,' said I. 'Then that goes to show that the man who made these fingerprints had been handling Japanese wax.'

'That is the obvious inference.'

'Does that throw any light on the man's personality or occupation? What is Japanese wax used for?'

'For a variety of purposes. Very largely for the manufacture of wax polishes for boots and furniture, for the preparation of foundry wax and the various waxes used by jewellers, engravers, and lapidaries. It is also used in pharmacy in the making of certain plasters and cerates.'

'Do you think,' I asked, 'that this man could have got it on his fingers by touching the furniture?'

'No,' replied Thorndyke. 'The cabinets were French-polished, and I saw no trace of wax polish on them. Besides, there is more wax than would have been taken up in that way.'

'Does the presence of this wax suggest anything to you?'

'Well,' replied Thorndyke, 'of course there are possibilities. But one mustn't expect to apply a fact as soon as it is discovered. We have ascertained what this substance is. Let us put this item of knowledge in its proper mental pigeon-hole and hope that we shall find a use for it presently.'

'I have a strong suspicion, Thorndyke,' said I, 'that you have found a use for it already. However, I won't press you. I know my place. The mantle of Jervis is on me – and trailing a few yards along the ground. I am not permitted to cross-examine my reverend senior.'

'There really isn't any need for you to do so,' said he. 'I have no exclusive information. You are in possession of all the facts that are known to me.'

106

'That is not strictly true, you know, Thorndyke,' I objected. 'We share the mere observed facts of this case, I admit; but you have a body of general knowledge which I have not, and which gives many of these observed facts a significance that is hidden from me. However, we will let that pass. You are the investigating wizard, I am only a sort of familiar demon. Which reminds me that I have been devilling for you this afternoon. I think you said that you would like to look over the documents relating to Miss Blake's claim.'

'Yes, I should be interested to see them.'

'Well, I've got a copy, which I have compared with the originals, and which I am to hand over Drayton. Would you like to have it now?'

'Yes; I have finished up here. Let us go downstairs and look over the documents together.'

'You had better take the copy down with you and run through it while I am having a wash. Then I will come down and hear your reverend pronouncements on the case.' I produced the manuscript book from my pocket and having handed it to him, retired to the bedroom of which I was tenant *ex officio*, while he descended to the sitting-room with the manuscript in his hand.

When I came down after a leisurely wash and brush up, I found Thorndyke sitting with the open book before him and a slip of paper and a pencil in his hand. Apparently he had finished the reading and was jotting down a few dates and other particulars.

'This is a singularly interesting story, Anstey,' said he, 'and extraordinarily picturesque in its setting. It enables us to understand Miss Blake's view as to her brother's claim, which sounded a little extravagant when baldly stated in her evidence. And, in fact, it looks as if that claim were a perfectly sound one. If it were only possible to produce satisfactory evidence of the marriage of Percival and Judith Blake and of the legitimacy of James, I should take the case into Court with perfect confidence – under suitable conditions, of course.'

'You mean, if there were any question as to the succession.'

'Yes. And such a question may arise at any moment if the present tenant is unmarried. It seems to me a matter of vital importance to find out as much as possible about this present tenant, Arthur Blake; I mean as to his heir, his relatives and connections generally, and the chances of his marrying. Miss Blake's brother is but a child, and many things may happen before he is a middle-aged man.'

'Yes,' I agreed. 'It would be a good deal more to the point than fussing about this ridiculous cat's eye. Miss Blake's keenness about that is a mystery to me.'

'Don't forget,' said Thorndyke, 'that the pendant is believed to bear an inscription that might be helpful to the possessor, though it is difficult to imagine in what way it could be.'

'Very difficult,' said I. 'But it isn't the inscription that she is so keen on, it is the thing itself. She has a sort of half-belief in some occult quality inherent in this jewel, in fact she is infected by the family superstition. It is incomprehensible to me.'

'It is always difficult for one temperament to understand another,' said he. 'But this state of mind is quite a common one. That absurd little bone of Halliburton's is a case in point, and quite a representative instance. It was obviously a mascot – that is to say, an object credited with occult properties and the power to influence events; and how many people are there who, openly or secretly, cherish similar charms or fetishes. The Stock Exchange, the Stage, and the Sporting Clubs are full of them.'

'Yes,' that is true,' I agreed; and then, suddenly remembering the mysterious woman, I said: 'By the way, a rather queer thing happened this afternoon. I accompanied Miss Blake home from Hampstead, but I got off the tram to get some tobacco and let her go on ahead. She had gone indoors before I arrived at the studio, and as I was approaching her house, I saw a woman cross the road and go deliberately up to the door and read the name on the plate.'

'Yes,' said Thorndyke, looking at me interrogatively.

'Well, the point is that that woman had followed us from Hampstead.'

'Indeed!' he exclaimed with sudden gravity. 'You are sure of that?'

'Yes. I recognised her before she crossed. You may have noticed her at the inquest, a brassy-haired baggage with a spotted veil and a face powdered like a clown's.'

'Yes, I noticed her. She was sitting near to you, by the door. I took particular note of her because she stood up while Miss Blake was giving her evidence, and seemed deeply interested in her and in you.'

'Well, that is the woman.'

'But this is very serious, Anstey. What a pity you didn't follow her and find out where she went to!'

'I had half a mind to, but Master Percy — Miss Blake's brother — came to the door at that moment and saw me, so it was hardly possible.'

'It is very unfortunate,' said Thorndyke. 'You see the importance of the matter? Miss Blake stood up in open Court and swore that she was confident she could identify the man who stabbed her. Now that man is not only a robber. He is, at least, an accessory to the murder of Andrew Drayton, and his apprehension would probably reveal the identity of the actual murderer — if he is not the murderer himself — to say nothing of the charge against him of wounding with intent. Of course, if the police are right about those fingerprints, there is not so much in it. They will arrest Moakey and probably get the other man as well. But if the police clue should fail — and I should not be surprised if it does — Miss Blake represents the whole of the evidence against these two men. Apart from her, a conviction would be impossible unless the men were taken with the stolen property in their possession, which they are not likely to be. Even if the men were arrested they could not be identified, excepting by her, and would have to be released. I consider that her position is one of extreme danger. Did you tell her of this incident?'

'No; I thought there was no use in making her uneasy.'

'She ought to be warned, Anstey. And she ought to be most cautious about exposing herself to the possibility of an attack of any kind. I am expecting a visit from Superintendent Miller — he sent me a note asking for an interview at seven o'clock, so he will be here in a few minutes. When we have seen him, we shall know how the case stands, but the fact of his wanting an interview suggests that the police bark has got into shoal water.'

Punctually at seven o'clock the Superintendent's characteristic official rat-tat announced his arrival, and as I let him in, a subtle something in his manner seemed to confirm Thorndyke's surmises.

'I suppose,' said he as he took the armchair and lighted the customary cigar, 'you've guessed what I wanted to talk to you about? It's this Drayton case, you know.'

Thorndyke nodded. 'Any new developments?' he asked.

'Well, yes, there are. We've got a bit of a setback. It seems that the fingerprint people made a mistake. Never known them to do such a thing before, but I suppose nobody is infallible. It turns out that those fingerprints are not Moakey's after all.'

As the Superintendent made this statement, he fixed a stony gaze on the opposite wall. Glancing at Thorndyke, I noted that my colleague's countenance had taken on that peculiar woodenness that I had learned to associate with intense attention not unmingled with suspicion.

'I can't think how they came to make such a stupid mistake,' the Superintendent continued, still staring fixedly at the wall. 'Might have got us into a horrid mess.'

'I should have thought,' said Thorndyke, 'that mistakes might easily be made with such multitudes of records. Whose fingerprints are they?'

'Ah!' said Miller, 'there you are. We don't know. They don't seem to have 'em at the registry. So our only clue is gone.'

'Haven't you opened up in any other direction?' Thorndyke asked.

'We've notified all the likely fences, of course, but that's no good. These coveys are not likely to try to plant the stuff with a murder charge hanging over them. Then we made some inquiries about that man Halliburton. But they turned out a frost. The chap has disappeared and left no address. We've got his signature, and we've got a dam silly rabbit bone that some fool has taken the trouble to cut a pattern on, that he left behind at the hotel; and as he seemed to value the thing, we put an advertisement in the papers saying that it had been found. But there are no answers up to the present, and not likely to be. And then Halliburton probably had nothing to do with the affair. So we're rather up a tree. And it's annoying, after thinking it was all plain sailing, and letting the papers give out that we were in full cry. Of course, they are all agog for the next act – and, by the way, one of them has got a portrait of you – I think I've got it. Yes, here it is.'

He produced from his pocket a copy of the *Evening Courier* and opened it out. On the front page was an excellent portrait of my colleague, with the descriptive title: 'Dr John Thorndyke, the famous criminal expert, whose services are being retained in the case.'

'That ought to help you, sir,' said the Superintendent with a grin. 'You won't be a stranger to our friends if you should happen to meet them. It is a pity their photographs can't be given, too.'

'Yes, it would be more to the point. But now, Miller, what is it that you want me to do? I assume that you have come to suggest some sort of co-operation?'

'Well,' said Miller, 'you are retained in the case, and I rather suspect that Sir Lawrence would like you to carry on independently. But there is no sense in our getting at cross-purposes.'

'Not the least,' Thorndyke agreed. 'It is a criminal case, and our objects are identical – to secure the offenders and recover the property. Do I understand that you are prepared to offer me facilities?'

'What facilities do you want?'

'At this moment I am not wanting any, excepting that I should like to look at the fingerprints. There would be no objection to that, I suppose?'

The Superintendent looked uncomfortable. 'I don't know why there should be,' said he, 'but you know what Singleton and his crowd are. They don't like unofficial investigators in their department. And,' Miller added with a grin, 'they aren't very fond of you, and no wonder; they haven't forgotten that Hornby case. But it wouldn't help you a bit if you did look at the prints. You can take it from me that Moakey is not the man. There's no mistake this time. They have checked the fingerprints quite carefully, and you can rely on what they say. So it would be no use your examining them – unless,' he added with a shrewd look at Thorndyke, 'you've got a fingerprint registry of your own.'

As a matter of fact it was known to me that Thorndyke had a collection in a card-index file, but it was a mere appendix to the reports of cases dealt with, which had no bearing on the present case.

'I daresay you are right,' Thorndyke agreed. 'One doesn't learn much from stray fingerprints. And you've nothing more to tell us?'

'Nothing,' was the reply. 'And you, sir? I suppose you haven't struck anything that would give us a lead?'

'I have not begun to work at the case,' said Thorndyke. 'I have been waiting for your report, to see if the case was as simple as it appeared.'

'Yes,' said Miller, 'it did look simple. Seemed as if there was nothing to do but make the arrest. And now we have nothing to go on at all. Well,' here he rose and began to move towards the door, 'if we can help you in anyway I hope you will let us know; and, of course, if you can put us on to anything we shall thank you kindly.'

As our visitor's footsteps died away on the stairs, Thorndyke softly closed the door and moved to the window, where he stood meditatively regarding the retreating officer as the latter crossed to Crown Office Row.

'That was a queer interview,' said he.

'Yes,' I agreed. 'I don't see why he made the appointment. He hadn't much to tell us.'

'I am not quite sure of that,' said Thorndyke. 'I have a sort of feeling that he came here to tell us something and didn't tell it – at least he thinks he didn't.'

'It seemed to me that he told us nothing,' said I.

'It probably seemed so to him,' replied Thorndyke. 'Whereas, if I am not mistaken, he has made us a free gift of a really valuable piece of information.'

'Well, it may be so,' said I, 'but for my part, I can't see that he gave us a particle of information excepting that the case against Moakey has fallen through. Perhaps it is a technical point that is outside my range.'

'Not at all,' he replied. 'It is just a matter of observation and comparison. You were present when Miller called last time and you have been present today. You have heard all that passed and have had the privilege of observing the Superintendent's by no means unexpressive countenance. Just recall the conversation and consider it by the light of all the known circumstances and see if it does not yield a very interesting suggestion.'

I recalled without difficulty the brief conversation and reflected on it in connection with the Superintendent's rather aggressively nonchalant air. But from that reflection nothing emerged but wonder at my colleague's amazing power of rapid inference. Finally I resolved to write down the conversation and think it over at my leisure.

'I take it,' said I, 'that you don't believe Miller is in such a fog as he professes to be?'

'On the contrary,' Thorndyke replied, 'I think that he is not only in a fog but hard aground. The fact that he meant to conceal and in effect disclosed (as I believe) is a leading fact. But I don't think he realises whither it leads. And, of course, it may not be a fact, after all. I may have drawn an erroneous inference. Obviously, the first thing to do is to test my hypothesis rigorously. In twenty-four hours I shall know whether it is true or false, since the means of verification are quite simple.'

'I am glad of that,' I said sourly, 'for the fog in which you assume that Miller is enveloped is clear daylight compared to that which surrounds me.'

'I think you will find that the fog will clear up under the influence of a little reflection,' said Thorndyke. 'But we are forgetting Miss Blake. You see the bearing of Miller's tidings on her position. Moakey is out of the case. The fingerprints are unknown, and therefore practically valueless. The police evidently have no clue at all. Miss Blake represents the only danger that threatens these men, and we may be pretty sure that they know it. If she could be eliminated their position would be absolutely secure. And, remember, these are desperate men to whom a human life is of no account when set against their own safety. It is an unseemly hour at which to call on a lady, but I think she ought to be warned without delay.'

'I entirely agree with you,' said I. 'We can't stand on ceremony; and after all, it is barely eight o'clock. A taxi will take us there in quarter of an hour.'

'Then let us start at once,' said he, stepping into the lobby for his hat and stick. Leaving a slip of paper on the table for Polton's information, we set forth together and walked rapidly up Inner Temple Lane to the gate. As we emerged, a taxi-cab drew up to deposit a passenger and we hurried forward to secure the reversion when the present tenant should give up possession. A few moments later we had taken our seats and were bowling up Chancery Lane to the soft hum of the taxi's engine.

Chapter Ten

A Timely Warning

As the cab rolled swiftly through the quietening streets I turned over once more the two statements that had been made by Superintendent Miller and compared them. Together they had yielded to the amazingly quick intelligence of my friend Thorndyke something that the speaker had not intended to convey. What was the something? The first statement had set forth that the fingerprints were those of Joseph Hedges – or Moakey, as his associates had nicknamed him; the second had set forth that the fingerprints were not his but those of some person who had yet to be identified. The two statements contradicted one another, of course, but the first was admittedly based upon a mistake. What was the fact that emerged from the contradiction?

I revolved the question again and again without seeing any glimmer of light. And then, suddenly, the simple explanation burst upon me. Of course! The prints were those of fingers smeared with Japanese wax. But Japanese wax is used for making furniture polish. There was the solution of this profound mystery. They were Mrs Benham's fingerprints – or perhaps those of the murdered man – made in the process of applying furniture polish to the cabinet. This, the only clue, evaporated into a myth and left Miss Blake's identification the only link with the vanished murderer.

'I think I have found the solution to the fingerprint problem, Thorndyke,' said I.

'Ah,' said he, 'I thought you would if you reflected on it. What is it?'

'They are Mrs Benham's fingerprints, or else Drayton's. They were made in the course of polishing the furniture.'

'An excellent suggestion, Anstey,' he replied, 'which doesn't seem to have occurred to the police. I suspected it as soon as I saw the waxy material of the fingerprints. It doesn't happen to be the correct explanation, I am glad to say, for it would be a singularly unilluminating one. I took the fingerprints both of Mrs Benham and the deceased this morning before the inquest, but I didn't think it necessary to mention the matter to the police. It is quite clear to me that they are not laying their cards on the table. In point of fact, they have only one card, and my impression is that they are mistaking the back of that for the face. But here we are at our destination.'

We sprang out of the cab, and having dismissed it, gave a pull at the studio bell. The wicket was opened by Miss Blake herself, and I hastened to make the necessary apologies.

'I have come back again, you see, Miss Blake, and with reinforcements. It is an unholy time for making a call, but we have come on a matter of business. Dr Thorndyke thought it advisable that you should be told something and given certain advice without delay.'

'Well,' she said graciously, 'you are both very welcome, business or no business. Won't you come in?'

'Is Percy in the studio?'

'Yes. He has finished his home lessons and is doing a little building before going to bed.'

'Then we had better say what we have to say here, or perhaps in the passage.' We stepped through the wicket and closed it, and as we stood in the dark entry, Miss Blake remarked: 'This is very secret and portentous. You are filling me with curiosity.'

'Then we will proceed to satisfy it. To begin with, do you remember a woman who jostled us rather rudely at the door when we were going in to the inquest?'

'Yes, I remember the incident, but I didn't notice the woman particularly, except that she gave me a rather impertinent stare and that she was a horrid-looking woman.'

'Well, she either lives about here or she followed us deliberately from Hampstead. She must have come on the same car as we did; for when I turned into Jacob Street I saw her prowling up the opposite side of the road, and when she came opposite this house, she crossed and looked at the number on the door and the name on your plate.'

'That was very inquisitive of her,' said Miss Blake. 'But does it matter?'

'It may be of no significance at all,' said Thorndyke. 'But under the special circumstances it would be unwise to ignore the warning that it may convey.'

'What are the special circumstances?' she asked.

'They are these,' he replied. 'You heard Inspector Badger say in his evidence this morning that the police have a very promising clue? Well, that clue has broken off short. I believe the police have now no clue at all, and the murderers pretty certainly know it. But you stated publicly that you are confident that you could identify the man whom you saw. That statement is certain to be known, or to become known, to these men; and they will consequently know that you are a serious menace to their safety, and the only one; that your ability to recognise one of them is the only circumstance that stands between them and absolute, perfect security. But for this one fact they could walk abroad, safe from any possible recognition. They could stand outside Scotland Yard and snap their fingers at the police. Now, I don't want to be an alarmist. But it is necessary to recognise a danger and take the necessary means to guard against it. You see what I mean?'

'I think so. You mean that if I were out of the way these men would be safe from any possibility of discovery, and that it is consequently to their interest to put me out of the way.'

'Yes, stated bluntly, that is the position. And you know what the characters of these men are.'

'They are certainly not persons who would stick at trifles. Yes, I must admit that your view of the position seems a reasonable one, though I hope things are not as bad as you fear. But what precautions could I take?'

'I suggest that, for the present, you don't go out after dark – at any rate, not alone; that you avoid going about alone as far as is possible, that you especially shun all unfrequented places where you might be suddenly attacked, and that, on all occasions, you bear this danger in mind in considering any unusual circumstances.'

'All this sounds rather alarming,' she said uneasily.

'It is alarming,' Thorndyke agreed, 'and I am extremely sorry to have to impress it on you. But I would further impress on you that you have friends – two of them are now present – who are deeply concerned as to your safety and who would consider it a privilege to be called upon at any time for help or advice. I am always at your service, and I am sure Mr Anstey is too, as well as Sir Lawrence Drayton.'

'Then,' said Miss Blake, 'the compensations are greater than the evil for which they compensate. I welcome the danger if it brings me such kind friends. And now you really must come in for a little while, or Percy will accuse me of gossiping with "followers" at the gate.'

She led the way down the paved passage and I steered Thorndyke with an expert hand past the scattered monoliths and the unfinished tombstone until we reached the door, where Miss Blake stopped to hold aside the curtain. As we entered Percy looked up from his work and then, in his quaint, self-possessed way came forward to welcome us.

'How do you like my tower now it's finished, Mr Anstey?' he asked, regarding his work complacently, with his head on one side.

We stood by him looking at the building – a model of a church tower some three feet in height – and I observed with a sort of proprietary pride that Thorndyke was deeply impressed.

'This is really a remarkable piece of work,' said he. 'Where do you get your bricks?'

'I make them of clay,' replied Percy, 'and let them dry hard. I make one as a model and make a plaster mould of it. Then all the rest are just squeezes from the mould. So I can get any shaped bricks that I like, and as many of them as I want. It's much cheaper than buying them, and besides, the bought bricks are no use for serious work.'

'No,' Thorndyke agreed, 'you couldn't build a tower like that with ready-made bricks, at least with none that I have ever seen. Are you going to be an architect?'

'Yes,' the boy replied gravely, 'if we can afford it. If not I shall be a mason. Mr Wingrave – out in the yard, you know – lets me do a bit of stone-cutting sometimes. I shouldn't mind being a mason, but I should like to work on buildings, not on tombstones. I love buildings.'

Thorndyke looked at the boy with keen and sympathetic interest. 'It is a good thing,' said he, 'to know what you want and to have a definite bent and purpose in life. I should think you ought to be a happy man and a useful one if you keep up your enthusiasm. Don't you think so, Miss Blake?'

'I do indeed,' she replied. 'Percy has a real passion for buildings and he knows quite a lot about them. His copy of Parker is nearly worn out. And I don't see why he shouldn't be an architect and make his hobby his living.'

As she was speaking, I looked at her and noticed that she was wearing the locket suspended from a bead necklace.

'I see you have taken your new acquisition into wear,' I remarked.

'Yes,' she replied. 'I have just hooked it to this necklace, but I must get some more secure attachment. Have you seen this locket, Dr Thorndyke?'

'No,' he answered, and as she unhooked it and gave it to him to inspect, he continued: 'This is what poor Mr Drayton used to call his "little Sphinx," isn't it?'

'Yes, because it seemed always to be propounding riddles. But the riddles are inside.'

'One of them is outside,' said Thorndyke, 'though it is not a very difficult one. I mean the peculiar construction and workmanship.'

'What is there unusual about that?' she asked eagerly.

'Well,' he replied, 'it is not ordinary jeweller's construction. The normal way to make a locket is to build it up of sheet metal. The sides would be made first by bending a stout strip into a hoop of the proper shape – nearly square, in this case – and joining the ends with solder. Then the back and front would be soldered on to the hoop and the latter cut through vertically with a fine saw, dividing the locket into two exactly similar halves. Then the hinge and the suspension ring would be soldered on, and the flange fastened in with solder. But in this case the method has been quite different. Each half of the locket was a single casting, which included half a hinge and one suspension ring. Probably both halves were cast from a single half-model and the superfluous part of the hinge filed off. Then each half was worked on the stake and pitch-block to harden the metal and the final finishing and fitting done with the file and stone. The engraving must have been done after everything but the hinge was finished.'

'It must have been very awkward to engrave that small writing inside, with the edges projecting,' said Miss Blake.

Thorndyke opened the locket, and taking his Coddington lens from his pocket, examined the writing closely. 'If you look at it through the lens,' said he, 'you will see that it is not engraved. It is etched, which would have disposed of the difficulty to a great extent.'

Miss Blake and I examined the minute writing, and through the lens it was easy to see that the delicate lines were bitten, not engraved.

'You were saying,' said Miss Blake, as the locket and lens were passed to Percy (who, having examined the inscription, extended his investigations to his fingertips and various other objects before reluctantly surrendering the lens) 'that the riddle of the construction is not a difficult one. What is the answer to it?'

'I think,' he replied, 'the inscription inside supplies the answer. That inscription was clearly put there for some purpose to which the original owner attached some importance. It apparently conveyed some kind of admonition or instruction which was hardly likely to be addressed to himself. But if the message was of importance it was worth while to take measures to ensure its permanence. And that is what has been done. There are no loose or separable parts, no soldered joints to break away. Each half of the locket is a single piece of solid metal, including the hinge and suspension ring. And you notice that the hinge is unusually massive, and that each half of the locket has its own suspension ring, so that if the hinge should break, both halves would still be securely suspended. And there was no loose ring to chafe through and break.'

'Don't you think,' she asked, 'that there was originally a loose ring passing through both of the eyes?'

'No,' he answered. 'If you look carefully at the two eyes you will see that the holes through them have been most carefully smoothed and rounded. Evidently the locket was meant to be suspended by a cord or thong, and the position of the eyes with a hole through from back to front shows that the cord was intended to be tied in a single knot where it passed through – a much more secure arrangement than a chain, any one link of which may, unnoticed, wear thin and break at any unusual strain.'

'And you think that the message or whatever it was that the inscription conveyed was really something of importance?' As she asked the question, Miss Blake looked at Thorndyke with a suppressed eagerness at which I inwardly smiled. The Lady of Shalott evidently had hopes of Merlin.

'That is what the precautions suggest,' was his reply. 'It appeared important to the person who took the precautions.'

'And do you suppose that it would be possible to guess what the nature of the message was?'

'One could judge better,' he replied, 'if one knew what passages the reader is referred to.'

'I can show you the passages,' she said. 'I have looked them up, and Mr Anstey and I went over them together and could make nothing of them.'

'That doesn't sound very encouraging,' said Thorndyke as she ran to the cabinet and brought out her book of notes. 'However, we shall see if a further opinion is of any help.' He took the note-book from her and read through the entries slowly and with close attention. Then he handed the book back to her.

'One thing is fairly evident,' said he. 'The purpose of the writer was not pious instruction. Whatever was intended to be conveyed did not lie on the surface, for the individual passages are singularly barren of

121

meaning, while the collection as a whole is a mere jumble of quotations without any apparent sequence or connection. The passages must have had some meaning previously agreed on, or, more probably, they formed the key of a code or cipher used for secret correspondence.'

'If they form the key of a cipher,' said Miss Blake, 'do you think it would be possible to work out the cipher by studying them?'

'I suppose it would be possible,' he replied, 'since a cipher must work by some sort of rule. But people who make ciphers do not take great pains to make them easily decipherable to the uninitiated. And then we are only guessing that they are the key to a cipher. They may be something quite different; some form of cryptogram that would be utterly unintelligible without some key or counterpart that we haven't got. Do you think of trying to decipher them or extract the hidden meaning?'

'I am rather curious about them,' she admitted, 'and rather interested in ciphers and cryptograms.'

'Well,' said Thorndyke, 'you may succeed. More probably you will draw a blank – but in any case I think you will get a run for your money.'

Once more with his lens he examined the locket inside and out, not omitting the hallmark on the back, on which he dwelt for some time. Then, still holding the locket in his hand, he said: 'You ought to have this cover-glass replaced. The hair is part of the relic and ought not to be exposed to loss or injury.'

'Yes,' said she, 'I ought to get it done, but I don't much like trusting it to an unknown jeweller.'

'Would you like Polton to do it for you?' Thorndyke asked. 'He is not a stranger, and you know he is a first-class workman.'

'Oh, if Mr Polton would do it I should be delighted and most grateful. Do you think he would?'

'I think he would be highly flattered at being asked,' said Thorndyke. 'I will take it back with me if you like, and get him to put in the fresh glass at once.'

Miss Blake accepted this offer joyfully, and taking the locket from Thorndyke, she proceeded, with great care and a quantity of tissue paper, to make it into a little packet. While she was thus engaged, the bell in the yard rang loudly and Percy ran out to open the gate. In less than a minute he re-entered the studio carrying a brown-paper parcel.

'Miss Winifred Blake,' he announced. 'Shall I see what's in it, Winnie?'

'I suppose you won't be happy till you do,' she replied, whereupon he gleefully cut the string and removed the paper, exposing a cardboard box, of which he lifted the lid.

'My eye, Winnie!' he exclaimed. 'It's tuck. I wonder who it's from. And it's for us both. "To Winifred and Percival Blake, with love." Whose love, I wonder. Can you spot the handwriting?' He passed a slip of paper to his sister and exhibited a shallow box filled with large chocolate sweets on which he gazed gloatingly.

Thorndyke, who had just received the little packet from Miss Blake and was putting it into his pocket, watched the boy attentively, interested, as I supposed, by the sudden descent from the heights of architectural design to frank, boyish gluttony.

'I don't recognise the writing at all,' said Miss Blake, 'and I can't imagine who can have sent this.'

'Well, it doesn't matter,' said Percy. 'Let's sample them.' He passed the box to his sister – still closely watched by Thorndyke, I noticed – and as she put out her hand to pick up one of the sweets, my colleague asked in a significant tone: 'Are you sure that you don't know the handwriting?'

The tone in which the question was asked was so emphatic that she looked at him in surprise. 'No,' she answered, 'the writing is quite strange to me.'

'Then,' said he, 'the writer is possibly a stranger.'

She looked at him with a puzzled expression, and I noticed that he was gazing at her with a strange fixity. After a pause he continued: 'We were speaking just now of unusual circumstances. Would not a gift of food from a stranger be an unusual circumstance?'

In an instant his meaning flashed upon me, and upon her too, for she took the box quickly from her brother and her face became deathly pale.

'I think, Percy dear,' she said, 'if you don't mind very much, we won't touch these tonight. Do you mind?'

'Of course I don't,' he replied, 'if you would rather keep 'em till tomorrow.'

Nevertheless the boy looked curiously at his sister, and it was clear to me that he saw that there was 'something in the wind.' But he asked no questions and made no comment, sauntering back to his tower and looking it over critically.

'It's really time you went to bed, Percy,' Miss Blake said after a pause.

'Is it?' he asked. 'What's the time?'

'It is getting on for ten, and you have to be up at half-past six.'

'It's always "getting on" for ten, you know,' said he. 'The question is, how far has it got? But there! It's no good arguing. I suppose I shall get chucked out if I don't go peaceably.' He offered a friendly hand to me and Thorndyke in succession, and having given his sister a hug and a kiss, took his departure. And again I thought I detected in his manner a perception of something below the surface that accounted for his sudden dismissal.

'I suspect Master Percy smells a fox,' said I, 'but is too polite to mention it.'

'It is very likely,' said Miss Blake. 'He is wonderfully quick and observant, and he is extraordinarily discreet. In most respects he is quite a normal boy, but in others he is more like a man.'

'And a very well-bred man, too,' said I.

'Yes, he is nice boy and the best of brothers. But now, Dr Thorndyke, about these sweets. Do you really think there is anything wrong with them?'

'I don't say that,' replied Thorndyke, 'but, of course, when you have swallowed one, it is too late to inquire. May I look at that paper?'

Miss Blake took the slip of paper from the box and handed it to him, and once more the lens came into requisition.

'Yes,' he said, after somewhat prolonged examination of the writing, 'this is not reassuring. It is quite clear that this writing was traced over a previous writing in lead pencil. A hard rubber has been used to take out the pencil marks, but the ink has fixed them in several places. If you look at the writing carefully through the lens you can see the fine, dark pencil line forming a sort of core to the broader ink line. And you can also distinguish several minute crumbs of blackened rubber – little black rolls with pointed ends.'

'But why should it have been written first in pencil?' Miss Blake asked.

'For the purpose of disguising the handwriting,' replied Thorndyke. 'It is a common practice. Of course, in the case of a forger copying a signature, its purpose is obvious. He takes a pencil tracing of the original signature, goes over it in ink and rubs out the pencil – if he can. But it is used in producing feigned handwriting as well. It is difficult to write direct with a pen in a hand which is quite different from one's own. But if a preliminary trial sketch is done in pencil, and touched up if necessary, and then traced over deliberately with the pen, the result may be quite unlike one's own handwriting. But, in any case, this underlying pencil writing is manifestly abnormal and therefore suspicious. Shall we see if there is anything unusual in the appearance of the sweets?'

She passed him the box, which he placed on the table under the gaslight and looked over systematically. Then he turned the sweets, one after the other, on their sides, and when they were all in this position, he again looked them over.

'It seems hardly possible,' said I, 'that the woman – if it is she whom you suspect – could have prepared a set of poisoned sweets in such a short time. It was past four o'clock when she came and looked at the plate, and it is not ten yet. There doesn't seem to have been time.'

'There has been about five hours,' said Thorndyke, 'and I see by the postmark on the wrapper that the parcel was posted in this neighbourhood barely two hours ago. That leaves three hours, which would have been sufficient. But she might have had the things prepared in advance, and merely waited for the inquest to get the name and particulars. And the sender may not be this woman at all. And again, there may be no poison in the sweets. We are only taking precautions against a possibility. But looking at these things all together, there seems to me to be a suggestion of their having been patched with liquid chocolate round the sides. If that is so, they will have been cut open horizontally and the halves fitted together again, and the purpose of the patching will have been to hide the join. Here is a very well-marked specimen. I think we will take it as a test case.'

He picked out the sweet, and with his pocket-knife, began very delicately to scrape away the outer coat of chocolate all round the sides, while we drew up our chairs and watched him anxiously. Presently he paused and silently held the sweet towards us, indicating a spot with the point of his knife; and looking at that spot where the outer coating had been scraped away, I could clearly make out an indented line. He then resumed his scraping, following the line, until he had worked round the whole circumference. And now it was quite obvious that the sweet had been divided into an upper and a lower half and the two parts rejoined.

'I am afraid it is a true bill, Thorndyke,' said I.

'I think so,' he agreed, 'but we shall soon see.' He inserted his knife into the encircling crevice, and giving it a gentle turn, raised the top half, which he then lifted off. At once I could see that the exposed surfaces of the white interior of the sweet were coated with a glistening white powder, worked into the soft material of the filling. Thorndyke produced his lens, and through it examined the cut surface for a few moments. Then he passed the half sweet and the lens to me.

'What do you suppose this stuff is, Thorndyke?' I asked, when I had inspected the sweet, and then passed it and the lens to Miss Blake. 'It looks like finely powdered china or white enamel.'

'It looks like – and I have no doubt is – arsenious acid, or white arsenic, as it is commonly called; and I should say there is rather more than two grains in this sweet. It is a heavy substance.'

'Is that a fatal dose?' I asked.

'Yes. And it is extremely unlikely that only one sweet would have been eaten. Two or three would contain a does that would produce death very rapidly.'

We were silent for a few moments. Suddenly Miss Blake burst into tears and buried her face in her hands, sobbing almost hysterically. Thorndyke looked at her with a curious expression, stern and even wrathful, and yet with a certain softness of compassion, but he said nothing. As to me, I was filled with fury against the wretch who had done this unspeakable thing, but, like Thorndyke, I could find no words that were adequate.

Presently Miss Blake recovered her self-possession somewhat, and as she wiped her eyes, she apologised for her outburst.

'Pray forgive me!' she exclaimed. 'But it is horrible – horrible! Just think! But for the infinitely unlikely chance of your coming in tonight Percy would have eaten at least two or three of those sweets. By now he would have been dead, or dying in agony, and I unable to help him! It is a frightful thought. Nobody would have known anything until Mrs Wingrave came in the morning and found our bodies! And the wretch may try again.'

'That won't matter much,' said Thorndyke. 'You are now on your guard. It will be best to think as little of this episode as you can. It has been a narrow escape, but it is past. You must fix your attention on the future.'

'But what can we do?' she asked despairingly.

'You must walk warily and never for one moment forget this implacable, ruthless enemy. No opportunity must be given. Do not go out after dark without efficient protection, and avoid going abroad alone at any time. You had better not to go to the gate after nightfall, neither you nor Percy. Can you not arrange for some one to answer the bell for you?'

'I could ask Mrs Wingrave, the sculptor's wife. Their rooms open on the yard. But what could I tell her?'

'You will have to tell her as much as is necessary. And, of course, Percy must be told. It is very unfortunate, but we can take no risks. You must impress upon him that under no circumstances whatever must he eat or drink anything that is given or sent to him by strangers or of which he does not know the antecedents. Does he go to school?'

'Yes. He goes to the Elizabeth Woodville Grammar School, near Regent's Park. He usually gets home about five o'clock. Sometimes I go and meet him, but he has some school-fellows who live near here and who generally walk home with him.'

'Then let him come home with them. There is no reason to suppose that he is in any danger apart from you. And let me impress upon you again that Mr Anstey and I are always at your service. While this danger lasts – I hope it will soon pass – don't scruple to make any use of us that circumstances may require. If you have to go anywhere at night, we can always arrange for you to have an escort. At a pinch, we could secure the help of the police, but we don't want to do that unless we are compelled. And – it seems contradictory advice to give you – but having taken all precautions, try not to think about this incident of tonight, or to dwell on the danger more than is necessary to keep your attention on the alert. And now we must wish you good night, Miss Blake. I will take these sweets with me for more complete examination.'

'I can never thank you enough for all your kindness,' she said, as he wrapped the box in its original paper, 'and I shall have no hesitation in treating you as the good and generous friends that you have proved tonight. I feel that Percy and I are in your hands, and we shouldn't wish to be in better.' She walked out with us to the gate, and at the wicket shook our hands warmly, and indeed with no little emotion. And when we had seen the wicket safely closed on her, and taken a look up and down the street, we turned westward and started on our way home.

CHAPTER ELEVEN

The Blue Hair

'What are you going to do, Anstey?' Thorndyke asked as we reached the corner of Jacob Street. 'Are you going to Hampstead or are you coming home with me?'

'What are you going to do tonight?' I asked in return.

'I shall make a rough qualitative test of the substance in that sweet,' he replied, 'just to settle definitely whether it is or is not arsenic.'

'Have you any doubt on the subject?' I asked.

'No,' he answered. 'But still it is not a matter of fact until it has been verified by analysis. My own conviction on the subject is only a state of mind which is not transferable as evidence. A chemical demonstration is a fact which can be deposed to in sworn testimony.'

'Then,' said I, 'I shall come home with you and hear the result of your analysis, although your certainty would be good enough for me.'

We walked down to the bottom of Hampstead Road where we boarded an omnibus bound for Charing Cross. For some time nothing more was said, each of us being immersed in reflection on the events of the evening.

'It is a horrible affair,' I said at length, assuming that we were still thinking on the same subject, 'and a terrible thing to reflect that the world we live in should contain such wretches.'

'It is,' he agreed. 'But the mitigating circumstance is that these wretches are nearly always fools. That is the reassuring element in the present case.'

'In what way reassuring?' I asked.

'I mean,' said he, 'the palpable folly of the whole proceeding. We have here no subtle, wary criminal who works with considered strategy under secure cover, but just the common arsenic fool who delivers himself into your hands by his own stupidity.'

'But what is the evidence of the stupidity?'

'My dear Anstey!' he exclaimed. 'Look at the crudity of method; the discharge, broadcast, of a boxful of poisoned food under manifestly suspicious circumstances, with the poison barely concealed; the faked writing, which a common policeman would have detected, the absence of any plausible origin of the gift, and the nature of the poison itself. That, alone, is diagnostic. Arsenic is typically a fool's poison. No competent poisoner would dream of using such a material.'

'Why not?' I asked.

'Because its properties are exactly the reverse of those which would make a poison safe to use. The fatal dose is relatively large – not less than two grains and for security, considerably more. The effects are extremely variable and uncertain, making necessary the use of really large doses. The material is rather conspicuous, it is only slightly soluble in water and still less so in tea or coffee; it is easily recognised by simple chemical tests, even in the minutest quantities. It is practically indestructible, and its strong preservative effects on the dead body make it easy to demonstrate its presence years after death. A man who poisons a person with arsenic creates a record of the fact which will last, at least, for the term of his own lifetime.'

'That isn't much benefit to the person who has been poisoned,' I remarked.

'No,' he admitted. 'But we are considering the poisoner's point of view. It is not enough for him to succeed in killing his victim. He has to avoid killing himself at the same time. A poisoner sets out to commit a secret murder, and the secrecy is the test of his efficiency. If his methods are easily detectable, and if he leaves a record which stands against him in perpetuity, he is an inefficient poisoner. And that is the case of the arsenic practitioner. He runs a great present risk, since the symptoms of arsenic poisoning are conspicuous and fairly characteristic; and he leaves traces of his crime which nothing but cremation will destroy.'

Our discussion had brought us to our chambers, where Thorndyke proceeded straight up to the laboratory, breaking in upon Polton, who was seated at his bench, putting the finishing touches to the large and elaborate pedometer.

'We need not disturb you, Polton,' said Thorndyke. 'I am just going to make a rough qualitative test for arsenic.'

Polton instantly laid down his watchmaker's glass and unlocked a cupboard on the chemical side of the laboratory. 'You will want a Marsh's apparatus and the materials for Reinsch's test, I suppose, sir?' said he.

'Yes. But we will begin with the liquid tests. I shall want a glass mortar and some hydrochloric acid.'

Polton put the necessary appliances on the bench and added a large bottle labelled 'Distilled Water,' while I seated myself on a stool and watched the analysis with a slightly vague though highly interested recognition of the processes that I had so often expounded to juries. I saw Thorndyke open the box, take from it the two halves of the divided sweet, and drop them into the little glass mortar, and having poured on them some distilled water and a little acid, rub them with the glass pestle until they were reduced to a muddy-looking liquid. This liquid he carefully filtered into a beaker, when it became clear and practically colourless, like water, and this watery-looking fluid formed the material for the succeeding tests.

Of these the first three were performed in test-tubes into each of which a small quantity of the clear solution was poured, and then to each was added a few drops of certain other clear liquids. The result was very striking. In two of the tubes the clear liquid instantly turned to a dense, opaque yellow, somewhat like yolk of egg, while in the third it changed to a bright, opaque emerald green.

'What are those precipitates?' I asked.

'The two yellow ones,' he replied, 'are arsenite of silver and arsenic sulphide. The green one is arsenite of copper. As there is sugar and some other organic matter in this solution, I shall not carry these tests any farther, but they are pretty conclusive. How are you getting on, Polton?'

'I think we are ready, sir,' was the reply; on which I crossed to the bench on which he had been at work. Here on a tripod over a Bunsen gas-burner, was a beaker containing a number of little pieces of copper foil and a clear, watery liquid which was boiling briskly.

'This is Reinsch's test,' Thorndyke explained. 'You see that this copper-foil remains bright in the dilute acid, showing that both the metal and the acid are free from arsenic. I shall now introduce a few drops of the suspected liquid, and if it contains arsenic the copper-foil will become grey or black according to the amount of arsenic present.' As he spoke, he took the beaker containing the filtered liquid from the mortar and poured about a tablespoonful into that containing the copper-foil. I watched eagerly for the result, and very soon a change began to appear. The ruddy lustre of the copper gradually turned to a steely grey and from that to a glistening black.

'You see,' said Thorndyke, 'that the reaction is very distinct. The quantity of arsenic present is, in an analytical sense, quite large. And now we will try the most definite and conclusive test of all – Marsh's.' He turned to the other apparatus which Polton had made ready, which consisted of a squat bottle with two short necks, through one of which passed a tall glass funnel, and through the other a glass tube fitted with a tap and terminating in a fine jet. The contents of the bottle – lumps of zinc immersed in sulphuric acid – were effervescing briskly, and the tap was turned on to allow the gas to escape through the jet. To the latter Polton now applied a lighted match, and immediately there appeared a little pale violet flame. Picking up a white tile which had been placed in readiness, Thorndyke held it for a moment in the flame and then looked at it.

'You see,' said he, 'that the tile is quite unsoiled. If there had been the smallest trace of arsenic in the bottle, a dark spot would have appeared on the tile. So we may take it that our chemicals are free from arsenic. Now let us try the solution of the sweet.'

He took up the beaker containing the solution of the disintegrated chocolate, and poured very slowly, drop by drop, about a teaspoonful into the funnel of the bottle. Then, after having given it time to mix thoroughly with the other contents, he once more picked up the tile and held it for an instant in the flame. The result was, to me, most striking. In the very moment when the tile touched the flame, there appeared on the white surface a circular spot, black, lustrous, and metallic.

'That,' said Thorndyke, 'might be either antimony or arsenic. By its appearance it is obviously metallic arsenic, but still we will make the differential test. If it is arsenic it will dissolve in a solution of chlorinated lime; if it is antimony it will not.' He removed the stopper from a bottle labelled 'Chlorinated Lime,' and poured a little pool of the solution on the tile. Almost immediately the black spot began to fade at the edges, and to grow smaller and fainter until at length it disappeared altogether.

'That completes our inquiry,' said Thorndyke as he laid down the tile. 'For the purposes of evidence in a court of law, a more searching and detailed analysis would be necessary. To produce conviction in the minds of a jury we should have to be able to say exactly how much arsenic was in each of the sweets. That, however, is no concern of ours. The criminal intention is all that matters to us. And now, Anstey, I must leave you for a while to entertain yourself with a book. I have to do some work in the office on another case. But we will take this ill-omened box down and put it in a safe place.'

He took the box of sweets, with its original wrapper, and when we descended to the sitting-room, he closed it up, sealed it, and signed and dated it; and having made a note of the particulars of the postmark, deposited it in the safe. Then he retired to the office, where I assumed that he had in hand some work of compilation or reference, for the 'office' was in fact rather a miniature law library, in which was stored a singularly complete collection of works bearing upon our special branch of legal practice.

When he had gone, I ran my eye vaguely along the book-shelves in search of a likely volume with which to pass the time. But the box of poisoned sweets haunted me and refused to be ejected from my thoughts. Eventually I brought out Miss Blake's manuscript from the drawer in which I had put it when Miller had arrived, and drawing an easy-chair up to the fire, sat listlessly glancing over the well-remembered pages, but actually thinking of the writer; of the brave, sweet-faced girl and the fine, manly boy to whom she was at once sister and mother. What, I wondered uncomfortably, was to be the end of this? Only by the merest hairbreadth had she and the boy, this very night, escaped a dreadful death. Soon the wretches who had contrived this diabolical crime would discover that their plot had miscarried in some way. What would they do next? It was hardly likely that they would try poison again, but there are plenty of other ways of committing murder. It was all very well to say that they were fools. So they might be. But they were unknown fools. That was the trouble. They could make their preparations unwatched, and approach unsuspected within striking distance. If your enemy is unknown it is almost impossible to be on your guard against him. In one direction only safety lay – in detection. In the moment when the identity of the criminals should become known, the danger would be at an end.

But when would that moment arrive? So far as the position was known to me, it was not even in sight. The police admitted that their clue had broken off short and apparently they had no other; at least that was Thorndyke's opinion. But what of Thorndyke himself? Had he any clue? My feeling was that he had not. It seemed impossible that he could have, for these two men had, as it were, dropped down out of the sky and then vanished into space. No one knew who they were, whence they had come, or whither they had gone. And they seemed to have left not a trace for the imagination to work on.

On the other hand, Thorndyke was – Thorndyke; an inscrutable man; silent, self-contained, and even secretive, in spite of his genial exterior. I thought of him, at this very moment, sitting calmly in the office with all his faculties quietly transferred to a fresh case, unmoved by the thrilling events of the evening, though it was he who had instantly seen the danger, he who had immediately suspected the 'Greek Gift.' And as I thought of him poring over his reports, and marvelled at his detachment, I recalled the many instances of his wonderful power of inference from almost invisible data, and found myself hoping that even now, when to me all seemed dark, some glimmer of light was visible to him.

It had turned half-past eleven when I heard a light but deliberate step ascending the stair. Instantly I stole on tiptoe to the office, and had just opened the door when a tapping – apparently with the handle of a stick or umbrella – on our 'oak' announced the arrival of a visitor.

'Shall I open the door, Thorndyke?' I whispered.

'Yes,' he answered. 'It is Brodribb. I know his knock. Tell him I shall have finished in a few minutes. And you might run up and tell Polton that he is here. He will know what to do.'

I accordingly went out and threw open the 'oak,' and there, sure enough, was Mr Brodribb, looking with his fine, rich complexion, his silky white hair, and his sumptuous, old-fashioned raiment, as if he had stepped out of the frame of some Georgian portrait.

'Good evening, Anstey,' said he, 'might even say "good night." It's a devil of a time to come stirring you up, but I saw a light in your windows, and I rather particularly wanted to have a word or two with Thorndyke. Is he in?'

'Yes. He is in the office surrounded by a sort of landslide of reports – assizes, Central Criminal, and various assorted. He will have finished in a few minutes. Meanwhile I will run up and let Polton know you are here.'

At the mention of Polton's name methought his bright blue eye grew brighter, and by the way in which he murmured 'Ha!' and smiled as he subsided into an armchair, I judged that – as our American cousins would say – he 'had been there before;' and this impression was confirmed when I made my announcement in the laboratory, where I found Polton dancing his pedometer up and down and listening ecstatically to its measured tick.

'Mr Brodribb,' said he. 'Let me see, it is the sixty-three that he likes. Yes; and Lord, he does like it! It's a pleasure to see him drink it.'

'Well, Polton,' said I, 'it is an altruistic pleasure, and if it would add to your enjoyment to see me drink some, too, I am prepared to make an effort.'

'You couldn't do it as Mr Brodribb does,' said Polton, 'and you haven't got the complexion. Still – I'll bring it down in a minute or two, when I've got it filtered into the decanter.'

On this I descended and rejoined Mr Brodribb, and having offered him a cigar, which he declined – no doubt with a view to preserving his gustatory sense unimpaired – sat down and filled my pipe.

'I looked in,' said Mr Brodribb, 'on my way home to ask Thorndyke a question. I met Drayton today – only saw him for a few moments – and he said something about wanting some information respecting Arthur Blake of Beauchamp Blake. I understood him to say that the matter arose out of the inquest on his brother; can't see how the devil it could, but that is what I gathered. Now, before I tell him anything, I should like to know what's in the wind. What's he after? Do you happen to know?'

'I think I do, to some extent,' said I, and I gave him a brief account of the circumstances and a summary of Miss Blake's evidence.

'I see,' said he. 'Then this young lady will be Peter Blake's daughter. But what does Drayton want to know? And why does he want to know it? He said something about Thorndyke, too. Now, where does Thorndyke come in?'

As if in answer to the question, my colleague emerged at this moment from the office, slipping a large note-book into his pocket. As he greeted our visitor, I found myself speculating on the contents of that note-book and wondering what kind of information he had been disinterring from those piles of arid-looking reports of assizes, quarter-sessions, and the Central Criminal Court. The greetings were hardly finished when Polton entered with a tray on which were a decanter, three glasses, and a biscuit jar; and having placed a small table adjacent to Mr Brodribb's chair, deposited the tray thereon with a crinkly smile of satisfaction, and departed after an instantaneous glance of profound significance in my direction.

Thorndyke filled the three glasses, and drawing a chair nearer to the fire, sat down and began to fill his pipe; while Brodribb lifted his glass, looked at it reflectively, took an experimental sip, savoured it with grave attention, and again looked at the glass.

'A noble wine, Thorndyke,' he pronounced solemnly. 'I don't deserve this after coming and routing you out at close upon midnight. But I haven't come for mere gossip. I've just been putting my case to Anstey,' and here he repeated what he had told me of his interview with Sir Lawrence. 'Now, what I want to know,' he concluded, 'is, what is Drayton after? He seems disposed to interest himself in Peter Blake's daughter – and his son, too, I suppose.'

'Yes,' said Thorndyke, 'and for that matter, I may say that I feel a benevolent interest in the young people myself, and so, I think, does Anstey.'

'Then,' said Brodribb, 'I'm going to ask you a plain question. Is there any idea of contesting the title of the present tenant of the Blake property – Arthur Blake?'

'I should say certainly not,' replied Thorndyke. 'Drayton's object is, I think, to ascertain whether there is any prospect of circumstances becoming favourable in the future for the revival of Peter Blake's claim – or rather Percival Blake's, as it would now be. He wants to know who the present heir is, what is his relation to the present tenant, and he would like to know as much as possible about Arthur Blake himself, particularly in regard to the probability of his marrying. And, as I said, Anstey and I are not uninterested in the matter.'

'Well, if that is all,' said Brodribb, 'I can answer you without any breach of confidence to my client. As to the heir, his name is Charles Templeton, but what his relationship to Arthur Blake is, I can't say at the moment. He is a pretty distant relative, I know. With regard to Arthur Blake, I can tell you all about him, for I have made some inquiries on my own account. And I can tell you something that will interest you more than the probability of his marrying – he is trying to sell the property.'

'The deuce he is!' exclaimed Thorndyke. 'I suppose I mustn't ask why he wants to sell?'

'I don't know that there is any secret about it. His own explanation is that he doesn't care for England and would like to get back to Australia, where he has lived nearly all his life; and I daresay there is some truth in that, for he is like a fish out of water – doesn't understand the ways of an English landowner at all. But I don't think that's the whole of it. He knows about this claim of Peter Blake's, and he knows that Peter Blake's son is living; and then – you know about the title-deeds, I suppose?'

'Yes,' said Thorndyke. 'Miss Blake has told us the whole story.'

'Well, I suspect that, with this claim in the air and the mystery of the whereabouts of the title-deeds, he feels that his tenure of the property is a little insecure. So he would like to sell it and clear off with the money. And, mind you, he is not entirely wrong. Peter Blake's claim was a *bona fide* claim. It broke down from the lack of documentary evidence. But it is always possible for documents to reappear, and if these documents ever should, the position would be very different. And, to tell the honest truth, I shouldn't be particularly afflicted if they did reappear.'

'Why wouldn't you?' I asked.

'Well,' Brodribb replied, 'you know, one gets a sort of sentimental interest in a historic estate which one has known all one's life. I am Arthur Blake's solicitor, it is true. But I feel that I have responsibilities towards the whole family and the estate itself. I have much more sentiment about the old house and its lands than Blake himself has. I hate the idea of selling an old place like that, which has been in one family since the time of Henry the Eighth, as if it were a mere speculative builder's estate. Besides, it isn't playing the game. An inherited estate belongs to the family, and a man who has received it from his ancestors has no right to dispossess his posterity. I told him so, and he didn't like it a bit.'

'What sort of man is he?' I asked.

'He's a colonial, and not a good type of colonial. Gruff and short and none too well-mannered, and, of course, he doesn't know anybody in the county. And I should think he is a confirmed bachelor, for he lives – when he is at home – in the new part of the house with three servants and his man, as if he were in a bachelor flat.'

'How did you manage to dig him up?' Thorndyke asked.

'I began to make inquiries as soon as it was certain that he would be Arnold Blake's successor. That was years ago. I ascertained his whereabouts and got into touch with him pretty easily, but I really never knew much about him until a few weeks back, when I came across a man who had just retired from the Australian Police. He knew all about Blake, so I took the opportunity to get a pretty full history of him and make out a little *dossier* to keep by me. You never know when a trifle of information may come in useful.'

'No,' Thorndyke agreed as he refilled our visitor's glass. 'Knowledge is power.'

'Quite so,' said Brodribb, 'and it is well to know whom you are dealing with. But, in fact, this fellow Blake is quite an interesting character.'

'So the police seem to have thought,' I remarked.

'Oh, I don't think there was anything against Blake,' said he, 'excepting that he kept rather queer company at times. My friend first heard of him at a mining camp, where the society was not exactly select, and where he ran a saloon or liquor bar. But he gave that up and took to digging, and he seems to have had quite good luck for a time. Then his claim petered out and he moved off to a new district and started a sawmill with some of his mining pals. There, I think, some of his partners had trouble with the police – I don't know exactly what it was, but he moved off again and rambled about doing all sorts of odd jobs – boat-building, farming, working as deck hand on a coaster, carpentering – he seems to have been able to turn his hand to anything – and finally he came across his last partner, a man named Owen, a fellow of his own type, who seemed to be able to do anything but stick to one kind of job. Owen was a colonial – he was born at Hobart – and by trade he was a photo-engraver, but he had worked a small type-foundry, run a local newspaper, and done some other jobs that weren't quite so respectable. Blake ran across him at a new town in a mining district, and the circumstances were characteristic of the two men. Owen had started a pottery, but he had just met with an accident and broken his knee-cap. Thereupon Blake took him in hand and fixed his knee-cap up in splints, and as it happened to be the left knee, so that Owen would not be able to work the potter's wheel for a long time, Blake took over the job, worked the wheel, and turned out the pots and pans, while a woman who was associated with Owen – I don't know what their relations were – helped with the kiln and sold the stuff in the town.'

'Why can't you work a potter's wheel with your right foot?' I asked.

'I don't know,' replied Brodribb, 'but I understand that you can't.'

'In an ordinary "kick-wheel," ' said Thorndyke, 'the "kick-bar," or treadle, is on the left side, and has to be if the potter is right-handed, to enable him to steady himself with the right foot.'

'I see,' said I. 'And how long did the pottery last?'

'Not long,' replied Brodribb. 'When Owen got about again, as he couldn't work the wheel, it seems that he got restless and began to hanker for something fresh. Then Blake got a tip from some prospector about some traces of gold in the hills in an outlying district, so they sold the pottery and the three of them went off prospecting; and I think they were engaged in some tentative digging when Blake got my letter telling him that Arnold Blake was dead and that he had come into the property. A deuce of a time he was, too, in getting that letter, for, of course, there was no post out there and they only rode into the town at long intervals.'

'And now,' said Thorndyke, 'he wants to sell the property and get back to his cronies. I should think they would be very glad to see him.'

'I don't know that he wants to join his pals again,' said Brodribb. 'As a man of property, I should think he would keep clear of people of that sort. But in any case, he couldn't. Owen is dead. He must have died soon after Blake left; must have met with an accident when he was alone, for his body was found only a few months ago at the foot of a cliff – just a heap of more or less damaged bones that must have been lying there for several years. The skeleton was found by the merest chance by another prospector.'

'How did he know it was Owen's body?' I asked.

'Well, he knew that Owen had been there and had not been seen for a long time, and he found a signet-ring – a rough affair that Owen had made himself and engraved with a representation of a yew-tree. That was recognised as his.'

'Why a yew-tree?' I asked.

'That was his private mark, a sort of rebus or pun on his Christian name, Hugh.'

'But how was it,' Thorndyke asked, 'that the woman hadn't reported his death?'

'Oh, she had left him quite soon after Blake's departure. The police had an idea that she had gone off with Owen to the South Sea Islands on one of the schooners. At any rate, she disappeared, and they weren't sorry to see the last of her. She was a shady character – and so, apparently, was Owen, for that matter.'

'What was there against her?' I asked.

'Well, I don't know that there was anything very definite, though there may have been. But she turned up rather mysteriously at Melbourne on a Russian tramp steamer, and the police surmised that she had left her country for her country's good and her own. So they entered her name – Laura Levinsky – on their books and kept an eye on her until she went. But, God bless me, what a damned old chatterbox I am! Here am I babbling away at past midnight, and giving you a lot of gossip that is no more your business than it is mine.'

'I think,' said Thorndyke, 'we have all enjoyed the gossip, and as to its irrelevancy, who can tell? At any rate, we gather that there is no immediate prospect of Blake's marrying, which really does concern us.'

'No,' said Brodribb, 'nor of his selling the property, though he has put it into the hands of Lee and Robey, the estate agents. But he won't sell it. Of course there's no magic in title-deeds, and his title is good enough, but no one would buy an important property like that with the title-deeds missing and liable to turn up in the wrong hands. And now I must really be off. You've squeezed me dry if you were out for information, and I've squeezed you dry,' he added with a complacent glance at the decanter, 'and a devilish good bottle of port it was. You can pass on what I've told you to Drayton, and I'll see if I can let you know what relation the heir, Charles Templeton, is to Arthur Blake. So goodnight and good luck, and my best respects to your wine merchant.'

When Brodribb had gone, I stretched myself and yawned slightly.

'Well,' I said, 'I don't feel sleepy, but I think I will turn in. One must go to bed some time.'

'I don't feel sleepy either,' said Thorndyke, 'and I shall not turn in. I think I will just jot down a few notes of what Brodribb has told us and then have another look at Miss Blake's manuscript before handing it over to Drayton.'

'Old Brodribb enjoyed the wine, didn't he?' I remarked. 'And, by Jove, it did set his old chin wagging. But he didn't tell us much, after all. Excepting the proposed sale, it was just mere personal gossip.'

'Yes. But the sale question is really important. We shall have to think over that. He mustn't be allowed to sell the property.'

'Can we prevent him?' I asked.

'I think,' replied Thorndyke, 'from what Brodribb said, that a threat to apply for an injunction pending an investigation of the title would make him draw in his horns. But we shall see. Goodnight, if you are off.'

By the time I had undressed, washed, and turned into bed, I began to suspect that Thorndyke had taken the wiser course. And as I lay in the dark, at first quietly but then with increasing restlessness, the suspicion deepened. The disturbing – indeed, alarming – events of the evening came crowding back into my mind and grew, minute by minute, more vivid. The scene in the studio arose before me with fearful reality, and worse still, the horrible catastrophe, barely averted by Thorndyke's watchfulness and wonderful prevision, actually seemed to befall before my eyes. The dreadful picture that Miss Blake had drawn in a few words, painted itself in my consciousness with the most frightful realism. I saw the sculptor's wife peering into the dim and silent studio in the early morning, and heard her shriek of horror as her glance fell on the brother and sister, lying there stark and dead; and Thorndyke's analysis in the laboratory took on a new and fearful significance. At last, after tossing in bed for over an hour, I could bear it no longer, and rose to go down to the sitting-room for a book.

As I entered the room, Thorndyke looked up from the note-book in which he was writing. 'You had better have stayed up a little longer,' he remarked. 'Now you are going to read yourself to sleep, I suppose.'

'Yes, I hope so,' I replied, and turned to the book-shelves to search for a work of a calm and cheerful tendency. The *Compleat Angler* appearing to fulfil these requirements most perfectly, I picked it out and was just about to move away when my glance lighted on the rather curious collection of objects on the table. They had made their appearance since I retired, and were presumably connected with some kind of investigation which my colleague had been pursuing while I was wooing Hypnos in vain. I looked at them curiously, and speculated on the nature of the inquiry. There was a microscope, and beside it lay the locket, opened and showing the broken glass, and a little, fat, greasy volume which examination showed to be a Latin Vulgate Bible.

I laid down the volume and glanced at Thorndyke, whom I found watching me with a faint smile. Then I peered through the microscope and perceived what looked like a thread of blue glass.

'Is this a thread of silk, Thorndyke?' I asked.

'No,' he replied, 'it is a hair. Apparently a woman's hair.'

'But,' I expostulated, 'it is blue – bright blue! Where on earth did you get it?'

'Out of the locket,' he replied.

I stared at him in amazement. 'What an extraordinary thing!' I exclaimed. 'A blue hair! I never heard of blue hair before.'

'Then,' said Thorndyke, 'my learned friend has made an addition to his already vast store of knowledge.'

'I suppose it was dyed?' said I.

'I think,' he replied, 'we may assume that the blue colour is adventitious.'

'But why, in the name of Fortune, should a woman dye her hair blue?' I demanded.

He shook his head. 'A curious question that, Anstey, a very curious question. I suggest that when my learned friend has satisfied himself as to the correct method of "daping or doping with a grasshopper for the chavender or chub," he might with advantage bring his colossal intellect to bear on it.'

'You are an aggravating old devil, Thorndyke,' I said with conviction. 'You know perfectly well what this thing means, and yet, when you are asked a civil question, you sit there wagging your exasperating old head like some confounded secretive effigy. I'd like to paint your cranium with Stephen's blue-black ink and then put it under the microscope.'

He shook the threatened head conclusively. 'It would be futile, Anstey,' he replied. 'As a method of producing blue hair it would be a complete failure. The effect of the tannate of iron − on exposure to oxygen − would entirely mask that of the indigo-carmine. No, my friend. Physical experiment is outside the range of a King's Counsel. Reflection is your proper province. And now take your book and go to bed. Consider the chavender or chub and also the possible connection between a blue hair and a gold locket; shun needless and inky strenuosities, and "be quiet and go a-angling." '

With this he returned to his note-book; and there being evidently nothing more to be got out of him, I picked up my book, and having shaken my fist at the impassive figure by the table, once more betook myself to bed, there to meditate fruitlessly upon this new and curious problem.

CHAPTER TWELVE

From the Jaws of Death

On the following morning it seemed natural that my steps should stray in the direction of Jacob Street, not only that I might relieve my anxiety as to my friend whom I had left overnight in so distressed a state, but also to ascertain whether any services that I could render were at the moment in request. As to the former, my mind was completely set at rest as soon as I entered the studio (to which I was conducted by Mrs Wingrave, who opened the wicket), for I found Miss Blake hard at work and looking as cheerful and interested as if poisoned sweets and brazen-haired Jezebels were things unheard of.

I explained, half-apologetically, the purpose of my visit, and was preparing a strategic retreat when she interrupted me.

'Now, Mr Anstey, I will not have these formalities. We aren't strangers. You have been, and are, the best and kindest of friends to me and Percy, and we are not only grateful but we value your friendship very much indeed. As to Percy, he loves you.'

'Does he?' said I, with an inward glow of satisfaction. 'I am proud to know that. And Percy's sister – ?'

She coloured very prettily and smilingly avoided the pitfall. 'Percy's sister,' she replied, 'takes an indulgent view of her brother's infatuation. But I am going to treat you as a friend. I am going on with my work, because it has to be done, even if I didn't like doing it; but it would be very nice and companionable if you would sit down and smoke a pipe and talk to me, that is, of course, if you can spare the time.'

'If I could spare the time!' Why, the whole Appeal Court, with the House of Lords thrown in, might have sat and twiddled their thumbs for all I cared. But, in fact, I had nothing to do at all.

'You are sure I shan't hinder you?' I said, feeling for my pipe.

'Perfectly,' she answered. 'I have done all the troublesome part, you see – posing and draping the model,' and she pointed with her pencil to a lay figure (it was an elaborate, 'stuffed' figure with real hair and a wax face and hands), dressed in the very height of fashion, which stood, posed in what Lewis Carroll would have called an 'Anglo-Saxon attitude,' simpering at us idiotically.

'That is a very magnificent costume,' I remarked. 'I suppose it is one of your own? Or do you keep a wardrobe for the models?'

'It isn't costume at all,' she replied with a laugh. 'It is just dress material draped on and tacked or pinned in position. You will see if you go round to the other side.'

I went round to the 'off-side,' and having thus discovered the fraud, asked: 'Is this a figure for a subject picture?'

She laughed softly. 'Bless your innocent heart, Mr Anstey, I don't paint pictures. I draw fashion-plates. I have to earn a living, you know, and give Percy a start.'

'What a horrid waste of talent!' I exclaimed. 'But I had no idea that fashion-plate artists took all this trouble'; and I pointed to the smooth card on her easel which bore a masterly, though rather attenuated, nude figure – in the Anglo-Saxon attitude – lightly drawn in pencil, and looking almost like a silver point.

'Most of them don't,' she replied, 'and perhaps it isn't really necessary. But I like to make a finished pencil drawing though it has all to be rubbed out when the pen work has been done over it.'

'And the preliminary nude figure,' said I; 'you do that from a model, I suppose?'

'No,' she answered. 'I can draw a nude figure well enough for this purpose out of my head. You see, I worked from the model for a long time at the Slade School, and I never threw away a drawing. I have them all bound in books, and I have copied them and drawn them

146

from memory over and over again. In practice, one must be able to rough out a figure out of one's head.'

As she talked, her pencil travelled easily and lightly over the smooth fashion-plate board, gradually clothing the nude figure in transparent habiliments, and I sat smoking with infinite contentment and watching her. And a very dainty, picturesque figure she made in her long blue pinafore, with her red-gold hair and waxen skin, as she stood gracefully poised before her easel, hand on hip and the drawing arm flung out straight and swinging easily from the shoulder. I contrasted her lithe form, in which every curve was full of life and grace, with the absurd rigidity of the lay-figure, her simple, dignified garments with the fussy exuberance of the fashionable costume (though, to be sure, that costume was her own creation), and was moved to comments on the effigy that might have lacerated its feelings if it had had any.

'How long will this drawing take you?' I asked presently.

'I shall have it done by this evening,' she replied, 'and tomorrow morning I shall take it to the office and deliver it to the Art editor.'

'Couldn't I take it for you?' said I.

'I am afraid not,' she answered. 'I must go myself to see that it is all right and to get instructions for the next drawings. Besides, why should you?'

'Didn't we agree that you were to keep indoors out of harm's way? Or at least not to go abroad without an escort? If you must take the drawing yourself, you had better let me come with you to see you safely there and back. Do you mind?'

'Of course I should like your company, Mr Anstey,' she replied, 'but it seems such a tax on you.'

'I wish all taxes were as acceptable,' said I. 'But I understand that you agree; so, if you will fix a time, the escort will assemble at the gate and the bugles will sound "fall in" with military punctuality.'

After a few more half-hearted protests she fixed the hour of half-past ten for the following morning, and I then took my leave, very well satisfied with the progress of this friendship that was becoming so dear to me, and even sensible of a dawning hope that a yet closer intimacy might some day become possible.

Punctually at the appointed time the Hampstead tram set me down at the end of Jacob Street, when I proceeded to collect the convoy and make sail for Bedford Street, Covent Garden, which was the abiding-place of the Art editor to whom the drawing was consigned. But if the outward voyage was characterised by business-like directness, it was quite otherwise with the homeward; which was marked by so many circumnavigations and interrupted by so many ports of call – including the National Gallery – that it was well on in the afternoon when the convoy shortened sail at sixty-three Jacob Street, and it became necessary for the escort to put into port and take in stores in the form of tea and biscuits. And even then, so satisfactory had the voyage turned out that (to pursue the metaphor to a finish) the charter-party was renewed and further voyages projected.

Expeditions abroad, however, could only be occasional, and even then on a plausible business pretext, for my fair friend was a steady worker and spent long days at her easel and drawing-desk; nor was I entirely without occupation, though Thorndyke made but the smallest demands upon my vacation leisure. In effect, not a day passed without a visit to Jacob Street, and whether my time was spent placidly watching the growth of a new drawing, in executing shopping commissions, or in escort duties, it was all equally pleasant to me, and day by day more firmly established my position as the indispensable friend of the little household.

Affairs had been on this footing for about a week when early on a certain afternoon I set forth from the Temple for my daily call, but with a more definite purpose than usual, for I bore with me the locket, in which Polton had fixed a new glass. I rang the studio bell with the customary pleasurable anticipation of the warm and evidently sincere welcome, and listened complacently to Mrs Wingrave's footsteps as she came along the paved passage, and as the wicket opened I prepared to step jauntily through. But the first words that the worthy lady spoke scattered in an instant all my pleasant thoughts and filled me with alarm.

'Miss Blake has just gone out,' she said. 'A most sad thing has happened. Poor Master Percy has had an accident. He has broken his leg.'

'Where did this happen, and when?' I asked.

'It must have happened about an hour ago,' she replied. 'I don't know where, but they have taken him into a house near Chalk Farm.'

'Who brought the news?' I demanded breathlessly; for, seeing that Percy would be at school at the time mentioned, the story was, on the face of it, highly suspicious.

'It was a lady who brought the message,' said Mrs Wingrave. 'She wouldn't come in, but she handed me a note, written in pencil and marked "urgent." Miss Blake showed it to me. It didn't give any particulars beyond what I have told you, and the address of the house.'

'What was the lady like?' I asked.

'Well,' Mrs Wingrave replied, 'I call her a lady, but she was really rather a common-looking woman; painted and powdered and very vulgarly dressed.'

'Did you notice her hair?'

'Yes; you couldn't help noticing it. Brassy-looking, golden stuff, frizzed out like a mop – and her eyebrows were as black as mine are.'

'Do you know where the note is?' I asked.

'I expect Miss Blake took it with her, but she may have left it in the studio. Shall we go and see?'

We hurried together across the yard and into the studio, where for a minute or so we searched the tables and the unfastened bureau. But there was no sign of the note.

'She must have taken it with her,' said Mrs Wingrave. 'But I think I can give you the address, if that is what you want. You don't think there's anything wrong, do you?'

'I am extremely uneasy, Mrs Wingrave,' said I, producing my note-book and a pencil, 'and I shall go straight to the house, if I can find it. What is the address? For Heaven's sake don't give me a wrong one!'

'I remember it quite clearly,' she replied, 'and I think I know the place. It is number twenty-nine Scoresby Terrace, a corner house; and the terrace turns out of Sackett's Road on the left side going up from here.'

I wrote this down in my note-book and then asked: 'How long has Miss Blake been gone?'

'She started less than ten minutes before you came,' was the reply. 'If you hurry you may possibly over-take her.'

We came out of the studio, and as we crossed the yard she gave me very full and clear directions as to how to find the place, some of which I jotted down. Passing a marble tombstone on which her husband had been working, I noticed a number of his tools lying on a sack, and among them a long chisel, almost like a small crowbar.

'May I borrow this, Mrs Wingrave?' I said, picking it up.

'Certainly, if you want to,' she replied with a look of surprise.

'Thank you,' I said, slipping it up my sleeve. 'I may have to force a door, you know,' and with this I let myself out at the wicket and strode away swiftly up the street.

I am habitually a rapid walker, and now I covered the ground at a pace that made other pedestrians stare. For Winifred, I felt sure, would have flown to her brother on the wings of terror, and hurry as I might, I should be hard put to it to overtake her. But her terror could have been nothing compared with mine. As I raced along the shabby streets, swinging the chisel openly in my hand – for its presence in my sleeve was a sensible hindrance – the sinister possibilities – nay, probabilities – that, unsought, suggested themselves one after another, kept me in a state of sickening dread. Supposing I failed to find the place after all! It was quite possible, for the neighbourhood was strange and rather intricate. Or suppose I should lose time in searching for the house and arrive at last, only to find – Here I set my teeth and fairly broke into a run, regardless of the inquisitive stares of idlers at doors and street corners. But, for all my terror and horrible forebodings, I kept my wits and held my attention firmly to Mrs Wingrave's directions, and I derived a faint encouragement from the fact that I had never lost touch of the landmarks and that every hurried step was bringing me nearer to my goal. At length, want of breath compelled me to drop into a walk, but a couple of minutes later, with a gasp of relief, I reached the corner of Sackett's Road; and even as I swung round into the long, straight, dreary street, I caught a glimpse of a woman, at the far end, hurrying forward in the same direction. It was only a momentary glimpse, for in the instant when I saw her she turned swiftly into a by-street to the left. But brief as was the vision, and far away as she was, no doubt was possible to me. It was Winifred.

I drew a deep breath. Surely I should be in time. And perhaps my fears might be groundless after all. The plot might be but the creation of my own uneasy suspicion. At any rate, I was nearly there, and it was hardly possible that in a few short minutes anything could happen – but here all my terrors came crowding on me again, and, breathless as I was, I again broke into a run.

As I reached the corner of Scoresby Terrace and looked at the corner house, my heart seemed to stand still. A single glance showed that it was an empty house, and the horrible desolation of its aspect was made more dreadful by the silence and the total absence of any sign of life. I flew across the road, and barely glancing at the number – twenty-nine – raced up the garden path and tugged furiously at the bell.

Instantly the hollow shell reverberated with a hideous jangling that sounded more ominous and dreadful from the vacancy that the discordant echoes bespoke. But it slowly died away and was succeeded by no answering sound. A deadly silence enveloped the ill-omened place. Not a creak upon the stair, not a sign of life or movement could I detect, though I held my breath to listen. Yet this was the house, and she was in it – and that other! Again I wrenched at the bell, and again the horrible jangling filled the place with echoes, like some infernal peal rung by a company of ghouls. And still there was no answer.

In a frenzy of terror I rushed down the side passage, and bursting open the flimsy gate, ran into the back garden and tried the back door. But it was locked and bolted. Then I darted to the back parlour window, and springing on the sill, shattered, with a stroke of the chisel, the pane above the catch. Passing my hand in through the hole, I drew back the catch and slid up the lower sash. I had noticed that the wooden shutters were not quite closed, but at the moment that I slid up the window-sash, the shutters closed and I heard the cross-bar snap into its socket.

For a moment I had a thought of running round to the front and breaking in the street door. But only for a moment. Rescue, not capture, was my purpose. A glance at the flimsy, decrepit shutters showed me the way in. Thrusting the edge of the long, powerful chisel into the crack close to the lower hinge, I gave a violent wrench, and forthwith the hinge came away from the jamb, the screws drawing easily from the rotten woodwork. Another thrust and another wrench at the upper hinge brought that away, too; at a push the whole shutter swung inward and I sprang down into the room. And at that moment I heard the street door shut.

I ran across the room to the door. Of course it was locked and the key was outside. But I was not a criminal lawyer for nothing. In a moment I had the chisel driven in beside the lock, and pressing on the long handle, drove the door back on its hinges, when the lock-bolt and latch disengaged from the striking-plate and the door came open at once.

I ran out into the hall, unlocked the front room, and looked in, but it was empty. Then I flew up the stairs and was about to unlock the door of the first room that I came to, when I became aware of a soft, shuffling sound proceeding apparently from the next room. Instantly I ran to that door, and turning the key, flung it open.

The sight that met my eyes as I darted into the room was but the vision of a moment, but in that moment it imprinted itself upon my memory for ever. Even now, as I write, it rises before me, vivid and horrible, with such dreadful remembrance that my hand falters as it guides the pen. In a corner near the wall she lay – my sweet, gracious Winifred – lay huddled, writhing feebly and fumbling with her hands at her throat. Her face was of the colour of slate, her lips black, her eyes wide and protruding.

It was, I say, but the vision of a moment, a frightful, unforgettable moment. The next, I was on my knees beside her, my open knife was in my hand, its keen edge eating through the knot at the back of her neck that secured the band that was strangling her. A moment of agonised impatience and then the knot was divided and the band hastily unwound – it was a narrow silken scarf – revealing a livid groove in the plump neck.

As I took away the scarf she drew a deep, gasping breath with a hoarse, distressful sound like the breathing of a croup-stricken child. Again and again it was repeated, growing quicker and more irregular, and with each succeeding gasp the horrible purple of face and lips faded away, leaving a pallor as of marble; the dreadfully protruding eyes sank back until they looked almost normal, though wild and frightened.

I watched these changes with a sense of utter helplessness, though not without relief – for they were clearly changes for the better. But I longed to help her, to do something active to advance her recovery. If only I had had Thorndyke's knowledge I might have been of some use. He would have known what to do. But perhaps there was nothing to be done but wait for her natural recovery. At any rate, that was all that I could do. And so I remained kneeling by her side with her head resting on my arm, holding her hand, and looking with infinite pity and affection into the frightened, trustful eyes that sought my own with such pathetic appeal.

Presently, as her breathing grew easier, the gasps began to be mingled with sobs; and then, suddenly, she burst into tears and wept passionately, almost hysterically, with her face buried against my shoulder. I was profoundly moved, indeed I was almost ready to weep myself, so intense was the revulsion now that the danger was past. In the tumult of my emotions I forgot everything but that she was saved, and that I loved her. As I sought to comfort her, to coax away her terrors, to soothe and reassure her, I cannot tell what words of tenderness I murmured into her ear, by what endearing names I addressed her. Stirred as I was to the very depths of my soul, I was aware of nothing but the great realities. In the stress of terror but now barely past and the joy and relief of the hardly hoped for recovery, the world of everyday was forgotten. All I knew was that she was here, safe in my arms, and that she was all in all to me.

By degrees her emotion expended its force and she grew calmer. Presently she sat up, and having wiped her eyes, looked nervously about the empty room.

'Let us go away from this dreadful place,' she said in a low, frightened voice, laying her hand entreatingly on my arm.

'We will,' said I, 'if you are well enough yet to walk. Let us see.'

I stood up and lifted her to her feet, but she was very unsteady and weak. I doubt if she could have stood without support, for I could feel her trembling as she leaned on me heavily. Still, with my help, she tottered to the door and crossed the landing, and then, very slowly, we descended the stairs. At the open door of the room which I had entered, we paused to adjust her hat and remove any traces of the struggle before we should emerge into the street. I was still holding the silken scarf, and now put it into my pocket to free my hands that I might assist her in settling her hat and the crumpled collar of her dress. As I looked her over to see that all was in order, I noticed three or four conspicuous golden hairs sticking to her right sleeve. I picked them off and was in the act of dropping them when it occurred to me that Thorndyke might be able to extract some information from them, whereupon I brought out my pocket-book and slipped them between the leaves.

'That is how I got into the house,' I said, pointing to the shattered window and the hanging shutter.

She peered fearfully into the empty room and said: 'I heard the crash of the glass. It was that which saved me, I think, for that brute heard it too, and rushed away downstairs instantly. How did you break open the shutter?'

'I did it with a chisel of Mr Wingrave's – and that reminds me that I have left the chisel upstairs. I must take it back to him.'

I bounded up the stairs, and running into the room, snatched up the chisel from the floor and ran out again. As I turned the corner of the staircase, I met her beginning to ascend the stair, clinging to the handrail and sobbing hysterically. I cursed myself for having left her, even for a few moments, and putting my arm around her, led her back into the hall.

'Oh, pray forgive me!' she sobbed. 'I am all unstrung. I couldn't bear to be alone.'

'Of course you couldn't,' said I, drawing her head to my shoulder and stroking her pale cheek. 'I oughtn't to have left you. But try, Winnie dear, to realise that it is now over and gone. And let us get out of this house.'

She wiped her eyes again, and as her sobs died away into an occasional moan, I opened the street door. The sight of the open street and the sunlight seemed to calm her at once. She put away her handkerchief, and clinging to my arm, walked slowly and a little unsteadily by my side down the garden path and out at the gate.

'I wonder where we can get a cab,' said I.

'There is a station not very far away, I believe,' said she. 'Perhaps some one can direct us.'

We walked slowly down Sackett's Road, looking about that curiously deserted thoroughfare for some likely person from whom to make inquiries, when I saw a taxi-cab draw up at a house and discharge its passengers. I managed to attract the notice of the driver, and a minute later we were seated in the vehicle travelling swiftly homeward.

During the short journey hardly a word was exchanged. She was quite composed now, but she was still deathly pale and lay back in her seat with an air of intense fatigue and exhaustion. When we reached the studio I helped her out of the cab, and having dismissed it, led her to the gate and rang the bell.

Instantly I heard hurried steps in the passage, the wicket was flung open, and Mrs Wingrave looked out eagerly. When she saw us, she burst into tears.

'Thank God!' she exclaimed. 'I've been in an agony of suspense. Directly Percy came home, I knew that Mr Anstey must be right – that the message about him was a trap of some sort. What has happened?'

'I'll tell you later, Mrs Wingrave,' Winifred replied. 'I don't want to talk about it now. Is Percy at home?'

'No. The two Wallingford boys were with him. He has gone home to tea with them. I thought it best to say nothing, and let him go. They live quite near here.'

'I am glad you did,' said Winifred, as we crossed the yard – where I replaced the invaluable chisel. 'Perhaps we needn't tell him anything about this.'

'It might be better not to,' said Mrs Wingrave. 'And now go and sit down quietly in the studio and I will bring you some tea. You both look as if you wanted some rest and refreshment.' She bustled away towards her own residence and Winifred and I entered the studio.

As I held the curtain aside to let her pass, my companion halted and looked round the great, bare hall with an air of deep reflection – almost of curiosity. 'I never thought to look upon this place again,' she said gravely; 'and I never should but for you. My life is your gift, Mr Anstey.'

'It is a very precious life to me, Winifred,' said I. And then I added: 'I can't call you Miss Blake.'

'I am glad of that,' she said, looking at me with a smile. 'It would sound very cool and formal now when you have held my life in your hands, and my heart is bursting with gratitude to you.' She laid her hand on my arm for a moment, and then, as if afraid of saying too much, returned abruptly to the subject of her brother. 'It is fortunate Percy was not at home. I don't think we need tell him, at least not just now. Do you think so?'

'I don't see any necessity,' I replied. 'He knows the general position and the precautions that have to be taken. Perhaps he can be told later. And now you must just sit on the settee and rest quietly, for you are as pale as a ghost still. I wonder you have not collapsed altogether.'

In a few minutes Mrs Wingrave brought in the tea and placed it on a table by Winifred's settee. I drew up a chair and performed the presidential functions in respect of the teapot, and under the influence of the homely ceremony and the reviving stimulant my patient began to recover something like her normal appearance and manner. I kept up a flow of more or less commonplace talk, avoiding, for the present, any reference to the terrible events of the afternoon, the details of which I decided to elucidate later when the effect of the shock had passed off.

The postponement, however, was shorter than I had intended, for when we had finished tea and I had carried the tray across the yard and restored it to Mrs Wingrave, Winifred opened the subject herself.

'You haven't asked me how this thing happened,' she said, as I re-entered the studio and sat down beside her in the vacant place on the settee.

'No. I thought you wouldn't want to talk about it just now.'

'I don't want to talk about it to Mrs Wingrave,' said she. 'But you are my deliverer. I don't mind telling you – besides you ought to know. And I want to know, too, by what extraordinary chance you came to be in that place at that critical moment. When I saw you come into the room, it seemed as if a miracle had happened.'

'There was nothing very miraculous about it,' said I, 'except that I happened to arrive at the studio a little earlier than usual.' And here I gave her an account of my arrival and my interview with Mrs Wingrave and my efforts to overtake her.

'It was very clever of Mrs Wingrave to remember the address so clearly,' said Winifred.

'It is a mercy that she did,' said I. 'If she had not – but there, we won't think of that. What happened when you got to the house?'

'I rang the bell and a woman opened the door. I hardly saw her until I had entered the hall and she had shut the door, and then – you know how dark the hall was – I couldn't see her very distinctly. But I noticed that she was a good deal powdered and that she had bright, unreal-looking golden hair, though that didn't show much as she had a handkerchief tied over her head and under her chin. And I also noticed that her face seemed in some way familiar to me.

'As soon as she had shut the door the woman said in a rather peculiar voice: "You must excuse the state of the house, we haven't properly moved in yet. The little man is with the nurse on the first floor, the second room you come to. Will you go up?"

'I ran up the stairs and she followed close behind me. When I came to the second room, I asked: "Is this the one?" and when she answered

"Yes," I opened the door and stepped in. Then, of course, I saw it was an empty room, and instantly I suspected that it was a trap. But at that moment the woman threw the scarf over my head and pulled it tight. I turned round quickly, but she dodged behind me and pulled me into the room, and there we struggled and kept turning round and round for hours, as it seemed to me, she trying to get behind me to tie the scarf, and I struggling to keep her in front of me. She still held both ends of the scarf, and though she was not able to pull it quite tight, it was tight enough to make my breathing difficult and to prevent me from calling out. At last I managed to turn quickly and seize her by the hair and the handkerchief that was tied over her head. But the handkerchief came away in my hand and the hair with it. It was a wig. And then, to my horror, I saw that this was not a woman at all. It was a man! The man who stabbed me that night at Hampstead. I recognised him instantly, and the shock was so awful that I nearly fainted. For a moment I felt perfectly helpless, and in that moment he got behind me and tied the scarf and pulled it tight.

'Then there came a tremendous pealing of the bell. The man started violently, and I could feel his hands trembling as he tried to finish tying the knot while I struggled to get hold of his wrists. But, of course, I could not struggle long, for the scarf was so tight that it almost completely stopped my breathing, and the horror of the thing took away all my strength. When the bell rang the second time, he broke into a torrent of curses mixed with a curious sort of whimpering, and flung me violently on the floor. He was just finishing the knot when I heard a crash of glass down below, and at that he sprang to his feet, snatched up the wig and handkerchief, and flew down the stairs.

'After this there seemed a long, long interval. Of course it was only a matter of seconds, I suppose, but it was agonising – that horrible feeling of suffocation. At last I heard a bursting sound down below. Then the street door shut, and then – just as I seemed to be losing consciousness – you came into the room, and I knew that I was saved.' She paused, and then, laying her hand on mine, she continued: 'I haven't thanked you for saving me from that horrible death. I can't.

158

No words are enough. Any talk of gratitude would be mere anti-climax.'

'There is no question of gratitude, Winnie,' said I. 'Your life is more to me than my own, so there is no virtue in my cherishing it. But I needn't tell you that, for I suspect that my secret has slipped out unawares already.'

'Your secret?' she repeated.

'That I love you, Winnie dearest. You must know it by now. I suppose I ought not to speak of it just at this time. And yet – well, perhaps I might ask you if you would take time to consider whether we might not, some day, be more to one another than we are now.'

She looked down gravely though a little shyly, but she answered without hesitation: 'I don't need to take time to consider. I can tell you at once that I am proud to be loved by such a man as you. And it is not a case of gratitude. I should have said the same if you had asked me yesterday – or even longer ago than that.'

'Thank you for telling me that, Winnie,' said I. 'It would have been an unworthy thing if I had seemed to presume on any small service – '

'It would have been an absurd thing to have any such idea, Mr Anstey.'

'Mr Anstey?' I repeated. 'May I humbly mention that I also have a Christian name?'

'I always suspected that you had,' she retorted with a smile, 'and I must confess to having speculated as to what it might be.'

'It takes the prosaic form of Robert, commonly perverted by my own family to Robin.'

'And a very pretty name, too,' said she. 'But you are a foolish Robin to speak in that way about yourself. The mistake you are making,' she continued, holding up an admonitory forefinger, 'is that you don't realise what an exceedingly nice person you are. But we realise it. Mrs Wingrave is quite fond of you; Percy loves you; and as for Percy's sister, well, she lost her heart longer ago than she is prepared to admit. So let us hear no more ridiculous self-deprecations.'

'There shall be no more, sweetheart,' said I. 'You have taken away the occasion and the excuse. A man who has won the heart of the sweetest and loveliest girl in the whole world would be a fool to undervalue himself. But it is a wonderful thing, Winnie. I can hardly believe in my good fortune. When I saw you that night at Hampstead, I thought you were the most beautiful girl I had ever seen. And now I know I was right. But how little did I dream that that lovely girl would one day be my own!'

'I say again that you are a foolish Robin,' said she, resting her cheek against my shoulder. 'You think your goose is a swan. But go on thinking it, and she will be as near a swan as she can manage, or failing that, a very faithful, affectionate goose.'

She looked up at me with a smile, half-shy but wholly endearing; and noting how her marble-white cheeks had grown pink and rosy, I kissed her; whereupon they grew pinker still.

It was all for our good that Percy lingered with his friends and left us to the undisturbed possession of our new happiness. For me the golden minutes slipped away unnumbered – sullenly and relentlessly checked, however, by my unconsulted watch – as we sat, side by side and hand clasped in hand. We talked little; not that we were, as Rosalind would say, 'Gravelled for lack of matter' (and even if we had been, Rosalind's admirable expedient was always available). But perfect companionship is independent of mere verbal converse. There is no need for speech when two hearts are singing in unison.

At last there came the expected peal of the bell. I might, I suppose, have gone out to open the wicket, but, in fact, I left that office to Mrs Wingrave.

'I don't think Percy will notice anything unusual,' said I. 'You look perfectly recovered now.'

'I suppose I do,' she answered with a smile. 'There have been restoratives, you see.'

'So there have,' I agreed, and *ex abundantia cautelae*, as we lawyers say, I added a sort of restorative codicil even as the quick footsteps pattered across the yard.

Whether Percy observed anything unusual I cannot say with certainty. He was a born diplomatist and a very model of discretion. But I have a strong suspicion that he detected some new note in the harmony of our little society. Particularly when I addressed his sister as Winnie did he seem to cock an attentive ear; and when she addressed me as Robin he cocked both ears. But he made no sign. He was a jewel of a boy. No lover could have asked for anything more perfect in the way of a prospective brother-in-law.

But my suspicion of that juvenile diplomat was confirmed – and my admiration of his judgment reached a climax – when the time arrived for me to go, and Winifred rose to accompany me to the gate. This had always been Percy's office. But now he shook hands with me without turning a hair and without even a glance at the studio door. It was a marvellous instance of precocious intelligence.

We had left the studio and were just crossing the yard when suddenly I bethought me of the locket which Thorndyke had entrusted to me for delivery, and which I had, up to this moment, completely forgotten.

'Here is another narrow escape,' said I. 'The special errand which, to the uninitiated, appeared to be the occasion of my visit here today, has never been discharged. I was to give you your locket, which the ingenious Polton has made as good as new, and had forgotten all about it. However, it is not too late,' and here I took the little bauble from my pocket and handed it to her.

'I am glad it came today, of all days,' she said as she took it from me. 'Now I can wear it as a sort of memento. If we had only known, Robin, we could have got Mr Polton to engrave the date on the back.'

'He can do that later,' said I. 'It is engraved on my heart already. I can never forget a single moment of this day. And what a wonderful day it has been! What a day of wild extremes! Within a few hours I have suffered the most intense misery and dread that I have ever experienced, and been blessed with the greatest happiness that I have ever known. And as to you, my poor darling – '

'Not a poor darling at all,' she interrupted, 'but a very rich and proud and happy one. A day of storm and sunshine it has indeed been, but the storm came first, and "in the evening there was light." And after all, Robin dear, you can't have a rainbow without rain.'

By this time we had reached the gate; and when I had taken her in my arms and kissed her, I opened the wicket and passed out. As it closed behind me I looked up and down the dreary street, but it was dreary to me no longer. I don't know who Jacob was — I mean this particular Jacob — but as I stopped to look back fondly at the factory-like gate, I felt that I was in some sort under an obligation to him as the (presumptive) creator of the sacred thoroughfare.

CHAPTER THIRTEEN

Thorndyke states his Position

Recalling the events of the evening after leaving the studio, I am sensible of a somewhat hazy interval between the moment when I turned the corner of Jacob Street and my arrival at the familiar precincts of the Temple. After the fashion of the aboriginal Londoner, I had simply set my face in the desired direction and walked, unconscious of particular streets, instinctively or subconsciously heading for my destination by the shortest route. And meanwhile my mind was busy with the stirring incidents of this most eventful day, with its swift alternations of storm and sunshine, its terror, its despair, and its golden reward. So my thoughts now alternated between joy at the attainment of a happiness scarcely hoped for and apprehension of the dangers that lurked unseen, ready to spring forth and wreck the life that was more to me than my own.

Thus meditating, I sped through by-streets innumerable and unnoted, crossing quiet squares and traversing narrow courts and obscure passages, but always shunning the main thoroughfares with their disturbing glare and noise, until I came, as it were, to the surface at the end of Chichester Rents and turned into Chancery Lane. There the familiar surroundings brought me back to my everyday world, and my thoughts took a new direction. What would Thorndyke have to say to my news? Had he any resources unknown to me for staving off this very imminent danger? And would the terrible episode of the empty house convey any enlightenment to him that I had missed?

Still revolving these questions, I dived down Middle Temple Lane and presently became aware of a tall figure some little distance ahead, walking in the same direction as my own. I had nearly overtaken him, when he turned at the entrance to Pump Court and looked back, whereupon a mutual recognition brought us both to a halt.

'I expect we are bound for the same port, Anstey,' said he as we shook hands. 'I am going to call on Thorndyke. You are still helping him, aren't you?'

'He says I am, and I hope it is true. At any rate Jervis has not come back yet, if that is what you mean. I suppose, Drayton, you haven't any fresh information for us?'

Sir Lawrence shook his head gloomily. 'No,' he answered, 'I have learned nothing new, nor, I fear, are any of us likely to. Those brutes seem to have got away without leaving a trace that it is possible to make anything of. We can't expect impossibilities even of Thorndyke. But I am not calling on him with reference to the murder case. I want him to come down with me to Aylesbury to help me with an interview. A question of survivorship has arisen, and he knows more about that subject than I do, so I should like him to elicit the facts, if possible.'

As we walked through Pump Court and the Cloisters, I debated with myself whether I should tell Drayton of the horror that this day had witnessed. He was an interested party in more than one sense, for he had the warmest regard for Winifred. But I knew that he would be profoundly shocked, and as he continued to talk of the case on which he wanted Thorndyke's advice, I said nothing for the present.

When I let myself and Drayton in with my latch-key, we found Thorndyke seated at the table with a microscope and a tray of reagents and mounting materials, preparing slides of animal hairs to add to his already extensive collection.

'I am ashamed to disturb you at this hour,' Drayton began. But Thorndyke interrupted him. 'You are not disturbing me at all. This kind of work can be taken up and put down at any moment.'

'It is very good of you to say so,' said Drayton, 'and I will take you at your word.' And thereupon he opened the matter of which he had spoken to me.

'When do you want me to come down to Aylesbury?' Thorndyke asked.

'The day after tomorrow, if you can manage it.'

Thorndyke reflected for a few moments as he picked up with his forceps a newly-cleaned cover-glass, and delicately dropped it on the specimen that floated in its little pool of balsam.

'Yes,' he said at length, 'I think we can arrange that. There isn't very much doing just now.'

'Very well,' said Sir Lawrence. 'Then I will call for you at ten o'clock, and I needn't trouble you with any details now. We can talk the case over on the way down.' He rose as if to depart, but as he turned towards the door, he stopped and looked back at Thorndyke.

'I am afraid,' said he, 'that I have rather neglected our friend Miss Blake. Has either of you seen her lately?'

Thorndyke gave me a quick look, and in the short interval before replying, I could see that he was rapidly debating how much he should tell Sir Lawrence. Apparently he reached the same conclusion as I had, that we could hardly conceal material facts from him, for he replied:

'Yes, we have both seen her quite lately; in fact, I think Anstey has just come from her studio. And I am sorry to say, we are both rather anxious about her.'

'Indeed,' said Drayton, laying down his hat and seating himself. 'What is amiss with her?'

'The trouble is,' replied Thorndyke, 'that she is the sole witness to the identity of the murderers, and they realise it, and they have determined, accordingly, to get rid of her.' And here he gave Sir Lawrence an account of the incident of the poisoned chocolates and the circumstances that had led up to it.

Drayton was thunderstruck. As he listened to Thorndyke's vivid and precise narration, he sat motionless, with parted lips and his hands on his knees, the very picture of amazement and horror.

'But, good God!' he exclaimed, when Thorndyke had finished, 'this is perfectly frightful! It is a horrible state of things. Something must be done, you know. It is practically certain that they will make some further attempt.'

'They have already,' said I. And as the two men turned to me with looks of startled inquiry, I recounted – not without discomfort in recalling them – the terrible events of that afternoon.

My two friends listened with rapt attention as I told the hideous story, and on each it produced characteristic effects. Sir Lawrence glared at me with a scowl of suppressed fury, while Thorndyke's face settled into a rigid immobility like that of a stone mask.

When I had concluded, Drayton sprang to his feet and began to pace the room in uncontrollable agitation, muttering and cursing under his breath. Suddenly he halted opposite Thorndyke, and gazing frowningly into his set face, demanded: 'Is it not possible to do something? Something radical and effective, I mean? I don't know what cards you hold, Thorndyke, and I am not going to embarrass you by asking for details, but are you in a position to make any kind of move?'

Thorndyke, who had also risen, and now stood with his back to the fire, looked down reflectively for a few moments. At length he replied:

'The difficulty is, Drayton, that if we move prematurely, we run a serious risk of failing, and we can't afford to fail.'

'Do I understand, then, that you are in a position to take action?'

'Yes. But it would be extremely unsafe, for if we fail once we fail finally. It would be a gamble, and we should quite probably lose. Whereas, if we can wait, we shall have these men to a certainty. We have taken their measure and we know now exactly what kind of persons we are dealing with. You see, Drayton,' he continued after a brief pause, 'secret crime most commonly comes to light through the efforts of the criminal to cover his tracks. That is so in the present case. All that I know as to the identity of these men I have learned from their struggles to conceal it. But for their multitudinous precautions I should have known nothing about them. And you see for yourself that they are criminals of the usual kind who will not let well alone. They keep making fresh efforts to secure their safety, and each time they make a move we learn something more about them. If only we can wait, they will surely deliver themselves into our hands.'

There was a brief silence. Then Sir Lawrence gave utterance to the thought that was in my own mind.

'That is all very well, Thorndyke, and as a lawyer I fully understand your desire to get a conclusive case before making a move. But can we afford to wait? Are we justified in using this poor young lady as a bait to enable us to catch these villains?'

'If that were the position,' replied Thorndyke, 'there could be but one answer. But we must remember that the capture of these men is the condition on which her safety depends. If we fail, we fail for her as well as for ourselves.'

'Then,' asked Drayton, 'what do you suggest? You don't propose to stand by passively until they make some fresh attempt to murder her?'

'No. I suggest that more complete precautions be taken to secure Miss Blake's safety, and meanwhile I hope to fill in one or two blanks in my collection of evidential facts and perhaps induce these men to make a move in a new direction. I think I can promise to bring the affair to a climax in one way or another, and that pretty soon.'

'Very well,' said Drayton, once more taking up his hat. 'But who is going to look after Miss Blake?'

'Anstey has taken that duty on himself,' replied Thorndyke, 'and I don't think any one could do it better. If he wants assistance or advice, he has only to call upon us.'

With this arrangement Drayton appeared to be satisfied, though he still appeared uneasy – as, indeed, we all were. But he made no further suggestion, and very shortly took his leave.

For some time after his departure not a word was spoken. The conversation that had just taken place had given me abundant food for reflection, while Thorndyke, who still stood with his back to the fire, maintained a grim silence. Evidently he was thinking hard, and a glance at his face – stern, rigid, inexorable – assured me that his cogitations boded ill for those who had aroused his righteous anger. At length he looked up and asked:

'What measures can you suggest for Miss Blake's protection?'

'I have told her that, for the present, she must not go out of doors on any occasion whatever unless accompanied by me – or, of course, by you or Drayton. She has promised to abide absolutely by that rule and to make no exception to it. She has also promised to keep the studio door locked and to inspect any visitors from the window of the bedroom adjoining before unlocking it.'

'If she keeps to those rules she should be quite safe,' said Thorndyke. 'They are not likely to try to break in. There is a man living on the premises, I think?'

'Yes. Mr Wingrave is about the place at his work most of the day, and, of course, he is always there at night.'

'Then, I think we may feel reasonably secure for the present; and I am glad you have made such complete arrangements, for I was going to suggest that you come down with us to Aylesbury.'

'With what object?' I asked. 'Drayton won't want me at the conference.'

'No. But it just occurred to me that, as we shall be within a mile or two of Beauchamp Blake and can easily take it on our way back, we might go and have a look at the place and see if we can pick up any information on the spot. I believe the question of the sale of the property is more or less in abeyance, but it would be just as well to make a few inquiries locally.'

I received the suggestion with some surprise but no enthusiasm.

'Doesn't it seem rather inopportune,' I said, 'with these imminent dangers impending, to be occupying ourselves in prosecuting this shadowy claim? Surely this is no time for building castles in the air. The chance of young Percival's ever coming into this property is infinitely remote, and we can attend to it when we have done with more urgent matters.'

'If we attend to it at all,' he replied, 'we must do so when we have the opportunity. Should the property be sold, Percy's chance will be gone for good. And the conflict between our two purposes is only in your mind. The fact of our keeping an eye on Percy's interests will not hinder our pursuit of the wretches who murdered poor Drayton and would now murder Percy's sister. You can trust me for that.'

'No, I suppose it won't,' I admitted. 'And you seem to take Percy's claim to this estate quite seriously.'

'It is impossible to do otherwise,' said he. 'It may be impossible to prove it, even if an opportunity should arise. But it is a real claim, and what little chance he has ought to be preserved. It mustn't be lost by our negligence.'

I was not keen on the expedition, but I knew what Winifred's sentiments would have been, and loyalty to her bade me assent, though in my own mind, I felt it to be a fruitless and somewhat foolish errand. Accordingly I agreed to form one of the party on the day after the morrow, a decision which Thorndyke received with more satisfaction than the occasion seemed to warrant.

CHAPTER FOURTEEN
Beauchamp Blake

Can there be any more pleasant place of human habitation than an English country town? I asked myself the question as I strolled round the market square of the little town of Aylesbury, gazing about me with a Londoner's pleasure in the restful, old-world aspect of the place. I had still more than half an hour to wait, but I had no feeling of impatience. I could spend that time agreeably enough, sauntering around, wrapped in pleasurable idleness provocative of reflection, looking at the handsome market-place with its clock-tower and its statues immortalising in bronze the worthies of more stirring times, or at the carriers' carts that rested unhorsed in the square and told of villages and hamlets nestling amidst their trees but a few miles away down the leafy lanes.

Presently my leisurely perambulations brought me opposite a shop of more than common smartness, and here – perhaps because the crowd of market folk was a little more dense – I paused and gazed somewhat absently into the window. I have no idea why I looked into that particular shop window. The wares exposed in it – ladies' hats – have no special attraction to the masculine eye – at least in the state in which they are presented by the milliner, bereft of the principal ornament which should be found underneath them. Nevertheless, I was not the only male observer. Another man had stopped and stood, nearer to the window than I, inspecting the gaily-flowered and feathered headgear with undeniable interest.

The incongruity of this eager scrutiny of things so characteristically feminine struck me with amused curiosity, and I watched the man with a half-suppressed smile. He was a small, slight man, neatly dressed in a suit of tweeds and a tweed hat, and the trouser-clips at his ankles suggested that he had cycled in from the country. I could not see his face, as I was standing nearly behind him; but apparently he became aware, after a time, of my presence — perhaps he saw my reflection in the window — and of the fact that I was observing him somewhat curiously, for he turned away with some suddenness, glancing up at me as he passed and then half pausing to look at me again before he bustled away and disappeared up an alley.

There was something very odd in that second look. The first had been a mere casual glance, but the second — quick, searching, even startled — suggested recognition, and something more than recognition. What could it have been? And who could he be? The face — a clean-shaved, thin, sallow face, not very young, seen only for a moment, left a clear mental image that still remained. And as I visualised it afresh I was conscious of a faint sense of familiarity. I had seen this man before. Where had I seen him; and who was he? And why did he look at me with that singular expression?

I stood where he had left me, cudgelling my brains for an answer to these questions. And even as I stood there, a cyclist passed swiftly across the end of the square and disappeared in the direction of the London Road. He was too far off for his face to be clearly recognisable; but he was a small man, he wore a tweed suit and hat, and trouser-clips, and I had no doubt that he was the same man.

Now who was he? The more I recalled the face, the more convinced I was that I had seen it before. But the identity of its owner eluded me completely. I couldn't place the fellow at all. Probably it didn't matter in the least who he was. But still it was exasperating to be baffled in this way. Unconsciously, I turned and stared into the milliner's window. And then, in a flash it came. The middle of the window was occupied by an enormous hat — a huge, bloated, fungous structure overrun with counterfeit vegetation and bristling with feathers; such a hat as might have adorned the cranium of a Hottentot queen. A glance at that grisly head-dress supplied the missing link in the chain of association. The face that had looked into mine was the face of the woman who had shadowed Winifred and me from Hampstead; who had lured her to the empty house, and had there revealed herself as a man in disguise. In short, this was the murderer of poor Drayton, and the would-be murderer of Winifred!

And I had held this wretch in the hollow of my hand and I had let him go! It was an infuriating thought. If my quickness of observation had only been equal to his, I should have had him by now safely under lock and key. No wonder he had looked startled. But he must have a remarkably good memory for faces to have recognised me in that instantaneous glance. For he had seen me only once – at the inquest at Hampstead – and then but for a moment. Unless he had got a glimpse of me at the empty house, or – which seemed more probable – had shadowed and watched me when I had been acting as Winifred's escort. At any rate he knew me, better than I knew him, and had managed very adroitly to slip through my fingers.

But what on earth was he doing at Aylesbury? Was it possible that he lived in this neighbourhood? If so, a description given to the police might even yet secure his arrest. I was turning over this possibility when the chiming of a clock recalled my appointment. I glanced up at the dial on the clock-tower and had just noted that the appointed hour had struck when I observed Thorndyke ascending the steps to the platform at the base. This was our rendezvous, and I forthwith hurried across the cobbled square and presented myself, bursting with my news and discharging them in a volley as soon as I arrived.

Thorndyke was deeply interested, but yet I found in his manner something slightly disappointing. He was an impassive man, difficult to surprise or move to any outward manifestation of emotion. Still, knowing this, I was a little chilled by the almost academic view that he took of the incident, and especially by his firm rejection of my plan for invoking the aid of the police.

'It sounds tempting,' he admitted, 'to swoop down on this man and put an end forthwith to all our dangers and complications, but it would be a bad move. Quite probably the police would decline to take any action. And then what sort of description could you give them. For the purposes of a search it is far too general, and a change of clothing would make it entirely inapplicable. And we must admit the possibility of your being mistaken. And finally, if we gave this information, we should almost certainly lose one man – whom none of us has ever seen, but who is probably the principal. We should have let the cat out of the bag, and all our carefully-laid plans would come to nought.'

'I didn't know that we had any carefully-laid plans,' said I.

'You know that we are engaged in investigating a murder; that our aim is to secure the two or more murderers and to elucidate the causes and circumstances of the crime, and that we have accumulated a certain number of data to that end.'

'You have,' I objected. 'I have practically no data at all. May I ask if you know who this sallow-faced little devil is?'

'I have a strong suspicion,' he replied. 'But suspicion isn't quite what one wants to take into a court of law. I want to verify my suspicions and turn them into conclusive evidence. So that when I play my card it shall be a trump card.'

To this I had no reply to make. I knew Thorndyke's methods. For years I had acted as his leading counsel, and always when I had gone into court I had taken with me a case complete to the last detail. Now, for the first time, I was realising the amount of patience and self-restraint that went to the making of a case of unassailable conclusiveness, and I found myself with difficulty overcoming the temptation to make a premature move.

While we had been talking, we had been making our way at an easy pace out of the town on to the London Road, and now Thorndyke, with the one-inch ordnance map in his hand, indicated our route.

'Beauchamp Blake,' said he, 'lies just off the Lower Icknield Way, on the left of the London Road. But there is no need for us to take the shortest way. The by-road through Stoke Mandeville looks more entertaining than the main road, and we can pick up the Lower Icknield Way at the crossroads below the village.'

Our route being thus settled, we set forth, turning off presently into the quiet, shady by-road. And as we swung along between the thinning hedgerows, with the majestic elms – now sprinkled with yellow – towering above us and casting athwart the road streaks of cool shadow, we chatted sporadically with long intervals of silence, for we were Londoners on holiday to whom the beauty of this fair countryside was reinforced by a certain pleasant strangeness.

'I have wondered from time to time,' I said, after one of the long pauses, 'what can be the significance – if it has any – of that blue-dyed hair that you extracted from Winifred's locket' (I had confided to Thorndyke the new relations that had grown up between our fair client and me).

'Ah,' he replied. 'A very interesting problem, Anstey.'

'I have also wondered what made you take the hair out of the locket to examine it under the microscope.'

'The answer to that question is perfectly simple,' said he. 'I took it out to see if it was blue. In the mass the hair looked black.'

'But do I understand that you thought it might be blue?'

'I expected to find it blue. The examination was a measure of verification.'

'But why, in the name of Fortune, should you expect to find blue hair in a locket? I had no idea that hair ever was dyed blue – except,' I added with a sudden flash of recollection, 'in the case of ancient Egyptian wigs, and I had an idea that they were not hair at all.'

'Some of them, I believe, were not. However, this was not ancient Egyptian hair. It was modern.'

'Then, will you tell me what it was that made you expect to find the hair in the locket dyed blue?'

'The expectation,' he replied, 'arose out of an inspection of the locket itself.'

'Do you mean those mysterious and obscure Biblical references engraved inside?'

'No; I mean the external characters, the peculiar construction, the motto engraved on the front, and the hallmark on the back.'

174

'But what,' I asked, 'was the connection between those external characters and this most extraordinary peculiarity of the hair inside?'

He looked at me with the exasperating smile that I knew so well (and was, in fact, expecting).

'Now, you know, Anstey,' said he, 'you are trying to pump me; to suck my brains instead of using your own. I am not going to encourage you in any such mental indolence. The proper satisfaction of a discovery is in having made it yourself. You have seen and handled the locket, you have heard my comments on it, and you have access to it for further examination. Try to recall what it is like, and if necessary, examine it afresh. Consider its peculiarities one by one and then in relation to one another. If you do this attentively and thoughtfully you will find that those peculiarities will yield some most curious and interesting suggestions, including the suggestion that the hair inside is probably blue.'

'I shan't find anything of the kind, you old devil,' I exclaimed wrathfully, 'and you know perfectly well that I shan't. Still, I will take an early opportunity to put the "little Sphinx" under cross-examination.'

While we had been talking we had passed through the village of Stoke Mandeville, and we now arrived at the crossroads, where we turned to the left into the ancient Icknield Way.

'A mile and a half farther on,' said Thorndyke, again consulting the map, 'we cross the London Road. Then we turn out of the Icknield Way into this lane, leaving Weston Turville on our left. I note there is an inn opposite the gates of Beauchamp Blake. Does that topographical feature interest you?'

'I think,' said I, 'that after another couple of miles, we shall be ready for what the British workman calls a "beaver." But it is probably only a wayside beerhouse.'

Another half-hour's walking brought us to the London Road, crossing which we followed a side road – apparently part of the Icknield Way – which skirted the lake-like reservoir and presently gave off as a branch a pleasant, elm-bordered lane on the right-hand side of which was a tall oak paling.

'This,' said Thorndyke, whose stature enabled him easily to look over the fence, 'is the little park of Beauchamp Blake. I don't see the house, but I see the roof of a gatekeeper's lodge. And here is the inn.'

A turn of the lane had brought into view a gatekeeper's lodge by the main gates of the park, and nearly opposite, the looked-for hostelry. And a very remarkable-looking hostelry it was, considering its secluded position; an antique, half-timbered house with a high, crinkly roof in which was a row of dormer windows, and a larger, overhanging gabled bay supported below by an immense carved corner-post. But the most singular feature of the house was the sign, which swung at the top of a tall post by a horse-trough in the little forecourt, on which was the head of a gentleman wearing a crown and a full-bottomed wig, apparently suspended in mid-air over a brown stone pitcher.

'It seems to me,' said I, as we approached the inn, 'that the sign needs an explanatory inscription. The association of a king and a brown jug may be natural enough, but it is unusual as an inn-sign.'

'Now, Anstey,' Thorndyke exclaimed protestingly, 'don't tell me that that ancient joke has missed its mark on your superlative intellect. The inscription on the parlour window tells us that the sign is the King's Head, and the pitcher under that portrait explains that the king is James the Second or Third – His Majesty over the water. This is evidently a Jacobite house. Does the sedition shock you? Or shall we enter and refresh? If the landlord's ale is as old as his politics we ought to find quite exceptional entertainment within, and perhaps pick up a trifle of local gossip that may interest us.'

I assented readily, secretly denouncing my slowness in the 'uptake.' Thorndyke's explanations were always so ridiculously simple – when you had heard them.

The landlord, who looked like a retired butler, received us with old-fashioned deference and inducted us into the parlour, drawing a couple of Wycombe armchairs up to the table.

'What can I do for you, gentlemen?' he inquired.

'Well, what *can* you do for us?' asked Thorndyke. 'Is it to be bread and cheese and beer?'

'I can let you have a cold fowl and a cut of boiled bacon,' said the landlord with the air of one who lays down the ace of trumps.

'Can you really!' exclaimed Thorndyke. 'That is a repast fit for a king – even for the king over the water.'

The landlord smiled slyly. 'Ah, you're alluding to my old sign, sir,' said he. ' 'Twouldn't have done to have had him swingin' up there time back. Some others would have been swingin' too. In those days he used to hang in this room over the fireplace, only there was a portrait of King George fixed over him with concealed hinges. When strangers came to the house there was King George – God bless him! – the same as the sign that used to hang outside; but when the villagers or the people from the Hall opposite sat in the room, then George was swung back on his hinges to bring James into view and a pitcher of water was put on the table to drink the toasts over. This was a thriving house in those days. They say that Percival Blake – he was the last of the old family and a rare plotter by all accounts – used to meet some of his political cronies in this very room, and I've no doubt a lot of business was plotted here that never came to anything.'

'Who has the place now?' asked Thorndyke.

'The present squire is Mr Arthur Blake, and a queerish sort of squire he is.'

'In what way queer?' I asked.

'Well, you see, sir, he's a Colonial – lived in Australia all his life, I understand. And he looks it – a big, roughish-looking man, and very short spoken. But he can ride, I'll say that for him. There isn't a better horseman in the county. Mounts from the off-side, too. I suppose that's their way out there, though it don't suit our rule of the road.'

As the landlord gave these particulars, he proceeded, with swift dexterity, to lay the table and furnish it with the materials for the feast, aided and abetted by an unseen female who lurked in the background. When he had put the final touch with a foam-crowned jug of 'nut-brown,' he showed a tendency to withdraw and leave us to our meal; but Thorndyke was in a conversational mood and induced him, without difficulty, to fetch another tumbler and proceed with his output of local lore.

'Is it true that the place is going to be sold?' Thorndyke inquired.

'So they say,' replied the landlord. 'And the best thing the squire could do if the lawyers will let him. The place is no good to him.'

'Why not?'

'Well, sir, he's a bachelor, and like to remain one it seems. Then he's a stranger to the place and don't appear to take to English ways. He keeps no company and he makes no visits; he don't know any of his neighbours and doesn't seem to want to. He has only kept on one or two of the servants, and he lives with his man – foreign-looking chap named Meyer – in a corner of the house and never uses the rest. He'd be more comfortable in a little farm house.'

'And how does he spend his time?' asked Thorndyke.

'I don't know, sir,' was the answer. 'Mostly loafing about, I should say. He takes photographs, I hear; quite clever at it, too, it seems. And he goes out for a ride every afternoon – you'll see him come out of the gate at three o'clock almost to the minute – and sometimes he goes out in the morning, too.'

'And as to visitors? Are strangers allowed to look over the house?'

'No, sir. The squire won't have any strangers about the place at all. I fancy what made him so particular was a burglary that occurred there about a couple of years ago. Not that there was much in it, for they got all the things back and they caught the burglar the very next day.'

'That was smart work,' I remarked.

'Yes,' our friend agreed, 'they did the thief very neatly. It was a one-man job and the burglar seems to have been a downy bird, for he worked in gloves so that he shouldn't leave any marks behind. But he took those gloves off a bit too soon, for, when they heard him making off and let the dogs loose, he had to do a bolt, and he dropped one of the things in the park – a silver salver it was, I think – and the police found it the next morning and found some finger-marks on it. They wanted to take the salver up to Scotland Yard to have it examined, but the squire wouldn't have that. He took a photograph of the finger-marks and gave it to the police, and they took it up to Scotland Yard; and the people there were able to tell them at once whose fingermarks they were, and they got the burglar that very evening with all the stolen goods in his possession. Wonderful smart, I call it.'

'Do you think,' Thorndyke asked, 'that we should be able to get a look at the house? Just the outside, I mean?'

'I'll see what can be done, sir,' the landlord replied. 'I'll have a few words with the lodge-keeper. I was butler to the last squire but one, so they know me pretty well. I'll just run across while you are finishing your lunch. But you'd better wait until the squire has gone out, because, if he sees you on the drive, like as not he'll order you out, and that wouldn't be pleasant for gentlemen like you.'

'I think we'll take the risk,' said Thorndyke. 'If he tells us to go, we can go, but I don't like sneaking in behind his back.'

'No, sir, perhaps you are right,' the landlord agreed, a little dubiously, and departed on his errand, leaving us to finish our lunch – which, in fact, we had practically done already.

In this long conversation I had taken no part. But I had been an interested listener. Not that I cared two straws for the small beer that our host had been retailing. What had interested, and a good deal puzzled me was Thorndyke's amazing inquisitiveness respecting the private and domestic affairs of a man whom neither of us knew and with whom we really had no concern. For the question of the succession to the property was a purely legal one – and pretty shadowy at that – on which the personal qualities and habits of the present tenant had no bearing whatever. And yet my experience of Thorndyke told me that he certainly had not been asking these trivial and impertinent questions without some reasonable motive. No man was less inquisitive about things that did not concern him.

But the discrepancy between his character and his conduct did not end here. As soon as the landlord had gone and we had filled and lit our pipes, he began to explore his waistcoat pockets and presently produced therefrom Polton's reproduction of Mr Halliburton's ridiculous mascot, which he laid on the table and regarded fondly.

'Do you usually carry that thing in your pocket, Thorndyke?' I asked.

'Not usually,' he replied, 'but this is a special occasion. We are on holiday, and moreover, we are seeking our fortune, or at least, hoping that something may turn up.'

'Are we?' I said. 'I am not conscious of any such hope, and I don't know what you expect.'

'Neither do I,' he replied. 'But I feel in an optimistic mood. Perhaps it is the beer,' and with this he picked up the mascot, and opening the split gold ring with a knife-blade, attached it to his watch-chain, closing the ring with a squeeze of his finger and thumb.

It was a singular proceeding. What made it especially so was Thorndyke's openly-expressed contempt of the superstition which finds expression in the use of charms, mascots and other fetishistic objects and practices. However, we were on holiday, as he had said, and perhaps it was admissible to mark the occasion by playing the fool a little.

In a few minutes the landlord returned and announced that he had secured the consent of the lodge-keeper to our making an inspection of the house, with the proviso that we were not to go more than a couple of hundred yards down the drive. 'I'll just step across with you,' he added, 'so that he can see that you are the right parties.'

Accordingly, when we had paid the modest reckoning, we picked up our hats and sticks and as our host held open the parlour door, we passed out into the courtyard, glancing up with renewed interest at the historic sign which creaked in the breeze. Crossing the road, we passed through the wicket of the closed gate, under the detached observation of the lodge-keeper; and here our host wished us adieu and returned to the inn.

A short walk down the drive brought us to a turn of the road where we came in sight of the house across a stretch of meadows in which a small herd of cows made spots of vivid colour. It was not a large mansion, but what it lacked in size it made up for in character and interest. The two parts were clearly distinct, the newer portion being a Jacobean brick building with stone dressings and quaint corbie-step gables, while the older part – not later than the sixteenth century – was a comparatively low structure showing massive timbers with pargetted plaster fillings, a high roof with wide-spreading eaves and a long row of picturesque dormer windows and large, clustered chimneys.

'It is a grand old house,' I said. 'What a pity it is that Blake is such a curmudgeon. The inside ought to be even more interesting than the outside.'

'Yes,' Thorndyke agreed, 'it is a splendid specimen of domestic architecture, and absolutely thrown away, if our host was not exaggerating. One could wish for a more appreciative tenant – such as our young friend Percy, for instance.'

I glanced at Thorndyke, surprised, not for the first time, at the way in which he tended to harp on this very unresonant string. To me, Percy's claim to this estate was simply a romantic instance of the might-have-been, and none too clear at that. His chance of ever inheriting Beauchamp Blake was a wild dream that I found myself unable to take seriously. But this was apparently not Thorndyke's view, for it was evident that he had considered the matter worth inquiring into, and his last words showed that it still hovered in his mind. I was on the point of reopening the discussion when two men appeared round the corner of the house, each leading a saddled horse. Opposite the main doorway they halted and one of them proceeded to mount – from the off-side, as I noticed. Then they apparently became aware of our presence, for they both looked in our direction; indeed they continued to stare at us with extraordinary attention, and by their movements appeared to be discussing us anxiously.

Thorndyke chuckled softly. 'There must be something uncommonly suspicious in your appearance, Anstey,' he remarked. 'They seem to be in a deuce of a twitter about you.'

'Why my appearance?' I demanded. 'They are looking at us both. In fact I think it is you who are the real object of suspicion. I expect they think you have come back for that silver plate.'

As we spoke, the discussion came to an end. The one man remained, holding his horse and still looking at us, while the other turned and advanced up the drive at a brisk trot, sitting his mount with that unconscious ease that distinguishes the lifelong, habitual equestrian. As he approached, he looked at us inquisitively and with undissembled disapproval, but seemed as if he were going to pass without further notice. Suddenly, however, his attention became more intense. He slowed down to a walk, and as he drew near to us he pulled up and dismounted. And again I noticed that he dismounted from the off-side.

CHAPTER FIFTEEN

The Squire and the Sleuth-hound

As Mr Blake approached with the evident intention of addressing us, it was not unnatural that I should look at him with some interest. Not that such interest was in any way justified by his appearance, which was quite commonplace. He was a tall man, strongly built, and apparently active and muscular. His features were somewhat coarse, but his expression was resolute and energetic, though not suggestive of more than average intelligence. But at the moment, as he bore down on us, leading his horse by the bridle-rein, with his eyes fixed on Thorndyke's face, suspicion and a certain dim suggestion of surprise were what I principally gathered from his countenance.

'May I ask what your business is?' he demanded somewhat brusquely, but not rudely, addressing Thorndyke and looking at him with something more than common attention.

'We really haven't any business at all,' my colleague replied. 'We were walking through the district and thought we should like to have a glance at your very picturesque and interesting house. That is all.'

'Is there anything in particular that you want to know about the house?' Mr Blake asked, still addressing Thorndyke.

'No,' the latter replied. 'Our interest in the place is merely antiquarian, and not very profound at that.'

'I see,' said Mr Blake. He appeared to reflect for a few moments and seemed to be on the point of moving away when he stopped suddenly and a quick change passed over his face. At the same moment, I noticed that his eyes were fixed intently on Thorndyke's ridiculous mascot.

'I take it,' said he,' that you had the lodge-keeper's permission to come inside the gates?'

'Yes,' Thorndyke replied. 'He gave us permission − through the inn-keeper, who asked him − to come in far enough to see the house. As far as we have come, in fact.'

Mr Blake nodded, and again his eyes wandered to the object attached to Thorndyke's watch-chain.

'You are looking at my mascot,' the latter said genially. 'It is a curious thing, isn't it?'

'Very,' Blake agreed gruffly. 'What is it?'

Thorndyke pulled the soft wire ring open, and detaching it from his chain, handed the little object to the other, who examined it curiously and remarked:

'It seems to be made out of a bone.'

'Yes; the bone of a porcupine ant-eater.'

'Ha. You got it somewhere abroad, I suppose?'

'No,' replied Thorndyke. 'I found it in London, and, of course, it isn't really mine. It belongs to a man named Halliburton. But I don't happen to have his address at the moment, so I can't return it.'

Mr Blake listened to this explanation with a sort of puzzled frown, wondering, perhaps, at my colleague's uncalled-for expansiveness to an utter stranger. But his wonder was nothing to mine, as I heard the usually secretive Thorndyke babbling in this garrulously confidential fashion.

When he had examined the mascot, Mr Blake handed it back to Thorndyke with an inarticulate grunt, and as my colleague hooked the ring on his watch-chain, he turned away, walked round his horse to the off-side, mounted lightly to the saddle and started the horse forward at a trot. As he disappeared round a bend of the tree-bordered road, I glanced at Thorndyke, who was once more gazing calmly at the house.

'Mine host was right,' I observed. 'Squire Blake is a pretty considerable boor.'

'His manners are certainly not engaging,' Thorndyke agreed.

'I didn't notice that he had any manners,' said I, 'and it seemed to me that you were most unnecessarily civil, not to say confidential.'

'Well, you know,' he replied, 'we are on his premises, and not only uninvited, but contrary to his expressed wishes. We could hardly be otherwise than civil. And after all, he didn't eject us. But I suppose we may as well retire now.'

'Yes,' I agreed, 'he is probably waiting to see us off his confounded land, and possibly speaking his mind to the lodge-keeper.'

Both these surmises appeared to be correct, for when we came round the clump of trees at the turn of the road, I saw the squire in earnest conversation with the keeper, who was standing at attention, holding the gate open, and, I thought, looking somewhat abashed. We passed out through the wicket, which was still unfastened, but though the lodge-keeper looked at us attentively, and even a little curiously, Blake gave no sign of being aware of our existence.

'Well,' said I, 'he is an unmannerly hog. But he has one redeeming feature. He is a man of taste. He *did* admire you, Thorndyke. While you were talking he couldn't keep his eyes off you.'

'Possibly he was trying to memorise my features in case I should turn out to be a swell cracksman.'

I laughed at the idea of even such a barbarian as this mistaking my distinguished-looking colleague for a member of the swell mob. But it was not impossible. And certainly the squire had scrutinised my friend's features with an intensity that nothing but suspicion could justify.

'Perhaps,' said I, 'he suffers from an obsession on the subject of burglars. Our host's remarks seemed to suggest something of the kind. I wonder what he was saying to the lodge-keeper. It looked to me as if the custodian was receiving a slight dressing-down on our account.'

'Probably he was,' replied Thorndyke. 'But I think that, if my learned friend had happened to be furnished with eyes in the back of his head – '

'As my learned senior appears to be,' I interjected.

' – he would already have formed a more definite opinion as to what took place. In the absence of the retrocephalic arrangement, I suggest that we slip through this opening in the hedge and sit down under the bank.'

Stooping to avoid the thick upper foliage, he dived through the opening and I followed, with no small curiosity as to what it was that my extraordinarily observant colleague had seen. Presumably some one was following us, and if so, as the opening occurred at a sharp bend of the road, our disappearance would have been unobserved.

'It is my belief, Thorndyke,' I said, as we sat down under the bank, 'that your optical arrangements are like those of the giraffe. I believe you can see all round the horizon at once.'

Thorndyke laughed softly. 'The human field of vision, Anstey,' said he, 'as measured by the perimeter, is well over a hundred and eighty degrees. It doesn't take much lateral movement of the head to convert it into three hundred and sixty. The really important factor is not optical but mental. That earnest conversation with the gatekeeper suggested a possibility, though a rather remote one. Ordinary human eyesight, used with the necessary attention, was quite sufficient to show that the improbable had happened, as it often does. Hush! Look through that chink in the hedge.'

As he concluded in a whisper, rapid footfalls became audible. Nearer and nearer they approached, and then, through my spy-hole, I saw a man in cord breeches and leggings and a velveteen coat walk swiftly past. The gatekeeper had been dressed thus, and presumably the man was he, though I had not observed him closely enough to be able to recognise him with certainty.

'Now, why is he following us?' I asked, taking the identity for granted.

'We mustn't assume that he is following us at all with a definite intent, though I suspect he is. But he may be merely going the same way. He may have business in Wendover.'

'It would be rather amusing to dodge him once or twice and see what his game is,' I said with the schoolboy instinct that lingers on atavistically in the adult male.

'It would be highly amusing,' Thorndyke agreed, 'but it wouldn't serve our purpose, which is to ascertain his purpose and keep our knowledge to ourselves. We had better move on now if he is out of sight.'

He was out of sight, having reached and turned down the Tring Road. We followed at a sharp walk, and as we came out into the Tring Road, behold him standing in the footway a couple of hundred yards towards Wendover, looking about him with a rather foolish air of bewilderment. As soon as he saw us, he lifted his foot to the bank and proceeded to attend to his bootlace.

'We won't notice him,' said Thorndyke. 'He is evidently an artless soul and probably believes that he has not been recognised. Let us encourage that eminently desirable belief.'

We passed him with an almost aggressive appearance of unconsciousness on both sides, and pursued our way along the undulating road.

'I don't think there is much doubt now that he is following us,' said I, 'and the question is, why is he doing it?'

'Yes,' said Thorndyke, 'that is the question. He may have had instructions to see us safely out of the district, or he may have had further instructions. We shall see when we get to the station. Meanwhile I am tempted to try a new invention of Polton's. It is slightly fantastic, but he made me promise to carry it in my pocket and try it when I had a chance. Now, here is the chance, and here is the instrument.'

He took from his pocket a leather case from which he extracted a rather solidly-made pair of spectacles. 'You see,' he said, 'Polton has long had the idea that I ought to be provided with some means of observing what is going on behind me, and he has devised this apparatus for the purpose. Like all Polton's inventions, it is quite simple and practicable. As you see, it consists of a rigid spectacle-frame fitted with dummy glasses – clear, plain glass – at the outer edge of which is fixed a little disc of speculum-metal worked to an optically true plane surface and set at a minute angle to the glass. As the disc is quite close to the eye, it enables the wearer, by the very slightest turn of the head, to get a clear view directly behind him. Would you like to try it?'

I took the spectacles from him and put them on, and was amazed at their efficiency. Although the discs were hardly bigger than split peas, they gave me a perfectly clear view along the road behind us – as if I had been looking through a small, round hole – and this with a scarcely appreciable turn of the head. Viewed from behind, I must have appeared to be looking straight before me.

'But,' I exclaimed, 'it seems a most practical device and I shall insist on Polton making me a pair.'

'That will please him,' said Thorndyke, and he added, reflectively, 'if only there were a few thousand more Poltons – men who found their satisfaction in being useful and giving pleasure to their fellows – what a delightful place this world would be!'

I continued to wear the magic spectacles all the way to Wendover, finding a childish pleasure in watching the unconscious gatekeeper who was dogging our footsteps and taking ludicrous precautions to keep – as he thought – out of sight. Only as we descended the long hill into the beautiful little town did I take them off, the better to enjoy the charm of the picturesque approach with its row of thatched cottages and the modest clock-turret, standing up against the background of the wooded heights that soared above Ellesborough. At the station we had the good fortune to find a train due and already signalled, but we delayed taking our tickets until our follower arrived, which he did, in evident haste, a couple of minutes later, being, no doubt, acquainted with the times of the trains. As soon as he appeared, Thorndyke sauntered to the booking-office wicket and gave him time to approach before demanding in clear, audible tones, two firsts to Marylebone. The gatekeeper followed, and thrusting his head and shoulders deep into the opening, as if he were about to crawl through, made his demand in a muffled undertone.

'We need not trouble ourselves about him any more,' said Thorndyke, 'until we get to London. Then we shall know whether he is or is not trying to shadow us.'

When we had settled ourselves in an empty compartment and began to charge our pipes as the train moved off, I returned to the question of our tactics.

'What do you propose to do, Thorndyke, if this fellow tries to follow us home? Shall we let him run us to earth, or shall we lose him?'

'I see no reason why we should make a secret of who we are and where we live. That is apparently what Blake wants to know – that is, if this man is really shadowing us.'

'But,' I urged, 'isn't it generally wiser to withhold information until you know what use is going to be made of it?'

'As a rule, it is,' he admitted. 'But it may happen that the use made of information by one party may be highly illuminating to the other. We may assume that Blake wants to know who we are simply because he suffers from an obsession of suspicion and thinks that we were in his grounds for some unlawful purpose. But he may have some other object, and if he has, I should like to know what it is; and the best way to find out is to let him have our names and address.'

To this I assented, though I was a little mystified. The man Blake was no concern of ours, and it did not seem to matter in the least what suspicions of us had got into his thick head. However Thorndyke probably knew his own business – and meanwhile the presence of this sleuth-hound provided an element of comedy of which I was far from unappreciative, and which my sedate colleague enjoyed without disguise.

When we alighted at Marylebone, we walked quickly to the barrier, but having passed through, we sauntered slowly to the main exit.

'Do you think Polton's spectacles would be very conspicuous?' I asked.

My colleague smiled indulgently. 'The new toy has caught on,' said he, 'and it would be undeniably useful at the present moment. No, put the spectacles on. The discs are hardly noticeable to a casual observer.'

Accordingly I slipped the appliance on as we strolled out into the Marylebone Road and was able, almost immediately, to report progress.

'He is watching us from the exit. Which way are we going?'

'I think,' replied Thorndyke, 'as he is a country cousin, we will make things easy for him and give him a little exercise after the confinement of the train. The Euston Road route is less crowded than Oxford Street.'

We turned eastward and started at an easy pace along the Marylebone Road and Euston Road, keeping on the less-frequented side of the street. I was a little self-conscious in regard to the spectacles, but apparently no one noticed them; and by their aid I was able to watch with astonishing ease our artless follower and to amuse myself by noting his conflicting anxieties to keep us in view and himself out of sight. We turned down Woburn Place, crossed Queen Square to Great Ormond Street and proceeding by Lamb's-Conduit Street, Red Lion Street, Great Turnstile, Lincoln's Inn, and Chancery Lane, crossed Fleet Street to Middle Temple Lane. Here we slowed down, lest the sleuth-hound should lose us, and as we were now in our own neighbourhood, I removed the spectacles and restored them to their owner.

At the entrance to Pump Court we separated, Thorndyke proceeding at a leisurely pace towards Crown Office Row while I hurried through the court; and having halted in the Cloisters to make sure that the sleuth was not pursuing me, I darted through Fig-Tree Court and across King's Bench Walk to our chambers, where I found Polton laying a sort of hybrid tea and supper.

To our trusty assistant I rapidly communicated the state of affairs (including the triumphant success of the magic spectacles, at which his face became a positive labyrinth of ecstatic wrinkles); and having provided ourselves with field-glasses, we stationed ourselves at the laboratory window, from whence we had the gratification of watching Thorndyke emerge majestically from Crown Office Row, followed shortly by the man in the velveteen coat, whose efforts to make himself invisible brought Polton to the verge of apoplexy.

'Hadn't I better follow him and see where he goes to, sir?' the latter suggested.

The suggestion was put to Thorndyke when he entered, but was rejected.

'I don't think we want to know where he goes from here,' said he. 'But still, seeing that he has come so far, it might be kind of you, Polton, to go down and give him a chance of obtaining any information that he wants.'

Polton needed no second bidding. Clapping on his hat, he set forth gleefully down the stairs. But in a minute or two he was back again, somewhat crestfallen.

'It's no go, sir,' he reported. 'I found him copying the names on the door-post in the entry, and I think he must have got them all down, for when he saw me, he was off like a lamplighter.'

Thorndyke chuckled. 'And to think,' said he, 'that our friend, the squire, could have got all the information he wanted by the simple expedient of asking for our cards. Verily, suspicious folk give themselves a deal of unnecessary trouble.'

CHAPTER SIXTEEN

Mr Brodribb's Embassy

There is a certain psychological phenomenon known to those financial navigators who have business on the deep and perilous waters of the Stock Exchange as 'jobbing backwards.' It is not their monopoly, however. To ordinary mortals – who describe it as 'prophesying after the event' – it has been familiar from time immemorial, and has always been associated with a degree of wisdom and certainty strangely lacking in prophecy of a more hasty and premature kind.

Reviewing the curious case of which this narrative is the record, I am tempted to embark on this eminently satisfying form of mental exercise. But when I do so, I am disposed to look with some surprise at the very conspicuous deficiency in the power of 'jobbing forward' which I displayed while the events which I am chronicling were in progress. Now, I can see that all the striking and significant facts (only they then appeared neither striking nor significant) which enabled Thorndyke, from the very first, to pursue a steady advance along a visible trail, were in my possession as much as they were in his. But, whereas in his hands they became connected so as to form a continuous clue, in mine they remained separate, and apparently unrelated fragments. At the time, I thought that Thorndyke was hiding form me what material evidence he had. Now it is obvious to me (as also to the acute reader, who has, no doubt, already pieced the evidence together) that he not only concealed nothing, but actually gave me several of the very broadest hints.

So, despite the knowledge that I really possessed, if I had only realised it, I remained utterly in the dark. All that I knew for certain was that Winifred was encompassed by dangers; that human wolves prowled about her habitation and dogged her footsteps when she went abroad.

But even these perils had their compensations, for they gave an appearance of necessity to the constant companionship that my inclinations prompted. It was not a mere pilgrim of love that wended his way daily to Jacob Street, but an appointed guardian with duties to discharge. In the personally-conducted tours through the town, on business connected with the drawings that Winifred continued to produce with unabated industry, I was carrying out an indispensable function, since she was not permitted to go abroad without an efficient escort; and thus duty marched with pleasure.

Intimate, however, as my relations with Winifred had become, and recognised now even by Percy, I abstained from any confidences on the subject of our investigation of the murder. That was Thorndyke's affair, and although he had made no stipulation on the subject, I had the feeling that he expected me to keep my own counsel, as he certainly did himself. Accordingly, in describing our visit to Beauchamp Blake – in which both she and Percy were intensely interested – I said nothing about the man whom I had seen in Aylesbury.

One exception I had nearly made, but thought better of it. The occasion arose one afternoon when we were examining and criticising her latest drawing. As we stood before the easel, a shaft of sunlight, coming in through the great window, struck a part of the drawing and totally altered the character of the colouring. I remarked on the change of colour produced by the more intense illumination.

'Yes,' said she, 'and that reminds me of a very odd discovery that I made the other day and that I meant to tell you about.' She unfastened the silken cord by which she wore the mysterious locket suspended from her neck, and opening the little gold volume, held it in the sunbeam so that the light fell upon the coil of hair that it enclosed.

'Do you see?' she asked, looking at me expectantly.

'Yes,' I answered. 'In the sunlight the hair seems to have quite a distinct blue tint.'

'Exactly!' she exclaimed. 'Now isn't that very remarkable? I have often heard of blue-black hair, but I thought it was just a phrase expressing intense blackness without any tinge of brown. But this is really blue, quite a clear, rich blue, like the colour of deeply-toned stained glass. Do you suppose it is natural? It can hardly be a dye.'

It was then that I had nearly told her of Thorndyke's discovery and his strange and cryptic utterances on the subject. But a principle is a principle. The fact had been communicated to me by him, and I did not feel at liberty to disclose it without his sanction, though, to be sure, there was nothing confidential about it. His examination of the locket had been, apparently, a matter of mere curiosity. For Thorndyke was so constituted that he could not bring himself willingly to leave a problem unsolved, even though its solution promised no useful result. To him the solution was an end in itself, undertaken for the pleasure of the mental exercise. And this locket evidently held a secret. To what extent he had mastered that secret, I could not guess. Nor did I particularly care. It was not my secret, and I had no taste for working out irrelevant puzzles.

'I should hardly think the blue colour can be natural,' said I, and then, by way of compromise, I added: 'but I expect Thorndyke could tell you. When you come to see us again you had better show it to him and hear what he says about it.'

I took the locket from her hand and looked it over with half-impatient curiosity, remembering Thorndyke's exasperating advice; and recalling his reference to the hallmark on the back, I turned it over and scrutinised the minute device.

'You are looking at the hallmark, or the goldsmith's "touch," or whatever it is,' said Winifred. 'It is rather curious. I have never seen one like it before. It certainly is not an ordinary English hallmark. Let me get you a magnifying-glass.'

She fetched a strong reading-glass, and through this I examined the mark more minutely. But I could make nothing of it. It consisted of four punch-marks, of which the first was a capital A surmounted by a small crown and bearing two palm-leaves, the second a kind of escutcheon bearing the initials AH surmounted by a crown, and over that a fleur-de-lis; the third bore simply a capital L, and the fourth the head of some animal which looked like a horse.

'It is a curious and unusual mark,' said I, handing back to her the locket and the glass, 'but it conveys no information to me beyond the suggestion that the locket is apparently of foreign workmanship, probably French or Italian. But,' I added, with a malicious hope of seeing my reverend senior cornered, 'you had better ask Thorndyke about it when you come. He is sure to be able to tell you all about it.'

'He seems to be a sort of human encyclopaedia,' Winifred remarked as she refastened the locket. 'I shall adopt your advice and consult him about that hair, but I shan't be able to come this week. There is quite a big batch of drawings to be done, and that means some long working days. Perhaps you can arrange an afternoon in the latter part of next week for the oracular tea-party.'

I promised to ascertain my colleague's arrangements and to fix a day, but the promise was left unredeemed and the 'oracular tea-party' was thrust into the background by new and more stirring events, which began to cast their shadows before them that very evening. For, when I entered our chambers, behold Mr Brodribb and Sir Lawrence Drayton settled in armchairs by the fire, in company with the small table and the inevitable decanter. Evidently some kind of conference was in progress.

'Ha!' said Brodribb. 'Here is the fourth conspirator. Now we are complete. I have been devilling for your respected senior, Anstey, and I have called to report progress. Also, as you see, I have captured Sir Lawrence and brought him along as he seemed to be an interested party.'

'He is a somewhat mystified party at present,' said Drayton, 'but probably some explanations are contemplated.'

'They are going to begin as soon as Anstey has filled his glass,' said Brodribb, bearing in mind, no doubt, the laws of conviviality as expounded by Mrs Gamp; and as the stipulated condition was complied with, he proceeded: 'It was suggested to me by Thorndyke a short time ago that the tenure of the Beauchamp Blake property would be put on a more satisfactory footing if the missing title-deeds could be recovered.'

'More satisfactory to the present tenant, you mean,' said Drayton.

'More satisfactory to everybody,' said Brodribb.

'That would depend on the nature of the documents recovered,' Sir Lawrence remarked. 'But let us hear the rest of the suggestion.'

'The suggestion of our learned and Machiavellian friend was that, since the documents are believed to be hidden somewhere in the house, it would be a good plan to have a systematic survey of the premises carried out by some person who has an expert knowledge of secret chambers and hiding-places.'

'Do you know of any such person?' Drayton asked.

Brodribb smiled a fat smile and replenished his glass. 'I do,' he replied, 'and so do you. Thorndyke himself is quite an authority on the subject; and, of course, the suggestion was that the survey should be made and the search conducted by him. Naturally. You can guess why, I suppose?'

'I can't,' said Drayton, 'if you are suggesting any reason other than the one you have given'

'My dear Drayton,' chuckled Brodribb, 'can you imagine Thorndyke embarking on a search of this kind without some definite leading facts? No, no. Our friend has got something up his sleeve. I've no doubt that he knows exactly where to put his hand on those documents before he begins.'

'Do you, Thorndyke?' Sir Lawrence asked, with an inquisitive glance at my colleague.

'Now,' the latter replied, 'I put it to you, Drayton, whether it is likely that I, who have never been in this house in my life, have never seen a plan of it, and have no knowledge whatever of its internal construction or arrangement, can possibly know where these documents are hidden.'

'It certainly doesn't seem very probable,' Drayton admitted, and it certainly did not. But still I noted that Thorndyke's answer contained no specific denial, a circumstance that apparently did not escape Brodribb's observation, for that astute practitioner received the reply with an unabashed wink and wagged his head knowingly as he savoured his wine.

'You can think what you like,' said he, 'and so can I. However, to proceed: the suggestion was that I should put the proposal to the present tenant, Arthur Blake, and expound its advantages, but, of course, say nothing as to the source of the inspiration. Well, I did so. I wrote to him, pointing out the desirability of getting possession of the deeds, and suggesting that he should call at my office and talk the matter over.'

'And how did he take it?' asked Drayton.

'Very calmly – at first. He called at my office yesterday and opened the subject. But he didn't seem at all keen on it; thought it sounded rather like a wild-goose chase – until I mentioned Thorndyke. Then his interest woke up at once. The mention of a real, tangible expert put the matter on a different plane; gave it an air of reality. And he had heard of Thorndyke – read about him in the papers, I suppose – and, of course, I cracked him up. So in the end he became as keen as mustard and anxious to get a start made as soon as possible. And not only keen on his own account. To my surprise, he raised the question of the other claimant, Peter Blake's son. Of course he knew about Peter Blake's claim, although it was before his time, and it seems that he read the newspaper report of the curious statement that Miss Blake – Peter's daughter – made at the inquest on Sir Lawrence's brother. Well, in effect, he suggested – very properly, as I thought – that Miss Blake might like to be present when the search was made.'

'I certainly think,' said Drayton, 'she should be, if not actually present, at least represented. There might be some documents affecting her brother directly.'

'That was his point, and he authorised me to invite her to be present and to make all necessary arrangements. So the question is, Thorndyke, when can you go down and find the documents?'

'I am prepared to begin the search the day after tomorrow.'

'And with regard to Miss Blake? You are acquainted with her, I think?'

'Yes,' replied Thorndyke. 'We can communicate with her. But my feeling is that it would hardly be desirable for her to be present while the actual survey is being made. It may be a tedious affair, and we shall get on with it better without spectators. Of course I shall know if anything is found and shall probably ascertain its nature; and in that case she can be informed.'

Drayton nodded, but he did not seem quite satisfied. 'I suppose that will do,' said he, 'though I would rather that she were directly represented. You see, Thorndyke, you are acting for Blake, and if Anstey goes with you, he is your coadjutor. I wonder if Blake would object to my looking in later in the day. I could, as I have to go down to Aylesbury the day after tomorrow. What do you say, Brodribb?'

'I see no objection,' was the reply, 'in fact, I will take the responsibility of inviting you to call and see what progress has been made.'

'Very well, then,' said Drayton, 'I will come about four. I shall go down by car, and when I have finished with my client, I can easily take Beauchamp Blake on my way home. And for that matter,' he added, 'I don't see why Miss Blake shouldn't come with me. My client's wife could entertain her while I am transacting the business, and then she could come on with me to the house. How does that strike you, Thorndyke?'

'It seems quite an admirable arrangement,' my colleague replied. 'She will be saved the tedium of waiting about and she will have the advantage of your advice if any delicate inquiries have to be made.'

Drayton's suggestion was accordingly adopted, subject to Winifred's consent – which I did not doubt she would give readily, notwithstanding the pressure of her work – and shortly afterwards our two friends took their departure, leaving me a little puzzled as to the origin and purpose of the conference and the projected expedition.

It had been a rather curious transaction. There were several points that I failed to understand. In the first place, what interest had Thorndyke in these title-deeds? Assuming him to take Percy's rather indefinite claim seriously – which he apparently did – was the establishment of the title desirable from his point of view? I should have thought not. It had appeared that Blake was anxious to sell the property and had been restrained only by the insecurity of the title. But if the title were made secure, he would almost certainly sell the estate, which was the last thing that Percy's advisers could wish. Then could it be that our shrewd old friend Brodribb was right? That Thorndyke had actually ascertained or inferred the whereabouts of the missing deeds. In the case of any other person the supposition would have seemed ridiculous. But Thorndyke's power of reasoning from apparently unilluminating facts was so extraordinary that the possibility had to be admitted, and his evasive reply to Drayton's direct question seemed to make it even probable.

'I don't see,' said I, with a faint hope of extracting some trifle of information from Thorndyke, 'why you are so keen on these title-deeds.'

'That,' he replied, 'is because you persist in thinking in sections. If you would take a larger view of the subject this proposed search would appear to you in a rather different light.'

'I wonder if there is really going to be a search,' I said craftily, 'or whether old Brodribb was right. I am inclined to suspect that he was.'

'I commend your respect for Brodribb's opinions,' he replied. 'Our friend is an uncommonly wide-awake old gentleman. But he was only guessing. Whatever we find at Beauchamp Blake – if we find anything – will be discovered by *bona fide* research and experiment. And that raises another question. Are you going down with Drayton or did you propose to come with me?'

'I don't want to be in your way,' I replied, a little piqued at the question. 'Otherwise I should, of course, have liked to come with you.'

'Your help would be very valuable,' said he, 'if you are willing to sacrifice the other attractions. But if you are going to help me, we had better take a little preliminary practice together. There is a set of empty chambers next door. Tomorrow I will get the keys from the treasurer's office, and we can put in some spare time making careful measured plans. The whole art of discovering secret chambers is in the making of plans so exact as to account for every inch of space, and showing accurately the precise thickness of every wall and floor. And a little practice in the art of opening locked doors without the aid of keys will not be amiss.'

This programme was duly carried out. On the morrow we conveyed into the empty chambers a plane table covered with drawing-paper, a surveyor's tape, and a measuring-rod; and with these appliances, I proceeded, under Thorndyke's direction, to make a scaled plan of the set of rooms, showing the exact thickness of all the walls and the spaces occupied by chimneys, cupboards, and all kinds of projections and irregularities. It was a longer business than I had expected; indeed I did not get it completed until the evening was closing in, and when at last I had filled in the final details and took the completed plan to our chambers for Thorndyke's inspection, I found my colleague busily engaged in preparations for the morrow's adventure.

'Well!' I exclaimed, when my plan had been examined and replaced by a fresh sheet of paper, 'this is an extraordinary outfit! I hope we shan't have to carry this case home after dark.'

It was certainly a most sinister collection of appliances that Thorndyke had assembled in the suitcase. There was a brace and bits, and auger, a bunch of skeleton keys, an electric lantern, a pair of telescopic jemmies, and two automatic pistols.

'What on earth are the pistols for?' I demanded.

'Those,' he replied, 'are just an extra precaution. Many of these hiding-holes are fitted with snap locks, and it is quite possible to find oneself caught in a trap. Then, if there should be no room to use a jemmy, it might be necessary to blow the lock to pieces.'

'Well,' I remarked, 'it is as well to take all necessary precautions, but if Blake sees those pistols they will need a good deal of explaining, especially as he will certainly recognise us as the two suspicious visitors.'

'We need not exhibit them ostentatiously,' said Thorndyke. 'We can carry them in our pockets, and the jemmies as well. Then if the necessity to use them arises, they will explain themselves.'

The rest of the evening we spent in a course of instruction in the arrangement and design of the various kinds of secret chambers, hiding-holes, aumbries, and receptacles for documents, sacred vessels, and other objects that, in times of political upheaval, might need to be concealed. On this subject Thorndyke was a mine of information, and he produced a note-book filled with descriptions, plans, sections, and photographs of most of the examples that had been examined, which we went over together and studied in the minutest detail. By the end of the evening, I had not only acquired an immense amount of knowledge on an obscure out-of-the-way subject, but I had become in so far infected with Thorndyke's enthusiasm that I found myself looking forward almost eagerly to the romantic quest on which the following day was to see us launched.

CHAPTER SEVENTEEN
The Secret Chamber

It was close on half-past eleven when our train drew up in Wendover Station. We had just finished our rather premature lunch and had packed up the luncheon baskets and placed them on the seats; and now, lifting down the suitcase and the plane table with its folding tripod, stepped out on to the platform.

'I wonder,' said I, 'if Blake has sent any kind of conveyance for us. I don't suppose he has.'

My surmise turned out to be correct. When we went out into the station approach, the only vehicle in sight was a closed fly, which we decided to charter; and having stowed our impedimenta on the front seat and given the driver the necessary directions, we entered and took possession of the back seat. The coachman climbed to the box and started the horse at a quiet jog-trot, turning into the Aylesbury, or London Road to avoid the steep hill down which we had come to the station on the last occasion. As we passed the fine, brick-towered windmill and came out on the country road, Thorndyke leaned forward and opened the suitcase.

'We had better put the more suspicious-looking objects in our pockets,' said he. 'We may not want them at all, and then they won't have been seen, whereas if they are wanted, the necessity will explain our having provided ourselves with them.'

He took out the bunch of skeleton keys and slipped them into his coat pocket, and then picked out the two telescopic jemmies, one of

202

which he handed to me while he bestowed the other in some kind of interior pocket – into which, I noticed, it disappeared with singular completeness, suggesting a suspicious suitability of the receptacle. Finally he took out the two automatic pistols, and having pocketed one, handed me the other after a careful and detailed explanation of its mechanism and the proper way to hold and fire it. I took the weapon from him and stowed it in my hip-pocket, very gingerly and with some reluctance, for I detest firearms; and as I placed it carefully with the muzzle pointed as far as possible away from my own person, I reflected once more with dim surprise on the circumstance that Thorndyke, whose dislike of these weapons was as great as my own, should have adopted this clumsy and dangerous means of dealing with a somewhat remote contingency. It seemed an excessive precaution, and I found creeping into my mind a faint suspicion that my colleague might possibly have had something more in his mind than he had disclosed, though that was even more incomprehensible, considering the very peaceful nature of our quest.

I was still turning these matters over in my mind when the fly reached the crossroads and entered the lane. Here the appearance of the inn just ahead recalled me to our immediate business, and old Brodribb's observation recurred to me.

'How are you going to start, Thorndyke?' I asked. 'I presume you have got some definite programme?'

'I shall be guided by what Blake has to tell us,' he replied. 'He may have a good plan of the house, and it is possible that he has made some explorations of his own which will give us a start. There is our old friend, the lodge-keeper, mightily surprised to see us.'

I caught a passing glimpse of the sleuth, staring at us in undisguised astonishment; then we swung round into the drive, and the old house came into view. We were evidently expected, for as we approached the house a man came out of the main entrance and stood on the wide threshold awaiting our arrival. Just as the fly was about to draw up opposite the portico, Thorndyke said in a low voice:

'If we are offered any refreshments, Anstey, we had better decline them. We have had lunch, you know.'

I glanced at him in amazement. It was a most astonishing remark. But there was no time to ask for any explanation, for at that moment the fly drew up, the driver jumped down from his seat, and the squire came forward to receive us.

'We have met before, I think,' said the latter as we shook hands. 'If I had known who you were I should have invited you to look at the house then. However, it isn't too late. I see you have brought your traps with you,' he added, with a glance at the plane table and its tripod.

'Yes,' said Thorndyke, 'we are prepared to make a regular survey, if necessary. But perhaps you have a plan of the house?'

'There is a plan,' replied Blake, 'though I fancy it is not very exact. I will show it to you. Probably it will give you a hint where to begin.'

As I had now settled with the fly-man, we entered the house, and Blake conducted us into a large room, furnished as a library and containing a considerable collection of books. On a table by one of the windows was a plan spread out and held open by paperweights.

'You see,' said Blake, 'this is an architect's plan, made, I think, when some repairs were contemplated. It is little more than a sketch, and doesn't give much detail. But it will help you to take a preliminary look round before lunch.'

'We have had lunch,' said Thorndyke. 'We got that over in the train so that we should have a clear day before us. Time is precious, and we ought to get to work at once. I suppose you have not made any sort of investigation on your own account?'

As Thorndyke mentioned our premature meal, the squire gave him a quick glance and seemed to look a little resentful. But he made no comment beyond answering the question.

'I have not made any regular examination of the house, but I have poked about a little in the old part and I have found one secret chamber, which I have utilised as a photographic dark-room. Perhaps you would like to see that first. There may be some other hiding-places connected with it which I have overlooked. There is a tall cupboard in it which I have used to store my chemicals.'

'We may have to empty that cupboard to see if there is anything behind it,' said Thorndyke. 'At any rate, we had better begin by overhauling it.'

He opened the suitcase and took from it the surveyor's tape, which he put in his pocket.

'Hadn't we better take the lamp?' said I.

'You won't want that,' said Blake. 'There is a portable lamp in the room.'

I was half-inclined to take it, nevertheless, but as Thorndyke shut the suitcase and prepared to follow our host, I let the matter rest.

From the library we passed out into a long gallery, one side of which was hung with portraits, presumably of members of the family, and some of them of considerable antiquity, to judge by the style of the painting and the ancient costumes. Then we crossed several rooms – fine, stately apartments with florid, moulded ceilings and walls of oaken panelling, on which I noticed a very respectable display of pictures. The rooms were fully furnished – very largely, I noticed, with the oak and walnut furniture that must have been put in when the new wing was built. But they were all pervaded by a sense of desolation and neglect; they were dusty and looked faded, unused, and forgotten. Nowhere was there a sign of human occupation, nor, I noticed, did we meet, in the whole course of our journey across this part of the house, a single servant or retainer, or, indeed, any living creature whatever.

A door at the end of a short passage, on being unlocked and opened, revealed a short flight of wooden stairs, and when we had descended these we found ourselves in a totally different atmosphere. This was the old timber house, and as we crossed its deserted rooms and trod its uncarpeted oaken floors, our footsteps resounded with dismal echoes among the empty chambers and corridors, conveying a singular sense of remoteness and desolation. The gloomy old rooms with their dirt-encrusted casements, the massive beams in their ceilings, the blackened wainscoting, rich with carved ornament but shrouded with the dust and grime of years of neglect, the gouty-legged Elizabethan tables and ponderous oaken chairs and settles; all these dusty and forgotten appurtenances of a vanished generation of men seemed to have died with their long-departed human associates and to be silently awaiting their final decay and dissolution. It was an eerie place, dead and desolate as an Egyptian tomb.

And yet, strangely enough, it was here that I saw the one solitary sign of human life. We were passing along a narrow gallery or corridor when I noticed, high up in the panelled wall, one of those small interior windows which one sees in old houses, placed opposite an exterior window to light an inner chamber. Looking up at this little window, I saw the face of some person looking down on us. It was the merest glimpse that I caught, for the window was coated with dust and the room behind it in darkness. But there was the face of some human creature, man, woman, or child, and its appearance in this remote, sepulchral place, so far from the domain of the living household, smote upon me strangely and seemed to make even more intense the uncanny solitude of the empty mansion.

I was still speculating curiously on who this watcher might be, when our host halted by the wall of a smallish room.

'This is the place,' said he, pointing to the wall. 'I wonder if you can find the door.'

The wainscoting in this room was nearly plain, the only ornament being a range of very flat pilasters and a dado moulding, enriched by a row of hemispherical bosses. Thorndyke ran his eye over the wainscoting, noting more particularly the way in which the pilasters were joined to the intervening panels.

'I suppose,' said he, 'we had better try the most obvious probabilities first. The natural thing would be to use one of these bosses to cover the release of the lock.'

Blake assented (or dissented) with an inarticulate grunt, and Thorndyke then proceeded to pass along the row of bosses, pressing each one firmly in turn. After about a dozen trials, he came to one in the middle of a pilaster which yielded to the pressure of his thumb, sinking in some two inches, in the fashion of a large electric-bell push. Holding the 'push' in with his thumb, he pressed vigorously against the adjoining panel, first on one side of the pilaster and then on the other, but in neither case was there any sign of the panel moving, though I added my weight to his.

'You haven't quite hit it off yet,' Blake informed us.

Thorndyke reflected for a few seconds. Then, keeping the boss pressed in, he put his other thumb on the next one of the series, which was at the edge of the panel, and gave a sharp push, whereupon this boss also sank in with an audible click and then the whole panel swung inward, disclosing a narrow and wonderfully well-concealed doorway.

'Good,' said Blake. 'You've solved the problem more quickly than I did. Just hold the door open a moment. It has rather a strong spring, and I generally prop it open with this block.' As he spoke he fetched a small block of wood from under an adjacent table and set it against the foot of the door.

'I had better go first,' said he, 'as I know where to find the lamp.' With this he entered before us, striking a wax match and shading it with his hand. The dim illumination showed a narrow, passage-like room, apparently a good deal more lofty than the low-ceiled room from which we had entered it, and dimly revealed a very high cupboard near the farther end. We had grouped our way after him a few paces when he turned suddenly. 'How stupid of me!' he exclaimed. 'I had forgotten that I had left the lamp in the next room. Excuse me one moment.'

He slipped past us, and kicking the block away, ran out, pulling the door sharply after him, when it slammed to with a loud click of the latch.

'What the deuce did he kick that block away for,' I exclaimed, 'and leave us all in the dark?'

'We shall probably find out presently,' replied Thorndyke. 'Meanwhile, stand perfectly still. Don't move hand or foot.'

'Why do you say that?' I demanded with something like a thrill of alarm, for there was something rather disturbing in the tone of Thorndyke's sharply-spoken command. And standing there in the pitchy darkness, locked in a secret chamber in the very heart of this great, empty mansion, there came to me a flash of sudden suspicion. I recalled Thorndyke's mysterious warning to take no food in this house; I remembered the loaded pistol that he had put into my hand, and I saw again that unaccountable face at the window, watching us as Blake led us — whither? 'You don't think Blake is up to any mischief, do you?' I asked.

'I can't say,' he replied. 'Perhaps he will come with the lamp presently. But we may as well see where we are while we are waiting.'

I heard a rustling as if he were searching his pockets. Then, suddenly, there broke out a bright light that flooded the little room and rendered all the objects in it plainly visible.

It was a queer-looking room, almost more like a rather irregularly-shaped passage, for none of the walls were straight, and the ceiling sloped up from a height of about eight feet at one end to nearly twelve at the other. Near the farther end was a very high wall-cupboard, and at the extreme end, facing us, was a small door, about three feet above the floor level and approached by a flight of five wooden stairs.

The appearance of the light was reassuring, and still more so was the evidence that it afforded of Thorndyke's foresight in having provided himself with this supplementary lamp. But much less reassuring was his next observation after having flashed his light all over the room.

'I suspect we have seen the last of our host – for the present, at any rate. Look at the top of the cupboard, Anstey.'

I looked at the cupboard. It was between eight and nine feet high, and was fitted with folding doors, of which the leaf nearest to us was half open; and on the top of the half-open door, near the free corner, a little board had been placed with one end resting on the door and the other insecurely supported by the moulding at the top of the cupboard; and on the board, delicately balanced over the door, was a large chemical flask, filled with what looked like water and fitted with a cork.

'What do you make of it?' Thorndyke asked, keeping his powerful inspection-lamp focused on the flask as I gazed at it.

'It looks like some sort of booby-trap,' said I. 'It is a wonder that flask wasn't shaken down when Blake slammed the door.'

'He probably expected that it would be, and it very nearly was, for you can see that it has jarred to the extreme edge. But failing the slam of the door, he no doubt assumes that we, being as he imagines in total darkness, shall grope our way along the wall until we come to the cupboard. Then, the instant we touch the door, down will come the flask. It is quite an ingenious plan.'

'But what is the purpose of it?' I demanded. 'It can't be a practical joke.'

'It isn't,' said he. 'Far from it. I should say it is very deadly earnest. If I am not mistaken, that flask is filled with some volatile poison. The instant that it falls and breaks, this room will become a lethal chamber.'

At these words, uttered by Thorndyke in tones as calm and emotionless as if he were giving a demonstration to his students, a chill of horror crept over me. My very hair seemed to stir. It was an appalling situation. I stared in dismay and terror at the flask, poised aloft and ready, as it seemed, at the slightest movement, or even a loudly-spoken word, to come crashing down and stifle us with its deadly fumes.

'Great God!' I gasped. 'Then we are in a trap! But is there nothing that we can do? The flask is too high up for us to reach it.'

'It would be sheer insanity to go near it,' said Thorndyke. 'But I don't think we need be very disturbed. There must be some way of getting out of this chamber. Let us go and reconnoitre the door, though I daresay our friend has attended to that.'

We tiptoed cautiously back to the door and examined its construction. The mechanism was very simple, but like most old locksmith's work, extremely massive. The two bosses outside evidently were the ends of two sliding bars and bolts of wood. The one which Thorndyke had pressed first apparently had a slot which, when it was brought opposite the massive latch, allowed the latter to rise. That at least was what Thorndyke inferred, for, as the latch was in the thickness of the great oaken doorpost (which had a slot to let it escape, when raised) the actual mechanism could not be seen. The second sliding bar, when pushed in, raised the latch itself by means of an inclined plane. Both the sliding bars had been provided with knobs on their inner ends, so that they could be pulled in from inside as well as pushed in from without; but whereas the knob still remained on the bar which raised the latch, that of the bar which released the latch and allowed it to rise had been removed. The end of the bar could be seen, nearly flush with the surface of the doorpost, and in it a small hole in which the knob had evidently been screwed.

'Would it be possible to hook anything, such as a skeleton key, into that hole?' I asked when we had examined it thoroughly.

'I think we can do better than that,' said he, hooking the bull's-eye of his inspection-lamp in a button-hole of his coat and feeling in his pocket. 'This is a more workmanlike appliance.'

He exhibited an appliance that looked like a kind of clasp-knife, but was actually a pocket set of screw-taps, such as are carried by engineers and plumbers. Drawing out the smallest tap, he tried it in the hole, but the latter was too small to admit it. Then, from the same appliance, he drew out a taper reamer, and on trying this in the hole he found that the point entered easily. He accordingly drove it in lightly, rotating it as he pressed, and continued to turn it until the sharp-cutting tool had broached out the hole to a size that would admit the nose of the tap, when he withdrew the reamer, and inserting the tap, gave it a few vigorous turns. Now, on pulling gently at the handle of the tap, it was seen to be fast in the hole, and the sliding bar began to move forward.

'I wonder if our host is hanging about outside,' said he.

'What does it matter whether he is or not?' I asked.

'Because I want to try whether we can open the door, and I don't want him to hear.'

'But, confound it,' said I, 'he will see us when we come out.'

'We are not going to come out that way if we can find any other.'

'Why not?' I demanded. 'We want to get clear of that infernal flask, and the sooner we are out the better.'

'Not at all,' said Thorndyke. 'If we come out and show ourselves, the game is up, and there will probably be trouble. Whereas if we can get out another way, we shall put him in a very pretty dilemma. Hearing no sound from us, he will probably assume that his plan has succeeded. And if Drayton should arrive before he has taken the risk of verifying our decease, his explanations should be rather interesting. At any rate, I should like to see what his next move will be, but we must make our retreat secure in case of accidents. I think we can raise the latch without making any noticeable sound. You observe that the pivot has been oiled – and also that the door-spring is new and has apparently been fixed on quite recently.'

In my heart I cursed his inquiring spirit, for I wanted to get out of this horrible trap. But I offered no objection, standing by sullenly while he proceeded with calm interest to complete his experiment. Grasping the tap-handle with one hand and the knob with the other, he pulled steadily at the former until the sliding bar was drawn inwards to its full extent, and then at the knob, which came in with similar ease and silence. But when I saw the latch rise and the door begin to swing inwards, I could hardly restrain myself from dragging it open and making a burst for freedom.

The next moment the opportunity was gone. With the same silent care Thorndyke reclosed the door, let the latch down, and slid back the release bar.

'Now,' said he, turning away but leaving the tap jammed in the hole, 'we can pursue our investigations at our ease. If there is no other exit, we can come out this way, and we have got a clear retreat in case of accidents. What does the appearance of this place suggest to you? I mean as to an exit.'

'Well,' I answered, 'there is a door at the top of those steps. Presumably its function is the ordinary function of a door.'

'I doubt it,' said he. 'It is too blatantly innocent. More probably its function was to occupy pursuers while the fugitive was gaining a start. Still, we will have a thorough look at it, as I expect our host has already done. We had better go one at time, and for Heaven's sake step lightly, and remember that if that flask should come down, you make a bee-line for the door and get outside instantly.'

211

Lighted by Thorndyke's lamp, I crept cautiously along the room with my eyes riveted on the flask and my heart in my mouth. Then Thorndyke followed, and together we ascended the steps to the door, and proceeded to examine it minutely. It was provided with plainly visible H-hinges but had no ostensible latch or lock. Around it were a number of projecting ends of tree-nails, but pressure on them, one after the other, produced no result, nor did the door itself show any sign of yielding; indeed, the form of the hinges suggested that it opened inwards – towards the room – if it would open at all.

'We are wasting time, Anstey,' Thorndyke said at length. 'The thing is a dummy, as we might have expected. Let us try something more likely. Now, from what I know of these secret chambers, I should say that the most probable exits are the cupboard and the stairs. Both, you notice, seem to be functionless. There is no reason for that great cupboard having been built in here, and these stairs simply lead to a dummy door. And cupboards with sliding shelves and concealed doors in the back, and stairs with movable treads were very favourite devices. The cupboard is unfortunately not practicable while that flask is balanced overhead, so we had better give our attention to the stairs. I suspect that there are two exits, in different directions, but either will do for us.'

We stole softly down the stairs, and stooping on hands and knees, brought the light to bear on the joints of the treads and risers; but the dirt of ages had settled on them and filled up any tell-tale cracks that might have been visible. To my eye, the steps looked all alike, and all seemed to be solid oak planks immovably fixed in their positions.

Suddenly Thorndyke dived into his inner pocket and brought forth the telescopic jemmy, which he pulled out to its full length. Then, laying the chisel end on the tread of the bottom stair, he drove its edge forcibly against the angle where the tread and the riser met. To my surprise, the edge entered fully half an inch into the joint, which the dirt had filled and concealed.

'Get your jemmy, Anstey, and push it in by the side of mine,' said he.

I produced the tool from my breast pocket, where it had been reposing to my great discomfort, and opening it out, I inserted its edge close to that of Thorndyke's.

'Now,' said he, 'both together. Push!'

We both bore heavily on the ends of the jemmies, and the sharp chisel ends entered fully an inch; and simultaneously a visible crack appeared along the foot of the riser. We now withdrew the jemmies and reinserted them at the two ends of the tread. Again we drove in together, and the crack widened perceptibly. On this, Thorndyke rose and closely examined the angle of the step above and then that of the third, and here, as he brought the bull's-eye close to the surface of the step, I could see that a narrow crack had opened between the step and the riser.

'It looks,' said I, 'as if the two steps had shifted.'

'Yes,' he agreed, 'and apparently the pivot, if there is one, is above. Let us get to work again.'

We reinserted the jemmies several times in different places, thrusting together and as forcibly as we dared with that horrible flask insecurely balanced above our heads; and at each thrust there was an appreciable widening of the crack, which had now opened fully a quarter of an inch, making it evident that the stairs were really movable.

'Now,' said Thorndyke, 'I think we might venture to prise.'

He reversed his jemmy and inserted the 'crow' end into the crack near one extremity, while I inserted mine near the opposite end. Then, at a word from him, we bore on the ends of the levers, and with a protesting groan, the step rose another inch. Thorndyke now laid aside his jemmy, and standing on the bottom step, thrust his fingers into the gaping crack; I did the same, and when we had got a fair grasp, he gave the word.

'Now, both together. Up she comes!'

We both heaved steadily but not too violently. There was a grinding creak as the long-disused joint moved; then suddenly the two steps swung up and stood nearly upright on their pivot, disclosing a yawning hole in which the light showed a narrow flight of brick steps.

Thorndyke immediately stepped in through the opening, and descending a few steps, turned and held the light for me, when I followed.

The steps fell away steeply down a kind of well with walls of brickwork, which was thickly encrusted with slimy growths of algae and fungi, and the steps themselves were slippery with a similar coating and were almost hidden, in places, by great fungous masses which sprouted from the joints of the brickwork. After descending about eight feet, we reached a level floor and proceeded along a narrow brick tunnel, stooping to clear the slime-covered roof. This extended some fifteen yards and ended in what at first looked like a blank wall. On coming close, however, and throwing on it the light of the lantern, I perceived an oblong space of planking about five feet long by three high and three feet above the floor, forming a rude door, very massive and clumsy and furnished with a simple, roughly-fashioned iron latch.

'I don't see any hinges,' observed Thorndyke, 'so there is probably an internal pivot. Let us prise up the latch first and then see how the door moves.'

He slipped the end of his jemmy under the latch, taking a bearing on the brickwork, and levered the great latch up without much difficulty in spite of the rust that had locked it in position. Then, inserting the chisel end into the crack between the door and the jamb, he gave a tentative wrench, when the door moved perceptibly, inwards at one end and outwards at the other.

'It is evidently pivoted in the middle,' said he. 'If you will prise the other end while I work at this, we shall get it open easily.'

We accordingly inserted our jemmies at the respective ends and gave a steady thrust; on which the door, with a deep groan and a loud screech from the rusty pivots, swung round on its centre, letting in a flood of cheerful daylight and fresh air, which I inhaled with profound relief. A vigorous pull on the edge brought the door fully open and disclosed a mass of foliage which blocked the view from within and no doubt concealed the door from outside. But in any case it would have been very inconspicuous, for we could now see that the solid planking was covered externally with counterfeit brickwork, very convincingly executed with slices of brick.

Thorndyke reached out and pulled aside a branch of the tree that obscured the view. 'This door,' said he, 'seems to open on the edge of the moat, so it was probably made at a time when the moat was full of water. However, we have found our way out, and it is a better one than the cupboard would have given us, for, if that has an exit in the back, it probably leads up to the garrets or the chimneys. Now all we have to do is to remove our traces from the chamber above and make our way out. But there is no need for you to come up.'

'I am coming up all the same,' said I, and as he turned to re-enter the tunnel, I followed, though I admit, with infinite reluctance. But I did not actually re-enter the chamber. I stood with my head out of the opening and a terrified eye on the accursed flask, while Thorndyke tiptoed across the room to the door. Here he withdrew the tap from the hole, and folding it, dropped it into his pocket. Then he stooped and blew away the wood-dust that had fallen from the reamer on to the floor, and having thus removed every trace (excepting the broached-out hole in the sliding bar), he stepped lightly back and re-entered the opening.

'The problem now,' said he, 'is to get these stairs back in their place without shaking down the flask.'

'Does it matter,' I asked, 'now that we have a means of escape?'

'Not very much,' he answered, 'but I would rather leave it there in evidence.'

The movable stairs were furnished with a rough wooden handle on the underside to enable a fugitive to replace them from below. This Thorndyke grasped, and with a steady pull, drew the stairs down into their original position, giving a final tug to bring the joints close together. Then once more we began to descend the slippery steps.

We were about half-way down when Thorndyke stopped.

'Listen, Anstey,' said he, switching off the light. And as he spoke, I caught the sound of footsteps somewhere overhead. Then I heard the door of the secret chamber open slowly – I could recognise it by the sound of the door-spring – and after a little interval, Blake's voice called out:

'Dr Thorndyke! Mr Anstey! Where are you?'

Again there was a short pause. The door slowly opened a little farther, the floor above creaked under a stealthy tread, and then I seemed to catch faintly another voice, apparently more distant.

'They are not here,' said Blake. 'They seem to have got out somehow. Here, catch hold of the lamp. Mind the door! Mind the – '

The door-spring creaked. There was a heavy thud, and an instant later the sound of shattering glass, followed by a startled shout and a hurried trampling of feet.

'The knob! The knob! Quick!' a high-pitched voice shrieked; and at that the very marrow in my bones seemed to creep. For the knob was useless now. Thorndyke's reamer had destroyed the screw-hole.

With the sweat streaming down my face and my heart thumping with sickening violence, I listened to the torrent of curses, rising to yells of terror and anguish and mingled with strange, whimpering cries. I could see it all with horrible distinctness: the two trapped wretches above, frantically turning the knob in the broached-out hole while the poisonous fumes rose remorselessly and encompassed them.

The cries grew thicker and more muffled, and mingled with dreadful coughs and gasps. Then there was a sound of a heavy body falling on the floor and a horrible husky screech broke out, whereat I felt the hair of my scalp stir like the fur of a frightened cat. Three times that appalling screech came through the floor to our pitch-dark lurking-place, the last time dying away into a hideous, quavering wail. Then, once more, there was the thud of a heavy body falling on the floor, and after that an awful silence.

'God Almighty!' I gasped. 'Can't we do anything, Thorndyke?'

'Yes,' he replied, 'we can get out of this. It is time we did.'

Even as he spoke I became aware of a faint odour of bitter almonds which seemed every moment to grow more distinct. It was undoubtedly time for us to be gone; and when, once more, the light of his lamp flashed down the stairway, I responded readily to a gentle push and began to descend the steps as rapidly as my trembling knees would let me.

The faint, sinister odour pursued us even to the tunnel and it was with a sigh of relief that I reached the open doorway and looked again on the sky-lit foliage and breathed the wholesome air. We crept out together through the long, low doorway, and grasping the branches of the trees and bushes outside, scrambled down the sloping bank to the dry floor of the moat.

CHAPTER EIGHTEEN

The Cat's Eye

When we stood up at the bottom of the bank, I turned to Thorndyke and asked:

'What are we going to do now? We must make some effort to let those poor devils out.'

'That,' he replied, 'is an impossibility. In the first place they are certainly dead by now, and in the second it would be certain death to attempt to open that door. The chamber is full of the vapour of hydrocyanic acid.'

'But,' I expostulated, 'we ought to do something. Humanity demands that we should, at least, make a show of trying to save them.'

'I don't see why,' he replied coldly. 'They are certainly dead, and if they were not, I would not risk a single hair of my head to save their lives. Still, if you have any feeling on the matter, we can go and reconnoitre. But we must look to our own safety.'

He struck out along the floor of the moat at a brisk pace, and I kept up with him as well as my trembling knees would let me, for I was horribly shaken by the shocking experiences of the last few minutes, and still felt sick and faint. Thorndyke, on the other hand, was perfectly unmoved, and as he strode along at my side, I glanced at his calm face and found in his quiet, unconcerned manner something inhuman and repelling. It is true that those two wretches who now lay stark and dead on the floor of that dreadful chamber deserved no sympathy. They had digged a pit for us and fallen into it themselves.

But still, they were human beings, and their lives were human lives; but Thorndyke seemed to value them no more than if they had been a couple of rats.

About a hundred yards farther along the moat, we came to a cross path, at each end of which was a flight of rough steps up the bank. We ascended the steps on the house side, and these brought us to a small door with a Tudor arch in the head. A modern night-latch had been added to the ancient lock, but it was a simple affair which Thorndyke's picklock opened in a few moments, and the door then yielded to a push. It opened into a corridor which I recognised as the one which we had passed through and where I had seen the face at the window – a dead face it was now, I suspected. We turned and walked along it in the direction in which Blake had led us, and as we neared the end I began to be sensible of a faint odour in the musty air; an attenuated scent of bitter almonds.

'We must go warily,' said Thorndyke. 'The next room, I think, is the one out of which the secret chamber opens.'

He paused and stood looking dubiously at the door; and as he stood hesitating, I pushed past him, and seizing the handle, flung the door open and looked into the room. But it was only an instantaneous glance, showing me the uninterrupted wall, the wooden block lying where Blake had kicked it, and close by, a dead rat. The sight of that little corpse and the sickening smell of bitter almonds that suddenly grew strong in the air as the door opened, produced an instant revulsion. My concern for our would-be murderers was extinguished by a thrill of alarm for my own safety. I drew the door to hurriedly and followed Thorndyke, who was walking quickly away.

'It is no use, Anstey,' he said, a little impatiently. 'It is mere sentiment, and a silly one at that. All we can do is to open these windows and clear off until the gas has diffused out. It won't take so very long with all the gaping joints in this old woodwork.'

'And what are we going to do meanwhile?'

'We must find the housekeeper, if there is one, and let her know the state of affairs. Then we must send information to the police at Aylesbury, and before they arrive, I think it would be well to prepare a written statement, which we can sign in their presence and which should contain all that we are prepared to say about the matter before the inquest.'

'Yes,' I agreed, 'that seems to be the best course'; and with this we proceeded to open the rusty casements of the corridor and then made our way back to the new wing of the house.

The inn-keeper had certainly been right. Squire Blake had been very far from lavish in the matter of retainers. One after another of the great, dusty rooms we crossed or peered into without encountering a single serving-man or maid. The house seemed to be utterly deserted. At last we came to the entrance hall, and here, as we stood commenting on this extraordinary solitude, a door opened and a faded and shabby elderly woman, looking like a rather superior charwoman, emerged. She looked at us curiously and then asked:

'Can you tell me, sir, if Mr Blake is ready for lunch?'

'I am sorry to say,' replied Thorndyke, 'that Mr Blake has met with a mishap. He has locked himself in his dark room and has poisoned himself accidentally with some chemicals.'

'Oh dear!' exclaimed the woman, looking at Thorndyke with a sort of stupefied dismay. 'Hadn't some one better go and fetch him out?'

'That is not possible at present,' said Thorndyke. 'The room is full of poison gas.'

'But,' the woman protested, 'he may die if no one goes to his assistance.'

'He is dead already,' said Thorndyke, 'and there is another person in the room with him, who is also dead'.

'That will be Mr Meyer, his valet,' said the woman, staring at Thorndyke with a sort of bewildered horror, puzzled, no doubt, by the incongruity between his tragic tidings and his calm, matter-of-fact demeanour. 'And you say they have both killed themselves! Lord! Lord! What a dreadful thing!' She clasped her hands, and gazing helplessly from one of us to the other, asked: 'What are we to do? Oh! what are we to do?'

'Is there any one whom we could send into Aylesbury?' asked Thorndyke, 'We ought to let the police know of the accident, and we ought to get a doctor.'

'There is only the lodge-keeper,' she whimpered shakily. 'He could go on Mr Meyer's bicycle. Dear! dear! what an awful thing it is!'

'If you will have the bicycle brought to the door,' said Thorndyke, 'I will write a note and take it up to the lodge-keeper myself. There are writing materials in the library I suppose?'

She supposed there were, and showed us into the room, where we found some notepaper and envelopes. Then she departed, wringing her hands and muttering, to fetch the bicycle.

'I shall not give any details in this note,' Thorndyke said as he sat down at the table and uncapped his fountain pen. 'I shall just tell them that Mr Blake and his valet have met their deaths – presumably – by poisoning; that it is a police case, and that the Divisional Surgeon had better accompany the police officer.'

With this he wrote the note, addressing it to the Superintendent or Chief Constable, and he had just closed and sealed it when the woman reappeared to announce the arrival of the bicycle, which had been brought to the door by a young woman, apparently a housemaid. Thorndyke mounted the machine and rode away swiftly up the drive, and I turned back into the house, followed by the two women, who, now that the first shock had spent itself, were devoured by curiosity and eager to extract information.

Their efforts in this direction, however, were not very successful, for, although the facts must very soon become public property, it seemed desirable at present to say as little as possible; while, as for any explanation of this extraordinary affair, I was as much in the dark as they were. So I maintained a discreet, though difficult, reticence until Thorndyke reappeared, when the two women retired and left us in possession of the room.

'I sent our friend off with the note,' said my colleague, 'and I told him enough to make sure that he will put on the pace. It is only about four miles, and as the police probably have a car, we may expect them pretty soon. I will just draft out a statement of the actual occurrences, and you had better write, on the same paper, a confirmatory declaration. We can read them to the officer and sign them in his presence.'

He proceeded to write out a concise, but fairly full, narrative of what had befallen us in this house, with a brief statement of the nature of our business here, and when I had read it through, I wrote at the foot a paragraph confirming the statement and accepting it as my own. This occupied some considerable time, and we had not long finished when there was a somewhat peremptory ring at the bell, and a minute later, the elderly woman – whom I assumed to be the housekeeper – entered, accompanied by a police officer and a gentleman in civilian clothes. The former introduced himself briefly and got to business without preamble.

'Concerning this note, sir,' said he, 'you have given no particulars. I suppose there is no doubt that Mr Blake and his valet are really dead?'

'I should say there is no doubt at all,' replied Thorndyke. 'But I have written out a statement of the particulars, from which you will be able to judge. Shall I read it to you?'

'I think the doctor had better see the bodies first,' was the reply.

'Certainly,' agreed the doctor. 'We don't want to waste precious time on statements. Where are they?'

'I will take you to them,' said Thorndyke, 'but I must tell you that they are shut in a room which is filled with the vapour of hydrocyanic acid.'

The two men gave a startled look at Thorndyke, and as he led the way out into the hall and across the new wing, they followed, talking together earnestly but in low tones. Presently they overtook us, and the officer remarked:

'This is a very extraordinary affair, sir. Has no attempt been made to get these men out of that room?'

'No,' replied Thorndyke.

'But why not?'

'I think you will see when you get there.'

'But,' exclaimed the doctor, 'surely some effort ought to have been made to save them! You don't mean to say that you have left them in that poisoned air and made no attempt even to open the doors and windows?'

'We have opened some of the neighbouring windows,' said Thorndyke; and he proceeded to give a description of the secret chamber and its surroundings, to which the doctor listened with pursed-up lips.

'Well,' he remarked dryly, 'you seem to have been very careful. Is it much farther?'

'It opens out of the next room but one,' replied Thorndyke, and as he spoke I detected in the air a very faint odour of bitter almonds. I fancy the doctor noticed it, too, but he made no remark, and when we reached the end of the corridor and Thorndyke indicated the door that gave access to the room, both men hurried forward. The doctor turned the handle and flung the door open, and he and the officer stepped briskly across the threshold. And then they both stopped short, and I guessed that they had seen the dead rat. The next moment they both backed out hastily and the doctor slammed the door behind him and followed us to the discreet distance at which we had halted.

'The vapour is as you say,' said the latter, visibly crestfallen, 'in an extreme state of concentration.'

'Yes,' agreed Thorndyke, 'but it is much less than it was. If you will go a little farther away, I will throw the door open and we can then retire and let the vapour diffuse out.'

'Do you think it safe, sir?' queried the officer. 'There's a fearful reek in there'; then, as Thorndyke approached the door, he and the doctor (and I) walked away quickly up the corridor; and looking back, I saw my colleague, pinching his nostrils together, fling the door wide open and hurry after us.

When we had retired to a safe distance, the officer halted and said:

'You were saying something about a statement, sir. Shall we have it now? I don't understand this affair in the least.'

Thorndyke produced the statement from his pocket and proceeded to read it aloud; and as he read, the two men listened with growing astonishment and not very completely concealed incredulity. When he had finished, I read out my statement, and then we both signed the document, the officer adding his signature as the witness.

'Well,' he said, as he put the paper in his pocket-book, 'this is a most extraordinary story. Can you give any kind of explanation?'

'At the moment,' replied Thorndyke, 'I am not proposing to go beyond the actual occurrence – certainly not until I have seen the bodies.'

The officer looked dissatisfied, and naturally enough. On the facts presented, he would have been quite justified in arresting us both on a suspicion of murder; and indeed, but for Thorndyke's eminent position and my own status as a King's Counsel, he would probably have done so. As it was, he contented himself with the expression of a hope that we should presently be able to throw some light on the mystery, on which remark my colleague offered no comment.

When about half an hour had passed, Thorndyke suggested that the vapour had probably cleared off from the room out of which the secret chamber opened and that it might now be possible to open the door of the chamber itself. Our friends were somewhat dubious, however. The sight of the dead rat had effectually dissipated the doctor's enthusiasm and engendered a very wholesome caution.

'Perhaps,' said Thorndyke, 'as my friend and I know where to find the concealed fastenings of the door, we could open it more safely. What do you say, Anstey?'

I was not much more eager than the doctor, but as Thorndyke would certainly have gone alone if I had refused, I assented with assumed readiness, and we started down the corridor, followed at a little distance by the other two. On entering the room, in which the odour of the poison had now become quite faint, Thorndyke opened both the casements wide and then slid the block of wood close up to the foot of the door.

'Now,' said he, 'when I say "ready," take a deep breath, close your mouth, pinch your nostrils, and then push in the right-hand boss. I will press the other one and open and fix the door. Ready!'

I pushed in the boss, and immediately afterwards Thorndyke pressed in the other one. The door yielded, and as we pushed it wide open, he thrust the block in after it. Glancing in, I had a momentary glimpse of the dark chamber with the two dead men lying huddled on the floor and an extinguished lantern by the side of the nearer one. It was but the vision of an instant, for almost as the door opened, I turned with Thorndyke and ran out of the room; but in that instant it was imprinted on my memory for ever. Even as I write, I can see with horrible vividness that dark, gloomy hold and the two sprawling corpses stretched towards the door that had cut them off in the moment of their crime from the land of the living.

The first breath that I took, as I came out of the room, made me aware that the poisonous vapour was pouring out of the chamber of death. Our two friends had also noticed it and were already in full retreat, and we all made our way out of the old wing back to the library, there to wait until the poison should have become dissipated. The officer made one or two ineffectual efforts to extract from Thorndyke some explanation of the amazing events set forth in his statement, and then we settled down to a somewhat desultory conversation on subjects criminal and medical.

We had been in the library rather more than half an hour and were beginning to discuss the possibility of removing the bodies, when the doorbell rang, and a few moments later the housekeeper entered, followed by Sir Lawrence Drayton, Winifred, and Mr Brodribb. The latter came in with a genial and knowing smile, which faded with remarkable suddenness as his eye lighted on the police officer.

'Why, what the deuce is the matter?' exclaimed Sir Lawrence as he also observed the officer.

'The matter is,' replied Thorndyke, 'that there has been a tragedy. Mr Blake is dead.'

'Dead!' exclaimed Drayton and Brodribb in unison. 'And what,' asked the former, 'do you mean by a tragedy?'

'Perhaps,' said Thorndyke, 'the officer would allow me to read you the written statement that I have given him. I may say,' he added, addressing the officer, 'that this lady and these gentlemen are interested parties and that they will all be called as witnesses at the inquest.'

This latter statement, utterly incomprehensible to me, seemed to be equally so to every one else present. Sir Lawrence and Brodribb stared in astonishment at Thorndyke, while the officer, with a frown of perplexity, slowly took the statement from his pocket-book and handed it to my colleague without a word. Thereupon the latter, having waited for the housekeeper to withdraw, read the statement aloud, and I watched the amazement growing on the faces of the listeners as he read.

'But, my dear Thorndyke!' Sir Lawrence exclaimed, when he had finished, 'this is a most astounding affair. It looks as if this search had been a mere pretext to get you here and murder you!'

'That, I have no doubt, is the case,' said Thorndyke, 'and that I suspected to be the object when Brodribb conveyed the invitation to me.'

'The devil you did!' said Brodribb. 'But why should you suspect that Blake wanted to murder you?'

'I think,' replied Thorndyke, 'that when we have seen the bodies you will be able to answer that question yourself. And I should say,' he added, turning to the doctor, 'that it would now be possible to get the bodies out. Most of the fumes will have blown away by this time.'

'Yes,' the doctor agreed, evidently all agog to see and hear the explanation of this mystery. 'We had better get a sheet from the housekeeper and then go and see if we can get those poor wretches out.'

He set forth in company with the officer, and as soon as the two strangers had left the room, Brodribb attacked my colleague.

'You are a most inscrutable fellow, Thorndyke. Do you mean to tell me that when you proposed this search, you were just planning to give this man, Blake, an opportunity to murder you?'

'To try to murder me,' Thorndyke corrected.

'And me,' I added. 'It begins to dawn on me that the post of junior to Thorndyke is no sinecure.'

Brodribb smiled appreciatively, and Sir Lawrence remarked:

'We seem to be navigating in deep waters. I must confess that I am completely out of my depth, but I suppose it is useless to make any appeal.'

'I should rather say nothing more at present,' Thorndyke replied. 'In a few minutes I shall be able to make the crucial test which I expect will render explanations unnecessary.'

I speculated on the meaning of this statement, but could make nothing of it, and I gathered from the perplexed expressions of the two lawyers that they were in a similar condition. But there was not much time to turn the matter over, for, very shortly, the police officer reappeared to announce that the bodies had been removed from the chamber and were ready for inspection and identification.

'It will not be necessary, I suppose,' said Drayton, as we rose to accompany the officer, 'for Miss Blake to come with us?'

'I think,' answered Thorndyke, 'that it is desirable and, in fact, necessary, that Miss Blake should see the bodies. I am sorry,' he added, 'that she should be subjected to the unpleasantness, but the matter is really important.'

'I can't imagine in what respect,' said Drayton, 'but if you say that it is, that settles the matter.'

On this we set forth, Thorndyke and the officer leading the way; and as we crossed the great, desolate rooms I talked to Winifred about the old house and the secret chamber to divert her attention from our rather gruesome errand. At the end of the long corridor, as we entered the large room, we saw the doctor standing by two shrouded figures that lay on the floor near a window, with their feet towards us. We halted beside them in solemn silence, and the doctor stooped, and taking the two corners of the sheet, drew it away, with his eyes fixed on Thorndyke.

For a moment we all stood looking down on the two still and ghastly figures without speaking a word; but suddenly Winifred uttered a cry of horror and started back, clutching my arm.

'What is it?' demanded Drayton.

'The man!' she exclaimed breathlessly, pointing to the body of the valet, which I had already recognised. 'The man who tried to murder me in the empty house!'

'And who stabbed you that night at Hampstead?' said Thorndyke.

'Yes, yes,' she gasped. 'It is he, I am certain of it.'

Sir Lawrence turned a look of eager inquiry on my colleague.

'This is an amazing thing,' he exclaimed. 'How on earth did this fellow come to be associated with Mr Blake?'

Thorndyke stooped over the dead squire, and unfastening the collar and neckband, drew the shirt open at the throat. There came into sight a stout, silken cord encircling the neck, which Thorndyke gently pulled up, when I saw that there was suspended from it a small gold pendant with a single large stone. As the little jewel was drawn out from its hiding-place, Winifred stooped forward eagerly.

'It is the Cat's Eye!' she exclaimed.

'Impossible!' Sir Lawrence ejaculated. 'Let me look at it.'

Thorndyke cut the cord and handed the pendant to Drayton, who turned it over in his hand, gazing at it with an expression of amazement and incredulity.

'It is,' he said at length. 'This is certainly the pendant that was stolen from my poor brother's house. I recognise it without doubt by the shape and colour of the stone, and there is the inscription on the back, "Dulce Domum," which I remember now. It is unquestionably the stolen pendant. But what does it mean, Thorndyke? You seemed to know that this man was wearing it.'

'The meaning of it is, Sir Lawrence,' replied Thorndyke, 'that this man' – he pointed down at the dead squire – 'is the man who murdered your brother. It was he who fired the pistol.'

Sir Lawrence looked down at the dead man with a frown of disgust.

'Do you mean to tell me, Thorndyke,' said he, 'that this man murdered poor Andrew just to get possession of this trumpery toy?'

'I do,' replied Thorndyke, 'though, of course, the murder was not a part of the original plan. But he carried the pistol with him to use if necessary.'

'He has got a pistol in his pocket now,' said the officer. 'I felt it as I was dragging him out of the secret room.'

He plunged his hand into the dead man's coat pocket and drew out a small automatic pistol, which he handed to Thorndyke.

'This seems to be the very weapon,' said the latter; 'a Baby Browning. You remember that we identified the pattern from the empty cartridge-case.'

I had noticed a peculiar expression of perplexity gathering on Mr Brodribb's face. Now the old solicitor turned to Thorndyke and said:

'This is a very unaccountable affair, Thorndyke. We didn't know a great deal about Arthur Blake, but it always appeared that he was quite a decent sort of man; whereas this robbery and murder that he actually did commit, and the murder that he was attempting when he met his death, are cases of sheer ruffianism. I don't understand it.'

Thorndyke turned to the doctor. 'Would you mind telling us,' said he, 'if there is anything abnormal in the condition of this man's left knee-cap?'

The doctor stared at Thorndyke in astonishment. 'Have you any reason to suppose that there is?' he asked.

'I have an impression,' was the reply, 'that there is an old fracture with imperfect ligamentous union.'

The doctor stooped, and drawing up the trouser on the left side, placed his hand on the knee.

'You are quite right,' he said, looking up at Thorndyke with an expression of surprise. 'There is a transverse fracture with a gap of fully two inches between the fragments.'

Suddenly Mr Brodribb broke out eagerly with a look of intense curiosity at my colleague: 'It can't be – What is it that you are suggesting, Thorndyke?'

'I am suggesting that this man was not Arthur Blake. I suggest that he was an Australian adventurer named Hugh Owen.'

'But,' objected Brodribb, 'Owen was reported to have died some years ago. His body was found and identified.'

'A mutilated skeleton was found,' retorted Thorndyke, 'and was identified as that of Hugh Own by means of a ring which was known to have belonged to Owen. I suggest that the remains were those of Arthur Blake; that he had been murdered by Owen, and that the ring had been put on the body for the purpose of ensuring a false identification.'

'That is perfectly possible,' Brodribb admitted. 'Then who do you suggest that this other man is?'

'I suggest that this other person is a woman named Laura Levinsky.'

'Well,' said Brodribb, 'that need not be left a matter of guesswork. I don't think I mentioned it to you, but that Australian police official told me that Levinsky had a tattoo-mark on the right forearm – the letters H and L with a heart between. Let us see if this person has such a mark.'

The police officer bent down over the dead valet, and unfastening the right wristband, drew the sleeve up above the elbow.

'Ha!' exclaimed Brodribb as there were revealed, standing out on the greenish-white skin as if painted in blue ink, the letters H and L with a small, misshapen heart between them, 'you are right, Thorndyke, as you always are. And I suppose she was a party to the murder?'

'I take it,' said Thorndyke, 'that these two wretches murdered Arthur Blake, removed all identifiable objects from the corpse, put Owen's ring on its finger, and tumbled it over the cliff, shooting down a mass of rocks and stones on top of it. Then they took possession of all Blake's papers and money and separated, coming to England on different ships. I assume that no measures were ever taken to verify Blake's identity?'

'No,' replied Brodribb. 'There was no one who could identify him. He sent a letter, in answer to mine, saying when he would arrive. He arrived about the date mentioned, and presented all the necessary credentials. The question of identity was never raised.'

For some moments we all stood looking down on the bodies of the two adventures in silence. Presently Drayton asked, holding out the pendant:

'What is to be done with this? It was stolen from my brother, but it seems that, as it is an heirloom, it should be handed to Miss Blake.'

'For the present,' said Thorndyke, 'it must remain in the custody of the police, as it will have to be put in evidence at the inquest. We will take a receipt for it. But as to its being the missing heirloom. I doubt that very much. It does not agree with the description, and I should suppose that the original jewel will have been hidden with the title-deeds.'

'That could hardly be,' said Winifred, 'though I agree with you that the inscription "Dulce domum" doesn't seem to be the right one. But you will remember that Percival's manuscript distinctly says that the jewel was taken away and given to Jenifer to keep for the child James.'

'That is not my reading of the manuscript,' said Thorndyke. 'But we can discuss that on another occasion. If we give our respective names and addresses to the officer, we shall have concluded our business here.'

At this hint, the officer produced a large, official notebook in which he entered the names and addresses of all the witnesses in the case, and when the doctor had once more covered the corpses with the sheet, we turned to retrace our steps to the library. As I walked along the corridor at Winifred's side, I glanced at her a little anxiously, for it had been a rather terrible experience. She met my glance, and resting her hand on my arm for a moment, she said in a low voice:

'It was a gruesome sight, Robin, that poor little wretch lying there with that awful, fixed stare of horror on her face. But I couldn't feel sorry for her, nor even for the man, though there was something very dreadful – almost pitiful – in the way in which his dead hand clutched that little brass knob. It must have been a frightful moment when he found that the knob was useless and that he and his companion were caught in their own hideous trap. But I can't be sorry for them. I can only think of the relief to know that you are safe and that I am free.'

'Yes,' said I, 'it is an unspeakable relief to feel that you can now go abroad in safety – that that continual menace is a thing of the past, thanks to Thorndyke's uncanny power of seeing through a stone wall.'

'I am not sure,' said she, 'that I am not disposed to quarrel with Dr Thorndyke for calmly walking you into this murderer's den.'

'I don't think there was ever any real danger,' I replied. 'They couldn't have murdered us by overt methods, and as to the other methods, I have no doubt that Thorndyke had got them all calculated out in advance and provided for. He seems to foresee everything.'

When we reached the library, and Thorndyke and I had replaced our pistols and jemmies in the suitcase (a proceeding which the police officer watched with bulging eyes and open mouth), Drayton asked:

'Have you two got any sort of conveyance? Because, if you haven't, and you don't mind a pretty tight squeeze, I can give you a lift to the station.'

We accepted the offer gladly; and having made our adieux to the officer and the doctor, we went out and packed ourselves and our impedimenta into the car as soon as the lawful occupants had taken their seats. As we moved off, I observed the housekeeper and two other women watching us with concentrated interest; and at the gate, as we swept past the lodge, I had an instantaneous glimpse of the keeper's face at the window, with another countenance that seemed reminiscent of the 'King's Head.'

The swiftly-gliding car devoured the mile or two of road to the station in a few minutes. We drew up in the station yard, and while the chauffeur was handing out our luggage, Drayton stood up, and laying his hand on Thorndyke's shoulder, said earnestly:

'I have spoken no word of thanks to you, Thorndyke, for what you have done, but I hope you understand that I am your debtor for life. Your management of this case is beyond my wildest expectations, and how you did it, I cannot imagine. Some day you must give me the intellectual satisfaction of hearing how the investigation was carried out. Now I can only congratulate you on your brilliant success.'

'I should like to second that,' said Brodribb; 'and talking of success, I suppose you didn't find those deeds after all?'

'No,' replied Thorndyke. 'They are not there.'

'Oh, aren't they?' Brodribb. 'Then, if you are so certain where they are not, you probably know where they are?'

'That seems a sound inference,' replied Thorndyke. 'But we can't discuss the matter here. If you care to come to my chambers tomorrow, at two o'clock, we might go into it further, and, in fact, conduct an exploration.'

'Does that invitation include me?' Winifred asked.

'Most undoubtedly,' he replied. 'You are the principal party to the transaction. And perhaps you might bring the Book of Hours with you.'

'I believe he has got the deeds stowed away in his chambers,' said Brodribb; and although my colleague shook his head, I felt no certainty that the old lawyer was not right.

When the car had moved off, we carried our cases into the station and were relieved to find that we had but a few minutes to wait for a train. I postponed my attack on my secretive colleague until we were snugly established in a compartment by ourselves. Not that I had any expectations. Thorndyke's reticence had conveyed to me the impression that the time for explanations had not yet come; and so it turned out when I proceeded to put my questions.

'Wait till we have finished the case, Anstey,' said he. 'Then, if you have not worked out the scheme of the investigation in the interval, we can review and discuss it.'

'But surely,' said I, 'we have finished with the case of the murder of Andrew Drayton?'

'Not entirely,' he replied. 'What you have never realised, I think, is the connection between the problem of the murder and the problem of the missing documents. This is a very curious and interesting case, and those two problems have a very strange connection. But for Owen's determination to possess the cat's eye pendant at all costs, those documents might have lain in their hiding-place, unsuspected, for centuries.'

This statement, while it explained Thorndyke's hitherto un-accountable interest in Percy Blake's claim, only plunged the other problem into deeper obscurity. During the remainder of the journey I tried to reconstitute the train of events to see if I could trace the alleged connection between the two problems. But not a glimmer of light could I see in any direction; and in the end I gave it up, consoling myself with the reflection that the morrow would probably see the last act played out and that then I might hope for a final elucidation.

CHAPTER NINETEEN

A Relic of the '45

At two o'clock punctually, on the following afternoon, our visitors made their appearance; and at the very moment when the last of them – Mr Brodribb – emerged from Crown Office Row, I observed from the window two taxi-cabs, which had entered successively by the Tudor Street gate, draw up before our door. I hailed their arrival with deep satisfaction, for the strange events of the previous day, together with Thorndyke's rather mysterious observations thereon, had made me impatient to see the end of this intricate case and intensely curious to hear how my inscrutable colleague had managed to fit together the apparently unrelated fragments of this extraordinarily complex puzzle. Throughout the morning – while Thorndyke was absent, and, as I suspected, arranging details of the afternoon's adventure – I had turned over the facts again and again, but always with the same result. There were the pieces of the puzzle, and no doubt a complete set; but separate pieces they remained, and obstinately refused to join up into anything resembling an intelligible whole.

'I see, Thorndyke,' said Mr Brodribb as he entered, smiling, rosy, and looking as if he had just come out of a bandbox, 'that I did you an injustice. You have not been sitting on the deeds. The chariots are at the door waiting, I suppose, for the band or the stavebearers. We shall be quite an imposing procession.'

'We won't wait for the band,' said Thorndyke. 'As we are all here, we may as well start. Will you conduct Miss Blake, down, Anstey?'

'Do I give any directions to the driver?' I asked.

'Yes. You can tell him to put you down at the north-east corner of the Minories.'

Accordingly I led the way with Winifred, and having given the destination to the driver, bestowed my charge and myself in the cab. The driver started the engine, and as the cab made a sweep round to the Tudor Street gate, I heard the door of the other cab slam.

'Have you any idea where we are going, Robin?' Winifred asked as the cab whirled round into New Bridge Street.

'None beyond what I have communicated to the driver,' I replied. 'Apparently we are going to explore the Minories or Aldgate or Whitechapel. It is an ancient neighbourhood, and in the days of Percival Blake it was somewhat more aristocratic than it is now. There are good many old houses still standing about there. You may have seen that picturesque group of timber houses looking on Whitechapel High Street. They are nearly all butchers' shops, and have been, at least, since the days of Charles the Second; in fact, the group is known as Butcher Row, though I think there is an old tavern among them.'

'Perhaps we are going to the tavern,' said Winifred. 'It is quite likely. Many of the old inns had secret hiding-places and must have been the favourite rendezvous of the conspirators of those times.'

She continued to speculate on the possibilities of the ancient tavern, which had evidently captured her romantic fancy, and as I looked at her – pink-cheeked, bright-eyed, and full of pleasurable excitement over our adventurous quest – I once more breathed a sigh of thankfulness that the dark days of ever-impending peril were over.

It seemed but a few minutes before the cab drew up at the corner of the Minories; and we had hardly alighted when the other vehicle arrived and disgorged its occupants at our side. The drivers having been paid (and having thereafter compared notes and settled themselves to watch our further proceedings), Thorndyke turned his face eastward and we started together along Whitechapel High Street. I noticed that, now, no one asked any questions. Probably each of us was busy with his own speculations; and in any case, Thorndyke maintained a sphinx-like reticence.

'Are those delightful old houses the ones you were speaking of?' Winifred asked as the ancient, plaster-fronted buildings came in sight.

'Yes,' I answered. 'That is Butcher Row.'

'Or,' said Thorndyke, 'to give it what is, I believe, its official title, "The Shambles," though the shambles proper are at the back.'

'The Shambles!' exclaimed Winifred, looking at Thorndyke with a startled expression. She appeared to be about to ask him some question, but at this moment he turned sharply into a narrow alley, into which we followed him. I glanced up at the name as we entered and read it aloud – 'Harrow Alley.'

'Yes,' said Thorndyke, 'quite a historic little thoroughfare. Defoe gives a very vivid description of its appearance during the Plague, with the dead-cart waiting at the entrance and the procession of bearers carrying the corpses down the narrow court. Here is the old "Star and Still" tavern, and round the corner there are the shambles, very little changed since the seventeenth century.'

He turned the corner towards the shambles, and then, crossing the narrow road, dived through an archway into a narrow paved court, along which we had to go in single file. This court presently opened into a squalid-looking little square, surrounded on three sides by tall, ancient, timber and plaster houses, the fourth side being occupied by a rather mean, but quaint little church with a low brick tower. Thorndyke made his way directly to the west door of the church, and taking from his pocket a key of portentous size, inserted it into the lock. As he did so I glanced at the board that was fixed beside the doorway, from which I learned that this was the church of St Peter by the Minories.

As the door swung open Thorndyke motioned to us to enter. We field in, and then he drew the door to after us and locked it from the inside. We stood for a few moments in the dim porch under the tower, looking in through the half-opened inner door; and as we stood there, Winifred grasped my arm nervously, and I could feel that her hand was trembling. But there was no time for speech, for as Thorndyke locked the door and withdrew the key, the inner door opened wide and two men – one tall and one short – appeared silhouetted against the east window.

'These are my friends, of whom I spoke to you,' said Thorndyke. 'Miss Blake, Sir Lawrence Drayton, Mr Brodribb, Mr Anstey – the Reverend James Yersbury. I think you have met this other gentleman.'

We came out into the body of the church, and having made my bow to the clergyman, I turned to the smaller man.

'Why, it's Mr Polton!' exclaimed Winifred, shaking hands heartily with my colleague's familiar; who greeted us with a smile of such ecstatic crinkliness, that I instantly suspected him of preparing some necromantic surprise for us.

'This is quite a remarkable building,' said Sir Lawrence, looking about him with lively interest, 'and it appears the more striking by contrast with the shabby, commonplace exterior.'

'Yes,' agreed the clergyman, 'that is rather characteristic of old London churches. But this is rather an ancient structure; it was only partially destroyed by the Great Fire and was almost immediately rebuilt, at the personal cost, it is said, of the Duke of York, afterwards James the Second. Perhaps that accounts for the strong Jacobite leanings of some of the later clergy, such as this good gentleman, for instance.'

He led us to a space between two of the windows where a good-sized tablet of alabaster had been let into the wall.

'That tablet,' said he, 'encloses a cavity which is filled with bones piously collected from the field of Culloden, and the inscription leaves one in no doubt as to the sentiments of the collector. But I believe it was covered with plaster soon after it was put up, to preserve it from destruction, by the authorities, and it was only discovered about fifty years ago.'

I read the brief inscription with growing curiosity:

'PRO PATRIA – PRO REGE
1745

'This Tablet was raised to the Memory of the Faithful by Stephen Rumbold, sometime Rector of this Church.'

'But,' said Winifred, 'I thought Stephen Rumbold was rector of St Peter by the Shambles.'

'This is St Peter by the Shambles,' replied Mr Yersbury. 'The name has only been changed within the last forty years.'

Winifred faced me and looked with eager delight into my eyes, and I knew that the same thought was in both our minds. Here, during all the slowly-passing years, the missing deeds had rested, securely hidden with the bones of those patriots at whose side Percival Blake had fought on the fatal field of Culloden. I looked round at Thorndyke, expecting to see some preparations to open this curious little burial-place. But he had already turned away and was moving towards the east end of the church. We followed him slowly until he halted before the pulpit, where he stood for a few moments looking at it reflectively. It was a very remarkable pulpit. I have never seen another at all resembling it. In shape it was an elongated octagon, the panels and mouldings of deep brown oak enriched with magnificent carving. But the most singular feature was the manner in which it was supported. The oblong super-structure rested on twin pillars of oak, each pillar being furnished with a handsome, floridly-ornamented bronze capital and a bronze base of somewhat similar character. But fine as the workmanship was, the design was more unusual than pleasing. The oblong body and the twin pillars had, in fact, a rather ungainly appearance.

'Here,' said Thorndyke, pointing to the pulpit, 'is another relic of the Reverend Stephen Rumbold, and one of more personal interest to us than the other. You notice these twin pillars. Aesthetically, they are not all that might be desired, but they serve a useful purpose besides supporting the upper structure, for each of them forms an aumbry, originally designed, no doubt, to conceal the sacred vessels and other objects used in celebrating Mass or Vespers or in administering Communion in accordance with the rites of the Church of Rome. One of them is still discharging this function. This pillar' – here he tapped the northern one of the pair – 'contains a chalice and paten, a thurible and a small pyx. This other pillar contains – well, Polton will show us what it contains, so I need not go into particulars.'

'Do I understand,' Drayton asked, 'that you have opened aumbries already and verified the existence and nature of the contents?'

'We have not yet opened the aumbries,' Thorndyke replied, 'but we have ascertained that the things are there untouched. Polton and I made an examination some days ago with an X-ray apparatus and a fluorescent screen. It was then that we discovered the plate in the second pillar. I wished Miss Blake to be present at the actual opening.'

At these words, like an actor taking up a cue, Polton appeared from somewhere behind the pulpit bearing a good-sized leather handbag. This he deposited on the floor, and as we gathered round, he took from it a small, rounded mallet, apparently of lead, covered with leather, and a tool of hard wood, somewhat, in shape, like a caulking chisel.

'Which pillar shall I begin on, sir?' he inquired, looking round with a sly smile. 'The one with church plate or – '

'Oh, hang the church plate!' interposed Brodribb, adding hastily: 'I beg your pardon, Mr Yersbury, but you know – '

'Exactly,' interrupted the clergyman, 'I quite agree with you. The church plate will keep for another half hour.'

Thereupon Polton fell to work, and we crowded up close to watch. The capitals of the pillars presented each two parts, a lower member, covered with ornament, and above this a plain, cylindrical space extending up to the abacus. It was to the lower part that Polton directed his attention. Having mounted on a chair, he placed the edge of the hardwood chisel against the lower edge of the ornamented member and struck it gently with the leaden mallet. Then he shifted the chisel half an inch to the right and struck another blow, and in this way he continued, moving the chisel half an inch after each stroke, until he had travelled a third of the way round the pillar, when Thorndyke placed another chair for him to step on.

'Have you oiled the surface?' my colleague asked.

'Yes, sir,' replied Polton, tapping away like Old Mortality; 'I flooded it with a mixture of paraffin and clock oil, and it is moving all right.'

We were soon able to verify this statement, for when Polton had made a complete circuit of the pillar, the plain space above had grown perceptibly narrower and a ring of lighter-coloured wood began to appear below. Still, the leaden mallet continued to deliver its dull sounding taps, and still Polton continued to creep round the pillar.

By the time the second circuit was completed, the sliding part of the capital had risen half-way to the top of the plain space, as was shown by the width of paler, newly-uncovered wood below. And now the sliding member was evidently moving more freely, for there was a perceptible upward movement at each stroke, so that, by the end of the third circuit, the upper, plain space had disappeared altogether and a narrow ring of metal appeared below; and in this ring I perceived a notch about half an inch wide.

'I think she's all clear now, sir,' said Polton.

'Very well,' said Thorndyke. 'We are all ready.'

He relieved Polton of the mallet and chisel and handed him a tool which looked somewhat like a rather slender jemmy with a long, narrow beak. This beak Polton inserted carefully into the notch, when it evidently entered a cavity in the top of the woodwork. Then he began cautiously to prise at the end of the lever.

For a moment or two nothing happened. Suddenly there was a grating sound; the end of the lever rose, and at the same instant about a quarter of the pillar began to separate from the rest and come forward, showing a joint which had been cunningly hidden by the deep fluting. Polton grasped the top of the loose panel, and with a sharp pull, drew it right out and lifted it clear, but as he was in front of the opening, none of us could see what was within. Then he stepped down from the chair, and Winifred uttered a little cry and clasped her hands.

It was certainly a dramatic moment, especially to those of us who had read the manuscript in the little Book of Hours. The pillar was a great shell enclosing a considerable cavity, and in this cavity, standing on the floor, was a tall leaden jar with a close-fitting, flat lid; and on the lid stood a great, two-handled posset-pot. It was all exactly as Percival Blake had described it, and to us, who had formed a mental picture from that description, there was something very moving in being thus confronted with those strangely familiar objects, which had been waiting in their hiding-place for more than a century and a half – waiting for the visit of Percival's dispossessed posterity.

For some time we stood looking at them in silence. At length Thorndyke said: 'You notice, Miss Blake, that there is an inscription on the jar.'

I had not observed it, nor had Winifred; but we now advanced, and looking closely at the jar, made out with some difficulty on the whitened surface an inscription which had apparently been punched into the metal letter by letter, and which read:

'The Contents hereof are the Property of Percival Blake, MD of Beauchamp Blake in Buckinghamshire, or the Heirs of his Body. AD 1746.'

'That,' said Sir Lawrence, as Winifred read the inscription aloud, 'settles the ownership of the documents. You can take possession of the jar and its contents with perfect confidence. And now perhaps it would be as well to see what is inside the jar.'

Polton, who had apparently been waiting for this cue, now lit a small spirit blow-pipe. The posset-pot was tenderly lifted out by Winifred and deposited on a pew-bench, and Polton, having hoisted out the jar and placed it on a chair, began cautiously to let the flame of the blow-pipe play on the joint of the lid, which had been thickly coated with wax. When the wax began to liquefy, he introduced the edge of the jemmy into the joint, and with a deft turn of the wrist, raised the lid, which he then took off.

Winifred peered into the jar and announced: 'It seems to be full of rolled-up parchments,' a statement which we all verified in turn.

'I would suggest,' said Mr Yersbury, 'that we carry the jar into the vestry. There is a good-sized table there, which will be a convenience if you are going to examine the documents.'

This suggestion was instantly agreed to. Polton took up the rather ponderous jar and made his way to the vestry under the guidance of the clergyman, and the rest of us followed, Winifred carrying the precious posset-pot. Arrived at the vestry, Polton set down the jar on the table, and Sir Lawrence proceeded at once to extract the roll of stiff and yellow parchment and vellum documents. Unrolling them carefully – for they were set into a rigid cylinder – he glanced over them quickly with the air of one looking for some particular thing.

'These are undoubtedly the title-deeds,' he said, still turning over the pages quickly with but a cursory glance at their contents, 'but – ha! Yes. These are what we really wanted. I had hoped that we should find them here.'

He drew out from between the leaves of the deeds two small squares of parchment which he exhibited triumphantly and then read aloud:

'I hereby certify and declare that on the thirteenth day of June in the Year of Our Lord seventeen hundred and forty-two, at the church of St Peter by the Shambles, near by Aldgate, the following persons were by me joined together in Holy Matrimony to wit
PERCIVAL BLAKE of Beauchamp Blake in the County of Buckinghamshire, Bachelor and
JUDITH WESTERN of Cricklewood in the County of Middlesex, Spinster.

STEPHEN RUMBOLD, MA,
Rector of the said Church of St Peter
by the Shambles. 20th May 1746.'

'That,' said Sir Lawrence, 'is what principally matters, but this second certificate clenches the proof. I will read it out:

'I hereby certify and declare that James the Son of Percival and Judith Blake of Beauchamp Blake in the County of Buckinghamshire was baptized by me according to the rites of Holy Church on the thirtieth of May in the Year of Our Lord

seventeen hundred and forty-three at the Church of St Peter by
the Shambles near by Aldgate.

> STEPHEN RUMBOLD, MA,
> Rector of the said Church of St Peter
> by the Shambles. 20th May 1746.'

'That,' continued Drayton, 'with the other certificates, which I
understand you have, establishes a direct descent. And seeing that the
estate is at present without an owner, this is a peculiarly opportune
moment for putting forward a claim. What do you say, Brodribb?'

'I should like,' said Brodribb, 'to have fuller particulars before giving
a definite opinion.'

'Oh, come, Brodribb,' Sir Lawrence protested, 'you needn't be so
infernally cautious. We're all friends, you know. Would you be
prepared to act for Miss Blake?'

'I don't see why not,' replied Brodribb. 'I am not committed to any
other claimant. Yes, I should be very happy to act for her.'

'Then,' said Drayton, 'we must arrange a consultation and find out
exactly how we stand. I will call at your office for a preliminary talk
tomorrow, if that will suit you.'

'Very well,' agreed Brodribb, 'come in at one o'clock, and we can
lunch together and talk over the preliminaries.'

While this conversation was proceeding, I had observed
Thorndyke peering inquisitively into the now empty jar. From this he
transferred his attention to the posset-pot which Winifred was
guarding jealously. It was a fine specimen of its kind, a comparatively
large vessel of many-coloured slip-ware. On the front was a sort of
escutcheon, on which was a heart surmounted by a B with the letters
H and M on either side and the date 1708 below. Just under the rim
was a broad band bearing the following quaint inscription:

> 'Here is the Gest of the Barly Korne,
> 'Glad Ham I the child is Borne.' – JM

'Isn't it a lovely old thing?' murmured Winifred. 'So human and
personal and so charming too.'

'Yes,' Thorndyke agreed, 'it is a fine piece of work. Old Martin was something more than a common village potter. Have you looked inside it?'

'No,' replied Winifred. She took the knob in her fingers and delicately lifted off the cover; and then she uttered a cry of surprise.

'Why,' she exclaimed, 'it is the Cat's Eye – the real cat's eye this time. And what a beauty!'

She lifted out of the pot a small pendant, curiously like the other one – so much so, in fact, as to suggest that the latter had been a copy. But, whereas the stone in the counterfeit had been a rather dull grey, this one was of a beautiful deep yellow with a brilliant streak of golden light. Attached to the pendant was a slender gold chain and a clasp, which, like the pendant itself, was smooth and rounded with years of wear. After gazing for a while at the flashing stone, Winifred turned the pendant over and looked at the back. The inscription was half-obliterated by wear, but we read without difficulty:

'God's Providence is Mine Inheritance.'

'It is extremely appropriate,' she commented when she had read it aloud, 'though it isn't quite what one expected. But what I don't understand is how it comes to be here. Percival distinctly says that he had the jewel and that he intended to give it to Jenifer to keep for the child.'

'Not the jewel,' Thorndyke corrected. 'He speaks of "the bauble" and "the trinket," never of "the jewel." '

'You think he was referring to some other trinket?'

'Obviously,' replied Thorndyke. And then, looking at Winifred with a smile, he exclaimed: 'O blind generation! Don't you see, Miss Blake, that events have shaped themselves precisely as Percival designed? Here is his descendant, the child of his children's children, coming to the hiding-place wearing the precious bauble around her neck and guided by it to the possessions of her fathers. Could anything be more complete?'

244

Winifred was thunderstruck. For a while she sat, motionless as a statue, gazing at Thorndyke in speechless amazement. At length she exclaimed: 'But this is astounding, Dr Thorndyke! Do you mean that this little locket is the trinket that was given to Jenifer and which she lost?'

'Undoubtedly,' he replied, 'and the really strange and romantic circumstance is that it was given into your hand by the very impostor who was seeking to rob you for ever of your inheritance.'

'Then,' exclaimed Sir Lawrence, who was almost as overcome as Winifred herself, 'it was actually poor Andrew's "little Sphinx" that gave you the clue to this hiding-place?'

'Yes,' replied Thorndyke, 'only the sphinx was really an oracle, just waiting for the question to be asked.'

Winifred's eyes filled. Impulsively she grasped my colleague's hand, murmuring shakily: 'What can I say to you, Dr Thorndyke? How can I ever thank you for all that you have done for my brother and me?'

'You need say nothing,' he replied, 'but that which is written on the back of the cat's eye.'

Our business being now concluded, Sir Lawrence carefully returned the precious documents to the jar and replaced the cover. From without, a dull tapping that had been audible for some time past, had told us that Polton was at work on the second pillar. But that was no concern of ours.

'What are we going to do now?' asked Sir Lawrence. 'It seems as if we should mark the occasion in some way.'

'I agree with you, Drayton,' said Thorndyke, 'and I have, in fact, arranged a little festival at my chambers; just a simple tavern dinner, since Polton was otherwise engaged. Will that satisfy the requirements?'

'It will satisfy mine,' replied Drayton, 'and I think I can answer for Brodribb.'

'Then,' said Thorndyke, 'if Miss Blake will consent to combine the function of hostess with that of principal guest, we will capture Polton and betake ourselves to the Temple.'

We strolled out into the church, where Polton and the rector were gloatingly examining the newly-recovered sacred vessels, and having thanked the friendly clergyman and bidden him a warm farewell, we went forth in search of conveyances, Polton heading the procession with the heavy jar under his arm, and Winifred tenderly carrying the posset-pot swathed in her silken shawl.

In Whitechapel High Street we had the unexpected good fortune to encounter an unoccupied taxi-cab, which was by universal consent assigned to Winifred, Polton, and me. In this we bestowed ourselves and were forthwith spirited away, leaving our companions to follow as best they could. But they were not far behind, for we had barely arrived in the chambers and disposed of our treasure-trove, when a second cab drew up in King's Bench Walk and our three friends made their appearance at the rendezvous.

Chapter Twenty

QED

To an enthusiastic and truly efficient gourmet it might be difficult to assess the respective merits of the different stages of a really good dinner; to compare the satisfactions yielded, for instance, by the first tentative approaches – the little affairs of outposts – with the voracious joy of the grand onslaught on tangible and manducable solids; or again with the placid diminuendo, the half-hearted rear-guard actions, concerned with the unsubstantial trifles on which defeated appetite delivers its expiring kick. For my own part, I can offer no opinion – at any rate, without refreshing my memory as to the successive sensations; but I recall that as our dinner drew to a close, signs of expectancy began to manifest themselves (in Mr Brodribb's case they seemed to be associated with the advent of the port decanter), and when Polton had evacuated the casualties to an aid-post established n the adjacent office, Sir Lawrence gave expression to the prevailing state of mind.

'I suppose, Thorndyke, you know what is expected of you?'

Thorndyke turned an impassive face towards his guest.

'On these triumphal occasions,' said he, 'I usually smoke a Trichinopoly cigar. On this occasion, I presume, I am expected to refrain.'

'Not at all,' replied Drayton. 'I think we can endure the Trichy with reasonable fortitude; what we can't endure is the agony of curiosity. We demand enlightenment.'

'You want to know how the "little Sphinx" answered its own riddle. Is that your demand?'

'I understood you to say,' said I, 'that the problem of the crime and that of the missing deeds were one and the same.'

'I said that they were closely connected. But if you want an exposition of the unravelment, it will be more convenient to take them separately and in the order in which they were presented. In which case we begin with the crime.'

He paused, and I saw him glance with an indulgent smile towards the office door which was incompletely closed, and from which issued faint sounds of furtive movement which informed us that Polton had elected to take his dinner within earshot of the exposition.

'We had better begin,' he proceeded, 'with the facts presented to us on the night of the tragedy. First as to the criminals. There were traces of two men, and only two. One of these was a tall man, as shown by the size of his feet. He appeared to suffer from some weakness of the left leg. The sound of his footsteps, as heard by Anstey, suggested a slightly lame man, but as he ran away rapidly he could not have been very lame. Yet there was some distinct disability, since he had to draw up a garden seat to enable him to get over a fence which we climbed easily; and the faint impression of the left foot under the fence showed that, when he jumped down, the weight was taken principally by the right. Examination of the cast of his left hand showed a depressed scar on the tip of the forefinger. We also gathered that he carried a Baby Browning pistol and appeared to be a skilful pistol shot.

'Of the other man we learned less. He was noticeably small and slight; he was left-handed; he had dark hair, and at the time of the robbery he was wearing gloves, apparently of kid or thin leather. But later, when examining the tuft of his hair that was found grasped by the deceased, we made an important discovery. Among those dark hairs was a single blonde hair – not white, but golden – which could not have come from his own head. Of its presence there seemed to be only two possible explanations: either it had been rubbed off, or had fallen from the head of some other person, or it had become detached from the inside of a wig. But the first explanation was ruled out – '

'How?' demanded Brodribb.

'By its appearance under the microscope. When you find an alien hair, on your coat-sleeve, for instance – '

'I don't,' said Brodribb, 'at my time of life.'

' – If you examine it under the microscope, or even with a strong lens, you will invariably find it to be a dead hair – a hair which has completed its growth and dropped out of its sheath. You can identify it by the presence of the complete bulb and the absence of the inner root-sheath (which would be adherent to it if it had been pulled out while growing). Well, this blonde hair had no bulb. It had both ends broken which suggested unusual brittleness, as if it had been treated with some bleach, such as chlorine or hydrogen peroxide. But the hair of wigs shows absence of bulbs and is commonly so treated and is usually somewhat brittle. Thus the probability was that this man had recently worn a wig of artificially bleached hair.

'These were our initial data concerning these two men. There were also some fingerprints, but we will consider those separately. The initial data included the character of the things stolen. These were of insignificant intrinsic value and were very easily identifiable. They were thus quite unacceptable to the ordinary professional thief, yet the evidence (of the suspicious visitor) suggested that they knew what they were stealing. One of the things stolen – the cat's eye pendant – was known to have an extrinsic value and to have been eagerly sought by other persons, and there was thus the bare suggestion that this pendant might have been the object of the robbery.

'We now come to the fingerprints. These presented some very remarkable anomalies. In the first place, they were not the fingerprints of either of the robbers. That was certain. The small man wore gloves, so they could not have been his; and the tall man had a depressed scar on the tip of his left forefinger, whereas there was no trace of any such scar on the corresponding fingerprint. But if they were not the fingerprints of either of the robbers, whose fingerprints were they? There was no trace of any third person, and it was practically certain that no third person was present.

'But there was another striking anomaly. Although there were numerous impressions, only six digits were represented – the forefinger and thumb of the left hand and the thumb and the first three fingers of the right. Every impression of the right hand showed the same four digits, every impression of the left showed the same two.

'Now what could be the explanation of this curious repetition? Anstey's very reasonable suggestion was that the man had soiled these particular digits with some foreign substance and that, consequently, the soiled digits alone had made prints. This suggestion received a certain amount of support from the fact that a foreign substance actually was present – it proved, on examination, to be Japanese wax. But though the presence of the wax accounted for the distinctness of the fingerprints that were there, it did not explain why the other fingers had made no mark at all. I examined the glass which bore the fingerprints with the utmost minuteness, but in no case was there the faintest trace of the other fingers. Yet those fingers, if they had existed, must have touched the glass, and if they had touched it they would have made marks. The only explanation seemed to be that there were no other fingers; that the prints were not real fingerprints at all, but counterfeits made by means of facsimile stamps of rubber, roller-composition, or – more probably – chrome gelatine.

'It seemed a far-fetched hypothesis. But it fitted all the facts, and there seemed to be no other explanation. Thus the use of a set of stamps would explain the existence of a set of fingerprints which were not those of either of the parties present; it would explain the repetition of the same group of digits (on the assumption that only six stamps were available which might easily be the case if these stamps were copies of a particular group of fingerprints); and lastly, it would explain the presence of the Japanese wax.'

'How would it?' I asked.

'Well, some foreign substance would be necessary. In a real fingerprint – on glass, for instance – the mark is produced by the natural grease of the fingers. But a rubber or gelatine stamp has no natural grease. It is quite dry, and would make no mark at all unless it were charged with some sticky or greasy material. Now Japanese wax is an ideal material for the purpose. It is markedly sticky and would consequently develop up splendidly with dusting powder; it has no tendency to spread or run, so that it gives very clear impressions; and it might easily be mistaken for natural skin-grease.

'The counterfeit fingerprints hypothesis was, therefore, the only one that explained the facts, and I adopted it provisionally, assuming that the stamps were probably thin plates of rubber or gelatine cemented on the finger tips of the gloves worn by the short man.

'A few days later I received a visit from Detective-Superintendent Miller who informed me that the fingerprints had been identified at the registry as those of a well-known "habitual" named Hedges, more commonly known as Moakey. Of course this did not alter the position since there was no evidence that Moakey had ever been on the premises. However, I decided to wait until he was arrested and hear what he had to say. But he never was arrested. A day or two later, the Superintendent called on me again, and this time he settled the matter finally. My impression was, and is, that he came intending to make a clean breast of the matter, but that at the last moment he shied at the responsibility of giving away official secrets. What he actually said was that there had been a mistake; that the fingerprints were not Moakey's after all.

'Of course this was absurd. A mistake might occur with a single fingerprint, but with a set of six it was incredible. What had happened appeared to me quite obvious. The fingerprints had been submitted to the experts, who had at once identified them as Moakey's. Then the executive had set out to arrest Moakey – and had discovered that he was in prison. If that was really what had happened, it furnished conclusive proof that the fingerprints were forgeries.

'At once I set to work to ascertain if it were so. I searched the lists of convictions at assizes, quarter-sessions, and so forth, and eventually ran Moakey to earth. He had been convicted six months previously and sentenced to two years' imprisonment with hard labour. So, at the date of the murder, he had been in prison about six months.

'We were now on solid ground. We knew that the fingerprints were forgeries. But we knew more than this. The forgery of a fingerprint, unlike that of a signature, is a purely mechanical operation, carried out either by photography or by some other reproductive process. The forged print is necessarily a mechanical copy of an existing real print. Whence it follows that the existence of a forgery is evidence of the existence of an original. And more than that, it is evidence that the forger had access to that original. Now these forgeries were copies of Moakey's fingerprints. It followed that we had to look for somebody who had had access to Moakey's fingerprints.

'Fortunately we had not far to look. At the first interview the Superintendent had referred to a previous exploit of Moakey's; a burglary at a country house, when that artist was apprehended and convicted on the evidence of his fingerprints, which were found on a silver salver. A photograph of these fingerprints was immediately taken by the owner of the house and given to the police, who took them straight to Scotland Yard. I looked up the report of that case and had the good fortune to find that the fingerprints were described. There were six of them, the thumb and first three fingers of the right hand, and the forefinger and thumb of the left hand.

'This was extremely interesting. But still more so was the fact that the house which was broken into was Beauchamp Blake, and the further fact that the owner who photographed the fingerprints was Mr Arthur Blake.

'I need not point out the importance of the discovery. It told us that Arthur Blake had had, and presumably still had, in his possession, a set of negatives with which it was possible to make the stamps of these very fingerprints. It did not, however, follow that he had made the stamps, for that would demand an amount of technical knowledge and skill far beyond that of an ordinary photographer; knowledge ordinarily possessed only by professional photo-engravers. He might have such knowledge or he might have employed some one else. At any rate, he had the negatives and had made them himself.

'But Blake was not only associated with the fingerprints. He was also associated with the stolen property. Of all the persons known to us, he was the most likely to wish to acquire the cat's eye pendant. So, you see, the investigation, which started with a certain connection with Beauchamp Blake, led us straight to Beauchamp Blake again. And there we will leave it for the moment and approach the problem from one or two different directions.

'First we will consider the mysterious woman who came into view on the day of the inquest and who presumably sent the poisoned chocolates. Who was she? And what was her connection with the case? Now, the first thing that struck me in the description of her was her hair. It was of that brassy, golden tint that one associates with bleaches such as hydrogen peroxide. I recalled the stray hair from the small man's head which had suggested that he had worn a wig of precisely this character. The obvious suggestion was that this woman and that small man were one and the same person. They appeared to be similar in stature, there were good reasons why they should be the same, and no reasons why they should not. But, assuming them to be the same (it was afterwards proved that they were) the question arose, is this woman a disguised man or was that man a disguised woman? The latter view was clearly the more probable, for whereas a woman, if she cuts her hair short, will pass easily for a clean-shaved man, a clean-shaved man does not pass so easily for a woman, especially if he is dark, as this person was. It seemed probable, therefore, that this was really a woman – a dark woman wearing a fair wig. But who she was, and what – if any – was her relation to Blake, remained for the present a mystery.

'We now come to the man Halliburton. Obviously he was an object of deep suspicion. His only known address was an hotel. He visited Andrew Drayton without any reasonable purpose. He tried unsuccessfully to purchase the cat's eye pendant, and within four days of his failure the jewel was stolen. Then he disappeared, leaving no trace.

'Anstey and I called at his hotel to make inquiries about him. There we obtained a photograph of his signature, which we have not used, but which will be produced at the inquest, and we acquired some information which has been invaluable. He had lost, and left behind, a mascot which he valued so highly that he offered ten pounds reward for its recovery. We got the loan of it, and Polton made this indistinguishable facsimile.' Here Thorndyke passed round Polton's masterpiece for inspection. 'Now,' he continued, 'in connection with this mascot, two very important facts emerged. One was that, as Anstey expressed it, this man was a superstitious ass, a man who believed in the occult properties of mascots and charms. The importance of that becomes evident when we remember that the cat's eye was, in effect, a mascot – an object credited with occult powers affecting the fortunes of its owner. It enables us to understand his anxiety to possess the cat's eye.

'The other important fact emerges from the nature of the thing itself. It is a neck vertebra of an Echidna, or porcupine ant-eater, decorated with aboriginal ornament. The Echidna is an animal peculiar to Tasmania and Australia, and the ornament is distinctive of the locality. This mascot, therefore, established some connection between Halliburton and Australasia. But Blake had lived most of his adult life in Australia. There was, however, a difficulty. Punched on the mascot – apparently with typefounder's steel punches – were the letters *o* and *h*. The name signed in the hotel register was Oscar Halliburton, and these letters seemed to be his initials. But if that was so, Oscar Halliburton would appear to be a real person and consequently could not be Arthur Blake.

'Thus, at this stage of the inquiry, on the hypothesis that the robbery had been committed by Blake, we had two persons whom we could not account for – the unknown woman (possibly a man) and Mr Oscar Halliburton.

'But just as we appeared to have reached an impasse, Mr Brodribb threw a flood of light on the problem. For different reasons, Sir Lawrence and I were anxious to obtain some particulars of Arthur Blake and his affairs, and these particulars Mr Brodribb was fortunately in a position to supply. The information that he furnished amounted to this:

'Arthur Blake appeared to be a decent, industrious man with nothing against him but the rather queer company that he had kept. He had been associated in Australia with a man named Hugh Owen, who was a person of shady antecedents, and who, on his side, was associated with a woman named Laura Levinsky who appeared to be definitely a bad character, and who, like Owen, was under police observation. These two persons seem to have separated immediately after Blake's departure for England, and both disappeared. Levinsky was lost sight of for good, but Owen's body – or rather unrecognisable remains – came to light some years later and was identified by a ring which was known to have belonged to Owen.

'Certain particulars that Mr Brodribb gave concerning Owen made a considerable impression on me. For instance, it appeared that Owen was originally a photo-engraver by trade and that he had later owned a small type-foundry. Also that he had fractured his left knee-cap and that this injury was certainly never completely repaired. But the first thing that struck me on looking at this party of three was that whereas Blake appears to have been a respectable man and most unlikely to have committed an atrocious crime such as the one we were investigating, the same could not be said of his two companions; and inevitably I found the question creeping into my mind: Is it certain that those remains were really the remains of Owen? Or may it have been that they were those of Arthur Blake? That these two criminals had murdered Blake when Brodribb's letter arrived: that Owen had taken the papers and credentials and come to England personating Blake, and that Levinsky had come by another route?

'It seemed, perhaps, a rather violent supposition; but it was quite possible; and the instant it was adopted as a working hypothesis, all the difficulties of the case vanished as if by magic. We could now account for the mysterious woman. We could also account for Halliburton, for the letters on the mascot could be read either way – *o h* for Oscar Halliburton or *h o* for Hugh Owen; and Owen had possessed and used in his type-foundry steel punches exactly like those with which the letters had been made; and further, Owen was a native of Tasmania and had lived many years in Australia. He fitted the mascot perfectly.

'Then Owen had been a photo-engraver; that is to say, he possessed the very kind of knowledge and skill that was necessary to make the stamps for the fingerprints; and he agreed with the taller of the two criminals in that he had a marked weakness of the left leg. In short, the agreements were so striking as to leave little doubt in my mind that our two criminals were Owen and Levinsky, and that the former was in possession of Beauchamp Blake, personating the murdered owner.

'One point only remained to be verified in order to complete this aspect of the case. We had to ascertain whether the man who was posing as Arthur Blake had, in fact, fractured knee-cap. I was casting about for some means of getting this information when the third attempt was made on Miss Blake's life, and it became evident that the danger to her was too great to admit of further delay. Just then Sir Lawrence asked me to go down with him to Aylesbury, and that proposal suggested to me the plan of visiting Beauchamp Blake and making an unmistakable demonstration. I had learned from Mr Brodribb something of the squire's habits, and I got further details from the landlord of the "King's Head." With the help of the latter I obtained access to the park at the time when the squire would be coming out, and I planted myself, with Anstey, where we were bound to be noticed.

'My object was twofold. First, I wanted to ascertain, if possible, whether the squire had any abnormal condition of the left leg, and if so, whether that condition was probably due to a fractured knee-cap; and secondly, I proposed to make such a demonstration as would convince him (if he were really Owen) that it was useless to murder Miss Blake until he had settled with me, and that it would be highly unsafe to make any further attempts. To this latter end I attached Polton's facsimile of the mascot to my watch-guard, where it could hardly fail to be seen, and then, as I have said, I planted myself on the road leading to the gate.

'Both purposes were achieved. I was able to verify with my own eyes the landlord's statement that the squire habitually mounted his horse from the off-side, a most inconvenient method of mounting, but one that would be rendered absolutely necessary by a fractured left knee-cap. Then, as I had expected, he recognised me instantly – no doubt from the portrait published in the newspapers – and dismounted to examine me more closely; and when he came near, he saw the mascot and it was obvious that he recognised it. I detached it and handed it to him, giving him such details as must have made clear to him that I knew its history and knew of his connection with it. His manner left me in no doubt that he fully understood the hint and that he accepted my challenge, and further proof was furnished by the fact that he sent a man to shadow us home and ascertain for certain who we were. So that matters were now on a perfectly definite footing, and I may add that further verification, if it had been needed, was supplied by the circumstance that, on this very day, Anstey caught a glimpse of Levinsky, disguised as a man, in the market square at Aylesbury. The rest of the story I think you all know.'

'Yes,' said Drayton, 'we gathered that from your written statement. But what is not clear to me is why you considered it necessary to thrust your head into the lion's jaws. You seem to have had a complete case against these two wretches. Why couldn't you have lodged an information and had them arrested?'

'I was afraid to take the risk,' replied Thorndyke. 'To us the case looks complete. But how would it have looked to the police? or to a possibly unimaginative magistrate? or, especially to a jury of ordinary, and perhaps thick-headed, tradesmen and artisans? Juries like direct evidence, and that was what I was trying to produce. I had no doubt that these two persons would try to murder me and Anstey, and that we should prevent them from succeeding. Then we could charge them with the attempt and prove it by direct evidence, after which we could have proceeded confidently with the second charge of the murder of Andrew Drayton.'

'I think Thorndyke was right,' said I, seeing that Sir Lawrence still looked doubtful. 'From my large experience of juries in criminal cases, I feel that this intricate train of inferential evidence would have been rather unconvincing by itself, but that it would have been quite effective if it had come after a charge supported by the testimony of eye-witnesses, such as we should have been.'

'Well,' said Drayton, 'we will agree that the circumstances justified the risk, and certainly the unravelment of this case by means of such almost invisible data is a most remarkable achievement. This exposition has whetted my appetite for the explanation of the other mystery.'

'Yes,' said Winifred. 'I am on tenterhooks to hear how you made the "little Sphinx" answer its own riddle. Shall I hand you the locket?'

'If you please; and the Book of Hours. And if we can get Polton to put the microscope on the table with the slide that is on the stage, we shall have all that we want for the demonstration.'

At this Polton emerged unblushingly from the office, and having put the microscope on the table, carefully adjusted the mirror and then, with brazen effrontery, took a long and intent look through the instrument, under the pretence of seeing that the specimen was properly lighted.

'There is no need for you to go back to the office, Polton,' my colleague said with a smile at his familiar. 'We shall want your help with the microscope presently. Draw up a chair for yourself.'

Polton seated himself opposite the instrument with a smile of intense gratification, and Thorndyke then resumed:

'This investigation was a much simpler affair than the other. You may remember, Miss Blake, showing me the locket that night when I called with Anstey at your studio, and you will remember that we noted the very unusual construction; the evident purpose of the maker to render it as strong and durable as workmanship could make it. This curious construction – which I pointed out at the time – caused me to examine it rather closely. And then I made a rather strange discovery.'

Winifred leaned forward and gazed at him with breathless expectancy.

'It was concerned with the hallmark,' he continued. 'There are, as you see, four punch-marks. The first is a capital A with two palm-leaves surmounted by a crown. The second is an escutcheon or shape with the initials AH surmounted by a crown and over that a fleur-de-lis. The third is a capital L, and the fourth is the head of an animal which looks like a horse. This grouping shows that the piece is French. The first mark is the town mark, the second the maker's mark, the third is the date letter, and the fourth is the mark of the Farmer of the Duty. Now, I happened to have had occasion to give some attention to the marks on old French plate, and I happened to have read, only an hour or two previously, the fragmentary narrative of Percival Blake. Accordingly, when I examined the hallmark and learned from it that this locket had been made in Paris in the year 1751, that fact at once arrested my attention.'

'How did you learn that from the hallmark?' Winifred asked.

'It is the function of the hallmark to give that information,' he replied. 'The town-mark of Paris is a capital A surmounted by a crown, but it varies in style from year to year. This one is a Roman capital with two palm-leaves and a very small crown. That is the form used in the middle of the eighteenth century, but the date is definitely fixed by the date-letter – in this case a capital L, which indicates the year 1751.

'It was, of course, a very remarkable coincidence that this locket should have been made at the place and in the year of Judith Blake's death, and it naturally caused me to look at the little trinket more narrowly. Hitherto I had assumed, as you did, that the object that Percival referred to was the cat's eye pendant. But I now recalled that he had not specifically mentioned the pendant, and that he had spoken of it as "the bauble" or "the trinket," never as "the jewel." It was thus just barely conceivable that this mysterious little object might be the one to which he was referring; and the instant the question was raised, the evidence supporting it began to run together like drops of water.

'First, there was the inscription, "O BIOC BPAXΥO H ΔE TEXNH MAKPH," "Life is short but Art is long." It was the motto of the practitioner of some art or craft. But artists and craftsmen almost invariably use the Latin form, "Ars longa, Vita brevis," "Art is long, Life is short." But there is one body of craftsmen who use the Greek form. It is the motto of the London College of Physicians, and moreover it is written by them in the same uncial characters, with the round, C-shaped sigma. Now Percival was a physician and a fellow of this very college, and he was an enthusiast who originally practised his profession for love and not from necessity or for a livelihood. What more natural than that he should use the motto of his own college?

'Then there was the construction of the locket – everything sacrificed to permanence and durability. It fitted the circumstances perfectly. And there were the unusual suspension rings, specially adapted to take a cord or thong. I recalled the enigmatic words "gave me a string form his bass viol, which he says will be the best of all." Remembering that the bass viol would be a viol da gamba or violoncello, not a double-bass, we see that this was true; the stout gut string would last for a century or more.

'Then again there were the scripture references which you showed me. The first was "And then shall he depart from thee, both he and his children with him, and shall return unto his own family, and unto the possession of his fathers shall he return." That was a most striking passage. It was an exact statement of Percival's aim – incidentally illustrating the way in which the other passages were to be treated; and when I noted that the principal word in the last reference was "parchments," I felt that a prima facie case had been made out. I had little doubt that this locket was the "precious bauble" that was handed to – and presumably lost by – Jenifer.

'But after all this was only guesswork. We had to get down to certainties. And, fortunately, there was available and excellent and conclusive test. If the locket was Percival's, the hair in it was almost certainly Judith's. Now there was something very unusual about Judith's hair. During her imprisonment it had undergone a most extraordinary change. Percival tells us that when she was released, "her hair, that had been like spun gold, was turned to a strange black." This was very remarkable. Judith was evidently a true blonde, and when she was arrested, she must have been getting on for thirty years of age. But the hair of a blonde adult does not turn black from ill-health and grief. It tends rather to turn white. What could be the explanation of the change?

'It is a very curious one. Judith had been labouring in the mines in the Harz Mountains. These mines yield a number of different metals, and some of them are extremely poisonous. They are ancient mines, and in the Middle Ages, when the properties of metals were less understood, the terrible condition to which persons who worked in them were reduced by chronic poisoning was put down to the influence of a race of malignant gnomes who were believed to inhabit the mines and who were known as kobolds. In particular, the influence of the kobolds came to be associated with a particular, uncanny ore from which no metal could be – in those days – extracted, and in the end this ore came to be known by the name of these mine-gnomes or kobolds, and that name it bears this day, in the slightly altered form of cobalt.

'Now, the metal, cobalt, has one or two very distinctive properties. One is that of imparting a powerful and beautiful blue colour to substances with which it combines. This was the value of the ore, and for this it has been prized from quite ancient times. We find it in use everywhere. The blue of all the Chinese porcelain is cobalt. The blue of the old Delf pottery is cobalt. The blue in all the old stained-glass windows – and modern ones too – is cobalt.

'Then this metal has another curious property which it shares with arsenic and one or two other metals. It is capable of being absorbed into the body and producing poisonous effects, and when so absorbed, it becomes deposited in the skin, or, more correctly speaking, in the epidermis and its appendages – the fingernails and the hair. But whereas the outer skin and the nails wear away and are cast off, the hair – especially a woman's hair – remains attached for long periods. Consequently, in chronic cobalt poisoning, the hair becomes charged with a cobalt compound – probably an oxide – and is stained blue.

'Bearing these facts in mind, we can now understand what had happened to Judith. She had been sent to labour in a mine which yielded cobalt, and probably nickel. Her hair had not turned black, it had turned blue, though, in the mass, it would appear black – a strange, unnatural black, as Percival tells us. Thus, if the hair in this locket was the hair of Judith Blake, it would appear blue when properly examined. I took an opportunity to get possession of the locket, and that very night I removed the remains of the cover-glass and picked out a single hair, which I mounted in Canada balsam and examined under the microscope. That hair is on the stage of the microscope now. Polton will bring it round and let you see it.'

Our assistant tenderly carried the microscope round and set it before Winifred, and having adjusted the light and the focus, stepped back to watch the effect.

'But how extraordinary!' she exclaimed as she looked into the eyepiece. 'It looks like a thread of blue glass! And how strange and romantic!'

Brodribb and Drayton rose from their chairs and came round, all agog to see this prodigy. In succession they gazed at it with murmurs of astonishment and then went back to their seats, still muttering.

'The appearance of that hair,' Thorndyke resumed, 'settled the question conclusively. This was Percival's trinket beyond a doubt, and all that remained was to read the message inside. As we now knew what to look for, this presented no difficulty at all. It was no cipher or cryptogram. It was simply a collection of texts, from each of which, as the first one showed, the instructed reader would have no difficulty in picking out the significant word or phrase. We may as well just run through them and see what they tell us.

'Number one, Leviticus 25.41, we have already considered. It is the preamble which indicates the purport of the remainder. I see you have your notebook. Will you read us out the next?'

'Number two,' said Winifred, 'is Psalms 121.1: "I will lift up mine eyes unto the hills, from whence cometh my help!" That is the passage, but it doesn't convey any intelligible meaning to me.'

'No,' said Thorndyke, 'it doesn't, because you have got the wrong Psalm. You looked up your reference in the English Authorised Version, overlooking the fact that Percival was probably a Catholic and certainly a resident in France, and also that the references were given with Latin titles, suggesting that he used the Latin Vulgate. This happens to be matter of vital importance in this case, as the Psalms are not numbered quite alike in the two Bibles. Psalm 121 in the Vulgate is 122 in the Authorised Version. Here is the Douay Bible, which is the official translation of the Vulgate, and if we refer to Psalm 121.1 in it, we find "I rejoiced at the things that were said to me; We shall go into the house of the Lord." That is quite illuminating. It tells us that we are concerned with a church, and the next reference tells us what church. It is Actus Apostolorum 10.5'

'Yes,' said Winifred, ' "And now send men to Joppa, and call for one Simon, whose surname is Peter." '

'That,' said Thorndyke, 'gives us the church of St Peter. The next,' he continued, glancing at the notebook which Winifred had handed to him, 'is Nehemias 8.4. "And Ezra the scribe stood upon a pulpit of wood" – we need not complete the passage. The pulpit of wood is obviously the significant part. Then we come to 3 Lib. Regum 7.41 – by the way, that third book of Kings might have given you a hint that you were not dealing with the Authorised Version. It reads: "The two pillars, and the two bowls of the chapiters that were on the top of the two pillars," etc. The meaning of this passage was not very clear. It had some connection with the pulpit of St Peter's Church, but what the connection was, it was not easy to guess. Of course, directly one saw the pulpit, the meaning was obvious.

'The next reference is to Psalm 31.7, and again you have taken the Authorised Version and got the wrong Psalm. Psalm 31 in the Vulgate is Psalm 32 in the Authorised Version. Your reading is "I will be glad and rejoice in thy mercy: for thou hast considered my trouble; thou hast known my soul in adversities." This, as you say, seems quite irrelevant, but if you had turned forward to Psalm 32.7, you would have read: "Thou art my hiding-place" or "refuge," as the Vulgate has it, which is very relevant indeed. The last reference is 2 Epist. ad Tim. "The cloak that I left at Troas with Carpus, when thou comest, bring with thee, and the books, but especially the parchments."

'Thus, taking the references together, they suggest to us the ideas of parchments, a hiding-place, and the two pillars (and their capitals) of the wooden pulpit of the church of St Peter. It was perfectly plain and simple to a reader who knew the kind of information that was being given and who knew of the existence of this particular church. To a stranger, on the other hand, it was perfectly meaningless and undecipherable.'

'It certainly looks very simple now that we have heard the explanation,' said Winifred, 'but it didn't seem so when I was trying to work it out myself. There didn't seem to be anything to go on.'

'No,' agreed Sir Lawrence, 'there didn't seem to be anything to go on in either case. The clues were perfectly invisible, and I don't believe any one but our friend would have discovered a particle of evidence.'

Brodribb chuckled and reached out for the decanter. 'I agree with you, Drayton,' said he. 'Thorndyke reminds me of that, probably fabulous, kind of Indian juggler who throws a rope into the air and proceeds to climb up it and pull it up after him. He can work without any visible means of support. However, he has conducted our various affairs to a highly satisfactory conclusion, and I propose that we charge our glasses in his honour and invite him to light the Trichinopoly, which, I believe, is his disgusting habit on occasions of this kind.'

Accordingly the glasses were filled, the toast pledged, and the virulent little cheroot duly lighted; with which mystical rite the case of the Cat's Eye was formally closed and dismissed into the domain of memory.

There is little more to tell. I am finishing this narrative in a pleasant, panelled room in the old mansion of Beauchamp Blake, one of a suite assigned by Percy to Winifred and me, in which we commonly spend our weekends – for our normal abiding-place is still the Temple. Percy is growing apace, and like his ancestor and namesake, refuses to abandon his professional ambitions. At present he is engaged, under the direction of a famous architect, in restoring the old house to its former comeliness, and only this morning I saw them together superintending the replacement of a perished fascia with a sturdy oaken plank, enriched with fine carving and bearing in raised letters the legend: 'God's Providence is Mine Inheritance.'

R AUSTIN FREEMAN

THE D'ARBLAY MYSTERY
A DR THORNDYKE MYSTERY

When a man is found floating beneath the skin of a green-skimmed pond one morning, Dr Thorndyke becomes embroiled in an astonishing case. This wickedly entertaining detective fiction reveals that the victim was murdered through a lethal injection and someone out there is trying a cover-up.

DR THORNDYKE INTERVENES
A DR THORNDYKE MYSTERY

What would you do if you opened a package to find a man's head? What would you do if the headless corpse had been swapped for a case of bullion? What would you do if you knew a brutal murderer was out there, somewhere, and waiting for you? Some people would run. Dr Thorndyke intervenes.

R Austin Freeman

Felo De Se
A Dr Thorndyke Mystery

John Gillam was a gambler. John Gillam faced financial ruin and was the victim of a sinister blackmail attempt. John Gillam is now dead. In this exceptional mystery, Dr Thorndyke is brought in to untangle the secrecy surrounding the death of John Gillam, a man not known for insanity and thoughts of suicide.

Flighty Phyllis

Chronicling the adventures and misadventures of Phyllis Dudley, Richard Austin Freeman brings to life a charming character always getting into scrapes. From impersonating a man to discovering mysterious trapdoors, *Flighty Phyllis* is an entertaining glimpse at the times and trials of a wayward woman.

R AUSTIN FREEMAN

HELEN VARDON'S CONFESSION
A DR THORNDYKE MYSTERY

Through the open door of a library, Helen Vardon hears an
argument that changes her life forever. Helen's father and a man
called Otway argue over missing funds in a trust one night. Otway
proposes a marriage between him and Helen in exchange for his
co-operation and silence. What transpires is a captivating tale of
blackmail, fraud and death. Dr Thorndyke is left to piece together
the clues in this enticing mystery.

MR POTTERMACK'S OVERSIGHT

Mr Pottermack is a law-abiding, settled homebody who has
nothing to hide until the appearance of the shadowy Lewison, a
gambler and blackmailer with an incredible story. It appears that
Pottermack is in fact a runaway prisoner, convicted of fraud, and
Lewison is about to spill the beans unless he receives a large bribe
in return for his silence. But Pottermack protests his innocence,
and resolves to shut Lewison up once and for all. Will he do it? And
if he does, will he get away with it?

OTHER TITLES BY R AUSTIN FREEMAN AVAILABLE DIRECT
FROM HOUSE OF STRATUS

Quantity		£	$(US)	€
☐	THE ADVENTURES OF			
	ROMNEY PRINGLE	6.99	9.95	13.50
☐	AS A THIEF IN THE NIGHT	6.99	9.95	13.50
☐	A CERTAIN DR THORNDYKE	6.99	9.95	13.50
☐	THE D'ARBLAY MYSTERY	6.99	9.95	13.50
☐	DR THORNDYKE INTERVENES	6.99	9.95	13.50
☐	DR THORNDYKE'S CASEBOOK	6.99	9.95	13.50
☐	DR THORNDYKE'S CRIME FILE	6.99	9.95	13.50
☐	THE EXPLOITS OF DANBY CROKER	6.99	9.95	13.50
☐	THE EYE OF OSIRIS	6.99	9.95	13.50
☐	FELO DE SE	6.99	9.95	13.50
☐	FLIGHTY PHYLLIS	6.99	9.95	13.50
☐	FOR THE DEFENCE: DR THORNDYKE	6.99	9.95	13.50
☐	FROM A SURGEON'S DIARY	6.99	9.95	13.50
☐	THE FURTHER ADVENTURES OF			
	ROMNEY PRINGLE	6.99	9.95	13.50
☐	THE GOLDEN POOL: A STORY			
	OF A FORGOTTEN MINE	6.99	9.95	13.50
☐	THE GREAT PORTRAIT MYSTERY	6.99	9.95	13.50
☐	HELEN VARDON'S CONFESSION	6.99	9.95	13.50

ALL HOUSE OF STRATUS BOOKS ARE AVAILABLE FROM GOOD BOOKSHOPS
OR DIRECT FROM THE PUBLISHER:

Internet: **www.houseofstratus.com** including synopses and features.

Email: **sales@houseofstratus.com**
info@houseofstratus.com
(please quote author, title and credit card details.)

OTHER TITLES BY R AUSTIN FREEMAN AVAILABLE DIRECT
FROM HOUSE OF STRATUS

Quantity		£	$(US)	€
	The Jacob Street Mystery	6.99	9.95	13.50
	John Thorndyke's Cases	6.99	9.95	13.50
	The Magic Casket	6.99	9.95	13.50
	Mr Polton Explains	6.99	9.95	13.50
	Mr Pottermack's Oversight	6.99	9.95	13.50
	The Mystery of 31 New Inn	6.99	9.95	13.50
	The Mystery of Angelina Frood	6.99	9.95	13.50
	The Penrose Mystery	6.99	9.95	13.50
	Pontifex, Son and Thorndyke	6.99	9.95	13.50
	The Puzzle Lock	6.99	9.95	13.50
	The Red Thumb Mark	6.99	9.95	13.50
	A Savant's Vendetta	6.99	9.95	13.50
	The Shadow of the Wolf	6.99	9.95	13.50
	A Silent Witness	6.99	9.95	13.50
	The Singing Bone	6.99	9.95	13.50
	The Stoneware Monkey	6.99	9.95	13.50
	The Surprising Experiences			
	of Mr Shuttlebury Cobb	6.99	9.95	13.50
	The Unwilling Adventurer	6.99	9.95	13.50
	When Rogues Fall Out	6.99	9.95	13.50

ALL HOUSE OF STRATUS BOOKS ARE AVAILABLE FROM GOOD BOOKSHOPS
OR DIRECT FROM THE PUBLISHER:

Tel: Order Line
          0800 169 1780 (UK)
          International
          +44 (0) 1845 527700 (UK)

Fax: +44 (0) 1845 527711 (UK)
          (please quote author, title and credit card details.)

Send to: House of Stratus Sales Department
          Thirsk Industrial Park
          York Road, Thirsk
          North Yorkshire, YO7 3BX
          UK

PAYMENT

Please tick currency you wish to use:

☐ £ (Sterling)   ☐ $ (US)   ☐ € (Euros)

Allow for shipping costs charged per order plus an amount per book as set out in the tables below:

CURRENCY/DESTINATION

	£(Sterling)	$(US)	€(Euros)
Cost per order			
UK	1.50	2.25	2.50
Europe	3.00	4.50	5.00
North America	3.00	3.50	5.00
Rest of World	3.00	4.50	5.00
Additional cost per book			
UK	0.50	0.75	0.85
Europe	1.00	1.50	1.70
North America	1.00	1.00	1.70
Rest of World	1.50	2.25	3.00

PLEASE SEND CHEQUE OR INTERNATIONAL MONEY ORDER
payable to: HOUSE OF STRATUS LTD or card payment as indicated

STERLING EXAMPLE

Cost of book(s):..................... Example: 3 x books at £6.99 each: £20.97

Cost of order:...................... Example: £1.50 (Delivery to UK address)

Additional cost per book:.............. Example: 3 x £0.50: £1.50

Order total including shipping:.......... Example: £23.97

VISA, MASTERCARD, SWITCH, AMEX:

☐ ☐

Issue number (Switch only):

☐ ☐ ☐

Start Date: Expiry Date:

☐ ☐ / ☐ ☐   ☐ ☐ / ☐ ☐

Signature: _____

NAME: _____

ADDRESS: _____

COUNTRY: _____

ZIP/POSTCODE: _____

Please allow 28 days for delivery. Despatch normally within 48 hours.

Prices subject to change without notice.
Please tick box if you do not wish to receive any additional information. ☐

House of Stratus publishes many other titles in this genre; please check our website (**www.houseofstratus.com**) for more details.